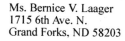

Belinda Alexandra has been published to wide acclaim in Australia, New Zealand, the United Kingdom, France, Germany, Holland, Poland, Norway, Russia, Spain, Turkey, Hungary and the United States. She is the daughter of a Russian mother and an Australian father and has been an intrepid traveller since her youth. Her love of other cultures is matched by her passion for her home country, Australia, where she is a volunteer carer for the New South Wales Wildlife Information Rescue and Education Service (WIRES). An animal lover, Belinda is also the patron of the World League for the Protection of Animals (Australia).

See Belinda Alexandra on Facebook at:
facebook.com/BelindaAlexandraAuthor

and at:
www.belinda-alexandra.com

Also by Belinda Alexandra

Belinda
Alexandra
Southern Ruby

HarperCollins_Publishers_

HarperCollins*Publishers*

First published in Australia in 2016
This edition published in 2017
by HarperCollins*Publishers* Australia Pty Limited
ABN 36 009 913 517
harpercollins.com.au

HarperCollins*Publishers*
Level 13, 201 Elizabeth Street, Sydney NSW 2000, Australia
Unit D1, 63 Apollo Drive, Rosedale, Auckland 0632, New Zealand
A 53, Sector 57, Noida, UP, India
1 London Bridge Street, London SE1 9GF, United Kingdom
2 Bloor Street East, 20th floor, Toronto, Ontario M4W 1A8, Canada
195 Broadway, New York NY 10007, USA

National Library of Australia Cataloguing-in-Publication data:

Creator: Alexandra, Belinda, author.
  Title: Southern Ruby / Belinda Alexandra.
  ISBN: 978 0 7322 9662 9 (paperback)
  ISBN: 978 1 7430 9832 5 (ebook)
  Subjects: Family secrets – Fiction.
  Hurricane Katrina, 2005 – Fiction.
  New Orleans (La.) – Fiction.
A823.4

Cover design by Jane Waterhouse
Cover images: Woman by CoffeeAndMilk / Getty Images; House by Stephen
Saks / Getty Images; Trees by Brennan Hilliard / EyeEm / Getty Images;
all other images by shutterstock.com
Author photograph by Elizabeth Allnutt
Typeset in Sabon 10.5/14 by Kirby Jones
Printed and bound in Australia by McPhersons Printing Group
The papers used by HarperCollins in the manufacture of this book are a
natural, recyclable product made from wood grown in sustainable plantation
forests. The fibre source and manufacturing processes meet recognised
international environmental standards, and carry certification.

For my father, Stan.
Always proud,
Always supportive,
Always there.

AUTHOR'S NOTE

Like many of my readers, I was brought up to believe that the correct and polite way to refer to American citizens of African ancestry was 'African-American'. However, when I was in New Orleans researching Southern Ruby I discovered people preferred to use, and be referred to, as 'Black American' or simply 'black'. For this reason, I have used that terminology for the modern story in Southern Ruby. The words 'coloured' and 'Negro' are not considered correct or polite these days. However in the 1950s and 1960s these were the descriptions used by everyone including Civil Rights supporters and black people themselves. For authenticity, I've adopted these terms in the past story. I hope that no offence will be taken as none is intended.

ONE

Amanda

Sydney, 2004

On Friday 17 September at 11.20 am, my life changed forever. I was standing in the master bedroom of a house in Mosman, staring at the queen-sized bed and deciding whether to dress it in neutral colours or go lavish with a silver-beaded satin throw, when my mobile phone rang, giving me a start. I was tempted not to answer it, but a glance at the number told me it was Tony from the real estate office.

'Amanda?' He sounded out of breath. 'Can you come back to the office? I need to talk to you now.'

Some people say that when something terrible has happened they had some sort of premonition of it: a sick feeling in their stomach; a lump in their throat they couldn't swallow; a prickle down their neck. I didn't feel any of those things. The breezy spring day and the stunning house with its panoramic view of Sydney Harbour had put me in an exuberant mood. Styling prestigious properties for sale wasn't the job I'd intended to end up in when I graduated from my Master of Architecture degree the previous year, but it beat being unemployed.

'Sure,' I told him. 'I'm at the Dennisons' property. The delivery team have already been so I can lock up and be there in fifteen minutes.'

When I climbed into the Holden Barina Nan and I shared, I could smell her perfume, Youth Dew, lingering in the air. I reapplied my Russian Red lipstick and smiled when I thought of Nan always imploring me to tone down my love of striking colours. While she sported the polished 'au naturale' look, I saw my style as 'luxe alternative' — dyed black bob, winged eyeliner, black nail polish and a tailored skater dress teamed with Doc Martens. Before I turned the key in the ignition I scrutinised the Dennisons' modernised home one more time: its Regency white and beige rendered exterior; the topiary plants leading to the front entrance; the plantation blinds in the windows, all evenly angled. It was my job to see that the house was presented perfectly to prospective buyers.

My gaze travelled to the house next door. It was a red-brown-brick Federation home, circa 1912, still occupied by an elderly lady who had been there since the 1930s. The slate-tiled roof was intact but badly in need of repair, as were the peeling window frames and sagging front veranda. Tony described the house as an 'eyesore', but to me it was a diamond in the rough. I imagined that inside it was a treasure trove of original cast-iron and tile fireplaces, high ceilings and picture rails. While Mosman Council had conservation guidelines, they allowed for significant adaptations. I had no doubt that as soon as the elderly lady died and the house went up for auction, its guts would be ripped out and replaced with indoor-outdoor living areas, open-plan rooms, rear dormer windows and Juliet balconies that had never been part of the original design.

Although I was addicted to my mobile phone, laptop and iPod, I was drawn to things with a sense of history like a bee is to flowers. My Master's had been in restoration architecture, and what I longed for was to take an old house and restore it to its former glory. Along the way I'd discover historical gems that told the story of the residence: wartime newspapers; rusted tools and cooking utensils; yellowing accounts printed in Spencerian script; and, most thrilling of all, a stash of love letters hidden away behind a skirting board. But Sydneysiders were as enthusiastic about capital gains as they were about renovating and my fantasy of a commission like that was a long shot. It was one of the reasons that, apart from a short stint with a senior architect converting a Victorian terrace in Surry Hills into a restaurant and some work experience with the Heritage Council, I'd been unable to find a permanent job.

As I turned onto Military Road and headed back to the Neutral Bay office, I wondered what Tony had wanted to see me about so urgently. I hadn't even thought to ask him. Another person might be worried they were about to be fired, but I had no such concerns. Tony was practically family. Nan had worked as his office manager for the past thirty years. She was also godmother to his now grown daughter, Tamara. When I was younger, I used to pretend to the girls at school that Tamara was my sister. I wanted to be like them, with parents and siblings, and didn't want them to know that Nan was all the family I had.

I parked my car in Nan's space, adjusting the seat back to her petite height like a well-trained husband leaving the toilet seat down, and took my style portfolio from the back seat. Julie wasn't at the reception desk, and by habit I glanced in the direction of Nan's desk. She wasn't there either. The orchids she'd bought at the beginning of the week still looked fresh in their crystal vase, but folders and Post-It notes were strewn over her desk and the floor. Her chair was pulled away from her desk. Nan was famous for her orderliness and the disarray was puzzling. But it was only when I saw Anne, one of the agents, crying in the kitchen that I knew something was wrong.

Tony was alone in his office, shuffling papers. As soon as he spotted me through the glass partition he rose from his chair, pale as a sheet, and fiddled with the middle button of his shirt. 'Amanda, you're here!' His voice had a high, tight edge to it.

He ushered me into his office and shut the door behind him. Steve, another one of the agents, watched us from his desk, his face frozen. The reception console rang but no-one made a move to answer it.

'Is everything okay?' I asked Tony.

He had trouble meeting my eyes and ran his fingers through his hair. A sensation of dread crept into my heart. Had something gone wrong with the business? Was he about to tell me the agency was in receivership and we were all out of jobs?

'It's Cynthia,' he said, turning even paler. 'She collapsed after this morning's sales meeting.' Tears came to his eyes and he struggled to continue. 'They couldn't revive her. She died on the way to hospital.'

I stared at him, not comprehending. He couldn't possibly be talking about Nan. We'd had breakfast together in Crows Nest before I'd dropped her off at the office and headed to the Dennisons' property. She'd been fine then: a woman in perfect health who looked fifteen years younger than her sixty-five years. She was going to retire in another two months and we planned to travel around Europe together. No, he couldn't be talking about Nan.

'Amanda,' his voice penetrated my thoughts, 'do you understand what I'm saying? Your grandmother had a fatal heart attack. There at her desk this morning.'

Steve joined us in Tony's office. 'I'm so sorry,' he said, squeezing my shoulder. 'It's a terrible shock! It happened so suddenly. We didn't even get a chance to call you ... and then she was gone.'

A cold, clammy feeling crept over my skin. I rushed from Tony's office towards Nan's desk, staring at it as if something would give me a clue as to why the world was spinning around me. Nan's handbag was there under her desk, and her sweater was hanging on the back of her chair. Maybe she'd gone to the ladies? Then I saw the needle caps scattered on the floor — left by the paramedics after trying to revive someone with adrenaline. The grim truth of what Tony and Steve were trying to tell me started to sink in, shutting off parts of my body and turning me numb.

'No!' I said, gasping for breath. 'Nan!'

Tony's arms were around me, guiding me into a chair. 'She's at North Shore Hospital. I'll take you to see her — they'll be waiting for your instructions.'

I stared at him, trying to come to grips with this new reality. When he said, *she's at North Shore Hospital*, he was talking about her body, wasn't he? Nan was gone. And I hadn't even had a chance to say goodbye. The terrible realisation hit me: while I'd been thinking about decorating themes in the Dennisons' house in Mosman, Nan had been lying here on the floor, dying.

The five days and nights after Nan's death that I spent alone in the house we'd shared were unbearable. Grief rocked me in waves and I struggled for breath as if I were drowning. I kept expecting to hear her key in the door or see her in the kitchen in the morning making omelettes or avocado on toast. Every time the telephone rang, I thought it might be her calling for me to pick her up from her embroidery class or to put the oven on in preparation for making dinner. But the sympathy bouquets of white lilies and roses that seemed to arrive by the hour were a reminder of what I found impossible to accept.

'Nan, I thought we'd have at least another twenty more years together,' I called to the empty rooms. 'Remember, you always said that you'd give me away at my wedding. You were supposed to be here to see your first great-grandchild.'

My grandmother would have been shocked at my slovenliness. She had been very proper and nothing was ever left out of place. Books had to be returned to bookshelves and I hadn't been allowed to study anywhere except at my desk. But after her death I wore the same clothes several days in a row, let the dishes pile up in the kitchen, and slept wherever the mood took me, which was usually in one of the olive green velveteen armchairs in front of the television. I was grateful that Tony liaised with the funeral director for me and Nan's best friend, Janet, took over the task of calling Nan's friends to inform them of her passing. Nan wouldn't have come apart like I did. She would have squared her shoulders and persevered, abiding by her favourite motto: *The show must go on.*

Janet and the ladies of the local Uniting Church seemed to anticipate that I wasn't made of the same sturdy material as they were. Like Nan, many of them were country girls who had come to the city to marry their bank manager and accountant husbands. At the wake after the burial, they laid out a feast of finger sandwiches, tea cakes and mini quiches on a lace cloth on Nan's walnut dining table, and left to me the task of opening the front door to welcome the mourners. Many of them expressed a shock that mirrored my own: 'But she'd never had a sick day in her life!'

The arrival of Tamara and her partner, Leanne, in their lemon-yellow Volkswagen was a welcome reprieve. Only Tamara, with her Italian colouring and her Slavic cheekbones, could carry off wearing a black tie-dyed jumpsuit to a funeral.

'For God's sake, sit down,' she told me. 'Leanne can let people in for you. Now what can I get you to eat?'

Despite my dazed confusion I was amused by the thought of Leanne, with her leather jacket and spiky blonde hair, welcoming Nan's prim friends into the house.

Eating was the last thing I felt like, but Tamara brought me a plate stacked with sandwiches and a cup of steaming tea.

'I don't know how you stand living here still,' she whispered. 'Whenever I visit Mum and Dad I have flashbacks of tennis lessons and pony club. Do you remember when we got suspended from school for dyeing our hair candy pink?'

Tamara and I had always been experimental with our fashion. I cringed when I remembered how much that sometimes upset Nan. When I was eighteen I'd had wings tattooed on my shoulder blades. Nan didn't speak to me for a week except to say: 'Why would you spoil your beautiful skin like that?' I couldn't tell her that they symbolised my freedom after surviving school and were done in memory of my mother, who I'd hoped was my guardian angel. It was difficult to talk to Nan about my mother. Even after twenty-two years, the mention of her brought tears to Nan's eyes.

'Oh my God,' giggled Tamara. 'Is that Reverend Edwards? Isn't he retired now?' I turned to look at the white-haired man who was speaking with Reverend Taylor, who had conducted the service. 'Do you remember when he told Dad that he shouldn't allow me to learn karate in case I came under the influence of "oriental philosophies"?'

'Just as well you gave up karate and became a lesbian then,' I quipped.

Tamara threw back her head and laughed. Even I managed a smile.

'You know, the people here might be old-fashioned but they are kind,' I told her. 'I have more frozen casseroles than I can possibly eat, and the ladies in Nan's embroidery class are working on a portrait of her.'

Tamara grimaced and I knew she'd never understand. Her family was intact, including two sets of grandparents, uncles and aunts, and cousins by the dozen. She couldn't appreciate how important any sort of connection to other human beings was to me, no matter how tenuous.

⚜

After everyone had left, I caught my reflection in a mirror and realised what an alien I looked like in the house. The week before Nan died, I'd had my hair coloured liquorice black and a blunt fringe cut into it. My eyeliner and foundation had disappeared with my tears at the service. The bluish tinge of the new colour was unnatural against my skin and made my vacant eyes stand out strangely. While Nan was alive, our home had been a haven, but now the plush beige carpet, striped wallpaper and pinch-pleat curtains felt dismal and smothering. It was no longer a home, just a dated Art Deco house. Many times, Tamara had offered me a room in her rental in Newtown; and the inner city, with its eclectic cafés and vegan food, was more suited to my personality than conservative Roseville, where my sequined tops and polka-dot skirts stood out among the linen pants and chambray button-up shirts. But I could never have left Nan. Now she had left me.

I sat down at the upright Beale piano and played a few bars of Scarlatti's Sonata in F Minor, which had been one of my pieces for my final music examination. Busy with my university studies and trying to establish myself in a career, I hadn't touched the instrument since I'd left school, although Nan still made sure it was tuned annually.

My grandfather, who died before I was born, had bought the piano for my mother to learn on when she was a child. According to Nan, my mother couldn't be persuaded to touch it, preferring tap dance and softball to studying music. It seemed ironic then that the top of the piano held so many photographs of her, like some sort of shrine. I gazed at the pictures that showed her as a baby in her bassinette, on her first day at the same school I'd gone to, and on the day she'd left for her road trip across the United States, where she'd met my father. That last photograph had always intrigued me. My mother had small, even features and the colouring of an English rose, but her peroxided-blonde hair stuck out in all directions. I couldn't help thinking that I'd inherited my rebellious streak from her, and that's what Nan had always been afraid of.

I transitioned from Scarlatti to 'Summertime' and remembered the first time I'd heard Ella Fitzgerald sing it — on a record at Tony's place. The music had moved something deep inside me: I fell in love with each phrase and every soft croon. Until then I had been addicted to Michael Jackson and Madonna.

But when Nan found me picking out the piece on the piano later she was furious. 'The only real musicians are classical musicians,' she scolded. 'Don't waste your time on any other rubbish.'

I knew even then that her comment had nothing to do with the quality of jazz musicians and everything to do with my father who had been a native of New Orleans, the birthplace of jazz. If not for a horrific twist of fate, I might have grown up in that Southern American city instead of Sydney. I might have been Amandine Lalande instead of Amanda Darby. I might have known my parents.

TWO

Amanda

'Your grandmother left everything to you,' advised Tony, who Nan had appointed as executor of her will. 'But you'd better hold on to the house for twelve months in case any long-lost relatives appear out of the woodwork and make a claim.'

Oh, God, I thought. *Somebody appearing, no matter how unlikely — a love child, a long-lost cousin, a prodigal sister — would be welcome. Anyone who could help to relieve this feeling of being cast adrift in the world.*

It took me six months to decide to rent out the house and go live with Tamara so I could figure out what to do next. It then took me a further four months to clear out the furniture and personal effects so tenants could move into it. I put sentimental items, like the piano, into storage but with every piece of furniture I sold or gave away it was as if I was destroying the life I'd had with Nan. The last room that I tackled was hers. I was tempted to leave it as it was and seal it up like a time capsule. Even when I worked up the courage to step inside, it was as if I was invading her privacy and shouldn't be there without her permission.

I opened her dressing-table drawers and the sight of her neatly folded underwear and the scented soaps between them was too much to bear. I sat down on the bed. *I might have to ask Tamara to help me*, I thought. But then I dismissed the idea. It would have made Nan uncomfortable to have someone other than me going through the intimate parts of her life. I steeled myself and began to empty the dresser drawers, sorting what needed to be given away or thrown out from what I wanted to keep.

Nan and I had very different tastes in jewellery. She thought only yellow gold was worthwhile, and I loved silver, white gold and platinum. She had been buried with her wedding ring, but she hadn't left any instructions regarding her dress watches, pearls and charm bracelets. I decided I would give them to Janet. She could keep anything she wanted and give the rest to the church. I was placing the jewellery in a box when I came across a heart-shaped Lucite pendant with a pink rose accented by green leaves in its centre. It wasn't an expensive piece but it was pretty. I remembered Nan telling me that my grandfather had given it to her when they were courting. It made me smile to think of Nan as a young woman in love, and I picked up the pendant and put it around my neck.

'I'll wear this in memory of you, Nan,' I said out loud.

The pendant seemed to give me a burst of strength, as if Nan was there telling me there was a job to do and to get on with it. She'd been born into a rugged farm life, where people accepted fate and were grateful to have food on the table and clothes on their backs and didn't endlessly analyse it when life dealt them a blow. They pressed on. So I pressed on too: emptying the bedside-table drawers and wiping away tears at the sight of her Bible and reading glasses; and deadening myself to the pain when I took her landscape paintings from the wall. I was packing away her life and the room gradually began to lose its personality — her personality.

The wardrobe was another matter. I knew that somewhere in there were letters from my mother along with photographs from New Orleans. I knew about them because when I was fifteen, Nan and I had a fight about them.

'For God's sake, Amanda! That man ruined our lives!' That's what Nan would say if I asked her about my father. That's what she always said.

I lay in bed and listened to her moving about in the kitchen, clinking plates and glasses as she stacked the dishwasher then locked the back door as she got ready to go to work. The sound of her pumps clomping down the hall sent me rolling onto my stomach and feigning sleep. She strode into the bedroom and put a list of chores on my bedside table, as she'd done each morning since last Friday when I'd been suspended from school. Nan had always been my greatest ally, my guide and my confidante, and I could talk to her about anything — except my parents, of course. Now she was mad at me.

'It's time to get up,' she chided. 'You can't lie in bed all day.'

'Okay,' I replied, rubbing my eyes. 'I'll get up in a minute.'

She kissed me on the cheek, giving me a whiff of Youth Dew. 'I don't know what possessed you and Tamara to do what you did, but I know you're good girls at heart.'

'Thanks,' I said, watching her hands as she patted down the sheets. I was fascinated by Nan's hands. They were thin and bony and translucently pale with freckles on the knuckles — not anything like my hands, which were long with tapering fingers that gave me an advantage on the keyboard but weren't very feminine. I had muscular hands that looked like I could crush an apple between my palms.

'Your grandad left me an insurance policy and this house, Amanda. I don't need to keep working,' Nan said, looking at me with her piercing green eyes. 'I'm doing it so you can get the best education possible. So don't pull any more stunts like that, all right?'

Ouch! Did I need to feel more guilty than I already did? The fees at the ladies college were hefty and Nan was putting aside money for my university studies as well. Dyeing my hair candy pink for the school sports carnival put me only two strikes away from getting expelled.

'I wouldn't mind going to the local school, Nan,' I said, sensing I was pushing my luck with the topic. 'They have a good music department. The master entered the school's rock band into the Kool Skools project and now they're getting assistance to record and package their own first album.'

I'd sung in Nan's church and even had some paid gigs at weddings and birthday parties but I longed to perform jazz like Ella Fitzgerald. What I wouldn't give to be making an album! But the only performing available at my school was in the corny school musical — where girls had to play the male parts as well — or in the choir.

Nan grimaced and hoisted her handbag onto her shoulder. 'Singing for the pleasure of your friends is one thing but the life of a musician is nothing but drugs, debauchery, divorce and ... death. A woman needs a profession these days and to get that you need a good education.' She kissed me on the forehead and headed out into the hall. Before she opened the front door she called back to me: 'Your art teacher faxed your assignment description. I've left it on the kitchen counter. I think Miss Ellis is rather fond of you. She said you'd make a first-class architect.'

I heard her 1984 Volvo warming up in the drive and went to the window to watch her leave. I'd normally be going with her, to be dropped off at school before she continued on to work. I glanced at my reflection in my dresser mirror and ran my hand through my thick hair, which had been dyed back to its natural dark brown by Nan's hairdresser.

'Life's a bitch,' I said. There was a stack of *Cosmopolitan* magazines on my desk. I picked up the top one and flicked through it. The girls were so pretty with their voluptuous Victoria's Secret bodies and sculpted features. I hadn't told Nan that I'd dyed my hair because I was sick of being bullied about my appearance by the other girls.

'Amanda came first in the freestyle today because she's got a nose like a dolphin!'

'Hey, beanpole, what's the weather like up there?'

The hair colour was reverse psychology: *Here, I'll give you something to really talk about ...*

I put the magazine down and turned my CD player on full volume. Sarah Vaughan singing 'Misty' filled the room.

A copy of Anne Rice's *Interview with the Vampire* lay in a hiding spot under my bed and I retrieved it to read it for the fifth time. I'd underlined the parts that described New Orleans. People found it hard to imagine that I might miss what I'd never had, but I did. I often fantasised about what it would have been like to be brought up by young parents and live in the lush, tropical atmosphere of New Orleans. I felt more affinity with Rice's descriptions of that languid and dark arts city than I did with Roseville and its neat houses and English-style hedged gardens. Sometimes I dreamed of a white house with a turret and a balcony that overlooked a garden scented with gardenias and verdant with palms and banana trees, but I didn't know if the picture was a memory or something that had come out of my imagination.

As a child, I'd wished that I could make Mother's and Father's Day gifts at school for my actual parents, like the other kids, as well as for Nan. My mother was visible around our house in the photographs on the piano and her sports trophies in the spare room, but my father was a taboo subject with Nan. 'A devil who drove drunk with his wife and young child in the car and ruined our lives!' It was obvious that my brunette looks and tall stature hadn't come from Nan or my mother with their petite figures and fair Anglo-Saxon features, which meant I must have inherited them from my father. He was half of me, and until someone told me at least one good thing about him, I'd feel despicable too.

Why couldn't I know something as simple as what he looked like or what he had done for a living? For the past year I'd been imagining that perhaps my father might have been an aristocratic vampire, like Louis de Pointe du Lac, and that was the real reason Nan wouldn't talk about him.

I spent the rest of the morning cleaning the kitchen and vacuuming the floors. In the afternoon, I lay on my bed with my stack of *Cosmopolitans* and read an article on rhinoplasty. Nan's friend Janet said with my height and striking features I should be a model, but the girls at school called me 'a freak'. My nose was horrible in every way: long, dorsal-humped, with a boxy tip. Corinne Doulton tormented me at least once a week by sketching it and then passing around her artwork for the other girls' amusement.

'It's the Leaning Tower of Pisa.'

'No, it's the Eiffel Tower after a lightning strike.'

'Ha haa!'

As I read the magazine article, it occurred to me that plastic surgery might change my life. I closed my eyes and pictured returning to school after the holidays with a pert ski-slope of a nose, no longer an ugly duckling but a beautiful swan. The younger girls would carry my books, and the boys from other schools would fall at my feet.

I was lost in this vision when something occurred to me. What if I'd inherited this nose from my father along with my colouring and long limbs? If that was the case, how could I ever change it? It would be like destroying the last vestige of him. But how could I find out?

I hovered at the door to Nan's chintz and rosewood bedroom with indoctrination and curiosity warring against each other inside me. I was a serial 'dresser up' as a child and after one incident, where I'd used up an entire tube of Nan's pricey Christian Dior lipstick to paint my face, I was banned from her room unless she was present. Even now I was fifteen she kept that rule. But I'd seen her pack away documents in archive boxes at the bottom of her wardrobe. Maybe there would be something about my father in one of those? My heart pounded as I approached the wardrobe although I tried to justify my actions: if Nan hadn't been so reticent about my father, this sneakiness would not be required.

But an hour of painstaking searching through the boxes, so as not to put anything out of order, yielded only copies of deeds to the house, my grandfather's death certificate — giving the cause of death as cancer — and my childhood vaccination records. But then as I opened the last box, I found a smaller shoebox inside.

When I took the lid off and saw a picture of my smiling mother holding my infant self, I had to catch my breath. We were wearing matching harlequin costumes — I guessed for the New Orleans Mardi Gras. Under the photograph was a stack of letters in airmail envelopes with a New Orleans return address. From the curvy feminine handwriting, I assumed they must be from my mother. I pressed them to my heart. There wasn't time to read them now, but I knew what I would be doing in the next school holidays.

There was a yellow envelope at the bottom of the box. I picked it up, surprised at its weightiness, and pulled out a stack of photographs. I shuffled through them and gasped at what I saw. There were dozens of pictures of my mother with me — on a vintage streetcar, looking at ducks in a pond, sitting under an oak tree. But the other person in the frame — my father — had been either cut out or scribbled over with black pen. In a couple of photographs a smooth tanned hand had escaped censorship, but nothing else. Nan had obliterated my father as deliberately from the photographs as she had from my life. But there was no mistaking it: my father's hand was exactly like mine.

'What are you doing?'

I turned around to see Nan standing in the doorway. Mortification paralysed me as I realised I'd lost track of time. Her eyes fell to the photographs. Her jaw tightened and her face turned dark. She didn't look like Nan at all. She looked like a tiger about to bite.

She snatched the photographs from me and threw them in the box. 'You're always asking me in what ways you're like your mother. Well, I can clearly see the similarity now. You are as stubborn as she was!'

I hung my head and my lips trembled as I tried to explain: 'I ... I wanted ... I wanted to see a picture of my father,' I stammered. 'To see if we have the same nose.'

'Nose? For God's sake, Amanda!' she said, stepping towards me. 'That man ruined our lives!'

It was no use trying to explain. 'You'll never understand!' I shouted, before fleeing to my room and slamming the door. The sight of the *Cosmopolitan* magazines on my bed enraged me and I began to tear out the pages. Not only were the girls pretty but they probably knew who they had inherited their prettiness from. I had no-one to talk to about my feelings. I was an outsider: I never truly belonged anywhere.

Nan knocked on the door. 'Mandy?' she called, opening it. Her gaze fell to the mess of magazine pages scattered on the floor. She sat on the end of my bed, no longer looking angry but stricken, like someone who's had the air knocked out of them.

'I'm sorry, Mandy,' she said, fighting back tears. 'What I said about you being stubborn isn't true. You're a good girl who does her best despite having been put in a difficult situation.'

'There isn't anyone in the world that I love more than you,' I told her. 'Why is wanting to know if I look like my father so wrong?'

She exhaled sharply and took my hand. 'When I argue with you, it's like arguing with Paula all over again. I'm too old for that. I don't want to argue any more — and I don't want to lose you like I did her. I told her to use the money she was saving from her job to put a deposit on an apartment and get a bit of security in her life first. She could travel later when she got married. But she was always ready to head off in any direction without knowing what was waiting for her at the other end.

'I drove her to the airport the morning she left for her "grand trip". She was young and lively and full of hope. As she went through the departure gate, she turned to wave at me and flashed her enchanting smile. That's my last memory of her. The next time I was at the airport, it was to collect her suitcases and you. I didn't even witness my only child being buried. She's lying in a tomb in a strange city I don't know and don't care to know either.' She lifted her eyes to look directly into mine. 'Your father was careless and selfish! Forget about him!'

I might have only been fifteen but I was wise enough to understand the truth when I heard it. Nan had destroyed my father in those photographs because she believed he'd destroyed her daughter.

The memory of that argument with Nan was still painful, even after so many years. I had become tired of arguing with her too, so I hid my feelings. But all that did was confuse me further. Now, with her gone, not only did I not fit in anywhere but I was totally alone in the world.

Nan wasn't able to hide the photographs from me now. I opened the wardrobe doors, but the sight of her neatly hung jackets and dresses hit me like a wave and I shut them again. I rubbed my hand over my face then tried another time. More than anything else in the room, Nan's clothes carried with them distinct memories: from the champagne lace dress she'd worn for my graduation to the Chanel-style suits she'd favoured for work. I took out an emerald-green cardigan and a pair of taupe pull-on pants and hugged them to me. They had been Nan's favourite winter loungewear. I saw us sitting together snuggled up under throw blankets on the couch, drinking tea and watching episodes of *Antiques Roadshow*. I couldn't understand how it was possible: how could all these things that Nan wore and were once such a part of her daily life still be here while she was gone?

I took the clothes out of her wardrobe and laid them on one side of her bed to deal with later. My eyes travelled to the bottom of the wardrobe where Nan kept her archive file boxes. I took them all out and lined them up along one wall, but the box that had contained the photographs and letters my mother had sent from New Orleans wasn't among them. A hollow sensation formed in the pit of my stomach. Was it possible that Nan had destroyed them?

I moved the stool from Nan's dressing table to the wardrobe and searched the top shelves. I spotted an archive box hidden behind a winter-weight quilt, and stretched and grasped it, then hugged it towards me as I climbed off the stool, and lowered it to the floor. The lid had been sealed shut with tape. I used my thumbnail to slit it open. When I saw the shoebox and yellow envelope inside, dizziness overcame me. I had to sit for a while and let my head clear.

After a few moments I gathered the courage to take out the envelope and look at the photographs of me with my mother in New Orleans. Tears blurred my eyes as I realised how hungry I was for any scrap of the brief life we'd had together. The photographs of us were tangible proof that our relationship had once existed.

Then I took out the letters my mother had written.

The first one I picked up was dated 12 October 1979 and was written on pink paper with a gingham border and a Betsey Clark waif child on a swing in the corner. The sweet musty smell of old paper made my nose twitch.

Hi Mum,
I've arrived in New Orleans! This place is like
no other! I'm staying in a hostel in the French
Quarter (or the 'Voo-car-eh' as the locals call it).
Outside my window a green parrot is squawking
in a palmetto tree, and across the road in a
pub — the bars are open all day and night here
and it's perfectly legal to walk up and down
the street with a drink in your hand — a Cajun
zydeco band is playing. A woman wearing a
metal washboard on her chest is beating out a
blues rhythm with thimbles on one hand and a
spoon in the other. I'm tapping my feet and my
fingers. It's crazy! This place is just crazy! It's
like a 24-hour party. I LUUUVVVV IT! But
everyone I talk to says that if I love it now, I
should come back for Mardi Gras ...

I stopped reading and pressed the letter to my heart. It was as though I'd heard my mother's voice in her writing: breathy, vibrant and revealing a personality ready for adventure. She sounded so young. Well, she had been young. She was nineteen when she went to the United States. Twenty when she gave birth to me. I was older now than my mother had been when she died. It was a strange feeling to know that I'd already outlived her in terms of age.

'Mum!' I said out loud, wondering what it would have been like to have called her that. I pictured her floating around the room like a girlish spirit, before settling next to me and looking over my shoulder as I continued reading.

After I started this letter, the maid wanted to vacuum the room so I took a break and went for a walk. On the corner of the street a woman in platform shoes and a straw hat was hula-hooping. Just hula-hooping! She didn't appear to be on drugs or trying to draw attention to herself, she was simply being herself. The people of this city don't seem to be self-conscious at all, and everyone more or less lets each other be. Can you imagine a woman hula-hooping in Roseville in the middle of the day? She'd be arrested and carted away to hospital. There was a hurricane warning when I arrived and do you think anyone was worried? The bars ran out of vermouth! The people here laugh at danger and carry on partying. What a way of life! I LUUUVVVV IT!

Kisses and hugs, Paulie XOXOXOXO

The tone of my mother's letter made me smile. I wished I'd known her. I could imagine talking to her about everything, from guys, to creative fashion, to music, without feeling anxious about garnering her disapproval. I wondered if I'd grown up in New Orleans, would I now be playing in a zydeco band or hula-hooping on a street corner in the middle of the day simply for the joy of it? I felt the weight of my own seriousness. I'd always thought the melancholy that haunted me came from having lost my parents so young, but maybe it was only the restraint of my stitched-up environment? Perhaps in a different place, I'd be a free spirit like my mother?

I put the letter back in its envelope and picked up the next one. My breath caught in my throat when I read its contents.

Hi Mum,
I'm in Luuuvvvv! His name is Dale Lalande!
I met him at Preservation Hall where he was
playing saxophone. We locked eyes and I didn't
take mine off him until the last note was played.
It was like being drunk on a magic potion from
the witchcraft store. We have a ball together, with
my eccentricities and his sense of humour. I've
listened to him play at the Maple Leaf Bar and
Snug Harbor. He sometimes breaks away from
the band to dance with a member of the audience
before picking up his sax again. You'd like him.
Off stage, he's quite sensible, especially for a New
Orleanian. In the middle of soul-food city he sticks
to a macrobiotic diet. And in a place where most
people are sloshed, he limits himself to a drink a
night ...

My face tingled and my throat felt dry. Apart from his name and that he lived in New Orleans I'd known nothing about my father. This was the most information I had ever been given. He'd been a musician! A jazz musician!

I held up my hands and hot tears burned my eyes. I had to wipe them away with the edge of my shirt so as not to smudge the ink on the letter. He'd been responsible and a moderate drinker? How on earth then could he have driven a car with his wife and young daughter in it as drunk as a skunk, as Nan had always told me?

> *... I fell in love with Dale's family as quickly as I did with him. They're posh and live in the Garden District. His father passed away in January and is badly missed. Dale's sister, Louise, is warm and welcoming to me and she 'oohs' and 'aahs' as if everything that Dale and I do is wildly exciting. Her husband, Johnny, is charming. He's a lawyer, but looks way too hip to be one in his denim jumpsuit and alligator boots. Then there's Dale's mother, Ruby. She is the most amazing character of all. A French Creole by birth, she apparently caused quite a stir when she married into an American family. Whatever the time of day or the occasion, she is exquisitely dressed. Dale says she was a 'Heroine of the Civil Rights Movement' and showed me the award she was given last year by the city in remembrance of that. Despite her refined appearance, she has a kind of mystique about her and I can't help thinking she's keeping a secret.*

My scalp prickled. It had never occurred to me that my father might have a family apart from my mother and me. Perhaps it was because there had only been Nan and me here in Sydney so it was difficult to picture anything other than a contained family unit. I'd assumed that with the death of my parents all ties to New Orleans had been severed — but I wasn't all alone in the world after all. There were still people related to me: another grandmother, and an aunt and uncle. The idea of it baffled me. It was as if everything I'd believed about myself was now being challenged.

I continued to read my mother's letters through the night, falling in love with this delightful, cheeky and adventurous young woman and the city she described. The announcement of her marriage startled me as it must have startled Nan:

I don't know how to begin this letter — so I'll jump right in. Dale and I got married yesterday. Louise and Johnny were our witnesses. You'll like Dale, Mum. It's impossible not to like him. He's exactly the kind of man you would want me to marry: responsible and kind.

Again that word 'responsible'. I picked up another letter and discovered the news of my birth:

Dear Mum,
You're a grandmother!!
*   Amandine came into the world three days ago, on 12 April. In rather a rush, I might add — she didn't even give us time to get to the hospital.*

Everybody here is beside themselves with joy and they want you to come over as soon as possible! Dale is the proudest father you could imagine! He positively glows every time he picks up Amandine ...

When I read the name my parents had given me — Amandine — a deep sense of loss washed over me. It was a name for another city and another time that was lost to me forever. I hadn't been aware that Nan had anglicised my name to Amanda until we applied for passports for our planned trip to Europe and I saw my real name on my birth certificate. I reread the sentence, 'He positively glows every time he picks up Amandine' several times, as if I could somehow conjure up an image of my mysterious father.

There were no copies of the replies from Nan, but clearly she hadn't been pleased by my mother's hasty marriage and was angry that she had decided to make New Orleans her home.

I know you think I'm selfish, Mum, but I never intended to hurt you. A big lavish wedding with all the trimmings was never what I wanted. I had no idea when I left Sydney that it would be for good. Please come and visit us here. I've talked non-stop about you and everyone wants to meet you. You would like the Lalande family too, they are old-fashioned and elegant and the house is beautiful ...

My mother's desire to make amends with Nan was palpable. I cringed at her attempts at appeasement:

I'm enclosing a gold bracelet for you, Mum.
I hope you'll like it!

And:

Here is a picture of me and Amandine during
Halloween. Everything fascinated her — all the
ghouls, witches and ghosts. They go all out here
— real skeletons and full on costumes. I've also
enclosed a picture of her in her high-chair eating
her grits. She's a true New Orleans baby.

I knew exactly what she was feeling. Nan was a good
woman who would do anything for the people she loved.
But if you displeased her, she could shut down on you in
a way that made your blood turn cold. It took her a long
time to forget a grudge. I didn't like to think anything
but good about Nan, especially now she was gone. But I
had to admit the truth, and the evidence was there in my
mother's letters.

The last line in the final letter brought tears to my
eyes again:

Please write to me, Mum. You can't stay mad
about this forever!

I glanced at the date: 3 September 1982. One month
before my parents died. Perhaps much of Nan's grief had
been that she and my mother never reconciled before the
accident.

'Oh, Nan!' I cried out. 'Why?'

I lay back on the bed and stared at the ceiling for
a long time. The journey to the past was exhausting.

Finally, I summoned the strength to gather my mother's letters into a pile and retied the ribbon around them. I was about to return them to the box when I noticed another letter inside. I was sure it hadn't been there when I'd looked in the box when I was fifteen because I would have remembered it.

The envelope was cream cotton fibre and had been closed with a wax seal. The writing wasn't my mother's loopy cursive, but graceful calligraphy. I examined the postmark and saw that it was dated March 2001. The letter didn't smell musty like the others, but gave off a hint of jasmine and patchouli when I opened it.

Dear Cynthia,
This may be the last letter I ever write to you.
I have been diagnosed with atrial fibrillation
and will undergo electric shock treatment for
it next month. Nobody knows how long I have
got. I may last for years yet, or I might be
gone tomorrow from a stroke or heart attack.
The date for my surgery is the same as sweet
Amandine's twenty-first birthday, April 12. Do
you expect that I could have forgotten her? I
think of her every day, and am sure my grief at
not seeing her grow up is what is slowly killing
me, not the irregular heartbeat that the doctors
have diagnosed. It is as if you took my soul along
with her to Australia.

I am sorry we fought over her. That was a
dreadful mistake that has cost me dearly. But we
were younger women then, foolish and selfish.
We should have come to some better compromise
than to involve lawyers and diplomats. Have the

*years and the ebbs and flows of life not brought
you to feel any pity for me? Just as Amandine is
your last contact with Paula, she is my last with
my beloved Dale. Yet you have denied me not only
all contact with her but any news of the young
person she is becoming. As a mother yourself, you
must understand the meaning of this?*

*You have a right to your anger, but by holding
on to it you have also deprived Amandine of a
large part of herself. She has a family here too:
people who love her and miss her and always
will. She also has a significant property that
will come into her possession when I pass away.
This property is of great sentimental value to
our family and I ask one more time that you will
allow her to come here so I might show it to her
myself and explain its history.*

*To get what you want is a responsibility: I
have learned that in life. You won, Cynthia. Why
then are you still afraid of me? What could I
possibly do to harm you ... or Amandine?*

Yours truly,

Ruby (Vivienne Lalande)

I was stunned. All the excuses and rationalisations I'd made
to justify Nan's behaviour collapsed. My father's family in
New Orleans hadn't forgotten me. They'd wanted me to
be part of their lives. And after the death of my parents,
there'd been a dispute about whether I should remain
with them or come to live with Nan in Australia. It went
part of the way to explain Nan's secrecy and her denial of
any details about my father. But as much as I tried to see
everything in a detached manner, I was furious.

'Nan!' I cried. 'How could you have done that to me? You must have understood how badly you were hurting me!'

I paced the room, rereading the letter. And what was this about an inheritance? How could I inherit something from people I'd never known? Gradually my anger gave way to a deep sense of loss.

By the time the sun rose, my conflicting feelings had been overshadowed by questions. Was this woman — my Grandmother Ruby — still alive? And if so, what kind of woman was she?

THREE

Ruby

New Orleans, 1953

Lord, my Aunt Elva was evil and I wished her dead! But I smiled sweetly instead and offered her another piece of Doberge cake.

'No, thank you,' she said, pursing those thin lips of hers and shaking her head so her double chin wobbled like a turkey's wattle. 'It's rather dry. When my Millie makes it, it practically melts in your mouth.'

I glanced at Mae, who stood in the doorway in her faded uniform and watched us with her mahogany eyes. Her pride would be hurt. We'd eaten gravy on bread all week to put on a good show for Aunt Elva. It wasn't Mae's fault our oven was old and she'd had to go easy on the butter. I could have killed Aunt Elva with my bare hands right then if it didn't mean I would hang and then burn in hell.

It was my gracious mother who saved the moment. 'More tea then, Elvie?' she offered, picking up the pot and pouring some into Aunt Elva's cup.

My heart sank at the sight of Maman's trembling hands. She was getting worse, and yet she had dressed up in her mauve-pink pleated dress, powdered her face and buffed her nails.

Aunt Elva studied the teacup with calculating rather than admiring eyes. It was Haviland Limoges France and had been a wedding gift to my grandparents. These days I usually hid anything of value when Aunt Elva visited, but Maman had insisted that we always offer our guests the best we had. I knew what Aunt Elva was thinking when she stared at the cup, and it wasn't how pretty the rose and violet pattern was.

What else does the old witch want? I thought, looking at the bare walls of our parlour where the collection of Degas paintings used to hang. *Our blood?*

I loved Maman fiercely and wanted to protect her like a lioness protects her cub. She was everything a Southern belle should be — pretty, unfailingly polite and always thinking of others. But she seemed to live in some time in the past and couldn't adapt to our present circumstances. Mae and I had been pawning things left and right the past year to keep us going, and Maman acted like she didn't even notice. In her mind, she was still living in a plantation mansion with a drive lined by oak trees.

'Excuse me,' I said, rising from my chair. I grimaced at Mae as I passed her on my way to Maman's bedroom.

Mae followed me, and gripped my hands after I'd punched the bed viciously several times. I didn't know from whom I'd inherited my fierce ability to see reality as it was, but it certainly wasn't from Maman or any of my de Villeray ancestors, who had almost without exception perished through embarking on romantic but doomed ventures.

'Miss Ruby,' Mae said in a hoarse whisper, 'you control your temper now ... for your mama's sake.'

'I'm going to kill that old witch,' I said under my breath. 'Why'd she come here without Uncle Rex? She's up to something! I can see it in her beady eyes.'

'You kill her and who's gonna look after your mama when they lock you up?'

I pulled away from Mae and sat on the bed, catching my reflection in Maman's bevelled dressing-table mirror. My eyes looked wild.

Everyone called me Ruby, but that was my pet name. My real name was Vivienne — Vivienne de Villeray. Maman said she couldn't remember how I'd gotten the name Ruby and it must have been because of the pretty gemstone, but Mae said it was because when I was a baby I used to scream and turn ruby red until I got what I wanted. The name stayed, although I could no longer scream for my demands.

I turned away from my reflection. I was only seventeen and yet I felt worldly compared to Maman. Couldn't she see that Aunt Elva was a bad woman who would steal the food off a baby's plate if she wanted it? If I was a man I would have thrown her out, but I was a young woman who'd been brought up to 'behave'. It was utterly ridiculous that I had to act like a charming and proper lady when we had no money to fund such genteel appearances.

My gaze fell to the row of medicine bottles lined up on the dressing table. When I was a child, enticing crystal perfume dispensers and a silver brush set used to sit there instead. The dresser and mirror would bring us a tidy sum, but I couldn't sell it. Maman loved beauty and I couldn't take every last vestige of it away from her, especially not now. She was one of those fragile, sensitive souls who needed beauty the way the rest of us needed food and water.

'Aunt Elva wants to send me to the convent,' I told Mae. 'I heard her talking about it to Uncle Rex. She said it was the only future for a "girl in my position".'

Mae put her arm around me and stroked my hair the way she used to do when she was my nursemaid instead of our housekeeper. 'Now, don't be silly,' she said, laughing gently. 'You in a convent? Lord have mercy on the sisters! No, your Uncle Rex won't allow that. He likes you and your mama too much. Besides, you're the prettiest girl in town. You're going to find yourself a good man to marry.'

Dear Uncle Rex. While my father had been a gadabout Southern dandy who wore his jet-black hair slicked behind his ears, Uncle Rex was stocky and wore pin-striped suits like a man of business. He spoke in measured tones and was polite without ever resorting to my father's honeyed flattery. In my mind, he was the only reliable man in the de Villeray family and I loved him for it. After my father died, my uncle started discreetly putting money for housekeeping and living expenses in a jar on our mantelpiece. But now Maman was sick, that money wasn't enough and Aunt Elva was watching him like a hawk.

'You don't give these people another cent,' she'd told him one day in front of us. 'If Desiree can afford to make a debutante dress like that for Ruby, then she can afford to pay her own way.'

Never mind that we'd sold our last pieces of silverware to pay for the dress material. I hadn't wanted to debut, considering our circumstances, but Maman had insisted.

'It's the most beautiful night of a young girl's life,' she'd told me.

'It was only right for Ruby to debut,' Uncle Rex had replied to Aunt Elva. 'She's beautiful and at the right age to marry.'

'Well, I don't see any suitors from good families knocking down the door for her hand!' his wife had retorted.

I cringed at the memory. I loved Uncle Rex for his kindness, but Aunt Elva was correct in her summing up of the situation. To the chagrin of the other debutantes, especially Aunt Elva's own frumpy daughter, Eugenie, I had been the belle of the ball. My dress had indeed been exquisite, far more stunning than the other debutantes', because Maman herself had sewn the pearl embroidery onto the strapless silk bodice. But while the young men all wanted to dance with me, their mothers had forbidden them to court me because I didn't have a dowry. The whole thing had been a humiliating disaster.

'Listen,' said Mae, lifting me to my feet and smoothing my hair, 'you go out there and help your mama put on a show for Mrs Elva. Remember what she always told you.'

'If you must do a thing, then do it graciously,' I parroted, then returned to the parlour to find Aunt Elva talking to Maman about the beaus who were courting Eugenie.

'That charming Leboeuf boy lights up whenever he's around Eugenie,' she was saying. 'When I saw him talking to her at the Rombeaus' annual garden party, he looked positively smitten. Then there's Harvey Boiselle, a good catch indeed ...'

I glanced at Maman. She used to be good friends with Lisette Rombeau; they'd grown up together. We hadn't been invited to the garden party this year and that was a snub if ever there was one. However, although Aunt Elva was doing her best to make a point of our fall in status, Maman took it all in serenely, firm in her belief that one day I would meet the right man and fall in love with him and all our misfortunes would be swept away.

I wished I could lose my worries about the future in romantic delusions. It would sure beat the humiliation I felt whenever Mae and I had to take something else to Mr Joseph's pawn shop.

Later in the afternoon, while Maman was taking her 'lady's nap', I wandered around the apartment, trying to think clearly. Everything was going to pieces. What were we going to do? The de Villerays were one of the oldest Creole families. We could trace our ancestry to a naval officer who had accompanied Jean-Baptiste Le Moyne de Bienville to found the city of New Orleans, and whose descendants had become wealthy plantation owners on the shores of Lake Pontchartrain. The apartment we now lived in had once been part of one of the many townhouses our family had owned, but lavish living by my forebears had gradually eroded the family's fortune. My great-grandfather had been famous for his duelling, but had gotten himself killed at sixty years of age by a younger man's bullet on account of some scandal over a woman's honour. My grandfather's reckless disregard for money and expenditure had left the family with nothing but debts. I only had a few recollections of my own father, also a gambler and womaniser, because he was often away somewhere involved in some swashbuckling scheme to regain the family's fortune. His last attempt was in Brazil, where he was convinced he'd make his millions rediscovering an old gold mine that had been abandoned by the British. The only thing he achieved was to contract malaria, and he died ten days later on my twelfth birthday.

I could hear Mae in the bathroom, washing our clothes with a scrubbing board. Why did she stay with us? Other maids had modern appliances like vacuum cleaners and washing machines to help them with their work, while she had developed painful fluid on the knee from polishing floors. I couldn't stand it any more. After picking up my hat and gloves from the stand, I walked out the front door and quietly closed it behind me.

Often when I felt sad and frustrated, I would ride on one of the streetcar routes until I felt better. That day I decided to go to Audubon Park, but when I reached Uptown, instead of heading to the park as usual I walked onto Tulane's campus and sat under a large oak tree watching students hurry to and from classes. Each year there were more girls coming here. I studied them with curiosity. They looked so confident in their Peter Pan–collared sweaters and circle skirts.

'What are you studying?' I asked one dark-haired girl. She wore light pink lipstick and her hair was cut fetchingly short.

'Architecture,' she answered and then smiled apologetically. 'I'm sorry, I can't stop to talk. I'm late for class.'

She's going to design buildings, I thought as she hurried away. *How wonderful would that be?*

I crossed over St Charles Avenue into Audubon Park as if in a dream. What was this strange curtain that separated me from those confident, self-determined girls? I knew the answer: they were middle class and as such were free to develop their minds and use their bodies any way they pleased. They didn't carry the weight of the

Creole aristocracy on their shoulders. I was sure they hadn't been taught from nursery age to recite their entire family tree.

I sat on a park bench and watched the ducks swimming on the pond. There had been some Creole women who'd run their own plantations and left them to their daughters, but the fortunes of the women of the de Villeray family had always been tied to their menfolk. And the men had squandered those fortunes and left us struggling to make ends meet. Well, except for prudent Uncle Rex; but he was twenty years older than Aunt Elva, and I was very aware that Maman, Mae and I would be out on the street the moment he drew his last breath.

Why is it this way? I asked myself, gazing at the trees. Did I really have no choice but to watch our family slowly sink into destitution in the same way some geologists declared that New Orleans was gradually sinking into the ocean?

I looked about me and saw a young woman selling watermelon slices from a vending cart. People came to the cart, she gave them a slice of melon and they handed her some money. I kept staring at those coins. It seemed to me that she wasn't doing so badly with nothing more than watermelons to sell. I noticed how she spoke cheerfully to people as they purchased their fruit and that seemed to encourage them to buy more. Her stock moved quickly and she was done by the early afternoon.

How hard can it be? I wondered. I'd been brought up to believe that women couldn't manage money, but that young woman seemed to be managing it very well.

On my trip home, it was as if my eyes had been opened: I noticed all the women vendors who worked in the French Quarter selling everything from alligator pears to jewellery to yo-yos. There were women working in beauty parlours, and demonstrating kitchen devices in department stores, and even female artists selling their paintings in Jackson Square. Who said women couldn't handle money?

By the time I reached our apartment, I'd made a decision. It wasn't marriage that was going to save us. It was money — and I had to learn how to make some. I, Vivienne 'Ruby' de Villeray, was going to do what no woman in my family had ever done before me. I was going to get a job.

'No good can come of this, Miss Ruby!' Mae warned as she helped me to dress. 'Not for a young lady in your position. Those women you saw the other day don't come from the same folk you do. God gave us all a place and we should be satisfied with it. Once you start questioning one part of your life, you start questioning everything.'

'Listen, Mae,' I said, fixing my hair in the mirror, 'God gave me two arms, two legs and a head and I intend to use them to get us out of this fix. Didn't you always teach me that God helps those who help themselves?'

Mae shook her head. 'Small people shouldn't get ideas above their station and grand people shouldn't get ones below theirs — that's what my grandmama used to say.'

'I've got to try something different from what we've been doing. Otherwise what will we do when there's nothing left to sell? Now you keep Maman occupied until I get home. Tell her I'm taking piano and singing lessons in exchange for keeping Adalie de Pauger company. She'll be pleased by that. You know that old widow is a recluse and doesn't see anybody except young people she thinks have exceptional talent.'

I'd found a job at Avery's Ice Cream Parlor down the South Rampart end of Canal Street, near where the new Civic Center was to be built. There was a lot of development going on around that part of town and the manager, an Italian man named Mr Silvetti, was happy to hire me on the spot without asking about my experience. The parlour was a cheerful place with black and white tiles on the floor and a long counter with chrome stools upholstered in pink and green vinyl. As well as ice cream it served vanilla shakes, root-beer floats and hot fudge sundaes. A jukebox in the corner played music by people I'd never heard of, like Frankie Laine and Johnnie Ray, but the tunes made me tap my feet in time to the beat.

I had never waitressed before and I didn't know anyone who had, so as I put on my pink uniform and white apron the first day I kept reassuring myself, *How hard can it be?* As it turned out, taking the customers' orders and serving their food wasn't any more difficult than hosting a morning tea and looking after your guests. The hard part was not being able to sit down. At the end of the day, my legs throbbed as if I'd been riding a horse up a mountain, and Mae, despite her disapproval of what I was doing, massaged them with castor oil.

'You're going to ruin those nice pins of yours, Miss Ruby,' she warned. 'You'll end up bow-legged and bent over like me.'

'Shh!' I told her. 'This isn't forever. Just till we can figure out something else to bring in money.'

'What's going to bring in money is you being pretty and finding yourself a nice husband.'

'Oh, don't bother me about husbands, Mae. We're in this mess because of all the de Villeray husbands.'

It wasn't the standing that was the most disheartening part of the job, but how little money I earned for being in the parlour most of the day. I was pleased that we had some extra so we could buy better food and put colour in our cheeks again, but every penny was hard earned and there was no money left over for anything nice like lace or scented soap. And then there was the mopping.

'*Dio buono!*' said Mr Silvetti the first time he saw me take a mop and bucket to the floor. 'It's just as well you're pretty, Ruby, otherwise I'd have to fire you. You've got water and muck all over the place. Have you never mopped a floor before?'

The truth was I hadn't, but I didn't tell him that. At least he'd recognised that my good looks were an asset. He kept commenting that he'd never had so many young men coming to the parlour until I started working there.

'Where do you live, Ruby? Will your father let me take you out?' the young men asked me.

They were nice enough boys with their crew cuts and plaid shirts, but not the sort I was used to. Young Creole men were more aloof and didn't act so eager. Besides, their mothers were always hovering to vet their choice of female companions. I couldn't tell the boys in the ice cream parlour that I was from an aristocratic Creole family, lived in a crumbling apartment in the Quarter and that my father had perished in Brazil. Instead, to deflect all the questions, I decided to invent a new life for myself. It wasn't hard: each day as I walked to work,

I felt that I was leaving behind Vivienne de Villeray and becoming someone else.

'I live with my parents and younger brother in Lakeview,' I told the boys when they pestered me. 'On one of the new estates there.' So convincing did I make my fictional life that I could see every detail myself as I related it: the sliding glass doors and patio of our modern home; my father leaving for his job at the telephone company every morning; my mother baking oatmeal cookies; our dog, Spud, playing in the garden. 'I'm saving up for college,' I even added boldly.

It was a good, simple and happy life that I invented and it made me feel better. My mother wasn't dying of diabetes, and I had a bright future and could marry freely for love, without obligation to traditions, fortunes and a family name. Pretending to be a carefree seventeen year old *made* me a carefree seventeen year old, for a few hours a day at least. It wasn't until I'd changed out of my uniform and was heading back towards Royal Street that the weight of the world bore down on me again.

Then one day something happened at the ice cream parlour to challenge my invented happiness.

As well as the counter that faced the milk bar, there were tables that ran the length of the tall windows. Customers could look out at the street and watch the passing parade of people and streetcars. But the section reserved for coloured folks wasn't so appealing: just four tables tucked away in the back corner. They couldn't even use the front entrance, but had to come in through a side door that opened onto a dingy laneway. The parlour had a restroom but it was for 'Whites Only'. The coloured customers had to go find a public restroom elsewhere on Canal Street or wait until they got home.

I'd lived in a segregated society all my life and had never questioned it. It was the way things were — white and coloured lived 'separate but equal' lives according to the law. White people had their restrooms, and coloured people had theirs. It was the same with drinking fountains, seats on the streetcars, lines in banks and vending machines. Once, as a child, I'd asked my mother why our servants — three then, including Mae — ate in the kitchen and not with us. 'Darling Ruby,' Maman had replied, stroking my hair, 'coloured folk are much more comfortable in their place. They don't want to mix with us either. It's how it is.' But for some reason, things started to bother me in the ice cream parlour. Perhaps it was because the place was so pretty for whites and so drab for the coloured people. How could that be separate but equal? Or perhaps it was because, as Mae had warned me, now that I was questioning one aspect of my life, I was starting to question everything.

We'd just finished the lunchtime rush and Betty, another waitress, and I were wiping down the counters and tables. A group of young men and women office workers from the Louisiana Life Insurance Company were the only customers left. They were celebrating somebody's birthday, loudly joking and laughing with each other. Then the front door opened and in walked three coloured men.

Betty was rinsing glasses and didn't notice, but I was surprised to see them coming in the 'Whites Only' entrance. All of them were tall and smartly dressed: they wore cinnamon suits with two-toned embroidered shirts and silk ties that complemented their coffee-toned skin. The oldest of them, who I guessed to be twenty-five, nodded to me and said, 'Good afternoon, miss.' The men didn't take a table in the coloured section but sat at one facing the window. I considered that they might be from the North, where segregation wasn't mandated. But whether they were from the North or not, as long as they could read English they must have been aware of what they were doing. They'd selected a table right under the gigantic *Whites Only* sign.

Well, what of it? I thought. *There's plenty of room now lunchtime is over. Why shouldn't they have a view of the street?* I picked up my order pad.

The man who'd spoken watched my approach, looking me directly in the eyes. I always appreciated an interesting face. Despite his young age, this man was dignified, with broad cheekbones and a strong chin. His eyes seemed ancient.

'What would you gentlemen like?' I asked, directing my question to him and speaking in a low voice.

The other two men glanced at me briefly, surprised that I hadn't challenged them, while the first man held my gaze as if sizing me up.

I glanced back at the group of office workers. It was their presence that was making me nervous rather than the three coloured men sitting in the wrong place. I longed for more people to arrive and distract attention away from the threesome. But my discretion was of no use. Mr Silvetti walked in from the back room and called out, 'Coloureds in the rear! You can't sit there!' He didn't say it in a malicious way, rather out of habit, in the tone one might use to instruct a dog to heel or to sit. But he'd drawn the attention of the office workers, who turned around to see what was happening.

I sucked in a breath, sensing trouble.

The coloured men didn't get up and move as they were told. Rather the dignified man turned to Mr Silvetti and answered in a calm voice, 'No, thank you, sir. We'd like to sit here.'

You could have heard a pin drop in the room.

One of the office workers, a man with a skinny neck and freckles, frowned. 'Hey, nigger, the man told you to move!'

'No, thank you, sir,' the coloured man repeated. 'We'd like to sit here.'

His composure was chilling. Coloured men didn't speak back to white men. They didn't look them in the eyes and address them as equals. They didn't stand their ground when told to move. If you were coloured and a white man approached you on the banquette, you'd better lower your eyes and step out of his way or you'd be ganged up on and beaten.

'You've been told to move, boy,' said one of the women in the group. 'Have you been up North, boy? You got Yankee ideas about your place now, boy? Those ideas mean nothing here!'

The coloured men ignored her and picked up the menus.

Now a Southern woman's honour had to be defended and the white men sprang into action. They rushed towards the rebellious threesome with their fists raised, but when they reached them they seemed less certain of what to do. A white man could beat a coloured man to death with no fear of the law, but something about these men, apart from their superior size, was unnerving. They seemed to possess an inner power.

Frustrated, one of the office workers picked up a melted marshmallow sundae from a table I hadn't cleared yet and poured it over the first man's head. Inspired, the others began throwing napkin holders and forks at them, screaming, 'Get lost, you dirty niggers! You'll be sorry when there's a noose around your necks!'

Still the coloured men didn't react, until the troublemaking woman walked over and put her lighted cigarette onto the back of the hand of one of the men. He flinched, but I imagined the pain would have caused a bigger reaction in a lesser man.

As the threats escalated, the three men finally stood up, still with solemn dignity. I looked at the first man, his beautiful suit ruined by the sundae. I grabbed a napkin and wanted to hand it to him so he could clean himself up, but my limbs wouldn't move. Fear of being labelled a 'nigger lover' kept me rooted to the spot.

The inflamed group of office workers shoved the coloured men out of the parlour, ironically through the 'Whites Only' door. The whole episode couldn't have taken more than ten minutes but my world had changed forever. I looked at the napkin in my hand. In not helping the man, even in a small way, I'd let some significant part of myself down.

I promised myself that if ever I was in a similar situation and another human being needed my help and sympathy, I wouldn't stand by silently.

FOUR

Ruby

Apart from the incident with the coloured men, working at Avery's Ice Cream Parlor was pleasant enough but I was worried about the low pay despite the tips I earned. Maman's physician, Doctor Monfort, was an old family friend who treated her for free, but the medicines he prescribed were expensive. I had to find a better-paid job, but what?

One morning when there weren't any customers in the parlour and I was in the kitchen scrubbing down the benches, I heard a familiar voice.

'Well, of course her husband spends all his time on Bourbon Street looking at the girls. She doesn't know how to control him.'

It was a nasty, droning voice that drained you of energy the moment you heard it. A voice like that belonged to a nasty, droning person: Aunt Elva!

I peered through the round window in the kitchen door and saw her taking a seat at the counter with some other matronly ladies, including Lisette Rombeau. Aunt Elva wiped down the stool with her handkerchief before placing her 'too good for the ordinary world' derriere on it. I'd never expected to see people Maman knew in the parlour. It wasn't close to where Aunt Elva and Lisette Rombeau lived in Metairie. What were they doing here?

'Service, please!' Aunt Elva called, turning to look at the kitchen door.

I ducked down, my heart racing. This was a disaster. I was the only waitress scheduled for that morning, and Mr Silvetti was out on an errand. I didn't even want to imagine the consequences if I went out and served those women. I was proud of myself for doing something to help our situation, but if Maman found out she would be ashamed — and worse, mocked and shunned by the other high-society Creoles. Her weekly ladies' bridge club was one of the few social pleasures she had left.

'Service, please!' Aunt Elva called again. 'Is anybody even here? What's taking you so long?'

I heard the sound of a chair scraping. She was coming to investigate. There was nothing to be done but make a run for it.

I grabbed my clothes and fled into the storeroom, out the delivery door and into the laneway. It wasn't until I reached home that I fully realised what a close call it had been. I couldn't go back to the ice cream parlour. It was too risky. I quickly changed out of my uniform behind a palm in the courtyard and threw it into a garbage can. When I entered the apartment, I heard voices and found Maman entertaining Babette Pélissier, the only friend who still called on her, with tea and cake. And what a cake it was! The icing was butter cream formed into a bouquet of pink and white roses. Mae must have bought it from the exclusive French patisserie across the street. Of course it was all for Babette: Maman wouldn't be able to touch it because of her diabetes.

'Babette has the most wonderful news!' Maman exclaimed, indicating for me to sit down next to her. 'Georgine is getting married! To Harvey Boiselle!'

While Babette still called on Maman, I hadn't heard from her daughter in over a year. Still, it pleased me to think Georgine had stolen one of Eugenie's beaus. Aunt Elva must be fuming! It was hard to keep the smile from my face despite what had happened at Avery's. Maman seemed to have forgotten that Aunt Elva had spoken about Harvey Boiselle in relation to her own daughter, otherwise she might have been more circumspect. Maman was forgetful of quite a few things these days. Doctor Monfort said it was the progression of her disease.

'Your mother has been telling me the most delightful story about the history of the house in Rue Ursulines,' said Babette, adjusting her fashionable demi-chapeau. 'I'd forgotten how good she is at relating a story.'

If there was one talent appreciated above all in New Orleans it was the ability to tell a good story. Why, it was as impolite to tell a story badly as it was to not greet an acquaintance on the street. Visitors said the reason it took so long to get things done in New Orleans was because everyone you met had a story they wanted to share with you. In a city of storytellers, Maman was the best, especially when she told tales about the history of the place. The animation in her face and the way she raised and lowered her voice at the right moments made it seem like the scene she was describing was unfolding before your eyes. Perhaps her talent had been handed down from the plantation days, when there was nothing to do during the hot, mosquito-ridden evenings except play cards, read poetry and tell each other stories.

Mae came to refresh the tea. She glanced from the cake to me and winked. Even though she didn't like me working, I guessed she was pleased that we could make Maman happy with the money I was earning. Then I realised that not only could I not return to the ice cream parlour after I'd run out like that and thrown away my uniform, but I hadn't picked up my current week's pay. It was going to be gravy and bread again if I didn't figure something else out quickly. *Curse, Aunt Elva*, I thought. *She's got a way of spoiling everything.*

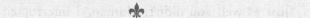

'Ruby,' Maman said that evening, when we were sitting together reading and listening to Chopin on the record player after dinner, 'you are looking more and more like your father every day.'

'Maman, that is not a compliment!' I cried, putting my book down.

'Pray, why not?' she asked, looking indignant. 'He was the handsomest man in town and you're the prettiest girl.'

'Because he left us and got himself killed by a mosquito. Being the handsomest man in town isn't much use if you aren't there for your wife and daughter.'

'Now that's no way to talk about your papa,' said Maman, taking off her mother-of-pearl spectacles. 'Your father was a passionate man and passion is a fine trait, even if it does get you into trouble sometimes.'

Despite the fact that my father had practically deserted us, Maman never said a bad word against him.

She had some strange points of view about the world, and being loyal to your husband, even if he was a cad, was one of them. She wasn't capable of seeing things any other way.

She pressed her lips together and frowned. 'It's true the de Villerays perhaps had more passion than most. But my branch of the Dreux family had none, and that made them weak. Both my parents were dead before they were forty and produced no heirs except me. Passion gives you the will to live. I think that's why I was so charmed by your father: he had a zest for living. Unfortunately, I couldn't keep up with his late nights and his festivities and his ideas —'

'Just as well you didn't, Maman,' I interrupted. 'Or you'd have gone on that foolish trip to Brazil and died with him.'

She sighed and changed the subject. 'Anyways, did I ever tell you about Nicolas Didier, a Creole aristocrat distantly related to the de Villeray family? Now there was a man who had some passion.'

Normally, listening to one of Maman's stories was my favourite way to pass time. But my mind was troubled and I only half paid attention to her tale about a French man and a beautiful quadroon woman back in the days when there were few white women in the colony. Maman spoke about the grand balls where mothers of mixed-blood women brought their daughters to meet prospective protectors in a system known as *plaçage*. The coloured women were given their own houses, and any offspring born of the union were formally educated. It was an arrangement that lasted until a suitably aristocratic wife was sent to the colony by the man's family for an official and legally recognised marriage. Maman described the ball gowns and the women 'with skin like butterscotch' in elaborate detail, but all I could think about was money. How was I going to earn it now that I no longer had a job at the ice cream parlour? Then something occurred to me.

'What an extraordinary story,' I said when Maman had finished. 'Why don't you write it down? You'd be a fine writer, and I bet a publisher would sign you up right away. You could be as famous as Margaret Mitchell.'

Maman lowered her eyes, flattered, then looked at me with a stern expression. 'Don't talk such nonsense, Ruby. I couldn't write a book and I wouldn't want to anyway. I've got you to take care of.'

'Why don't you approve of women working?' I asked. 'Sometimes they just have to. Many of the students at Tulane University are young women now.'

Maman smoothed her skirt. 'Oh, I understand that some women find themselves in a position where they have to work. But, Ruby, a lady — a real lady — never works outside the home. Those girls going to university might make fine careers for themselves, but in the end they're going to come home to a dark and empty house.' My dismay must have shown on my face because her eyebrows rose in alarm. 'Ruby, honey, promise me that you'll never work. I've given my all to raise you to be a proper lady and to make a good marriage. After your papa's death, it was all I had to live for. Promise me you'll never do anything to ruin that. A woman's first priority is her husband and children. A gentleman won't marry a woman he doesn't think is committed to him and the home first.'

Later, as I lay in my bed, I heard Maman coughing and Mae going to her room to take her some hot water with lemon. Doctor Monfort had warned that the diabetes could affect Maman's breathing. If the coughing persisted, she would need more medicines and for that we'd need money. Uncle Rex hadn't been to see us in a while. Aunt Elva was keeping him away, I suspected. How were we going to afford those medicines if I didn't work?

Maman had some lofty ideas but no practical sense and, as much as I loved her, it frustrated me. I thought about my father. It seemed to me that a woman could do better for herself than to tie her fate to the whims of a male member of the species. But Maman would never understand that, and as much as I hated sneaking around, that was what I was going to have to do.

Maman's cough was worse in the morning. I called Doctor Monfort, but he wasn't able to make a house call until later in the evening, so he told me to come to his office in Jefferson Parish and he'd give me some medicine to soothe Maman's respiratory tract.

When I stepped off the bus, I marvelled at how much Jefferson Parish was changing. It used to be a sleepy community with chickens and cows wandering about, but now there were housing developments and roads springing up everywhere. Factories, shops, hotels and even casinos stood where before there'd only been pastures.

As I was leaving Doctor Monfort's office with the medicine, I bumped into Uncle Rex on South Carrollton Avenue. My uncle, usually so precisely dressed, was unshaven and wearing a creased jacket with his tie askew. I wondered if he and Aunt Elva had argued and she'd thrown him out for the night. But that didn't feel right: Aunt Elva would never do anything that would 'get the neighbours talking'.

'Hello,' I said, stopping in front of him.

He looked at me kind of funny, then his eyes opened wide as if he'd suddenly recognised me. 'Ruby! What brings you to this part of town?'

'Doctor Monfort has his office near here. Maman was sick last night with her breathing and I had to come and pick up some medicine.'

I was hoping he'd offer to pay for the medicine, but he didn't, and I was at a loss about how to approach the subject because he'd always put the money in the jar on the mantelpiece without making a big song and dance of it. Had Aunt Elva truly gotten to him about not giving us anything? If that was the case, we were in trouble, because the medicine had cost ten dollars and I'd had to get it on credit. I was trying to help myself, but Aunt Elva kept thwarting me at every turn. I couldn't win for losing.

Uncle Rex and I talked about the weather and how it was finally starting to turn cold. Then, out of politeness, I asked about Eugenie, even though she wasn't an ounce nicer than her mother and I didn't really care how she was doing. 'I can't believe it's almost a year since we made our debut. How is she?'

Uncle Rex shifted uneasily on his feet and didn't reply.

I hadn't had any offers of marriage, but that was to be expected. I was surprised that Eugenie mightn't have either. Aunt Elva had made out that Pierre Leboeuf was very taken with her, and even though Eugenie wasn't the most attractive of girls she did have a sizeable dowry.

'There are plenty of men who would love to have a pretty girl like you for a wife,' Uncle Rex said, not jovially as he usually would have but with a tone of desperation. 'Don't restrict yourself to the Creole community, even if your mother tells you to. There are plenty of fine men out there — you just have to find the right one.'

He tipped his hat and hurried off. It was the strangest conversation I'd ever had with him.

I went straight home to give the medicine to Maman, then I sat on the gallery for a while, mulling over our money problems. Everyone was telling me that a man was my ticket out of genteel poverty, but if I married, I hoped it would be for love not money. For me, work was the obvious solution. Why then did things have to be so darn complicated? Taking control of one's destiny seemed like a fine characteristic to me, but in Creole society a woman working was akin to walking the slippery road to hell. I had to work but I had to hide it, and that made most of the jobs I could apply for out of the question.

Mae brought me a cup of tea, and I sipped it while watching people going about their business on Royal Street. A young woman holding a flag on a stick caught my eye. A group of tourists — smartly dressed in twin-sets, tweed suits and two-toned saddle shoes — was following her. Tour groups were a common sight in the French Quarter, but something about this guide caught my attention. Then I recognised her: she was the architecture student I'd spoken to outside Tulane University. Out of curiosity, I went downstairs and joined the group.

'This is an excellent example of a Creole cottage, built in 1793,' she said, pointing to a building behind her. 'Note the steeply pitched roof and the dormer windows, and the tall shuttered doors designed to increase the airflow or keep out the heat.'

Next she led the group to look at the matching red-brick Pontalba Buildings on either side of Jackson Square, and explained that they'd been commissioned by Micaela Almonester, Baroness de Pontalba, an aristocrat and a real estate developer.

'Baroness de Pontalba was known as a shrewd and vivacious woman with an excellent head for business,' the girl told us. 'These two buildings were the most ambitious of their kind at that time in America, and the Paris-influenced cast-iron grillework came to define the aesthetic of the buildings in the French Quarter from then ŏn, giving the area its uniquely feminine character.'

The story of Baroness de Pontalba was one of Maman's favourites to tell. A Spanish Creole born in the late 1700s, she was placed into an arranged marriage with her French cousin Célestin, who plotted with his father to get their hands on her fortune, which the Baroness's mother had been astute enough to protect when her daughter moved to Paris. Frustrated by their efforts to break her down, Célestin's father shot the Baroness four times before committing suicide. She survived, and obtained a legal separation from her husband so that she could return to New Orleans to develop property there. Although Maman was fascinated by the savvy Creole aristocrat, she didn't relate her independence to our lives at all. Maman would think that being described as a 'shrewd and vivacious woman with an excellent head for business' was an insult. But I admired Baroness de Pontalba. She had verve — and that's what I needed too.

The girl finished her tour by thanking the group, then added, 'In the 1930s, the city wanted to demolish the French Quarter and replace it with modern housing, but a small group of citizens saw the historic value of the area and fought that decision. I'm proud to say that my mother was one of those preservationists and I'm delighted to have been able to show you around the area today.'

The tourists gave her a round of applause and slipped money into her hand before dispersing. It looked like she'd made more in tips alone than I had in a day at the ice cream parlour.

'Do you do this every day?' I asked the girl, fascinated by what I'd seen.

'No, only a couple of times a week to help with my college tuition,' she replied, putting the money into her purse.

'It seems like a good job,' I said. 'You're making good money for an hour's work.'

She smiled sheepishly. 'I do all right, but my friend Sally, who does the ghost tours, makes more than me. The haunted tours draw bigger crowds.'

'Really?' I replied, my mind ticking over. Perhaps I could be a guide? I didn't know much about architecture, but I did know a lot about the history of New Orleans, thanks to Maman.

'She's doing one early this evening if you're interested,' the girl said. 'It starts outside the Cabildo at six o'clock.'

I waited for Sally outside the museum on Jackson Square. In the fading light the place was eerie and I recalled Maman's stories about rebellious slaves being hanged in the square as a warning to others. What an atmospheric place for a ghost tour! I was surprised then when a mousy-looking girl in a V-neck sweater and cigarette pants arrived, sold tickets to the dozen or so people who had gathered for the tour, and led us directly to Saint Louis Cathedral without mentioning the square itself.

She showed us an alley that was supposed to be haunted by Père Antoine, once the pastor of the church. 'But he's a very benign ghost,' she said in a high-pitched, strained voice. 'He came to the city in 1774 as part of the Spanish Inquisition, but never got into the spirit of things.'

She continued from building to building around the Quarter, telling us stories in a mediocre way. *This girl is awful*, I thought. If her Northern accent didn't give her away, you could tell by the flat way she told stories that she wasn't from New Orleans.

When she came to the intersection of Royal and St Ann streets, she rattled off the story of 'Julie's Ghost' in the same monotone she'd used for all her other stories. Julie had been an exotic octoroon whose protector had given her a beautiful home with servants and fine jewellery, but it wasn't enough for her. After her protector's wife died and Julie was pregnant with his child, she pestered him to make her his legal wife. One freezing and damp December night, when her protector grew tired of her begging, he joked that if she stayed on the roof naked until the dawn, he would marry her. Knowing her love of comfort, her protector never expected Julie to take his dare seriously and he spent the evening playing cards and drinking with friends in the parlour. When he retired in the early hours of the morning, he couldn't find Julie anywhere. Terrified, he climbed to the roof and found her frozen and naked corpse. The protector was shattered and, driven to drink, died the following year.

It was a heartbreaking story, but instead of being moved the tourists glanced at their watches. Sally had missed an opportunity to milk the tale for all it was worth. Maman would have told the story with tears choking her voice. Any decent storyteller would have!

The tour came to an end and, despite looking less than satisfied, the tourists tipped Sally with notes not coins. Those people hadn't signed up for a ghost tour like that, I thought, as I walked home. If they were interested in facts, they would have taken a historical or architectural tour. Instead they'd wanted to hear about objects moving by themselves, lights turning on and off, mysterious footsteps, and transparent figures appearing at the foot of a bed. They'd chosen a ghost tour because they wanted to be scared out of their wits. I knew I could run a better tour than Sally had.

The following day, I jotted down ideas for ghosts who would interest tourists. There was no use taking them around the French Quarter, where I would be recognised by people who knew me and Maman, so I settled on the Garden District, which had plenty of grand and spooky homes of its own. It was a hundred and fifty years since the French had sold New Orleans to the Americans, and yet we Creoles still maintained our superior attitude towards them. The Americans had been industrious people who worked around the clock and lived prudently in order to make money. We were people who valued leisure and frivolity above all other pursuits. These days, with a sick mother to think about and the de Villeray fortune a thing of the past, perhaps a bit of prudence wasn't a bad thing.

As I gathered material for my stories, I decided that I would need to dress the part of a ghost tour guide. My pale skin and dark hair would work well for an 'otherworldly' style; all I had to do was wear dark red lipstick and a black velvet dress Maman kept in the back of her wardrobe and hadn't worn for years.

I had business cards printed up and left them at luxury hotels like the Roosevelt and the Monteleone:

Selene Moon

Specialist Ghost Tour Guide — The Garden District

Three o'clock, Tuesday and Thursday afternoons

Corner of St Charles Avenue and Washington Avenue

'Oh!' said Mae, shaking her head when she learned what I was up to. 'No good can come of this, Miss Ruby. No good at all! All those stories you're making up will catch you out one day. Besides, you don't even have a licence from the city.'

'Don't be so pessimistic,' I told her. 'Of course good will come of it. Wouldn't you like to see Maman better? Wouldn't you like a washing machine?'

To my delight, on my first day twenty tourists turned up at the intersection of St Charles and Washington avenues. As they stepped off the streetcar, I sized them up. The women's eyes sparkled with excitement, but the men stood with folded arms, aloof and superior.

I asked the tourists to say where they were from. A couple from New York seemed like hard nuts, while two sisters from Wisconsin shifted from foot to foot eagerly. The others — Texans, Washingtonians and Californians — were difficult to read. It was a varied group to deal with, and I knew that like in a game of vingt-et-un I had to get the upper hand quickly.

'Ghosts are everywhere in this city,' I told them before we embarked on the tour. 'We New Orleanians talk about them as naturally as you might speak about the weather or the price of oil. They are part of the fabric of the city.' I leaned forward and added in a whisper, 'The wraiths of New Orleans will sit with you in a restaurant and all you'll feel is a chill on your arm; they'll stand behind you while you watch the parades and whisper in your ear; they'll ride with you on the streetcar and the only clue will be a breeze playing in your hair. Most of the time these spirits are harmless but there are evil ones too — those who have performed grim and ghastly deeds in their earthly life and want to take you back into hell with them. That is why you must stick with me at all times.' I touched the talisman of herbs I wore around my neck and affected a shiver.

The man from New York shot a glance over his shoulder. He didn't look so smug now. A woman from San Francisco giggled nervously, while the couple from Washington DC huddled closer to each other. I had them in my grasp.

I walked towards Coliseum Street and the tourists hurried along behind me, no-one wanting to be left behind lest one of 'the strange shapes that float around the walls of Lafayette Cemetery' tapped them on the shoulder and whispered to them, 'as they are known to do'.

Although it was the first tour I'd ever run, I made up supernatural experiences that had occurred on my earlier tours. I told them that once when I was walking with a group down Coliseum Street, a little girl joined the tourists and took the hand of one of the women. She bent down to ask the girl where she'd come from, but when the girl opened her mouth to speak water poured out of it. Then she faded away.

'Good Lord!' cried a woman from Texas, gripping onto her husband's arm.

'That was the ghost of a little girl who drowned in a pond when the Garden District was part of the Livaudais plantation,' I told the group. 'Some say she left the house and disappeared into the sugar cane, called by the spirits of slaves who'd been mistreated on the plantation and wanted their revenge.'

I stroked my talisman again and this time the woman from New York swallowed hard. I could see that the group was entranced — except for two young men from Los Angeles. No matter how many stories I told about dim shapes, apparitions of men in Civil War uniforms, eerie violin music or mysterious carriages that disappeared at dawn, they didn't look as fascinated as the others. *They're used to the dramatics of Hollywood*, I thought.

When we came to the last house on my schedule and the men still weren't impressed by my story of the star-crossed lovers who had leaped from its roof and whose heart-wrenching death cries could still be heard on summer evenings, I was ready to admit defeat. Until a pretty Victorian mansion on Prytania Street caught my eye. On my tour, I'd deliberately chosen antebellum houses or ones that were falling into decay, but this house was immaculate and the garden was a magnificent display of spring roses, honeysuckle and day lilies in full bloom. *Everyone is unnerved by a creepy house*, I thought, *but what could be scarier and more unexpected than an angry ghost inhabiting a home as pretty as this one?* It occurred to me that the men from Los Angeles didn't want to be scared, they wanted to be horrified. A story formed in my mind, drawing on Aunt Elva and Uncle Rex as characters. I brought my group to a stop.

'This is the last house on our tour,' I said, lowering my voice to an ominous whisper. 'A couple named Parkinson bought this beautiful home in 1897, but they were unhappily married. He was a kind, generous man, but she was the sort of woman who wouldn't even spare a few pennies for a limbless Confederate veteran. The couple had a niece whose family had fallen on hard times and whose mother was sick. When the wife found out her husband had been giving this niece money to help with expenses, she became so enraged that she cut her husband's throat while he lay sleeping, decapitating him.'

The woman from San Francisco gasped. The others rolled their shoulders or rubbed their necks as if trying to resist prickly feelings of horror. I glanced at the two men from Los Angeles. One of them had his mouth wide open while the other shivered noticeably. I looked down at the ground for a moment to compose myself so they wouldn't catch me smiling.

'When people asked Mrs Parkinson where her husband was, she answered that he'd deserted her and gone to Chicago. Given her cantankerous disposition, nobody found the story too incredible to believe or questioned that Mr Parkinson's tolerance might have finally broken. But for years afterwards, on the anniversary of the murder, a headless ghost appeared in the neighbouring houses, pointing to the blood dripping from its neck and beckoning the occupants to follow it. Of course, people were terrified and made all sorts of bedlam to scare away the ghost.

'One night, two young men who were visiting an elderly aunt saw the hideous apparition in her parlour.

One of the men shot at the wraith with his pistol, but the other said he was sure the ghost was trying to tell them something. He followed the eerie figure out the door and down the steps, struggling to keep up with its supernatural speed. It led him to the house you see here, to its back porch, before it disappeared. Although it was summer and the garden was alive with the scents of jasmine and magnolias, the young man detected a whiff of a foul odour. The next morning he went to the police, convinced there was a body under that porch.

'Sure enough, when the police investigated they found the decayed corpse of Mr Parkinson — but not his head. The wife was found guilty of murder and hanged for her crime, but even as she went to the gallows she refused to say what she'd done with her husband's head. Some say she burned it in the fireplace. Others say she cooked it and served the flesh to the niece as a chicken jambalaya.'

I paused, readying myself for the clincher. One of the Los Angeles men was opening and closing his fists, the other was staring at me, waiting for what was going to come next.

I turned and pointed to a live oak tree in the garden. 'But one thing is for certain: people around here say that on that same night once a year, Mr Parkinson's severed head appears in that tree there and laughs raucously, knowing that his death has been avenged.' I stared at the tree as if I was seeing a vision, then turned back to the group. 'Today is the anniversary. Who dares to come back here with me tonight?'

Everyone looked very uneasy and slipped me their tips quickly before slinking away. But when the men from Los Angeles tipped me five dollars each I knew that Selene Moon had triumphed!

I gave most of the money I earned from my growing tour business to Mae for the housekeeping, but once I kept a little back to buy Maman a lilac satin and lace slip and a chiffon peignoir to replace the ones that were worn and frayed. The delighted expression on her face when she found them hanging in her wardrobe made me feel like we were in high cotton again. If I could keep up my success as Selene Moon, maybe I could slowly get us out of our money problems.

What could possibly go wrong? I thought, lying on my bed and dreaming up more ghost stories. But as Mae always said, it wasn't a good idea to count your chickens before they hatched.

FIVE

Amanda

Sydney, 2005

'Amandine,' repeated Tamara. She sipped her carrot juice and stared at the exposed brick walls and pipework of the Newtown café, deep in thought, before turning back to me with an air of appraisal. 'It sounds exotic. It suits you. But I'm wondering why you've waited so long before telling me about your Grandmother Ruby's letter?'

'Anything to do with my past always brings up complicated feelings that I need to process first,' I explained. 'It's a big name — one that probably comes with an aristocratic history and a sense of duty. I'm not sure I can live up to it.'

Tamara put down her glass. 'You could grow into it,' she replied, grinning. 'I'm picturing a Southern belle in a satin and lace gown sitting in a rose-covered summerhouse and surrounded by ardent beaus.'

I grimaced. 'That's because we were addicted to *Gone*

with the Wind when we were younger. I don't know how many times we watched that together.'

Our kelp noodles and zucchini pasta arrived, and we took a few mouthfuls of the food before Tamara said, 'So are you going to contact your grandmother in New Orleans?'

Part of me had wanted to rush off to New Orleans in search of my remaining family as soon as I'd read Grandmother Ruby's letter. She sounded intriguing, and her mention of a historical family property was like dangling a carrot in front of a donkey for someone who'd specialised in restoration architecture. But old habits die hard. Even thinking about my father's family made me feel disloyal to Nan. Although she was dead, I couldn't bear the idea of hurting her.

'I keep wondering how Nan felt when she got that letter,' I said. 'Obviously she didn't want me to go to New Orleans or she'd have shown it to me. But why did she keep it then? Do you think she was conflicted — torn between her desire to keep me and sympathy for Grandmother Ruby's request?'

'I don't know,' replied Tamara. 'And you'll never know either. But you shouldn't be worrying too much about your nan's feelings now. You have to decide what *you* want to do. It's your life.'

Easier to say than do, I thought. My whole life had been directed by Nan. I'd studied architecture instead of becoming a musician on her advice. When she had shut down the subject of my father, I'd obeyed her. She might be dead, but that only increased my sense of obligation.

'Reverend Taylor said at Nan's funeral that the departed let go of their worldly anger and forgive everyone from their greater perspective,' I said. 'Do you think Nan might have forgiven my father and his family?'

Tamara frowned. I knew she hated any sort of traditional religion. 'I don't know, but I do know you were the best granddaughter you could have been to your nan when she was alive. It's time to make your own path now, Mademoiselle Amandine Desiree Lalande, and figure out who you are for yourself.'

A week after that conversation, I lay in Tamara's spare room with the bedside light still on. Since Nan's death I'd developed a loathing of going to sleep in the dark and preferred to keep reading until I fell asleep.

I cast my eye over the items in the room — the odd bits and pieces that Tamara and Leanne didn't want but for some reason couldn't part with. There was a bicycle that had only been ridden once; a hideous pair of coral pink ceramic table lamps left by the previous renters; and a computer desk with a wobbly top shelf. Tamara's early experiments in photography lined the walls, including a black-and-white picture of me taken four years ago in the Central Station concourse. I was standing in front of the train timetables with my arms folded, staring down at the lens, my expression proud, haughty and confident. I resembled a young Anjelica Huston. But I've never felt proud, haughty or confident in real life.

I studied my face in the photograph — those high cheekbones and full lips. Somehow the picture gave me the courage to do something I'd been thinking about ever since reading my mother's letters. I pulled my laptop from under the bed and connected it to the telephone line. The static bonging sound of the dial-up was so loud that I was worried that I'd wake up Tamara and Leanne who were asleep in the next room. I strained my ears but nobody stirred. They were sound sleepers. I had known my father's name since I was a child as it had been required on all my school applications, but it was only since reading my mother's letters that I'd learned of his profession. There might be something about him on the internet that would add to the little I knew.

I typed *Dale Lalande jazz musician New Orleans* into the search engine and winced from the tight knot of anxiety that formed in my stomach. Only two results appeared. The first was a souvenir poster for a show at Preservation Hall in 1979 with the listing *Dale Lalande and his Band*. The second result was a list of well-known New Orleans jazz artists of the 1970s. Would my father's name really be included among them?

I scrolled down the page and reeled back when I saw not only my father's name but a head-and-shoulders photograph of a young man with tawny eyes and dark brown hair: a man who looked uncannily similar to the photograph on the wall, although not so haughty. I waited for the buzz in my head to clear before scrutinising the image more closely. My father had been a masculine version of myself. Our angular features and squarish Egyptian noses were identical. After years of looking at my face and wondering who I resembled, the answer was right in front of me. I used the zoom option to magnify the picture and smiled. While I was 'creative' in my dress sense, my father looked like the perfect clean-cut college boy. He was wearing a tan jacket over a striped shirt, and his hair was short and parted severely at one side.

The description next to the photograph was brief: *Dale Lalande is a young up-and-coming jazz musician.*

*His unique style is relaxed, swinging and exuberant all
at once. He mesmerises his audiences with a repertoire
that ranges from traditional Dixieland clarinet to a
piano style that incorporates Brazilian and Cuban
rhythmic influences.*

I read the description over again slowly, my heart
thumping so loudly in my chest I could hear it. *His
unique style is relaxed, swinging and exuberant all at
once.* It was as if my father had appeared from a thick
fog and was now taking form alongside my mother.

I rushed to my suitcase and grabbed the box of letters
I'd brought with me. Grandmother Ruby's letter was
on top. Printed in the left-hand corner was an address
and telephone number. After checking the time in New
Orleans — eight o'clock in the morning — I dialled the
international code and then the number. What would I
say to her? How would I even begin?

After five rings a woman with a Spanish accent
answered: 'The Lalande residence.'

I opened my mouth to say something but my nerves
got the better of me and I hung up.

My mind turned over at a million miles per hour.
Had that been Grandmother Ruby who'd answered the
telephone? No, that couldn't have been her. My mother
had described her as a French Creole and that woman's
accent had been decidedly Latino: maybe Puerto Rican or
even Mexican. But she had said 'The Lalande residence'.
I lay back on the bed and took in gulps of air. Given my
overwrought state, a telephone call out of the blue was
probably not the best way to re-establish contact with
my New Orleans family. If it had ruffled me, what might
it do to Grandmother Ruby with her weak heart? If I
wrote first, she would have time to digest the shock of

hearing from me and decide how to respond. I stared at the ceiling, working myself up to a decision. After nearly an hour of deliberation, I took out my notebook and wrote:

Dear Grandmother Ruby,

I am sure you will be surprised to hear from me after all these years. My grandmother, Cynthia Darby, passed away last year and I came across some correspondence from you to her regarding my coming of age.

I understand the relationship between the both of you wasn't good, and I didn't know of your existence until I read the letter. I am very sorry to learn of your condition and hope that you remain well.

I will understand if you don't wish to have contact with me now that so much time has passed, but I would very much like to speak with you and to learn more about my family, especially my father, who I know very little about. I hope that you will agree to meet with me should I come to New Orleans.

Yours sincerely,

Amanda (Amandine) Darby

My words seemed woefully inadequate for the occasion, but they were the best I could muster. I enclosed a graduation photograph of myself, and included my address, my email and my telephone numbers on the letter. When I posted it the next day, I had a strange sensation of having cast myself out into the unknown. I prayed Grandmother Ruby would reply, because no response would be unbearable.

The rent from Nan's house and the money she had left me provided a modest monthly income and I no longer had to work at the real estate office. But I wanted to do something to keep myself occupied. Tamara introduced me to the manager of an Italian restaurant on King Street and I got a gig singing cabaret numbers on Thursday, Friday and Saturday nights. One morning, after a late night singing at the restaurant, I slept past my usual rising time and found that Tamara and Leanne had already left for the day. I made myself a cup of green tea and sat on the couch with it for a few moments before I turned on the television.

Oprah Winfrey was interviewing Mariah Carey and her mother, Patricia, about the challenges of being an interracial child in the United States. Patricia said the family had originally lived in a mixed-race neighbourhood, but both the black and the white children shunned Mariah. They thought things would get better if they moved to a more affluent white suburb, but someone poisoned their dog and they were shot at through their front window.

'What?' I said out loud and put my cup down on the coffee table. Guessing from Mariah's age, it must have been in the 1970s. I'd have thought the people of the United States would have resolved their conflicts over interracial mixing after Martin Luther King, Junior.

The telephone rang. I got up to answer it but before I could reach it the ringing stopped. I looked at the caller ID but no number appeared. Either the battery was flat or it was one of those annoying marketing calls we were always getting. I returned to the couch and to the *Oprah Winfrey Show*. Mariah's story intrigued me. Through my architectural course I'd met a Eurasian girl, Yumi, who had an Australian mother and a Japanese father. I thought she was the most exquisite human being I'd ever seen with her almond-shaped eyes, silky chocolate brown hair and smooth even-toned skin. It was Yumi who'd given me the courage to play up my unusual features rather than disguise them.

'Stop hiding your hands,' she told me one day when we were exploring Paddington Markets together and I'd shied away from trying on some papier-mâché bracelets she was enamoured with. 'Paint your nails vibrant colours so everyone will notice them. My grandmother always said to take what magazines would have you believe is a fault and make it your most fabulous feature.'

Under Yumi's tuition I transformed myself from a social outcast to the School of Architecture's avant-garde 'It' girl. I bobbed my hair, wore heavy eyeliner and drew attention to my unusual hands with bold shades of nail polish and giant amethyst power rings. I may not have looked like a Victoria's Secret model, but that didn't mean I had to hide myself away. Instead of being shunned as I had been at school, I found that boys flirted with me and girls wanted to know where I bought my clothes. The other students began taking my lead on the hippest nightclubs, the best house music and where to get their tattoos done.

The telephone rang again, giving me a start. I picked up the receiver. 'Hello?' I answered, impatiently waiting for the inevitable marketing spiel about a better telephone company or a 'once-in-a-lifetime' real estate investment offer.

There was a pause. Then a woman with an American accent came on the line. 'Could I speak to Amanda Darby, please?'

My fingers tingled. 'This is Amanda.'

The woman paused again as if to catch her breath. 'This is your Aunt Louise,' she said. 'We got your letter. Momma is too emotional to speak right now so she asked me to call. We want to see you as soon as you can come to New Orleans, darling. We want to tell you all about your father. When do you think you can come?'

The blood drained from my face. Although I'd given my telephone numbers I hadn't expected Grandmother Ruby — or Aunt Louise — to call. I'd thought they'd lack courage like me and write first. It took me a moment to find my voice and even then I could barely get the words out. 'I'm sort of a free agent now,' I told her. 'I can come anytime.'

Aunt Louise gave a warm chuckle. 'I'm delighted to hear that,' she said. 'I know it must be strange for you after all this time and it's difficult for me to say all I'd like to on the telephone. I'm going to email you the details of our travel agent. She'll book everything for you. Johnny and I will pick you up at the airport. We'll have so much to say to each other then and I'm looking forward to showing you our New Orleans hospitality.'

I thanked her and then we exchanged some small talk: Aunt Louise asked about Sydney and what I was doing; I told her about my university studies and what the weather was currently like. It wasn't a very in-depth conversation but I did feel an underlying rapport with her. When we ended the call I sat back down on the couch with my head in my hands. Had that all really happened — and so easily?

A key sounded in the door and I looked up to see Tamara and Leanne, their arms loaded with grocery shopping.

'What's up with you?' Tamara asked, peering at me over a bunch of spinach. 'You look like you've seen a ghost.'

'I'm going to New Orleans!' I told her.

'When?'

'As soon as I can get a ticket.'

SIX

Amanda

New Orleans, 2005

No sooner had I stepped into the arrivals area of Louis Armstrong Airport than a woman's voice called, 'Amanda!'

I scanned the crowd waiting for passengers and found a woman in her late forties waving to me. She stood out from the tropical smorgasbord of tee-shirts, micro sundresses, shorts and flip-flops with her tailored beige dress and wedged hairdo. As we got closer, we stared intently at each other's face as if searching for something. With her rounded figure and fair skin she was the antithesis of me in physical appearance. She wore a necklace of silver glass beads while I wore Nan's vintage rose pendant. Her earrings were discreet Akoya pearl studs, mine were Betsey Johnson crystal encrusted skulls. Yet it was there in the light in her eyes: a recognition of kin.

She threw her arms around me. 'Welcome back to New Orleans, darling! I'm your Aunt Louise.'

A trim man in pressed chinos and a button-front shirt joined us. 'I'm Jonathan,' he said, heartily shaking my hand. 'You've flown a long way to get to New-OAR-linz.'

He was softly spoken and his Southern accent was so striking that it took me a second to understand him. I remembered how my mother had described him as 'hip'. With his moisturised skin and chiselled sideburns he was simply well-kept now.

'Almost an entire day,' I said, brushing my fingers through my hair. 'But I changed planes in Los Angeles.'

'Well, let's get you back to the house,' he said, grasping the handle of my wheeled suitcase. 'You must be exhausted.'

Aunt Louise linked her arm with mine and we followed Uncle Jonathan. She was no longer a disembodied voice on the telephone, but a real human being with her flesh pressed to mine.

'I'm so glad you came,' she said, beaming from ear to ear. 'Momma is beside herself with excitement, and I hope you and I will laugh as much together as your mother and I did.'

Her natural affection put me at ease, and the way she described her relationship with my mother gave me a fluttery sensation in my heart. I'd thought our first meeting might be awkward, but I felt like I'd just grown another two inches. I'd never had an aunt before. I'd only had Nan.

'How is my grandmother?' I asked. 'She's had some trouble with her heart?'

'She has to take four different types of medication, but she's tougher than she looks,' Aunt Louise assured me. 'Her physician, Doctor Wilson, says that she'll die young. "You might be eighty, ninety or one hundred when you finally go, Ruby," he jokes. "But you'll still be young."'

'I'm glad,' I said, more keen than ever to meet my Grandmother Ruby. She would be able to tell me more about my father than anybody.

The air outside the terminal hit me like a burst from a hairdryer. The humidity was more oppressive than Sydney mid-January and the sun stung my winter skin. We reached Uncle Jonathan's car, a red Mustang convertible.

'I'll leave the top up,' he said, hoisting my suitcase into the boot. 'The weather's been oppressive today. We might get a storm on the way into town.'

He opened the door and pulled the front passenger seat forward so I could climb in the rear.

'No, look at her legs,' Aunt Louise told him. 'She's got Dale's height. She should sit in the front.'

The casual mention of my father's name was a shock. I had only known him as the man who had 'destroyed our life' and taken my mother with him to an early grave. Now, maybe, I would see him in another light. After all, these were the people who had loved him.

'No, that's fine,' I assured Aunt Louise. 'I'll be good in the back.'

I removed my denim vest and adjusted my halter top before getting in the car. Aunt Louise gave a start when she saw the tattoos on my shoulders, but then she smiled.

'Wings! How beautiful! It's like you're an angel.' To my surprise, her eyes filled with tears as she added, 'A beautiful angel who has come back to us.'

As the car sped along Interstate 10, I stared out the window and tried to imagine what my mother's first impression of the city had been. From the air, New Orleans was broken up by swampland, oil refineries and canals, with the mighty Mississippi weaving through it. But from the ground, it looked much like the outskirts of any city, with billboards, airport motels, car yards and shopping malls.

As we approached the city centre, however, we passed an old cemetery with the above-ground tombs that I knew were a feature of the place. Further on, Uncle Jonathan pointed out the Superdome. 'The home stadium of the Saints football team,' he said with pride.

We exited the interstate and drove along St Charles Avenue into the Garden District. Immediately, a strange sensation came over me: as if I'd been away on an alien planet and now I was returning home.

The first thing I noticed was the light — it was my favourite kind: dainty lacework patterns of sunlight broken up by the canopy of the gigantic live oak trees that stretched their twisted branches across the avenue. The gardens beneath the trees were lush blends of shade-loving azaleas, crimson impatiens and lilies of every variety. In place of lawns, the ground was covered with ivy edged neatly at the borders. The trees and verdant gardens created an atmosphere of seductive mystery that suited the Greek Revival and Italianate mansions. A streetcar passed by down the centre of the avenue. New Orleans was casting its spell on me. It was like slipping into a dream from the past, back to the place where I was born.

We turned at a quiet intersection and passed another ancient cemetery, where the above-ground tombs seemed to peer over the high wall that surrounded them.

'That's Lafayette Cemetery,' Aunt Louise explained. 'During the yellow fever outbreaks the city suffered in the mid-1800s, the bodies were piled up outside the gates.'

'New Orleans is supposed to be the most haunted city in the United States,' added Uncle Jonathan, turning to wink at me. 'Who knows, maybe it is. But I've lived here all my life and nothing supernatural has ever happened to me.'

I looked at the houses again. What I hadn't noticed in my earlier rapture I now saw clearly: while many of them had been restored, others were sinking and settling. The sight of their sagging balconies and roofs, rotting shingles and deteriorating sidings was heartbreaking. The area gave off an air of decadent decay and some of the houses were plain creepy. I noticed the broken dormer window of one peeling and lopsided house, and half expected to see a ghost staring back at me.

Fortunately, the number of pickup trucks with restoration construction company signs on their doors and the rubbish skips in driveways lifted my spirits. It would cost hundreds of thousands of dollars to restore one of these houses properly, but clearly there were residents who were passionate about saving the Garden District. It occurred to me that if I'd studied restoration architecture at Tulane University instead of Sydney, I might never be out of work.

'And here we are,' said Uncle Jonathan, turning into a shaded driveway bordered by magnolia and crepe myrtle trees. Bright blue agapanthus blooms and hedges of gardenias led the way to the front steps.

I stared at the Queen Anne Victorian mansion with its bay windows, porches, ornamental spindles and turret, and my breath caught in my throat. I stepped out of the car, my head spinning. The scent of jasmine was intoxicating and the buzzing of summer insects in the trees was deafening. My thoughts rushed at me all at once. I knew this house, but how could I possibly have remembered it? Then my eye fell to the name plate near the front door: *Amandine*. The link between me and the house was clear. I had been named after it.

'The house was built by my great-great-grandfather in 1890,' said Aunt Louise, getting out of the car and standing beside me. 'It's been our family home ever since. My father was born in that room,' she pointed to the second tier of the turret, 'and so were you.'

I turned to her in astonishment. 'Me?'

Uncle Jonathan chuckled as he lifted my suitcase out of the boot. 'Now don't think we're so backward here that we were still birthing our children at home in the eighties. But your mother went into labour so quickly we didn't have time to call an ambulance. You slid straight out into your father's hands.'

This time I couldn't maintain my composure. The thought of my father being the person who'd held me in the first moments of my life was too much. A deep ache clenched my heart and I staggered. Uncle Jonathan caught me by the elbow.

'It's the heat,' said Aunt Louise. 'It can get to you if you aren't used to it, especially as you've come from winter in Australia and all.'

The front door opened and out stepped a petite woman in a periwinkle-blue dress with her grey hair twisted into a chic updo. In the crook of her arm rested a plump white rooster. The woman lifted her chin with the haughty imperiousness of a grande dame. Her posture was graceful, like a dancer awaiting her curtain call, and her long neck and delicate heart-shaped face added to the effect. Her beauty was so striking that I felt myself and Aunt Louise pale by comparison.

But then her expression crumpled and she gave a cry, rushing down the steps towards me and placing her cool, tiny hand on my arm. 'Amandine!' she said softly, tears filling her violet-coloured eyes. 'You've come back!' Her grip tightened. 'You've come back to me. I knew you would. I am your Grandma Ruby.'

I was captivated by her. It was as if I'd stepped into a fantasy and she was the queen of this magical place. How could these three people standing with me in this tropical garden in front of this fairytale house be real? They had seen me come into the world, had raised me until I was two years old, and then vanished from my life like fairies. Now here we were, united again. I was Alice returned to Wonderland.

'We'd better get Amanda some water,' Aunt Louise told her mother. 'The heat today is unbearable.'

Grandma Ruby touched my cheek and smiled. Then seizing my hand with a physical strength that belied her size, she yanked me up the porch stairs and into the house, with Aunt Louise and Uncle Jonathan trailing behind.

She led me to a parlour with salmon-pink walls, mahogany trimmings and a grandfather clock that struck twelve midday right at that moment. My gaze drifted from a red velvet sofa with cabriole legs and trifid feet to the Aubusson rug that covered part of what appeared to be the original oak floors. I'd been a subscriber to *Antiques Collector* magazine for years. Now the treasures from its glossy pages were here in front of my eyes.

Then it occurred to me that these objects were the first things I'd seen as a baby. I probably crawled around on that carpet and stared open-mouthed at the crystal chandelier suspended from an ornate plaster medallion. Nobody in Australia had understood how a well-crafted piece of furniture could send me into a state of euphoria, but suddenly it made perfect sense.

'Amandine?' I turned to see Aunt Louise holding out a tray with glasses of iced water and lemon. 'Oh,' she said, colouring slightly, 'I meant to say "Amanda". I keep forgetting.'

'No,' I told her, 'please call me Amandine. I like it.'

'Amandine' had sounded like a pretentious name in Sydney, but here it fit me like a second skin. Perhaps it was the name of the person I was always meant to be — and soon I would discover who that person was. At my reply, everyone seemed to let out a collective sigh that they'd been holding since my arrival. It was as if by accepting my birth name I had agreed to return to the fold.

The conversation was polite as we progressed from the parlour to drinking mint juleps in the garden's summerhouse when the afternoon cooled off. My last meal had been breakfast at Los Angeles airport, and whether it was the effect of bourbon on an empty stomach, the heat, or the heady scent of the wisteria vine that shaded the summerhouse, the past seemed to peel away as Grandma Ruby, Aunt Louise, Uncle Jonathan and I mapped our way from the time I'd left New Orleans to the present.

My aunt and uncle, I learned, were real estate lawyers with their own practice in the central business district. As they spoke about their work, I was distracted by the rooster Grandma Ruby now had perched on her lap. At first I was anxious that the bird was going to be beheaded for a welcoming meal for me — I had heard that the food in New Orleans could be savage — but it soon became obvious from the way Grandma Ruby stroked him, and the adoring manner in which he gazed at her, that the rooster was a pet. She even kissed him and addressed him by name: Flambeau.

Aunt Louise noticed my interest in the bird. 'Two years ago, Momma and I were watching a documentary on factory farming on PBS. When the chicks hatched, the male ones were thrown alive into a meat grinder. Momma was so shocked she demanded that Johnny go to a chicken farm and find a male chick for her to raise as a recompense for the cruelty of the human race. Momma's always been a compassionate person.'

'He's very handsome,' I said.

As if he'd understood, Flambeau jumped down from Grandma Ruby's lap and strutted towards me. I reached out to scratch him and he turned himself into various poses so that I could reach his favourite spots.

'Your neighbours don't mind you having a rooster?' I asked. I was partial to the sound of a rooster crowing in the morning. It created an atmosphere of waking up somewhere romantically rustic, like Provence. But if anyone acquired one in Roseville the other neighbours would get a petition up to the council about 'the noise'. Children screaming all day and leaf blowers destroying peaceful Sunday afternoons were acceptable in Sydney's suburbia, but a rooster crowing a few times in the morning was not.

'It's illegal to have a rooster in the city of New Orleans,' explained Uncle Jonathan, 'but people here are pretty laid-back about things like that. And besides,' he said with an affectionate glance in his mother-in-law's direction, 'if something is illegal, forbidden or frowned upon it only makes it more attractive to Ruby.'

Grandma Ruby grimaced, but I could tell by the way she stuck her chin in the air that she was pleased by the description. Flambeau leaped onto my lap and I scratched his head.

'He likes you,' Grandma Ruby said. 'He's a flock bird. He's used to protecting his lady friends. Until now he's only had one henny — me — but now he's got you too.'

'Do you have any pets in Sydney?' Aunt Louise asked me.

I shook my head. I'd longed for a dog or a cat, as many only children did, but Nan had grown up with animals on her family's farm and didn't like them as pets. She thought they made too much noise and created too much mess.

Aunt Louise swirled her glass thoughtfully for a moment. 'It's incredible that you studied restoration architecture,' she said. 'You are going to love New Orleans. The neighbourhoods are so different from each other. The Garden District was built by Americans after the Louisiana Purchase. They weren't welcomed by the aristocratic Creoles of the French Quarter so they settled here.'

Uncle Jonathan stretched out his legs. 'Growing up in an antebellum house cured me of the desire to ever live in a historic home myself,' he said. 'I hated sitting in the same rock-hard armchair my great-great-grandmother had sat in, and the slave quarters gave me the creeps, although the house servants were all gone of course by the time I came into the world. We only had two maids, and they lived in their own homes and weren't required to whistle while carrying food to prove they weren't eating it. Not everything about the past is idyllic, and there's a lot to be said for a house that stays put, has windows and doors that close properly, and can be heated or cooled in minutes.'

I noticed the way Aunt Louise gazed at Uncle Jonathan when he spoke, as if every word he uttered was brilliant. I also saw how Grandma Ruby regarded both of them with amused interest. Uncle Jonathan had voiced an objection to historic buildings I'd heard hundreds of times, so I didn't take any offence.

'I do like classic design though,' said Aunt Louise. 'Our house in Lake Terrace is built in the French provincial style. It has all the appealing proportions of an historic house but without the need for constant repairs and the inconvenience.'

Grandma Ruby winked at me. 'Amandine is starting to look tired,' she said to her daughter and son-in-law. 'Why don't you two hurry along now, and we'll get together again for dinner tomorrow night.'

'Good idea,' said Uncle Jonathan, standing and straightening his shirt cuffs. 'We can eat at our place.'

We moved back into the house, where Aunt Louise retrieved her handbag.

'I've stocked up the fridge for you,' she said. 'Momma has a maid, Lorena. If you want any specific type of food ask her. She does the shopping.'

Grandma Ruby and I waved Aunt Louise and Uncle Jonathan off as they went down the drive. Then she turned to me with a mischievous smile. 'You'll see their house in Lake Terrace tomorrow, but I have a feeling you'll like this one much better. Would you like me to show it to you now?'

It was difficult to take my eyes away from Grandma Ruby. As she stood in the dappled light of late afternoon, her long neck and ivory skin gave her an ethereal beauty that transcended age. But I sensed a contradiction between her lilting Southern accent and the fiery glint in her eyes; I felt there was a complex duality to her.

She lowered Flambeau to the floor to let him run free, and led me to a music room with a Baldwin grand piano that looked the same age as the house. An open-armed statue of the Madonna by the window and a painting of a saint with the Christ child on the opposite wall were at odds with the otherwise Victorian-period style of the house. But then I remembered that New Orleans was a predominantly Catholic city, which made it different from the rest of the United States.

'Your father used to play this piano,' Grandma Ruby said. 'My husband, Clifford Lalande, was a lawyer, as the men in this family have been for generations. But I knew Dale would be a musician. Even as a small child, he would listen to something playing on the radio and then I'd find him in here, picking out the tune on the keyboard.'

I stroked the yellowed keys of the piano and was again overcome with the feeling that my father was stepping out of the shadows. I imagined him as a small boy, his feet swinging from the piano stool as he intently worked out the tune in his head. I glanced up to see Grandma Ruby watching me.

'You're more like your father than your mother,' she said. 'Paula was a firecracker, always ready to thrill us with her bright colours. Dale was quieter, more considered. The night they died, they say I screamed like a crazy woman and wouldn't stop. Yet despite my sorrow, I'm thankful your parents died together. I don't think one of them could have borne to go on living without the other.'

I felt a catch in my throat and couldn't bring myself to speak. The description of my parents' bond moved me. Nan had always given me the impression that the marriage was a hasty infatuation that wouldn't have lasted more than a few years.

But if my father was so calm, considered and responsible, as both Grandma Ruby and my mother in her letters had described him, how come he'd driven drunk with his wife and daughter in the car? Despite Grandma Ruby's vibrant personality, I heard the brokenness in her voice. I couldn't bring myself to ask her about the accident — not yet. *Let me get to know him better first*, I thought, *before I have to judge him*.

Grandma Ruby directed me to a sitting room that overlooked a circular lawn with a cottage on the left; and then to a grand dining room where the mahogany table was laid with Georgian silver and Waterford crystal.

'I like to leave the table set,' she explained. 'Although it creates more work for Lorena, it makes me feel that all the family are still in the house.'

I tried to imagine what dinner must have been like when my parents lived here: the conversation, the laughter, the lavish meals. As I took in the splendour around me, I wondered what my mother had made of it all. It was so different from the house in Sydney we'd both grown up in with its comfortable but simple furnishings. Had she been as dazzled as I was now by the stained-glass feature windows and Venetian chandeliers?

There was no air conditioning on that I could discern, yet the house was cool compared to the sticky atmosphere outside. One of the papers I'd written as an undergraduate had been on the poorly designed 'Tuscan villas' that were appearing all over Sydney, especially on its outskirts: oversized, energy-inefficient homes with eaveless roofs, poor orientations and treeless, paved gardens. The architect who had designed this home, with no computer programs or modern building materials to work with, had created an airy space with high ceilings and windows situated opposite each other for cross-ventilation. The inclusion of balconies and porches made it perfect for the climate, and the canopy provided by the live oak trees would prevent the hard surfaces from becoming such conductors of radiant heat that you could fry an egg on them.

'Would you like to see your parents' room?' Grandma Ruby asked. 'I've hardly changed a thing about it since they stayed there — except for your cot. I couldn't bear looking at that after you were taken away.'

I touched Nan's pendant. It was the first thing Grandma Ruby had said about that time and the bitterness in her tone was palpable. But I couldn't be disloyal to Nan. It was an agreement I'd made with myself before I left Australia.

Grandma Ruby met my gaze and regained her self-control, nodding as if she understood. She led me up the grand oak staircase to the second floor, then down a corridor with a door at the end of it. I followed her into the room, and the first thing I noticed was a wing-back chair and footstool in the part of the room where the turret created a curved space. Dusk had fallen and Grandma Ruby switched on the table lamps, casting a cosy glow on the walls. One side of the room was taken up with shelves stacked with books; the other by a four-poster double bed with a Renaissance-style crucifix on the wall above it. A saxophone and a clarinet were propped on stands near a desk.

'We usually keep Dale's instruments in their cases,' she said. 'But Johnny took them out for you. He thought you'd like to see them.'

I ran my finger over the smooth brass of the saxophone. The tranquillity of the room gave me a sense of my father's personality. Although I'd grown up without my mother too, there'd been pictures of her in the house and Nan, Janet and Tony had told me things about her. Yet my father still felt evasive. I was trying to guess what kind of animal he'd been from the tracks he'd left behind.

'My father liked to read?' I asked, moving to the bookshelves. There were collections of works by Charles Dickens, Edgar Allan Poe, Oscar Wilde and Edith Wharton. I noticed a copy of Hunter S. Thompson's *Fear and Loathing in Las Vegas*. It was one of my favourite books. My father had been eclectic in his tastes.

'Oh, yes,' replied Grandma Ruby. 'I don't remember him ever being without a book. He even used to read between sets.'

I ran my hand along the spines of the books, thrilled to know that my father had once touched them. On one shelf, next to a copy of *The World According to Garp*, I found a small portrait in a frame. It was of my parents with me; I was wearing a white christening dress. My mother looked angelic, her wild hair tamed and stylishly parted to one side. But it was my father who held my attention. He was gazing at me with pure love. My vision blurred with tears and I blinked them away.

'Why don't you lie down for a while?' Grandma Ruby suggested. 'Then come down for dinner. I eat late. It's a habit I've never been able to change. I believe Johnny put your bags in the cupboard there.'

After Grandma Ruby left, I took off my boots and lay down on the bed. It was thoughtful of her to give me this room rather than one of the guest rooms. As my gaze travelled from the botanical print curtains, to the tall chest with the hurricane lamp on top of it, and finally rested on the chandelier above the bed, I tried to fathom that this was the room I'd been born in and where, for the first two years of my life, I had slept with my parents.

My eyelids drooped. I'd intended to nap for only half an hour, but when I woke up and checked my watch, it was two in the morning. I'd slept well past dinner time. I hoped Grandma Ruby would understand.

The hallway was quiet, but the wall sconces were lit. I followed the lights to the top of the stairs. Jazz music played softly somewhere. Was Grandma Ruby still awake?

I crept down the stairs and noticed that the sound was coming from the dining room. The door was open and I peered in to see Grandma Ruby sitting at the table wearing a glamorous pearl satin nightgown and peignoir set. The candelabra on the table were lit and she was staring at the place setting next to her, moving her lips silently as if in prayer. I had intruded on a private moment and was about to move away when she looked up.

'Amandine! I checked on you earlier but you were out cold.'

'I'm sorry. It's the jetlag.'

She gestured to the place setting diagonally opposite her. 'Sit there. That was your mother's place. I'll fix you a po' boy if you're hungry.'

I had no idea what a 'po' boy' was, but didn't want to put her to any trouble. 'I'm fine,' I said, but my stomach rumbled right on cue and betrayed me.

'You stay here,' she said. 'I'll be back in a minute.'

She disappeared in the direction of the kitchen while I took my mother's place at the table. I realised that Grandma Ruby had been looking at a photograph in a frame, but the image was turned away from me.

I glanced about the room. Uncle Jonathan had said that New Orleans was supposed to be the most haunted city in the United States, and if the sensations I was experiencing were anything to go by, the Lalande home was full of ghosts. But they weren't the type that appeared on stairways or floated through doorways. They didn't make themselves visible at all, but I could smell them in the scent of the cypress-wood wainscoting and sense them in the air.

Grandma Ruby returned with a sandwich made of crusty French bread on a gold-edged plate. My mouth watered at the sight of the sliced tomato and chargrilled eggplant.

'Good?' she asked, after I'd taken a few mouthfuls. 'I make the aioli myself.'

I nodded. 'Very good!'

She picked up the photograph frame and turned the picture towards me. It showed a handsome young man in a white linen suit.

'That's my husband, Clifford,' she said, smiling fondly. 'That's about the age he was when I met him. Do you want to hear about him?'

My heart raced. Clifford Lalande was my grandfather.

'Yes, please,' I said. 'I want to know about the whole family.'

I was starving for information about my New Orleans relatives even more than I'd been starving for the sandwich. With every little piece I learned, it was as if nerve connections had started to re-form and parts of me were coming back to life.

Grandma Ruby seemed pleased by my answer. 'Well,' she said, sitting back in her chair and tapping her manicured hand on her lap, 'let's begin with Clifford. When I was a young woman, my family had financial difficulties and I used to run a ghost tour ...'

SEVEN

Ruby

One day, after a month of taking ghost tours around the Garden District, I'd led my group to the Victorian mansion and was relating the gory tale of Mr Parkinson's murder, when a dark-haired young man dressed in a white linen suit appeared from around the corner and joined us. I was reaching the climax of the story and didn't want to stop to ask him what he was doing or explain that the next tour was on Thursday, so I ignored him.

The tourists applauded when I finished the story and tipped me before making their way to the streetcar. But the young man remained, regarding me with an inquisitive expression. He was in his late twenties with a square face, tanned skin and grey eyes that turned down at the corners, giving him the sweet countenance of a puppy.

'You say that this house is haunted by the ghost of old Mr Parkinson?' he asked, bending a little so his tall height better matched mine. 'And sometimes his missing head appears in that tree over there?'

'That's right,' I replied.

'Killed by his own wife and buried under the porch?'

I nodded, thinking that if he wanted me to relate the whole story again, he was going to have to buy a ticket.

'Fascinating!' he said, putting his hands in his pockets and scanning the garden.

'Yes, it is,' I said.

He turned back to me as if suddenly struck by an idea. 'I would like to invite you to tea. Do you care to join me?'

The merry sparkle in his eyes was fetching, but an invitation without a formal introduction wasn't proper. I found his American brashness both disconcerting and strangely appealing.

'I have to get back to the Quarter,' I said, unconvincingly.

'Oh, we don't have to go far,' he replied, opening the gate to the garden and beckoning me in. 'I thought you might like to come in and see the house for yourself.'

I hesitated. What I had taken as flirtation seemed to have another motive.

He grinned at my confusion. 'You see, I live here. This is my house.'

A flush of heat burned my cheeks and my spine stiffened. I suddenly felt foolish, and forced a laugh to hide my embarrassment. I'd been telling false and horrific stories about his home but I still resented his playing with me. My irritation dissipated when he reached out his hand to shake mine heartily. His expression was so good-natured that it smoothed my ruffled feathers.

'I am Clifford Lalande, but all my friends call me Cliff,' he said, the dimples on his face springing to life as he smiled. 'And you are?'

For a moment I was tempted to stay aloof and say my name was Selene Moon. But he'd already seen straight through me and didn't seem to care. His tongue-in-cheek manner hinted at a penchant for fun and adventure. It appealed to my own sense of mischief.

'I'm Vivienne de Villeray,' I said, regarding him as if we were now conspirators. 'But you may call me Ruby.'

I couldn't have discovered a more American boy than Clifford Lalande. He was good-looking, earnest and energetic in that way only Americans can be. When he showed me into his family home, leading the way with a springy gait, it was like being escorted towards a festive Christmas tree by an excited child.

'Come in! Welcome!' he said, giving me less than a second to admire the ornately carved front door with its lion's head knocker. The entrance hall was a combination of oak floors and mahogany panelling. A marble bust of the Venus de Milo was perched on a pedestal in one corner, while a chalkware plaster statue of Jesus sat between two Boston ferns. The air was filled with a rich, buttery aroma. Someone had been baking.

'I hope you don't mind me taking off my jacket,' said Clifford, opening a door to a closet under the stairs and placing it on a hanger. 'The weather's cooling, but it's still humid for this time of year.'

Before he shut the closet again I caught a glimpse of tennis racquets, baseball mitts and golf clubs spilling over the shelves.

'Hello!'

I looked up to see a young woman coming down the stairs. With her pixie haircut and outdoorsy good looks, I knew that she was Clifford's sister even before he introduced us. Her grey eyes and dimples were a perfect match to his and her smile radiated the same vivacity.

'Oh, there you are, Kitty,' said Clifford, ushering her towards me. 'This is Miss Vivienne de Villeray, the charming tour guide I was telling you about.'

Despite her petite size, Kitty grabbed my hand like a man and shook it vigorously. 'I'm Cliff's sister. He's been watching you from his window with a pair of binoculars.'

'Oh, come on, Kitty, don't say that,' Clifford chided her. 'You make me sound like a spy with the House Un-American Activities Committee.'

'Or you're a sandwich short of a picnic,' Kitty quipped.

Clifford winked at me. 'Sisters! Do you have one yourself? If not, you can have mine.'

He and Kitty led me into a parlour with a carved wooden mantelpiece and a Régence-style gold-leaf mirror above it and two orderly oak bookshelves on either side.

'This house has been in our family since 1890,' Clifford said. 'I've travelled all around Europe and I've never found anywhere as wonderful as home.'

Everything I laid eyes on — the cluster of family photographs in gilt carved frames on the mantelpiece, the monogrammed stationery and the Montblanc pen and stand on the writing desk, the long silk curtains at the windows — radiated wealth. But not shallow wealth. Rather the house had an air of quiet prosperity that created ease and suggested it valued good books and conversation more than it did showiness. It was as lovely on the inside as it was on the outside.

'Please sit down,' he said, offering me a place on the carved walnut sofa. 'I can smell that Mother has made her famous chocolate cake.' He turned to Kitty. 'Go ask Philomena to make us some tea and let Mother know that we have a guest.'

Although the apartment I shared with my mother and Mae was crumbling around us, the atmosphere at home was always formal. At Maman's insistence, we all dressed before leaving our rooms, and had our meals at set times. Visitors only came by invitation, which were issued on cream-coloured cards with the family crest at the top. Although there was nothing in the Lalandes' home that was shabby or in need of repair or painting, the mood was decidedly informal. I had a sense that anything could happen.

And it did. Having completed her errands, Kitty returned wearing a white dress and veil.

'Mother is on her way,' she told Clifford. 'I want to show off my wedding dress. It was finished today.'

Clifford grinned at me. 'I do believe my sister has taken a liking to you. It's a compliment. She's usually harshly judgemental, especially of other women.'

Although being asked to view the wedding dress of a woman I'd just met was an unfamiliar experience for me, I stood up to admire the floral lace of the tea-length skirt.

'The portrait neckline is so sweet on you,' I told Kitty. 'When are you getting married?'

'In March,' she said, smoothing her lace sleeves. 'Here in the house. My parents were married in this room, and I hope Eddie and I will be as happy.'

'I'm sure you will be,' I told her.

A Labrador retriever ran in and around the room before stopping in front of each of us in turn to sniff at our feet. His wagging tail knocked a bowl of wrapped candies to the floor, but neither Clifford nor Kitty batted an eye. The dog disappeared back into the hall, panting excitedly, and returned a few minutes later at the side of a tall woman in a teal blue dress.

'I'm sorry it's taken me a while to come down,' said the woman, smoothing her hair. 'I've been on the telephone all afternoon.'

Clifford and I stood as he introduced us. 'Mother, this is Vivienne de Villeray.'

Mrs Lalande's gaze fell to the voodoo charm around my neck. I'd forgotten about it. I was tempted to cover it with my hand, but to my surprise Mrs Lalande smiled.

'You're a Creole!' she said. 'How positively charming.'

Mrs Lalande wasn't as attractive as her children. Her ash-brown hair was unkempt, and although the wing-collared dress she wore was made of expensive silk, the flared skirt was crushed and the sleeves were rolled up as if she'd been involved in manual work. Yet when she smiled, her eyes lit up and her face shone in a way that made her captivating.

'Well, do sit down, Miss de Villeray,' she said, seating herself on the sofa and patting the place next to her. 'I've been speaking with the Mayor this afternoon and I'm bored of it. I want to know how an adorable young lady like you has come to grace us with her lovely presence.'

Mrs Lalande was catching me in her spell. I wasn't used to being spoken to so kindly, except by Maman of course. Most of the women in our circle had always been cold to me, seeing my beauty as a threat to their daughters' marriage prospects. Since my debut of course, they merely gloated.

'Call me Ruby, please,' I told her. Although I was brought up to always use proper names except between family and close friends, the immediate intimacy with which the Lalande family had embraced me made it seem natural to drop that formality and let her address me as Ruby.

'Ruby leads walking tours around the Garden District,' Kitty explained to her mother. 'She's been stopping by our house on the way.'

'Is that so?' said Mrs Lalande, glancing at her daughter and not seeming in the least perturbed that Kitty was wearing her wedding dress. She turned back to me. 'Well, then we must give you a history of this house. It has a rather fascinating past. It was built in 1890 by my husband's grandfather who wanted to create a charming house for his equally charming wife, Amandine. We have some pictures from that period that we must show you one day when you have a lot of time. My husband loves history and will talk your ear off if you let him.'

A coloured maid wearing horn-rimmed glasses arrived pushing a trolley holding teacups and a teapot and a rich-smelling chocolate cake on a crystal platter. After the mini-feast was served, we all fell quiet as we delighted in the decadent moist cake.

'This is certainly the best chocolate cake I've ever eaten,' I told Mrs Lalande sincerely.

'The coffee and vanilla elevate the flavour of the chocolate,' she explained. 'And I use only the best-quality chocolate. If you use the best of anything, you don't need to eat so much to be satisfied.'

After we'd finished our slices of cake, Mrs Lalande insisted that Clifford and Kitty give me a tour of the rest of the house.

'I'll have to excuse myself, Ruby,' she told me. 'I have many letters to write this evening. We are trying to convince the Latter Memorial Library to integrate and it's taking some persuasion to convince the board that giving coloured folks inferior libraries means they can't get the same quality of education as white people do.'

'Mother and Kitty are members of the Urban League,' Clifford said proudly.

I'd heard about the organisation. They were a mixed-race group working towards improving opportunities for coloured people.

'Well, I wish you the best of luck,' I told her. 'It's been a pleasure to meet you.'

'The pleasure has been all mine, I assure you,' said Mrs Lalande. She turned to the Labrador who was chewing on a ball in the corridor. 'Come, Theodore, we have some work to do.'

The rest of the Lalande home was as beautifully appointed as the parlour. Clifford and Kitty showed me the elegant dining room with its twelve-foot-long table and Prince of Wales chairs, a sitting room with two fireplaces, and a breakfast room with lace curtains and a view of the garden.

'The furnishings have come from all over the United States and Europe,' Kitty explained. 'Each generation adds something of their own to the mix.'

'Our present generation's contribution is the Frigidaire and our television set!' said Clifford, grinning.

Indeed the kitchen, where the Frigidaire was located,

was the only room that had been modernised, with enamelled steel cabinets and an electric range.

We returned to the parlour for another round of tea and chocolate cake.

'Have you been guiding long, Ruby?' Kitty asked me. 'I think it's marvellous that young women like yourself show visitors around our special city and raise funds for civic causes. I've often thought of taking it up.'

I realised that Kitty had assumed I was a volunteer guide, like the socialite women who ran tours at the Louisiana State Museum. I wished that were the case. I was the descendant of a family who had once been favourites of the French king: a woman of my distinguished bloodline did not tramp around the streets for money. But that was exactly what I was doing.

It was too awkward to tell the truth so I went along with Kitty's assumption. 'It is very rewarding, but I haven't been doing it long.'

'Well, I think Cliff and I should join you one afternoon. It would be most entertaining.'

While I was wondering how I was going to prevent that ever happening, the grandfather clock struck five thirty and I seized the opportunity.

'Goodness me, is that the time?' I said, checking my watch. 'I'd better be getting home. My mother will be expecting me.'

'I'll escort you to the streetcar,' said Clifford, standing. 'But first let me quickly show you the garden.'

'Gosh, it is late,' said Kitty. 'Eddie's coming over for dinner and I can't let him see me in my wedding dress. I'd better hurry and get changed.' She shook my hand again with the same vigour as when she'd greeted me.

'Cliff's really taking you out into the garden because he wants to impress you with the gymnasium he's set up for himself,' she said with a parting wink.

'You have a gymnasium?' I asked as I followed him into the garden.

'Well, that's a bit of an exaggeration,' he said, leading me past beds of gardenias and azaleas towards a potting shed. He opened the door for me to look inside. 'I've commandeered this from the gardener for my own purposes.'

Inside the shed was a stand with weights and a set of parallel bars. A punching bag was suspended from one of the roof beams.

'That's a fine set-up,' I said. 'You must be fit.'

'I used to be a scrawny kid and uncoordinated too,' Clifford explained. 'When a boy pushed Kitty over at a children's party, I took him on and got myself hammered. I learned right then that if I intended to be chivalrous in life I needed to back it up with physical strength. I tried baseball, football and basketball and was hopeless at all of them. Then I tried boxing and discovered that I was surprisingly good at it. It's the only thing I do with any sort of grace.'

On one wall was a shelf filled with trophies and ribbons, a testament to his skills.

'Are you a professional boxer now?' I asked him. 'Surely you can't be an amateur. Look at all your awards!'

He grinned. 'I guess in a way I am a professional boxer. I'm a lawyer. I used to work in the district attorney's office, but now my father is planning to retire I've taken over his practice.'

My only experience of lawyers had been with those representing the creditors who had made Maman divide our house into apartments after my father's death in order to pay off his debts. I didn't have a high opinion of them.

'But doesn't that mean you end up defending the strong against the weak?' I asked. 'A lawyer always represents his client's best interests, even if that client is guilty of causing harm to another party.'

Clifford's face turned serious when he answered me. 'I served in the war. Believe me, what I experienced in Nazi Germany left an impression on me. You've got to do what's right, even if it hurts you, otherwise the human race is headed for disaster.'

I remembered the day in Avery's Ice Cream Parlor when I hadn't helped the coloured man whose suit was ruined by the white people attacking him.

'It takes a courageous person to stand up for others,' I said. 'When I was eight years old, my mother took me for a trip to Avery Island. We stopped at a drugstore along the way and the sales clerk offered Maman postcards showing pictures of lynchings. Most of them seemed historical, but you could tell from the clothing of the spectators in one of them that it was recent. "There's a discount if you buy more than ten," the clerk told her. Maman left the things she was going to purchase on the counter and hurried out of the store, pulling me after her. It was the first time I heard the term "nigger lover" — that's what the clerk shouted at Maman as we ran away.'

Clifford was thoughtfully quiet as he guided me around a pond towards the summerhouse.

'I know you don't have much time, Ruby,' he said, indicating for me to take a seat with him in the summerhouse, 'but do you mind if I ask you a question? I'm curious about something.'

Oh dear, here it comes, I thought. *He's going to ask me if I'm really a volunteer guide, or why I'm wearing black, or why I have a voodoo charm around my neck.* But Clifford didn't ask any of those things.

'When Mother said she was writing letters to integrate the Latter Memorial Library ... well, you didn't look at all surprised.'

I hesitated at the unexpected question. 'Why should I have been surprised?'

'You do understand what she meant, don't you?' he asked. 'She wants coloured people to be able to use the same facilities we do.'

Now it was my turn to be curious. What was Clifford trying to say?

'I didn't act surprised because your mother is right. Coloured people *should* be able to use the same facilities we do.'

Clifford's eyebrows shot up. 'Forgive my questions, but you see, women like my mother and Kitty are rare ... and well, I've never met another young woman before who supports integration. May I ask how you came to form that opinion?'

I considered his question a moment. 'Perhaps it's my heritage. Unlike the American planters, Creoles didn't treat their slaves like livestock. They didn't separate children from their parents or husbands from wives. The slaves were allowed to read and write if they wanted to, and could eventually buy their own freedom. Taking away someone's freedom was a terrible thing to do no matter who was the owner, but the slaves of Creoles were at least regarded as human. Perhaps that's why I'm more open to the idea of equality than American women my age — it's something that's come down the generations to me.'

Clifford's already beaming face became still more radiant. 'I think it's also got something to do with your character,' he said. 'I've listened to a lot of arguments for and against integration, but you've expressed the situation in the simplest terms. Coloured or white, we are all human beings.'

It would be an odd person who didn't like Clifford Lalande, I thought. His heart was in the right place, and he embodied the finest traits of the Constitution: not only in his zest for life but also in his desire that the world be a fair place.

A twinge of guilt at my deceitful tales pained me and I pointed to the live oak tree where Mr Parkinson's head was supposed to appear. 'I hope I haven't offended you with my ghost stories. Your home is charming. Your mother and sister too. It's just that ... I had to spice things up a bit. That's what tourists want.'

Clifford threw back his head and laughed. 'A good entertainer gives her audience exactly what they want. And besides, you're raising money for a civic cause.' He stood up and offered me his hand. 'Now, I've detained you long enough. I'd better get you on that streetcar and back to your mother.'

Something about Clifford's easy manner made me want to confess that I'd been guiding to make money for myself, not for a civic organisation, but I decided against it. What would he think of me? Instead I let him walk me to the streetcar stop on St Charles Avenue.

'Ruby, it's been a pleasure talking with you,' he said, as the streetcar appeared in the distance. 'Your next tour is on Thursday, isn't it? Please do come by when you finish. I'd certainly like to talk with you more, and I know Mother and Kitty would feel the same.'

I had never met anyone like Clifford before. I was taken by him, and couldn't imagine anything more pleasurable than visiting him again and seeing Kitty and his mother too. They were so utterly different in a refreshing way.

The streetcar arrived and I climbed on board. I could feel Clifford's eyes on me. He was giving me the same admiring appraisal the Creole boys had at the debutante ball and I couldn't say I didn't like it. But as wonderful as his mother was, what would she say when she discovered that I didn't have any money?

I took a seat by the window and waved to Clifford. He beamed a smile at me. *Oh my, he is nice-looking*, I thought. *And smart too.*

'See you Thursday!' he called out as the streetcar pulled away.

'Till Thursday!' I called back, fully believing that I would be spending another delightful afternoon with Clifford and his family.

But 'Thursday' never happened.

I knew something was wrong as soon as I entered the courtyard of our building. There were no familiar cooking smells wafting from our kitchen, and the lamp in the window of the sitting room where Maman liked to read before dinner wasn't lit. I climbed the stairs to our apartment with mounting anxiety.

'Maman!' I called as I stepped into the entrance way. I didn't even bother to remove my hat and gloves before running from room to room in search of her. 'Maman!'

'Is that you, Miss Ruby?' I heard Mae call from the kitchen. I found her sitting at the table looking lethargic and dejected. 'Oh, thank the Lord you're home! It's been a terrible day!'

The blood drained from my face. In my world there was only one truly terrible thing that could happen. 'What is it, Mae?' I clutched her arm. 'Tell me. Don't torture me!'

My distress forced Mae to regain control of herself, and she stood and helped me into a chair. 'It's all right, Miss Ruby, I didn't mean to frighten you. Your dear mother is still with us. It's just that I've been here waiting for you and you're much later than usual and I've got myself worked up. Mrs Desiree collapsed right after I brought her afternoon tea. Doctor Monfort sent her to the hospital. They're taking X-rays because her breathing was real odd. I stayed with her as long as I could in the ambulance, but they wouldn't let me into the white ward. So I came back here to wait for you.'

I put my head in my hands. Every time something happened to Maman, some further complication of her disease, my heart sank lower. How could God be so cruel? Didn't he hear my prayers every night before I went to bed? Maman was the kindest person in the world. Why was she suffering so when that old witch Aunt Elva never even caught a cold?

'Which hospital is she in?' I asked Mae. 'I'll go straight away.'

'The ambulance took her to Charity —'

'Charity!' I cried with horror, rising from the chair. That was a hospital for the poor of the city. Of course all the doctors and nurses there did their best, but it was no place for Maman. A de Villeray didn't go to a hospital for the disadvantaged!

'Now, Miss Ruby, what else was Doctor Monfort to do?' said Mae, patting my arm. 'We ain't got no money.'

No, we didn't have any money. The little I made on my ghost tours was just enough to meet our daily needs and buy the occasional luxury, and the only things of value we had left to pawn were the chairs we sat on, Maman's dressing table and our crockery. Financial troubles were nothing new to us, but now things were truly desperate.

'What about Uncle Rex?' I asked. 'Did you tell him?'

Mae looked at her feet and nodded.

'And what did he say?' I tried to keep my voice steady. Surely Uncle Rex wouldn't completely desert us? Not now!

Mae began to cry softly. 'He said, "I've helped all I can. It seems to be the Lord's will that my dear sister-in-law is not much longer for this earth."'

I gasped like a drowning person who'd grabbed for an oar only to be shoved back into the water by the very person who should be rescuing her. I remembered the day I'd met Uncle Rex in Jefferson Parish. Something in his attitude towards us had changed. If he would no longer help us, then we were lost. Truly lost.

I stood up and walked to the sitting room, my mind a swirl of desperate thoughts. I noticed Maman's empty chair. No! I couldn't imagine life without her.

I stared at my reflection in the mirror above the fireplace. 'I won't be defeated,' I said, clenching my teeth. 'I won't.'

I didn't know what I was going to do, just that I was going to have to do something. But first I'd go see Maman.

❦

I sat in the Charity Hospital's reception area, waiting for a nurse to escort me to the women's ward. My head pounded, and the pain was made worse by the inane conversation of the two women sitting next to me.

'You know, they don't separate the blood up North,' one of the women said. 'You get in an accident up there and need a transfusion, you won't know if they're giving you white blood or Negro blood.' When her friend gave a suitably horrified gasp, she continued, 'I know! Negro blood! Can you imagine? They may as well give you the blood of a monkey!'

For the first time since I'd learned of Maman's collapse, I thought of Clifford Lalande and our conversation. It seemed like it had taken place years ago, not a few hours earlier. I remembered the way his eyes sparkled with interest when I told him I shared his belief that coloured people should have the same rights and facilities as white people did. But listening to the two women next to me, I realised what a fight that would be. Too many Southerners wanted coloured people to remain inferior.

A nurse came and took me to the ward where Maman was being treated. When I arrived I saw Doctor Monfort speaking with another doctor who looked young enough to be an intern. Doctor Monfort excused himself and took me to one side.

'It's very serious, Ruby,' he said, holding up an X-ray. 'She's developed an abscess on her lung. The only way to save her is to remove the entire lung.'

The news pierced me as if a blade had been jabbed into my heart. The shock was so great that I barely heard Doctor Monfort explaining that bacterial infections were common in people with immune weaknesses and if the abscess ruptured it would spread the infection to other vulnerable organs, but I snapped to attention when he said, 'They can do the operation here, but it would be much better if my colleague Doctor Emory performed the procedure. He's a specialist in the field. It's a complicated and dangerous operation with a long recovery time. Unfortunately ...'

'Unfortunately what?' I demanded.

He hesitated, then said, 'He only operates at his clinic in Uptown. He won't operate here.'

My chest tightened. It was money that was stopping Maman being treated by the best doctor for her condition. Uncle Rex had already refused to help. What was I to do?

Out of the corner of my eye, I saw Maman being propped up by a nurse so she could have a sip of water. My sense of powerlessness abated and the fight returned to me. I didn't care what I had to do. I'd rob a bank if that's what it took. I would find a way to get the best treatment for Maman.

'Book her in with Doctor Emory,' I told Doctor Monfort.

He stared at me in wonder. 'But ...?'

'But nothing! If Doctor Emory is the best surgeon to do the operation then he is the one who will do it. Only will he let me pay in instalments?'

Doctor Monfort's shoulders relaxed. He was clearly relieved that I had agreed to Doctor Emory performing the surgery. 'It's not his usual practice but I'm sure it can be arranged. I will speak to him personally about it.'

After Doctor Monfort left, I approached Maman's bed. Her face was drawn and she was struggling to breathe. But when she saw me standing there she smiled.

'My darling Ruby,' she said in a hoarse whisper. 'You were my only little baby to survive. How strong you were. How much you wanted to live. Now your little brother and sisters are waiting for me in heaven. Your father too.'

I gritted my teeth. 'Don't talk like that, Maman. You aren't going to heaven just yet.' I reached out and stroked her burning forehead. 'Everything's going to be all right. You'll see. Don't you worry one bit. I'll always take care of you, Maman — always.'

EIGHT

EIGHT

Amanda

Iwoke up later that morning with my birth name on my lips: Amandine Desiree Lalande. I'd been named Amandine after the house, and Grandma Ruby had bestowed her mother's name on me too. I recalled my conversation with Tamara in Sydney, how I'd thought 'Amandine Desiree Lalande' a grand name that was too big for me. Now I realised I'd been given that name because I was cherished by my New Orleans family.

I slipped out of bed and moved to the window, where I had a view of the garden gate. I'd been fascinated by historic houses for as long as I could remember, but 'Amandine' was something else. Here, the story of my family was coming to life before me like a surround-sound 3D movie. I imagined a young Grandma Ruby standing there in her black dress, telling her tales, while Clifford Lalande watched her, perhaps from this very window, and fell in love.

I could have listened to Grandma Ruby's story all

night, but when dawn broke in the sky she told me she would continue it at a later time and that we'd better go to bed. Although I'd been disappointed, it was probably for the best. I was taking in so much about my family that it was both exhilarating and exhausting. I was rapidly realising that everything I thought I knew about myself had only been part of the story and I had to pace myself to hear the rest.

When I went into the ensuite bathroom, I caught sight of my reflection in the mirror. *My father used to look at himself in this mirror*, I thought, *and when he did, he saw these tawny eyes, this angular face, this smooth, even skin.*

After my shower, I applied tinted moisturiser, mascara and lip gloss, which was far less make-up than I would normally wear. Apart from my dyed black hair and silver nail polish, it was the most natural I'd looked in years. I'd suddenly lost the need to radically alter my appearance and put on a mask.

A blue and white tube dress was the first item of clothing I found in my suitcase, and I paired it with white sandals. On my way down the stairs I noticed there were no telltale cracks in the walls or dips in the floors to suggest that the house was shifting unchecked. It pleased me to know that 'Amandine' was being maintained.

I passed the parlour and a rich, delicious aroma reached my nostrils. It made me think of Mrs Lalande's chocolate cake but I realised it was the smell of brewing coffee. In the kitchen I found a dark-haired woman in a blue tunic pantsuit. She was laying out dishes on the breakfast counter.

'Good morning,' she said, in a Latino accent. 'You must be Amandine? I'm Lorena. I missed meeting you yesterday because I was running errands. Your grandmother has already had her coffee and beignets in bed, but your aunty told me that you'd like to eat healthy food.'

I eyed the fresh peaches, blueberries and sliced watermelon Lorena was arranging on a platter. I'd heard that Southerners ate 'fried for breakfast, fried for lunch and fried for dinner'. I didn't know how Aunt Louise had guessed that I preferred lighter food, but was glad she had. I thanked Lorena and sat down to eat. She handed me a copy of *NOLA Life News* before she disappeared into the adjacent laundry.

Judging from the number of murders, shootings, robberies and rapes reported in the newspaper I understood why the city was often described as dangerous. But looking out at the beautiful garden and sipping chicory-flavoured coffee, it seemed to me that nothing bad could happen in this lovely part of the world.

I flipped through the paper and a feature article caught my eye: *The Big One*.

> *It's only a matter of time before New Orleans is hit by a major hurricane that could decimate the city. But even a moderate storm could cause flooding that will kill thousands of people ...*

The journalist went on to argue that despite a system of levees, sea walls, pumping systems and satellite storm-tracking, the city was in danger of a major catastrophe.

> *Coastal erosion, ironically caused by flood protection efforts, has now made areas inland more vulnerable to tropical storms than they were a century ago. As things presently stand,*

*the only effective life-saving strategy would be
to evacuate the city entirely, but given the large
population involved, that task is fraught with
problems. A spokesperson for the American
Red Cross said the organization cannot build
emergency shelters in the area because of the risk
to volunteers and evacuees ...*

I was aware that New Orleans was prone to hurricanes
in the same way I was aware that Italy was prone to
earthquakes and the United Kingdom had experienced
flash flooding. The threat of a hurricane hadn't deterred
me from making travel plans; after all, what was the
chance of a natural disaster occurring on my trip? But
what the article reported sounded serious.

Lorena returned carrying a pile of folded towels. 'Oh,
you're reading about the "Big One",' she said when she
passed me. 'They have been predicting it for years: the
big storm that's going to wipe out New Orleans.'

'What a load of scaremongering!'

I turned to see Grandma Ruby coming into the
kitchen, a distinct sashay in her stride. She was wearing
yellow capri pants and a white fitted blouse. Her hair
was rolled into a Grace Kelly chignon. I wondered how
she managed to look so glamorous on so little sleep.

'Don't worry, Amandine,' she said, taking a seat next
to me at the counter and moving her arm in dramatic
arcs. 'I'm seventy years old and I've lived through many
hurricanes. Everybody's so serious these days with their
meteorological reports and models of potential damage.
We had two hurricanes in July, which everyone thought
were tropical storms until the weather bureau officially
classified them as hurricanes. In the old days when a

tempest was coming, we would barricade ourselves in our houses and party until it passed. We never stocked up on batteries and water. We used to buy vermouth and champagne.'

I thought about my mother's letter: partying during a hurricane sounded like gallows humour to me. Maybe the danger was what made the New Orleanians live so vibrantly.

Lorena placed four medicine bottles in front of Grandma Ruby, who took a pill from each one. It was a lot of medication but she seemed in good health. Anxiety pricked me. So had Nan! I couldn't bear the thought of losing Grandma Ruby now that I'd found her again.

'I'll take you for a stroll to Magazine Street before it gets too hot,' she said to me. 'My boyfriend has a shop there.'

Lorena and Grandma Ruby exchanged a smile, from which I deduced the 'boyfriend' was not quite that.

When Grandma Ruby went to the hall cupboard to get her handbag, Lorena took two bottles of water out of the fridge and handed them to me. 'Make sure she drinks plenty,' she said. 'She's not as tough as she acts.'

On our way down Prytania Street, I was again taken by Grandma Ruby's gait. Toes pointed and hips slightly thrust forward, it was something between a dancer's walk and a circus performer's strut. It was leisurely too. I had to keep slowing my own pace otherwise I was in danger of toppling over.

As we walked I took in the beautiful houses around us. It was incredible to me that so many antebellum mansions could exist together side by side yet there wasn't a flashy Mercedes or BMW in sight. Most of the cars we saw were dinted Toyotas and Chevrolets.

It wasn't only the kinds of cars the people of the Garden District favoured but how they were driving that caught me off guard. Nobody was doing more than forty kilometres per hour, and their calm manner wasn't broken once by whatever was the New Orleans equivalent of a P-plater hoon or impatient tradie. Nobody gave us the finger either for having to stop so we could use the pedestrian crossing, as had happened to me many times in the Sydney CBD.

Another thing I noticed was that the roots of the live oaks were breaking up the footpaths. 'Don't you have people trying to sue the city because they tripped on a tree root?' I asked.

Grandma Ruby looked aghast at the idea. 'Oh, no-one's going to cut these trees down,' she said. 'I mean, can you imagine this place without them?'

'I'm glad,' I told her. 'People on Sydney's North Shore used to think that way too. But as new people move in, they call out the loppers if so much as a leaf drops in their pool. The area's losing its unique charm.'

'We don't get rid of things in New Orleans because they're old and may not be one hundred per cent convenient. Look at the St Charles Avenue streetcar: it's been in continuous operation since 1835. The seats are wooden and the "air conditioning" comes from opening a window. But my, what a civilised way to travel compared to a bus. All of us in the district still use the streetcar. You know you're part of something when you ride on it. On a bus, you could be anywhere.'

'I'm not sure Uncle Jonathan would agree,' I said with a grin.

'Oh, you picked that up? Well, let me tell you a little bit about Johnny's gripe with old houses. He grew up in a grand Italianate villa Uptown. When he was a young boy his father, Judge Barial, decided the family ought to have a swimming pool but when the workmen went to dig the hole for the pool they discovered two skeletons buried in the garden.'

'Really?' I liked the way Grandma Ruby told a story, her lilting accent emphasising certain words. 'Who did they belong to?'

'There was a lot of speculation about that. Judge Barial's opponents suggested there had been a murder in the family and demanded a full investigation but the most popular theory of the day was that the two had been victims of a mafia assassination. The mob in those days had a practice of burying bodies in the gardens or under the houses of respectable citizens, where they knew the police were unlikely to search for them. But in the end it was proven that the skeletons were very old and belonged to slaves who had died from natural causes before the Civil War. The whole area used to be plantations and as more digging was done more skeletons were found. The Barial mansion had been inadvertently built over an old slave cemetery!'

'I can't imagine Uncle Jonathan being happy about that,' I said, with a giggle.

Grandma Ruby smirked. 'He makes out that he doesn't believe in the supernatural but you only have to say "Boo" to scare Johnny. That's why he and Louise live out at Lake Terrace.'

We turned onto a street lined with small stores — an art gallery, a chocolatier, a florist and a beauty spa — before arriving at a Greek Revival mansion with a blade sign in French typography out the front: *Galafate Antiques.*

Grandma Ruby opened the door and indicated for me to follow her inside. The shop was a treasure chest crammed with antiques and I was struck by the glint of the mirrors that seemed to cover every inch of the walls. Some were Italian rococo style, while others were baroque. None of them were reproductions. One was a walnut trumeau mirror with an oil painting of a courting couple in eighteenth-century dress. My gaze drifted up from it to the chandeliers and lanterns that dangled from the ceiling like grapes from a vine.

Once I became accustomed to the dazzling atmosphere, I noticed other items: a pair of Venetian blackamoor side tables; a porcelain Cavalier King Charles spaniel in a glass box; a Steinway grand piano. I approached a pair of silver gilt grotto armchairs and spotted the price tag: $34,000. Wow!

The store was crowded and yet everything worked sumptuously together. There was no musty smell or a speck of dust anywhere. How did the owner manage it?

'I think I've died and gone to heaven,' I said.

Although I had a passion for antiques, I didn't own any. The shabby-chic vintage furniture that was often passed off as antique had never appealed to me. It was the real deal or nothing. Of course I couldn't afford the real deal, so I satisfied myself with the pictures in *Antiques Collector* magazine. A slim black man in his late thirties, wearing a blue blazer, polka-dot cravat and oxford shoes, came down the stairs from the first floor and flounced towards us. 'Madame Ruby!' he cried. 'What a beautiful surprise!'

'Blaine, you handsome devil!' replied Grandma Ruby, accepting a kiss on each cheek from him. 'I've brought Amandine to see you. She loves history and beautiful objects too.' Turning to me, she said, 'Amandine, this is Blaine Galafate. The Galafate family has a long history of friendship with the Lalandes.'

Blaine reached for my hand and brought it to his lips. '*Enchanté*, Mademoiselle Amandine.'

His manner was highly affected and very camp. I liked him immediately. He was as theatrical as Grandma Ruby.

'Amandine arrived yesterday,' Grandma Ruby told him. 'From Australia.'

Blaine's eyebrows shot up as if it had suddenly occurred to him who I was.

'Well,' he said, bringing his palms to his cheeks, 'I think that calls for a celebration, don't you, Madame Ruby? I've got some champagne in the fridge.'

'Good idea, Oscar,' she exclaimed.

He disappeared out the back and I turned to Grandma Ruby. 'Oscar? Didn't you say his name was Blaine?'

'Oh,' she said, waving her hand, 'that's a New Orleans custom. We give our close friends pet names. Mine's always been Ruby. Louise's friends call her Lucy. Even New Orleans has a few different names: The Big Easy; The Crescent City; The City That Care Forgot.' She grinned at me. 'You can have a special name too. What would you like to be called?'

I shook my head. 'I'm still getting used to Amandine.'

After Blaine had returned with a bottle of Bollinger and proposed a toast to my visit, I asked him about the store. 'Where do you obtain these pieces? They're exquisite.'

He sat down at a sales desk and invited me and Grandma Ruby to take the seats opposite. 'I travel to France and Italy five or six times a year to attend the fairs and private estate sales.'

My eyes fell to a pair of Famille Rose peacocks on his desk. There were many elegant homes in the Garden District, and I imagined there would be more in other affluent areas of New Orleans, but if the other two floors of the shop were anything like the ground floor, Blaine must have a few million dollars worth of merchandise. Surely the locals in New Orleans and the wealthy tourists wouldn't be enough to keep him in business?

'Who are your customers?' I asked.

He nodded towards the desktop computer. 'These days I sell mainly over the internet. Americans have a passion for European antiques, but my other big markets are France and Italy.'

Firstly, I was surprised that anyone would buy an antique online. Surely you'd want to see the object for yourself, to touch it, to admire its lines, to fall in love with it before investing in it? But then I remembered that there were people in the world with more money than I could ever imagine possessing, and for them buying an eighteenth- or nineteenth-century antique over the internet was no different from me shopping on eBay for a pair of earrings. But the second part of what Blaine had said bamboozled me.

'You mean you buy these items in France and Italy, ship them here, and then sell them back to customers in France and Italy?'

He smiled wryly. 'It takes time to develop a good eye for what is not only beautiful but will hold its value too. If inexperienced people go to fairs, it's very likely they'll buy things that are overpriced and not genuine. I've gotten to know my clientele well over the years and they trust me to make good decisions. I never buy anything I wouldn't be happy to live with myself.'

'I knew you two would get along like a house on fire,' said Grandma Ruby. 'Now, Blaine, you have to promise me that you'll take Amandine out to all the exciting places in New Orleans. You know I don't do much of that any more.'

'It will be my pleasure. There's always something happening in New Orleans and Amandine will be charming company.'

The shop's telephone rang and Grandma Ruby told him to answer it, indicating that we were going back home.

Outside on the street, she took my arm. 'I want you to fall in love with New Orleans, Amandine. I don't want you to ever leave again. I'll marry you off to Blaine if I have to.'

I leaned towards her and said in a conspiratorial whisper, 'I don't think Blaine is the marrying type.'

'No?' she answered, raising her eyebrows mockingly. 'But you two have so much in common — and your children would be beautiful!'

After a late lunch of cornbread with tomatoes, black-eyed peas and green peppers, Grandma Ruby and I took a nap before Aunt Louise arrived in her Toyota Prius to pick us up. On the way to her house in Lake Terrace we passed City Park and I marvelled at its avenues of live oaks draped with Spanish moss.

'It used to be the favoured place to have duels,' Grandma Ruby told me. 'An activity of which Creole men were particularly fond. I lost a few ancestors that way.' Then she pointed to the long body of water running parallel to the park. 'The Bayou St John is the reason New Orleans exists. The French sought a shorter route from the Gulf of Mexico to the Mississippi River and the Choctaw Indians led them to this waterway. It was once lined with plantations, and the free women of colour would hold voodoo ceremonies on the banks, which scared the hell out of the Europeans.'

The Spanish and the French Creoles were gone now, as were the free people of colour and the African slaves, and yet something of their essence remained in the languid atmosphere, I thought, as the essence of the Lalande family remained in the house in the Garden District. It was as if the divide between the dead and the living was very thin in New Orleans.

That impression dissipated the closer we got to the newer suburbs near Lake Pontchartrain. The original houses in the area were 1950s ranch-style bungalows, while the newer ones replacing them were contemporary takes on Georgian, Acadian and Cape Cod styles. The area was open and set out in a modern garden city plan, with arterial roads circling it and the interior streets ending in cul-de-sacs. Street trees were in abundance, but the gardens were mostly lawns with a few shrubs. I remembered Grandma Ruby's comment that when you rode on the streetcar you knew you were part of something, but on a bus you could be anywhere. This area was pleasant but it wasn't quintessentially New Orleans. We could have been driving through any suburb in America. We could even have been somewhere in Sydney.

Aunt Louise turned the car into a street of prestige homes and then into the driveway of one with a steeply pitched roof and dove-grey stucco exterior walls. The parapet mouldings and the keystones were French provincial style but the tall multi-paned windows, devoid of blinds or curtains, were a modern touch. She pushed the remote door opener and drove the car into the triple garage.

'Welcome to our home,' she said, ushering us from the car into a hallway that led to a spacious kitchen. It was an impressive room with a chef's stove and ornamental carvings on the kitchen island and cabinets. A chandelier dangling above added to the glamorous ambience.

'Wow!' I said, admiring the granite benchtops and the white porcelain double sink. We followed Aunt Louise out into a family room with a natural stone floor and a view over a garden of clipped hedges and topiary rose bushes.

To an architect's eye, the home was opulent with a well-thought-out flow between the rooms. Most people would be ecstatic to live in a beautiful home like this, but it was too glitzy for me. I preferred the house in the Garden District with its associations with the past. Then I smiled when I recalled what Grandma Ruby had told me about old houses freaking Uncle Jonathan out. At least in this house, which looked to be only two or three years old, he could be sure nobody had died within its walls.

Uncle Jonathan appeared from the garden with a bunch of fresh thyme and handed it to Aunt Louise.

'Well, hello!' he said, grinning from ear to ear. 'It's lovely to see you again, Amandine.' He kissed me on the cheek and greeted Grandma Ruby the same way. 'While Louise is starting on dinner, let me show you around the house.'

From my experience of styling houses in Mosman, most owners of French-inspired homes decorated them with gilt mirrors, cupid statues and reproductions of

Monet's paintings in distressed white frames. As Uncle Jonathan led us through a formal lounge my eye was taken by an oil painting of a slave cabin covered in snakes and an Andy Warhol–like pop art painting of Louis Armstrong. It was an interesting juxtaposition of styles. He took us to the entertaining area, which was decorated in South-Western style with glazed plastered walls and exposed ceiling beams. 'This is amazing!' I said, examining a feathered headdress perched on top of a life–sized driftwood sculpture of a Native American chief. Next to it, a glass cabinet housed a collection of arrowheads and antler pipes.

'Ever since he was a boy, Johnny has been fascinated by Native American culture,' said Grandma Ruby, guiding me to a couch covered in a Navajo rug. 'I think it was because his father used to read him stories about the Old West. But as Judge Barial was famous for his empathy for the underdog, he must have taught Johnny to root for the Indians instead of the cowboys!'

Uncle Jonathan laughed. 'Louise became interested in Native American culture too when we married but her approach is more academic than mine. In our library upstairs one wall is taken up with law books and the other three with her books on Native American history and culture.'

'They're going to a Mojave Indian Ranch for their anniversary next week,' Grandma Ruby added with a wink. 'Then they're going to trek out into the desert. How romantic is that?'

Uncle Jonathan cleared his throat. 'Maybe not,' he said.

'Why not?' asked Grandma Ruby, looking surprised. 'You've been talking about it for months!'

Uncle Jonathan shifted on his feet. 'Well, we have our niece here now and we want to spend time with her.'

It was my turn to feel embarrassed. I had come to New Orleans on short notice. 'Oh, please don't cancel because of me,' I pleaded. 'I'm planning to be here a while.'

Uncle Jonathan nodded but didn't answer me. He moved behind the bar. 'We need to welcome you properly with a traditional New Orleans cocktail,' he said, taking out three rocks glasses and filling them with ice and chilled water. Then he filled another three glasses with a sugar cube each, before smothering the cubes with bitters, crushing them and mixing them with water, and adding a measure of whiskey.

'Johnny makes a Sazerac the way it's supposed to be made,' Grandma Ruby said. 'None of this syrup stuff. Though originally the French Creoles used cognac instead of rye whiskey, which was more elegant, and the liquor was absinthe.'

'Absinthe was banned in 1915 because it was thought to be a dangerous hallucinogen,' Uncle Jonathan explained. 'So we use an anise-flavoured liquor called Herbsaint instead.' He held up the bottle and pointed to the label. 'It's an anagram of "absinthe" except for the "r".'

Uncle Jonathan emptied the glasses filled with ice, swished some Herbsaint in each of them, then tossed them individually into the air before catching them and shouting 'Sazerac!' He then strained the mixture into the chilled glasses, and added a piece of lemon peel to each before serving them.

'Santé!' he and Grandma Ruby said in unison as we clinked glasses.

The cocktail was both spicy and sweet — and very potent! We had toasted to our health, but I was beginning to wonder about my liver. I was only an occasional drinker in Australia; perhaps one glass of wine if I was out for dinner with friends. Was the New Orleans lifestyle of champagne at breakfast, mint juleps in the afternoon and cocktails in the evening going to turn me into a lush?

'By the way,' said Uncle Jonathan, taking a sip of his drink, 'I should explain that "Creole" has quite a different meaning to most people these days than it did when Ruby was a young woman. Originally "Creole" referred only to the descendants of Spanish and French colonial settlers. "Creoles of colour" referred to those who had some African blood due to racial intermarriage. But nowadays, "Creole" almost always implies someone with mixed heritage. So if you are going to say that your grandmother is a Creole, you are going to have to explain that she is of French Caucasian ancestry.'

Dinner was served out on the patio. The outdoor table and chairs were rustic ironwork, and the surrounding garden was mainly topiary plants in terracotta urns. The water fountain caught my eye: instead of the ubiquitous lion's head you saw in French provincial-style homes, the water flowed into the pond from an upturned tuba.

Aunt Louise noticed me looking at it. 'Johnny and I like to blend things,' she explained. 'Just like New Orleans is a blend: highbrow and crass; religious and rowdy; exotic and homespun; equally obsessed with living and death. We enjoy having the unexpected among the everyday items.'

'The ethnic, linguistic and cultural mix is what makes New Orleans distinctive from the rest of the

United States,' added Uncle Jonathan. 'First there were the Choctaw Indians, then the French colonised the area before it became a Spanish territory. It reverted to the French again for a brief time, but Napoleon sold it off to the young American Union which saw the value in its port. Canadians fleeing the British settled here, and both whites and free people of colour arrived from Cuba and Santo Domingo, and of course there were slaves to work on the plantations.'

'Not to mention the people of all the other nationalities who migrated here, including Germans, Irish and Italians,' chimed in Aunt Louise. 'We are the most diverse city in the South and certainly the most interesting.'

'Diversity does not always make for tolerance,' Grandma Ruby said quietly. 'That was the mistake we made when we thought school integration would go smoothly in New Orleans.'

I was fascinated that Grandma Ruby had played a role in the Civil Rights Movement. Apart from a documentary I'd seen about Martin Luther King Junior and Malcolm X, I knew little about it. But she didn't elaborate on her comment, and Aunt Louise quickly filled in the silence.

'Well, speaking of blending,' she said, taking the lid off a tureen, 'I present to you my okra gumbo with chickpeas and kidney beans.'

Uncle Jonathan passed around the rice while Aunt Louise served the thick stew. The air became fragrant with the aromas of paprika, thyme and bay leaves. The gumbo was tangy and I savoured every mouthful.

'This is delicious,' I told Aunt Louise. 'Will you teach me how to make it?'

'I would love to,' she said, offering me more rice. 'It's a favourite of Momma's, although these days I go easy on the okra because of her medication.'

Dessert was crème brûlée, silky and heady with vanilla and served alongside a glass of sherry.

Uncle Jonathan pointed to the tuba fountain and said to me, 'New Orleans has a tradition of parades. Some say it's because of the Latin heritage and the plethora of brass instruments left behind by marching bands after the Civil War. When I was a young boy I fancied myself as a trumpet player, but in my first parade I stepped in a pothole and split my lip. That was the end of my musical career.'

We all laughed. It was clear that Uncle Jonathan loved New Orleans and its history; he just had a different way of expressing it from Grandma Ruby.

'I wanted to play the harp,' Aunt Louise said with a giggle. 'Momma got me one and arranged for lessons with New Orleans' finest teacher, but at the first sign of calluses I gave up.' She smiled at me. 'I didn't have your father's talent for music, Amandine. Dale was a natural, but he was persistent too, which is why he was successful so young. Daddy used to take him to see the big names play, and Dale would find some way to get himself on stage while they took a rest. Eventually people were paying to come see him.'

'Dale had passion,' agreed Grandma Ruby. 'And passion makes all the difference. Yes, he was naturally talented, but he perfected his talent by practising for hours until he produced the most beautiful tone on whatever instrument he was playing — and there wasn't an instrument that he couldn't master.'

Hearing Aunt Louise and Grandma Ruby talk about my father was a soothing balm to my soul. Whatever his faults, he'd had admirable qualities too and I was finally learning about them. Perhaps if he'd lived, my father might have been someone I looked up to, and someone who would have encouraged me. I was a good musician, but maybe I could have been a great one if I'd had the discipline to practise for hours.

When it was time to go, and Grandma Ruby had gone to the bathroom while Aunt Louise brought the car out the front, I asked Uncle Jonathan something that had been on my mind ever since I'd arrived in New Orleans.

'I'd like to see where my parents are buried,' I told him. 'But I'm uncomfortable asking Grandma Ruby or Aunt Louise. I don't want to upset them.'

An expression of sympathy formed on his face. He squeezed my arm. 'The family tomb is in Saint Louis Cemetery. Louise goes often but Ruby never does, not even on All Saints Day. It upsets her too much. Louise will take you.'

After Aunt Louise had helped Grandma Ruby into the front seat of the car, Uncle Jonathan told her what I'd requested.

'Of course, darling,' said Aunt Louise, opening the rear door for me. 'I'm free the day after tomorrow. I'll take you, and then we'll go to lunch somewhere nice afterwards.'

I kissed Uncle Jonathan good night and got into the car. I'd only met him, Grandma Ruby and Aunt Louise a day ago but already they were feeling like family.

Back at the house in the Garden District, Grandma Ruby made a tisane of rose petals, lavender and chamomile, and we drank it together in the dining room.

I was sitting in my mother's place again and was tempted to ask which place setting had been my father's: next to her or next to Grandma Ruby? I was pierced with a longing to know about my parents' daily lives in New Orleans. Every detail mattered. But I hesitated, remembering what Uncle Jonathan had said about Grandma Ruby never going to the cemetery. Perhaps that was why she was so attached to this house. It was a place to remember everyone without having to think about how they'd died.

'I love Louise with all my heart,' Grandma Ruby suddenly offered, 'but sometimes I wonder if I really gave birth to her. We are like chalk and cheese. But she has an inherent goodness that I admire. She got that from her father. Clifford was an honourable man.'

I held my breath, hoping that she would recommence her story about Clifford. I was thirsty to hear more.

Grandma Ruby stared at the space in front of her, as if thinking deeply about something, then she stood and gathered our empty cups and saucers to take them to the kitchen.

'Well, to bed,' she said when she returned, standing by the light switch and waiting for me to follow her upstairs.

My heart sank. Things seemed to happen slowly in New Orleans. I'd have to be patient and wait.

NINE

Amanda

Blaine arrived at the house the following morning wearing a banana yellow suit and a paisley shirt. He told me he was taking me to a funeral.

'You should go,' said Lorena, stacking the breakfast plates in the dishwasher. 'Funerals in New Orleans are something to see.'

Grandma Ruby had left a note to say that she'd gone to a dental appointment, so I didn't have her to come to my defence. I didn't want to go to a funeral, especially for someone I didn't know. My grief over Nan was still raw and I was afraid that seeing other people's pain would trigger my own depressed feelings again. At the same time, I didn't want to offend Blaine, who had obviously taken seriously Grandma Ruby's request to show me the sights of New Orleans.

'I only brought one black dress with me,' I said, fishing for an excuse, 'and it's far too short for the occasion.'

'Oh, you don't wear black to this kind of funeral,' replied Blaine, pointing to his own bright outfit. 'The more colour, the better. It's for a member of a family who were clients of your grandfather's law firm,' he added. 'I know that Ruby would appreciate it if you went on her behalf. She hasn't attended a funeral since Dale and Paula died.'

Wearing colourful clothes to funerals, releasing balloons into the sky and calling the service 'a celebration of a life' had become trends in Australia too. But death was always a loss and I found it hard to be cheerful about it no matter how it was represented. Then it occurred to me that Blaine might be talking about a jazz funeral. I'd seen one on a re-run of the James Bond film *Live and Let Die* and had been curious enough to look up jazz funerals on the internet. The ceremony was a tradition unique to Louisiana. A band led the mourners through the streets in a slow dancing march step with dirges and hymns; however, once the funeral service was over and the body entombed, the band played upbeat music and the mourners danced wildly to celebrate the soul's ascent to heaven. Although I still didn't like the idea of going to the funeral, I had to admit that participating in a jazz funeral would be a unique part of my discovery of New Orleans.

'All right,' I told Blaine. 'Give me a minute to get ready.'

After my anticipation of a funeral parade, I was disappointed when Blaine and I arrived at an ordinary-looking funeral parlour with curtained French windows and azaleas in planter boxes bordering the driveway.

'Traditionally the wake was held the night before the funeral,' Blaine explained, leading me into the marble foyer and signing the memorial register on behalf of both of us. 'But these days we do the viewing, service and burial all together.'

The viewing! My mind raced. I'd been brought up a Protestant, and to me a wake meant tea and sandwiches after the funeral service. But Catholics were different, weren't they? I remembered an Italian girl at university describing how she'd been taken to view her grandmother's body before the coffin was closed and had to kiss her cheek. She'd described her grandmother as looking like a shrivelled potato. My jaw tightened. The sight of Nan's pale and lifeless body in the morgue at the hospital had been traumatic enough.

'Isn't the viewing for family members only?' I asked. 'Maybe I should wait outside until the service?'

'Oh, no,' said Blaine, guiding me into the reception room. 'Estée was the most gregarious person I've ever known. She knew she was dying and planned this funeral herself. She wanted everyone to come!'

I became lightheaded as we followed the other mourners into the softly lit room. Although it was air-conditioned to a refrigerator-like chill, I was sweating. I scanned the crowded space for the coffin. But all I could see were vases of brightly coloured flowers: crocuses, dahlias, asters and hyacinths. *The coffin must have been in another room. Maybe I wouldn't have to view it at all.*

I had been self-conscious about coming to a funeral in a sky-blue skater dress, but the other mourners were also brightly attired. We looked more like we were celebrating Mardi Gras than attending a sombre event. A guitar and double bass duo played jazz in one corner; and a woman dressed like a gypsy and wearing sunglasses sat at a table to one side of the room, with a deck of tarot cards spread out before her and illuminated by a beaded lamp. People were lining up in front of her — I assumed to get their fortunes read. How had I ended up at this bizarre funeral with people I didn't know?

'This wake is Estée down to a tee,' said Blaine, nodding towards the fortune-teller. 'She came from one of the wealthiest families in New Orleans but liked nothing better than to sit in Jackson Square on Sundays and read the palms of tourists. Wasn't that a marvellous life?'

A waiter carrying a tray of cocktails offered us drinks.

Blaine picked up a couple of glasses and handed one to me. 'Have you tried a Hurricane before? It's the quintessential New Orleans drink.'

I wondered how many 'quintessential' drinks New Orleans had. It seemed irreverent to be drinking at somebody's funeral, but my nerves were getting the better of me and I sipped the red-coloured liquid. From the orange wheel garnish, I'd expected the cocktail to be fruity but the caramel taste of rum burned my throat and went straight to my head.

'What's in it?' I asked, coughing. 'Besides the rum?'

A man standing behind me heard my question. 'Grenadine,' he answered in a casual and friendly voice. 'But it's got healthy content too — orange juice with lime and passionfruit thrown in.'

I turned to find myself face to face with a man in his early thirties wearing a Hawaiian shirt. His eyes were the colour of blue chintz and stood out against his dark eyebrows and fair skin. I hadn't intended to lock gazes with him but it was unusual for me to share the same eye level with anyone — I usually towered over people. I resisted the temptation to run my hand through his glossy brown hair, which fell to his shoulders in waves and was enough to make any girl envious. Instead, I discreetly placed my drink behind a vase. While getting drunk at a funeral might be forgivable, I doubted throwing up would be.

'Well, hello, Professor Elliot,' said Blaine, shaking the man's hand daintily. 'This is my friend Amandine, fresh from Australia.'

'Australia?' repeated Elliot. He looked at me for what seemed an eternity, then smiled. 'One of my graduate students is from Australia — Melbourne. He's writing his thesis on Don Burrows.'

'Professor Elliot Davenport teaches music theory and jazz history at the University of New Orleans,' Blaine told me.

Jazz history? Elliot was too young to have heard my father play but he might know something about him. I was about to ask him, when the funeral director, dressed in a white suit with an orange gerbera in his lapel, stepped onto a podium and the chatter in the room quietened.

'Dear family and friends of our beloved Estée,' he said. 'We are going to take her away soon to prepare her for the service. If you haven't said your last goodbyes, could you kindly do so now.'

I glanced around, expecting some of the mourners to leave the room to pay their respects to the corpse wherever it was displayed. No-one did. Instead they lined up in front of the table where the fortune teller was reading cards. My blood turned cold. I stared at the woman. She hadn't moved. It wasn't simply that she hadn't got up from her chair, turned her head or reshuffled her cards. She hadn't moved at all — not a twitch or a tremor. She was as still as a statue.

'Oh my God,' I said under my breath. 'She's dead!'

'Yes, my dear,' chuckled Blaine. 'That's why we're here.'

He linked his arm with mine and directed me into the line that was heading towards Estée's corpse. I looked back to Elliot as if he might somehow save me, but an elderly woman in a bejewelled kaftan had engaged him in conversation. She was digging her long fingernails into his forearm and scrunching up her face. He glanced at me and grinned ruefully before turning back to the woman who was determined to have his full attention. Meanwhile, people were kissing Estée and telling her how well she looked. Others were touching her hands. I was horrified but I couldn't turn away.

As it came closer to our turn to pay our respects, I was twitching from head to foot. I wanted to run away but my legs were like lead. Then I noticed something. As each person touched Estée, whatever was propping her upright in the seat started to give way. At first it was a slight lean, but then she slipped sideways when someone patted her head. An elderly man made a grab for her, but her deadweight was too much for him and she toppled to the floor with a thud that sent the room into a stunned silence.

The funeral director and an assistant rushed forward to set her back upright, but as they lifted her, the sunglasses slipped from her face and we were treated to the sight of her flattened, half-opened eyes staring at us.

'Well, that's awkward,' said Blaine, nudging me. 'Can I get you another drink?'

The burial was in Lafayette Cemetery. I'd thought such a historical place would be well-maintained, but many of the tombs had been vandalised or were falling into disrepair. If Estée's family was so wealthy, why, I wondered, did her family's tomb look like it was on the verge of crumbling? The door of the tomb next to it had already collapsed; and while the priest was conducting the burial service, I tried to ignore what looked like a femur bone poking out of the gap.

The funeral assistants took forever to line up the coffin properly on the top platform. The woman in the bejewelled kaftan fainted from the heat and I thought I might drop next. I was glad when Blaine suggested we skip the luncheon and go see the French Quarter.

We were making our way back to his red Mini Cooper when Elliot caught up with us. 'Would you two like to get a bite to eat somewhere?'

'I was going to show Amandine the French Quarter,' Blaine said. 'Why don't you join us?'

'Sure!' Elliot agreed.

When we reached the car, I turned to him and said, 'I think you'd better take the front seat.' We were the same height, but he was built like a bear, with broad shoulders and muscular legs.

'A gentleman would never allow a lady to sit cramped in the back,' he said. 'Besides, the Quarter is only ten minutes away with Blaine driving.'

I'd seen pictures of the French Quarter many times but it was another thing to lay eyes on the old town centre for myself. The Spanish colonial townhouses that dominated it, with their ornate galleries and arcaded walls, gave the narrow streets an air of romance and mystery. It seemed fitting that Grandma Ruby had grown up here.

Blaine parked the car in front of a dusky pink and green-shuttered house in Royal Street with a gift shop on the ground floor. Nearly all the townhouses had some sort of commercial business at street level — art galleries, restaurants, antiques stores and souvenir shops. As we walked along the street, I caught glimpses of inner courtyards with banana trees and palms: little oases from the oppressive New Orleans heat.

Blaine prodded me. 'Ruby said you studied restoration architecture? Seeing all this must be getting your fire started.'

'Is this the first time you've been to the Vieux Carré?' Elliot asked. 'Well, it couldn't be more different from the Garden District.' He pointed to a crown of vicious-looking spikes near the top of one of the gallery posts. 'That's called a Romeo pole. The Creoles constructed them to prevent amorous young men climbing up the posts to reach their daughters.'

'Ouch!' I giggled.

'Elliot lives in the Quarter,' Blaine said. 'In an apartment that's certified haunted.'

'It's a friendly ghost of an old woman who still likes living there, so I don't mind,' Elliot said with a shrug. 'She doesn't disturb me so I don't disturb her.'

'It must be amazing to be surrounded by so much history,' I said to him. 'As soon as I can, I'm going to take an architectural tour.'

We entered a bar that was so dark inside it could have been night-time. The oriental carpet and green walls reeked of stale beer, and the patrons were dressed in shorts and flip-flops, but at least it was a cool relief from the heat outside. We took a table near the window and I studied the menu:

Gator meatballs

Drunk squirrel

Coon

Garfish

'What would you like to eat?' Blaine asked me.

'Do you really eat squirrels and racoons here?' I asked, flustered. 'Those were the animals that inhabited Snow White's forest in my favourite childhood Disney film. I can't imagine eating them.'

'I was wondering about the choice of restaurant myself,' said Elliot. He leaned towards me and mock whispered, 'Blaine's ancestors were from the Caribbean: he'll eat anything that comes out of the swamp. But don't worry, they also serve salads with French fries.'

Blaine threw back his head and laughed good-naturedly. 'Well, if it was up to Elliot we'd be at some dive on Frenchmen Street listening to poetry readings and chewing on kale. I don't usually eat here — it's for tourists and I don't recommend it. But they've got a good selection of beer. Why don't you try the Lazy Magnolia Jefferson Stout?' he said, before adding with a wink, 'it's the ideal Southern stout: dark and chocolatey. But I won't make the obvious joke. We can have a drink here and then walk to the French Market for something to eat.'

The waitress arrived and we placed our orders for drinks. A trombonist, bass player and saxophonist started setting up in the corner.

I watched them for a moment before turning back to my companions. 'Was that a normal funeral for New Orleans?'

'Well, it wasn't your typical Catholic service,' said Elliot with a wry grin. 'But it was what Estée wanted, and in New Orleans we aim to please.'

'But that tomb?'

'A lot of people are under the impression that we bury above ground because of our high water table,' said Blaine, missing my point. 'They say the coffins float up in heavy rains. But our above-ground tombs are actually an environmentally friendly form of slow cremation.'

I gritted my teeth, sure he was going to tell me something I didn't want to hear.

'In the tropical heat, it can get up to three hundred degrees Fahrenheit inside those tombs,' he continued. 'After a year and one day, the official waiting time, there isn't much left of the deceased but bones and dust. Whatever is left of the coffin is disposed of, and the remains are swept to the back of the tomb where there's a space for them to drop to the bottom of the vault. Then the tomb can be used for another family member. Some of those tombs hold dozens of people. Tell me that's not a great space-saver!'

I must have been pulling a face because Elliot glanced at me sympathetically. 'You'll have to forgive us, Amandine. We New Orleanians tend to forget that other people aren't as comfortable with death as we are. Death is as much a part of this city as a nose is part of a face. Four years after the colony was first settled, it was wiped out by a hurricane. In the 1700s it was destroyed twice by fires; and later, more than forty-one thousand people died from yellow fever. I think our history of death is the reason why we make merry today and don't worry too much about tomorrow.'

The waitress brought our drinks. I took a sip of mine. It tasted like a blend of roasted chocolate, coffee and caramel; more like a dessert than a beer.

'My grandmother told me that in her day when a hurricane was approaching, they used to party,' I said, glad to get away from the subject of cemeteries and funerals.

Elliot grimaced and turned serious. 'New Orleans was smaller then, and the wetlands were still intact. Professor Ivor van Heerden, a friend of mine, is a hurricane expert at Louisiana State University. He's been warning the city authorities that New Orleans is poorly prepared for a category four or five storm. He predicts even a category three hurricane could potentially destroy the city and surrounding areas.'

'I saw an article about that in *NOLA Life News*,' I said. 'But I didn't understand how that could be possible.'

'New Orleans is below sea level and, according to Ivor, with climate change even a slow-moving hurricane could create a storm surge into Lake Pontchartrain and flood the industrial areas,' Elliot explained. 'The waters, full of toxic chemicals, would then flow into the city, which would fill up like a soup bowl. The poorer, lower lying areas will be the worst hit. There are thousands of families who don't own cars in this city and many homeless, elderly and disabled people who won't have a way out if the city rapidly floods.'

'Don't you have levees to prevent the flooding?' I asked.

'We do have levees,' he replied. 'Just badly designed and poorly maintained ones.'

'Anyways,' said Blaine, throwing up his hands, 'if there is another hurricane I'm going to lock myself in my shop and blow away to oblivion with all the antiques. I got caught up in all the doom and gloom hoo-ha last year over Hurricane Ivan. All that happened to me was I got stuck in traffic on I-10 for four hours, forgot to turn the air-con off, and had to leave the car by the side of the road and hitch a ride with some Christian evangelists. I still can't get the words of "How Jesus Loves Us" out of my head.'

Elliot and I laughed and the mood instantly lightened.

'Blaine could be right,' said Elliot, leaning back and taking a sip of his beer. 'Look at the millennium bug. There was talk about planes falling out of the sky and the end of civilisation as we knew it, and absolutely nothing happened.'

The musicians started up a lively jazz riff and we turned to face them. 'I wonder if my father ever played here,' I mused out loud.

'Your father was a musician?' asked Elliot.

'His name was Dale Lalande. I never got to hear him play because I was only two years old when he died.'

'Your father was Dale Lalande?' Elliot looked impressed.

'Have you heard of him?'

'Sure! He was a talented musician and composer. He died way too young. Only I didn't know he had a daughter in Australia.'

I stared at him in amazement. So my father really hadn't been some run-of-the-mill bar musician. He'd been well-respected.

'You wouldn't happen to have a recording of him ... or something like that?' I asked.

'There could be something in the faculty's library.' Elliot reached into his pocket and took a card from his wallet. He handed it to me. 'I'm back there next week for summer classes. Why don't you give me a call and I'll let you know if I can find anything.'

I lowered my gaze so he and Blaine wouldn't see what I was feeling. The possibility of hearing my father on a recording was more than I'd anticipated. But how could they understand? How could anyone understand what it was like to only now be learning that my father wasn't the scum I'd been brought up to believe. But I couldn't explain all that to people I'd just met.

After eating po' boys at the French Market, we walked back to the car so Blaine and I could return to the Garden District.

'I look forward to hearing from you next week,' Elliot said, and smiled at me in a way that made my stomach flutter, even though he wasn't my type. My 'type' so far had been angst-ridden artists who never painted anything, or unemployed cybergoths. I wasn't sure how I'd relate to a cute university professor, but I was glad he was willing to help me learn more about my father.

Back at the house, Lorena was vacuuming the rugs. 'Your grandmother is having a lie-down,' she told me.

'Is she all right?'

Lorena scrunched up her face. 'She has turns sometimes, but I don't know if it's her age or her heart. She'll never say anything is wrong. Louise came by this afternoon and we both said how glad we are that you're staying with Ruby now. It used to drive Louise crazy worrying about her mother in this big old house by herself at night.'

I went up to my room and lay down on the bed, thinking about the funeral and Elliot Davenport, and worrying about Grandma Ruby. Nan's death had taught me that everything could be fine one minute and harrowing the next.

I got up and took from my suitcase the framed photograph of Nan I'd brought with me. I wanted to place it on the bedside table next to the picture of my parents and me, but then I thought about how much she would have hated to be part of this place and I hesitated. I missed Nan, but I was conflicted about her too.

'Why couldn't you forgive him?' I asked her image before returning it to the sleeve of my suitcase. 'I know you were hurt, but you hurt me too.'

After my experience at Lafayette Cemetery, I was apprehensive the following day when Aunt Louise turned up to take me to see my parents' tomb. On the way, she pulled up outside a florist on Magazine Street.

'Go inside and choose something,' she said. 'Put it on the Lalande account. I'll wait for you here.'

As soon as I stepped inside the florist shop I felt like a little girl who'd discovered a fairy grotto. The profusion of colours and scents bursting from the displays of hyacinths, daphne, cherry blossoms, lilacs and rambling guelder-roses was intoxicating. Nan loved flowers and had passed on her passion to me. I'd always enjoyed styling houses when there was a budget for fresh flower displays.

A summery arrangement of sunflowers, orange roses and lilies caught my eye. I chose them for my mother. The florist was on the telephone talking about wedding flowers, so I took the opportunity to wander among the leather leaf and accordion palms to find something masculine for my father. I spotted some deep purple irises in the cooler, and when the florist was free I asked her to team them with some yellow solidago. Somehow I felt it was the perfect arrangement for my father, although he was still an enigma to me.

'Beautiful!' said Aunt Louise when I showed her my selection. 'The fleur-de-lis — the symbol of New Orleans — is a stylised iris. It represents hope and courage.'

When we reached Saint Louis Cemetery, I was relieved to see that it was better maintained than Lafayette. The tombs were freshly whitewashed, and their uniform size and the straight avenues that ran between them gave the cemetery the bizarre appearance of a miniature housing estate.

'There are actually three Saint Louis Cemeteries,' Aunt Louise explained. 'Number One is the most popular with the tourists because it includes the tombs of the voodoo queen Marie Laveau, and Delphine LaLaurie, a sadistic slave owner. But I like this one the best. It's peaceful and doesn't attract vandals. It's got a few notables too, like Paul Sarebresole, the ragtime composer, and Ralston Crawford, the abstract painter. But the average tourist wouldn't have a clue who those men were.'

We came to a tomb set slightly higher than the others, and Aunt Louise crossed herself. At the top of it, a statue of an angel spread out its wings. At its feet, the words *The Lalande Family* were carved into the stone. Two black granite tablets covered the entrance, carved with a list of names in gold lettering, but the first I saw were those I'd come searching for:

Dale Stanton Lalande
Paula Jane Lalande

Seeing my parents' names, and knowing this was their final resting place, brought a lump to my throat. They'd only been together for a few vibrant years, and now they were entombed here together for eternity.

My vision blurred and I began to weep. I hardly ever cried in Sydney, but in New Orleans tears seemed to come quickly. Perhaps I was becoming less Amanda, with Nan's tough Scottish ancestry, and more Amandine, the sensitive French Creole.

Aunt Louise put her arm around my shoulders. She was my only link to my parents now, along with Grandma Ruby.

'I can't imagine what it's been like for you not knowing your parents,' she said. 'When I look at you, I think I'm seeing Dale's female twin. You look much more like his sister than I ever did.'

I smiled through my tears, remembering how the photograph I'd found of my father on the internet had impacted on me.

'Were we alike in other ways?' I ventured.

Aunt Louise grinned. 'Once you're over your jetlag I'll know for sure. Even when we were young, Johnny and I were settled, but your parents could go to sleep in a different town every night and not think a thing of it. If someone offered them a trip to the moon they would have taken off right away, while Johnny and I would still be writing out our packing list. They had so much zest for life; it was almost as if they knew they would die young and were making the most of everything.'

She turned to the granite urns on either side of the tomb. They were filled with gardenias that had wilted and turned brown from the heat. 'Someone besides me always brings flowers,' she said, lifting out the finished bouquets. 'I think it's either one of Dale's fans or someone who is grateful to my father for the help he gave the Civil Rights Movement.' I kneeled beside her to refresh the water in the urns with water from my drinking bottle, then I arranged the flowers I'd brought with me in them.

'Your parents were on their way to Florida with you and the band on the night they were killed,' Aunt Louise said, her expression growing sombre. 'No-one knows what happened except that the car suddenly left the road. There was nothing that could be done for your parents, but by some miracle you survived with only a scratch to your forehead.'

Instinctively I touched my head. There had never been a scar there. The scars were all in my heart.

'Why didn't Nan come for the funeral?' I asked. Could she really have been so angry she refused to see her only child laid to rest?

'There wasn't time,' Aunt Louise explained. 'According to New Orleans law, the deceased must be buried, embalmed or cremated within twenty-four to thirty-six hours. We offered to hold a special memorial service for your grandmother, but she cut off all communication with us, except through her lawyers.'

We were moving onto shaky ground and this wasn't the time or place for it. I stood up and ran my fingers over the list of family members buried with my parents. There were twenty of them. I tried not to think about Blaine's explanation of what happened to the bodies after entombment, but then thought perhaps it was fitting for them all to eventually mingle as one.

My finger stopped on *Clifford Benjamin Lalande*. It was strange to be standing in front of the final resting place of a man I'd never met but who Grandma Ruby had brought to life with her story. It was stranger still to think that everyone in this tomb had once lived in the house on Prytania Street. If I stayed in New Orleans and never married, would I one day be interred here too?

'Did my grandfather mind that my father became a musician rather than a lawyer?' I asked, remembering how adamant Nan had been that I should become an architect and not pursue music.

Aunt Louise shook her head. 'Daddy was real open-minded that way, and he respected Dale. New Orleans can get wild. From a young age, Dale played in bands and saw a lot of things — drugs and prostitution. While he never judged anyone for what they did, he never got into bad things either. And of course he was the apple of Momma's eye.'

'Did that make you jealous?'

'Oh, no, not at all.' She indicated with a nod of her head that we should start making our way back to the car. 'Dale was charming and energetic. He brought creative people to the house — musicians, painters, writers, actors and dancers — and their company made Momma come alive. She was brought up in the Quarter. It was quite a thing for her to marry an American and move to the sedate Garden District. She was friendly with the American society ladies, but I think they bored her.'

We reached the car and Aunt Louise unlocked it. 'It wasn't that Momma neglected me or was cruel,' she added thoughtfully once we were seated inside. 'She was always very interested in my education. But it's not easy for a young girl to find her place in the world when she has such a stunning mother. When I was a teenager I wished I had a mother that was more ... you know, ordinary. Not to mention the fact that she was a heroine of the Civil Rights Movement — a Great Lady of New Orleans — while I was just an average girl. It was difficult for us to find sympathy with each other, but Dale's death brought us closer together. We realised that all we had left in the world was each other, and Johnny of course.'

'I admire your lack of bitterness,' I told her. 'I knew a girl at university who blamed all her problems in life on the fact that her parents had taken more baby pictures of her older sister than of her.'

Aunt Louise laughed. 'Well, Daddy more than made up for any shortfall. He treated me like a princess. He was the kindest person I've ever known. He never raised his voice. He never had to. I would have done anything he asked. But then isn't every girl a little enamoured of her father?'

I nodded in agreement although I didn't know. How could I?

For lunch, Aunt Louise took me to Commander's Palace, a swanky restaurant located in a turquoise and white Victorian mansion. Inside were tables dressed with starched white tablecloths, gilt mirrors and a troop of dutiful waiters. After the maître d' had seated us, Aunt Louise nodded to the sommelier, who appeared a few moments later with two martinis. One sip of mine and the menu became blurry. I decided that if I was going to stay in New Orleans for an extended period, I'd have to limit myself to one drink a day.

'Johnny usually has the spring pea gazpacho and the citrus salad,' Aunt Louise said. 'Would you like that too? I can see you're into fitness by looking at your biceps.'

While it was true I liked to run a few times a week and go to the gym, even when I didn't exercise my arms and legs stayed toned. That must have been something else I'd inherited from my father besides my height and facial features.

I agreed, and Aunt Louise ordered those dishes for me, and the seafood cakes and Louisiana shrimp and grits for herself.

'You know that Momma is going to leave the house in the Garden District to you,' she said, buttering her bread roll.

My stomach turned. I hadn't come to New Orleans to sniff around for an inheritance. I'd simply wanted to meet my father's family and learn more about him. Grandma Ruby's letter to Nan had mentioned that she intended to leave some property to me, but I hadn't anticipated it to be the family home.

'I don't expect that,' I said.

Aunt Louise was unperturbed. 'Johnny and I want you to have it. I was delighted to learn that you've studied restoration architecture — you're the right family member for it. I love the old house but don't have the patience to give it the attention it needs; and Johnny would never live there.' She smiled and patted my hand. 'Please don't think you're causing trouble in the family. Momma has provided generously for me and Johnny in other ways.'

Our food arrived, and Aunt Louise changed the subject to the Brennans, the famous family of restaurateurs who owned the Commander's Palace, and the doyenne of the family, Ella Brennan, who was a master of haute Creole cuisine. But I barely heard a word she said. Grandma Ruby wanted me to have

'Amandine'? Owning a historic house was beyond my wildest dreams, but I felt overwhelmed too. It was a greater responsibility to bear than an aristocratic-sounding French name.

The waiter returned and Aunt Louise recommended the bread pudding for dessert. 'It goes straight to your hips but you simply have to try it. They spike it with whiskey!'

After our meal, Aunt Louise had an appointment to attend so she dropped me off at the front gate of the house. Before I got out of the car, I turned to her. 'Uncle Jonathan said that you'd planned to go to Arizona for your anniversary next week. Please don't cancel because of me. At the moment I don't have any commitments in Australia to rush back to and I can look after Grandma Ruby.'

'That's very generous of you,' replied Aunt Louise. 'I'd feel comfortable leaving her with you. I know you'll take good care of her. Let me discuss it with Johnny.'

We kissed each other goodbye and I watched her drive down the street.

The bread pudding had been delicious but I could feel it sitting in my stomach so I decided to walk around the garden before going inside.

I'd only seen the garden from the perspective of the summerhouse up to now, but as I strolled along the paths and across the lawn I fell in love with its magic. Squirrels were scampering along the branches of the crepe myrtle trees, and there was a dovecote with several beautiful white fantails sitting on its perches. The plants and garden design were in historic agreement with the house, and I looked forward to meeting the gardener, who, Lorena had told me, came two or three times a week depending on the season.

I stopped by the potting shed and peered inside. It only held gardening tools now, but I thought of Clifford and his boxing gym and smiled. If I was going to inherit the house, I wanted to know every bit of its history.

I approached the back porch, and it was only then that I discovered a major problem. While the porch was freshly painted and decorated with wicker chairs and pots of Boston ferns, those touches were cosmetic. The roof was in reasonable condition, but the end grains of the floorboards and the bases of the columns were showing signs of rot. Underneath, there were indications of real trouble. The lattice that covered the crawl space had deteriorated from the damp, and the tilt of the porch suggested it was on the verge of tearing loose from the house entirely. It was hard to fathom the reason for the neglect. While it was true that many people were so fixated on the interiors of their homes that they failed to notice exterior issues, the rest of this house was impeccably maintained and the front porch was in good repair. Then an idea came to me. I went to my room and rummaged in my suitcase for the sketch pad and pencils I'd brought with me. I'd seen a measuring tape in one of the kitchen drawers and I took it and spent the next half hour measuring up the porch and making a sketch of what we needed to do to fix it. I'd look into finding a suitable carpenter. The restoration of the porch would be my gift to Grandma Ruby and a project that would allow me to learn more about the building techniques in the Garden District.

I found Grandma Ruby sitting in the parlour reading *The Pursuit of Love* by Nancy Mitford.

'Did you have a nice lunch with Louise?' she asked, looking at me over the top of her reading glasses.

'The food was very nice and the martinis too – I think I'm still a bit tipsy.'

I'd intended to approach the subject of the porch diplomatically but I was so excited about my potential project I couldn't contain myself. 'You know the back porch is in pretty bad condition,' I blurted out. 'It needs to be repaired as soon as possible. I've taken the measurements and I'd love to fix it for you. It can be my pet project.'

Grandma Ruby slipped her reading glasses further down her nose. 'I hadn't noticed. It gets painted every five years like the rest of the house, but we never sit out there.'

Her lack of enthusiasm deflated me. 'Nobody uses the porch?' I asked. 'But it catches the afternoon breeze and the view of the garden from it is so pretty. But it's not structurally safe. If it tears away from the house it'll take part of the exterior wall with it.'

Grandma Ruby pursed her lips and put her book down. 'Clifford's mother died there one morning, Amandine. It was a sudden and severe stroke. The porch was her favourite spot to sit and read, or to type her letters about civil rights to the various governors. Nobody sat there after her death. It was too heartbreaking for us.'

The explanation was given gently, but I felt chastised. I should have brought up the subject more sensitively. But a porch in that condition could do structural damage to the house, which might not be so easy to repair.

Grandma Ruby regarded me curiously. 'You love this house, don't you? I saw it in your face the afternoon that you arrived. Amandine has come home to care for "Amandine", I thought.'

The warmth in her eyes eased my embarrassment. I realised that while I was getting to know her and bond with her again, she had never stopped loving me.

It touched me deeply to know that I had someone in the world who cared for me like that. I would drop the subject of the porch — for now.

I sat down next to her and pointed to her book. 'Are you enjoying it?' I asked. 'Mitford's novel *Love in a Cold Climate* is a favourite of mine.'

Grandma Ruby shrugged. 'I don't know,' she said. 'It's something Louise gave me to read. I'm finding the characters too ordinary.'

I stifled a chuckle. Only Grandma Ruby could find a story about an eccentric British uppercrust family that 'hunts' its own children with bloodhounds 'too ordinary'.

Lorena had left us pasta tossed in Cajun alfredo sauce for dinner, and Grandma Ruby and I ate it in the dining room, with a side dish of sautéed mushrooms and toasted French bread. My eyes kept wandering to the other place settings and inwardly I willed her to tell me more of her story, but instead she returned to the subject of the house.

'You are the only person who can inherit this house. I'd rather it burn to the ground than be bought by some visiting Hollywood star who'd paint its interiors white and sell off the furniture to Blaine to be distributed around the world.' She looked at me keenly. 'But with this house comes great responsibility, Amandine. When you inherit it, you'll not only have to maintain its beauty; you'll become the keeper of its secrets.'

'Secrets?'

A storm had started outside. Rain beat against the windows and thrummed on the porch roofs. Grandma Ruby rose and switched off the lights so that only the candles illuminated the room. She placed her hands on the table in front of her.

'The moment we die we become nothing more than a memory,' she said. 'I can't let that happen to the people I loved. I can't let them be nothing more than names and dates on a tombstone.' Her lips trembled, and my own legs began to quiver, as if something ominous was happening. 'There are things only I know,' she continued, 'and I can't share them with Louise. She wouldn't understand. But now that you're here, perhaps we won't all fade as quickly as I'd feared ... especially not him.'

I assumed she was referring to my father.

'He can't fade, and neither can you,' I told her. 'I carry you in my heart and in my genes. Besides that, you're a heroine of the Civil Rights Movement: a Great Lady of New Orleans. You're not going to be forgotten.'

She looked at me in a fierce, trancelike way. 'I want to tell you something. Something you should know because it concerns you directly.'

I held my breath. I could see from the set of her jaw that this was something significant, but I had no idea that everything I had believed about Grandma Ruby up to that point was about to be turned on its head.

TEN

Ruby

Mae and I sat on the floor of our empty parlour and stared at the ceiling. To pay for Maman's operation at Doctor Emory's private clinic plus the first two weeks of her convalescence, I'd had to pawn everything. Everything! All we had now were our clothes. There were no chairs to sit on, no paintings on the walls and even no dishes to eat from. But it was worth it to have gotten Maman safely through her operation. All I had to do now was figure out a way to buy our things back and pay for the rest of Maman's stay at the clinic, which Doctor Emory had warned me might extend to months, maybe even a year.

The task seemed insurmountable; even thinking about it left me exhausted. But there was nothing to do but face each day as it came. There was no point worrying about the future. If I did, I'd give up before I even started.

'Miss Ruby,' Mae said, with a pained expression on her face, 'I've been thinking. With your mama being looked after at the clinic, you don't need me so much around here.'

I guessed what was coming: Mae was going to leave. Well, how could I resent that? I didn't even have enough money to provide adequate food for her. But her going would be a blow to Maman, who loved her, and to me too. I'd known Mae all my life. But she was fifty-five years old. If she didn't find herself a new position now, she might never find one.

'I've been thinking about getting a job in the new laundry that's opening on St Claude Avenue,' she said, fixing her gaze on me. 'They're looking for coloured workers. I can pay you a little rent for my room and help you and your mama that way.'

I brought my hands to my face. 'Oh, Mae! You have a heart of gold! But I can't ask you to do that. You're a free woman. You have to get yourself a better position.'

Mae cringed as if I'd slapped her. That wasn't the reaction I'd been expecting. I'd thought she'd be relieved to know I was letting her go with my blessing.

Instead tears filled her eyes. 'Don't you want me no more, Miss Ruby?'

'Want you?' I cried, grabbing her arms. 'You're like family to me! But I'm trying to think what would be best for you.'

She lifted her chin, but there was a tremble in her voice when she replied, 'What's best for me is to stay in the only place I want to be — with you and your mama. I'm figuring out a way to do that.'

I looked at her incredulously.

She took my hands from her arms and held them in hers. 'Did your mama ever tell you how I came to work for her?'

I shook my head.

'I was born eighty miles out of New Orleans, in sugar-cane country. My grandpa continued to work on plantations after the Civil War, but that wasn't good enough for my daddy. He worked hard, taught himself reading and arithmetic, and got himself a small goods store. When he started to do all right, he sent me and my three brothers to school. Although it was near impossible for coloured folks to register to vote in Louisiana, my daddy did because he could read and he had property. Not only that, he used to tell customers that one day one of his sons would run for government. Now if a coloured man wants to enrage white folks, all he has to do is put on airs and graces.' Mae clenched my hands tighter, and tears came to her eyes. 'There was a no-count white hussy who set her sights on my daddy, who was a fine-looking man. When he refused her advances, she accused him of rape. It was the excuse the townsfolk were looking for. My daddy was dragged from our house, castrated, branded, hung from a tree and set on fire.'

Mae's story hurt me like a sharp kick in the stomach. I balled up my fists. It was a tale I'd heard too often growing up. Lynchings were rare in New Orleans but they'd happened all over the rural South ever since the end of the Civil War. I'd like to see those mobs get a taste of their own medicine, but all too often the local sheriff was in on it.

I blew out a breath to calm myself. 'How old were you when they killed your father, Mae? And what happened to the rest of your family?'

Mae wiped her eyes with her sleeve. 'I was thirteen years old. The townsfolk locked us in our store and set it alight. I broke a window and escaped to the garden, but I couldn't save my mama and my brothers. They were trapped in the kitchen. A coloured farmer gave me a ride into New Orleans, but after that I was on my own. That's when I met your grandma. Your mama was only four years old then and when I went to see your grandma about the position she'd advertised, your mama hung onto my leg and wouldn't let go. "Can't argue with that," said your grandma. "Dee Dee has chosen you." Even though I looked like something the cat had dragged in, your grandma took me in and trained me. Sometimes my nightmares would wake the entire household but instead of getting rid of me, she'd come and comfort me. "There's nothing to be afraid of here, Mae," she'd tell me. "We won't let anything bad happen to you." After she died and your mama got married, your mama brought me here to look after you.' Mae straightened herself and looked into my eyes. 'So you think I'll up and leave just 'cause you and your mama have fallen on hard times? The men in your family might have been fools, but the women have always been fine Christians.'

I looked at Mae as if seeing her for the first time and realised that I'd taken her for granted. I hadn't thought of her as having a past or a childhood before she'd been with my family, and we'd never discussed such things. I'd get impatient with her for always being nervous and never wanting to try new things, but now I understood. What had happened to her family had made her terrified of the consequences should she ever lift her head or step out of line.

I wondered what Mae would have been like if she wasn't kept low by white people. I thought of the three men I'd seen in Avery's Ice Cream Parlor and how they'd been treated for wanting nothing more than to sit at a decent table. What would the whole coloured race be like if they weren't subjected to discrimination and terror?

I stood and pulled Mae up with me. 'I don't want you sweating in some laundry for low wages. You're better than that. Let me figure something out.'

She looked at me askance. 'What are you fixing to do, Miss Ruby? I hope nothing bad. You got nothing left but your reputation. Don't sully that — for your mama's sake.'

I thought about Mae's warning as I peered into the window of a tobacco shop on Canal Street and admired my best day dress in the reflection: red wool with a black velvet trim. To work was to 'sully' my reputation but what else could I do? I needed to make money to pay for Maman's treatment, and I needed to make it fast. Only finding a job that would pay me more than waitressing or tour guiding proved difficult. Demonstrating kitchen gadgets at Woolworths paid only fifty cents an hour with no commission for goods sold. A sales clerk earned sixty cents an hour; a telephone operator, twenty-five dollars a week. If I'd paid more attention to my piano lessons I might have been able to teach, but the reality was I had no skills and no outstanding talents beyond my ability to tell an enthralling story. I couldn't even type — not that a secretary's salary would get us out of hot water either.

I considered begging Uncle Rex on my knees. But even if Aunt Elva was struck by a lightning bolt and allowed him to lend us the money, she would expect it back, and with interest, so credit from them wasn't a long-term solution to our problems. I couldn't be sure that sometime in the future Maman might not need another major operation.

I stopped outside a hairdressing salon. Women in white uniforms moved about inside, fussing over customers sitting under conical dryers. One manicurist was buffing a matronly looking woman's fingernails while another was massaging her feet. But what most caught my eye was a sign on the reception desk: *Shampooist Wanted. Whites Only Apply.*

I could give that a try, I thought. *After all, it's only washing hair. How hard can it be?*

I smoothed my skirt and straightened my collar before entering and asking the receptionist if I could see the manageress. She pointed to a woman with short peroxided hair who was sitting at a desk at the back of the salon and giving instructions to an apprentice.

I walked over to her and said, 'Good morning, ma'am.'

'We're fully booked today,' she replied in a voice heavy with boredom. 'Did you make an appointment?'

'Oh, no,' I said, pointing at the sign on the reception desk, 'I'm inquiring about the job. The shampooist.'

Her eyes travelled over my dress. 'Do you have any experience?' she asked with a sneer.

Maman had always taught me that even if someone was very rude I must never sink to their level. But I'd never been one for tolerating insolence. I stared at the manageress's overly tight curls and was tempted to reply, 'No, do you?' But my desperate circumstances tamed my sassiness.

'I'm willing to learn,' I said.

The manageress moved her tongue around her mouth as if she was trying to get something out of her teeth. Then her eyes narrowed.

'You are kind of pretty,' she said, with the disdain of someone assessing a cheap dress on a rack. 'The job is ten dollars a week plus tips.' She nodded towards the women sitting under the dryers. 'But I have to warn you, the customers around here aren't too generous.'

Ten dollars! I was instantly deflated. Before Maman had gotten sick, I'd never thought so much about wages or how hard people worked for so little money.

'Can't you please pay me more?' I asked. 'My mother's sick and I've got a lot of bills to pay.'

The manageress sat back in her chair then raised one of her over-plucked eyebrows. 'Who do you think you are, Miss Uppity, to ask me to pay you more? I'm not a charity!' Then a cruel smile formed on her face. 'If you want more money, there's another profession you could try.'

One of the hairdressers sniggered and accidentally sprayed lacquer into her customer's eyes. The woman cursed.

My cheeks blazed. I knew what profession the manageress was talking about. Anyone who lived in the Quarter couldn't be unaware of the seedy side of New Orleans. The prostitution and gangster activity were out in full view every night.

Some of the customers joined in with their own jeers. 'I'm sure there are men who'd pay her plenty to massage their heads,' shouted out one.

Her remark sent the others into howls of laughter.

My stomach lurched and I stepped back, bumping into a display of shampoos and making it wobble. The women laughed harder and my face burned with shame. I didn't wait for things to get any worse and made a run for the door. *Dear God*, I thought, walking quickly along Canal Street, *what am I going to do?*

Around me, mothers pushed babies in prams, and men chatted easily with each other, but I felt all alone.

The women's laughter rang in my ears. Why did they have to kick me when I was already down?

'Hey, honey, stop a moment,' a woman's voice called.

I turned to see a plump woman with rollers in her hair and a rubber cape around her shoulders rushing towards me. She must have come from the salon.

'You walk too fast,' she panted when she reached me. She waved a piece of paper in the air. 'Those women were jealous 'cause you're pretty! I know of a job that will pay well for a nice girl like you. My daughter has left her position at a gentlemen's club on Frenchmen Street to get married. The owner is looking for a hostess to replace her.'

'A gentlemen's club?'

'A nice one,' she said, nodding her head vigorously as if to reassure me. 'Classy. All above board. You have to be well-dressed and have good manners. Rich men go there. Nancy said they're respectful.' She pressed the piece of paper into my hands. 'There's the address for you. The owner's name is Rolando Perez. Tell him Gina sent you.'

The Havana Club: Gentlemen Only the sign on the door read. I wasn't too sure about seeking work in any gentlemen's club. What did men do there that they didn't want their wives to see? Smoke? Gamble? Swear? Seduce other women? I was on the verge of walking away, but then I reasoned with myself that I didn't have too many options available to me and Gina had seemed genuine. I stared at the Spanish columns set among banana trees in the entrance way. 'Classy' was the word Gina had used to describe the club. I was doubtful about that, but I entered anyway.

The place was empty except for some waiters setting up the tables for the evening and a cleaner mopping the mosaic-tiled floor. The interior wasn't as gaudy as I'd been expecting. Round tables decorated with linen cloths and beaded lamps faced towards a stage with a red velvet curtain. A carved horseshoe bar dominated the centre of the room and the scent of whiskey and expensive tobacco lingered in the air. I tried to imagine what kind of men came here.

'Are you here for me?'

I turned to see a swarthy man in a purple jacket and bow tie. His broad smile was as flashy as the diamond rings he wore on each of his fingers.

'Mr Perez? Gina suggested I come. She said you're looking for a hostess?'

The man smoothed back his cowlick. 'Please, call me Rolando. And remind me to thank Gina.' He showed me into his office and told me to take a seat. 'What's your name?' he asked, taking a cigar from a box on his desk, and clipping it before lighting it.

'Vivienne de Villeray,' I told him.

'Vivienne de Villeray.' He whistled under his breath to demonstrate he was impressed. 'What do your friends call you, Vivienne?'

'Ruby.'

'Well,' he said, blowing puffs of aromatic smoke into the air, 'Ruby is very nice. Why don't we stick with that? It sounds friendlier, and we're all friends here.'

A reproduction of Titan's erotic *Venus of Urbino* hung on the wall behind Rolando. I sat up straight to appear confident and mature, but beneath my bravado a worry gnawed. Mae had warned me not to do anything to compromise my reputation.

'I don't want to do anything shameful,' I told him. 'I need to be sure that hostessing is all that's expected of me.'

Rolando frowned. 'I can assure you that I don't employ whores. If any of my girls goes with a customer, I fire her. Likewise, if a customer gets fresh with one of my girls he's asked to leave. I look after everyone who works for me as if they were my family. All I expect of you is to be friendly and to make sure that the customers are having a good time.'

'And by a good time you mean ...?'

'You encourage them to drink, Ruby. That's what a hostess does. I pay you thirty dollars a week, but you'll earn the rest by what your customers purchase. You encourage a gentleman to buy a thirty-dollar bottle of champagne, you get ten dollars. You get him to order a hundred-dollar bottle of champagne and you get a third of that.'

Goodness me, it was the most lucrative job offer I'd had so far! It wasn't going to turn us into millionaires, but it was a start to getting us out of debt. How hard could it be? My entire education had been about how to charm men to lure them into marrying me. Surely charming them to drink would be simpler. But there was still the problem of someone recognising me. Even if I wasn't doing anything immoral, just being seen in a gentlemen's club would be enough to get the gossips talking.

'Do you get many Creole men coming to the club?' I asked.

He looked surprised. 'Why do you ask that? This is New Orleans — we get everybody. Tourists, locals and yes, some Creole men too.'

I struggled between the hope of helping Maman and the fear that my plan could go belly up and ruin us all. I stared at my hands, not sure how to ask the question.

'You see, Mr Perez ... Rolando, I've kind of fallen on hard times. I don't want to be recognised.'

'Oh, I see,' he said, pausing for a moment to think. 'Well, recognise you someone might, but I doubt very much that they'd tell anyone they'd seen you here.'

'Why's that?'

'Well, Ruby,' he shifted in his seat, 'you could say it's because of the entertainment.'

'The entertainment?'

His slick smile returned. 'Why don't you start tonight, and then you can see for yourself.'

The terms exotic dancer, burlesque queen, peeler, bump-and-grinder or effeuilleuse meant nothing to me. If Rolando had come straight out and told me that the entertainment at the club was strippers, I would have been better prepared for Rocky Mountains' performance. When the statuesque blonde appeared on stage, I thought she was going to sing. After all, she was decked out in a gorgeous evening gown of flaming red satin beaded with crystals and edged with feathers. Diamantés glittered around her neck and in her platinum-coloured hair.

'Wow!' I said to my male companion after I'd ordered him another glass of brandy. 'She's beautiful!'

'Almost as lovely as you,' he replied.

I smiled demurely. Rolando had warned me not to ask customers too many personal questions, just to listen to them as if every word they said was the most enlightening or amazing thing I'd ever heard. I didn't know much about this gentleman, except with his grey hair and furrowed brow he looked like he might be some sort of politician. But he had a taste for fine St-Rémy brandy and that was all right by me.

After a few minutes of sashaying back and forth across the stage to the accompaniment of the jazz band and not a note sung, Rocky Mountains began to slowly remove her opera-length gloves. First she clenched her pinky finger in her mouth and pulled the glove loose with her teeth, then continued with the other fingers until she had loosened the glove enough to peel it off and fling it off stage. She repeated the action with the other glove. The men in the audience cheered and applauded.

'I had no idea that taking off one's gloves was considered so entertaining,' I whispered to my companion.

He raised his eyebrows and looked highly amused. 'Ruby, you are funny! Next you'll be asking me why they call her Rocky Mountains!'

Rocky turned her back to the audience and, little by little, undid the zipper at the back of her dress before wiggling out of it to stand before us in only a beaded bra and a sheer skirt and panties. My jaw dropped. I thought she might be drunk or had lost her mind, and expected that Rolando would appear at any moment to pull her off stage. But nothing like that happened. Instead, every eye in the room remained on Rocky as she continued to disrobe one item at a time, until eventually all she wore were her high heels, a net bra with jewels covering her nipples, and rhinestone G-string panties.

'Now you can't expect me to take these off,' she said, winking at the audience. 'I'd catch a cold.'

The lights dimmed, and when they came on again Rocky had vanished like a dream. The men stood up, wolf-whistled and clapped enthusiastically.

I stared at the stage, trying to take in what I had seen. A beautiful woman had removed items of clothing one by one in a roomful of men and for a few minutes it had seemed the most fascinating thing in the world. I was astounded, not disgusted. Rocky had been a vision of feminine magnificence. Although the men had whistled and cat-called, not one of them had dared to stand up and touch her or shout anything disrespectful.

My companion nudged me. 'I think you need a drink more than me,' he said, indicating to the waiter to bring me a brandy.

'You are right there,' I told him. 'Eau-de-vie is exactly what I need.'

The waiter arrived with my drink: a flat Coca Cola. The beverages served to the hostesses were never the alcohol that the customer paid for. Still, I sipped the 'brandy' and smiled as if it were the real thing. I hadn't done too badly with my drinks commission on my first night.

Over the next month and a half, as I worked at the club and made enough money to keep Maman at the clinic and buy back some of our furniture, I watched a variety of strippers do their acts. The cheap, gimmicky ones made me cringe, but I was captivated by the classy ones. There was a star act named White Lily who was trained in ballet and did an elegant number about a girl getting ready for bed after an evening at the opera. Another dancer performed with doves that tugged at her clothes and helped her undress.

As Rolando had promised, he looked after me and all the other girls. The customers were usually well-behaved, and, to my relief, nobody showed up that I knew. The club was nice but it wasn't ritzy enough for the Creole social crowd. The men who came were mostly business executives and middle managers in town for conferences, and sometimes lonesome retirees. I didn't feel bad that I was encouraging them to spend big on drinks because they seemed to enjoy my company.

Some of the customers knew what the game was though. One man from New York insisted on tasting my drink to check it really was wine and not grape juice. 'If I'm paying for Mouton Rothschild, then Mouton Rothschild better be what you're drinking!' Luckily for me he was all talk and knew nothing about French wine. I was able to convince him by waxing lyrical about the 'layers of wild berries and anise flavours' that my grape juice was indeed claret.

Rolando was so impressed he gave me an extra five dollars for the night. 'You can spin a story, Ruby. That's for sure.'

I didn't realise that the strippers didn't like other women watching their acts and learned that lesson the hard way. One night, when I was leaving the club, a stripper named Buxom Maximus leaped out of a doorway at me brandishing the stem of a broken champagne glass. I jumped out of her reach in time to avoid her attack, but she moved menacingly towards me again.

'I'm going to teach you a lesson,' she screamed. 'You're trying to steal my act!'

Rolando and one of the club's bouncers saw what was happening and grabbed her in time to stop her slashing me.

'You tell that B-girl to stop watching my act!' she squealed, wrestling with the men and pointing at me. 'She wants to steal something.'

'B-girl?' I repeated. I'd never heard the term.

'Yeah,' she said, baring her teeth. 'Bar girl: just drinks, no talent.'

I bristled at her tone. Did this little hussy from some hick town think she was better than me? Infuriated, I went home and imitated her bumps and grinds in my bedroom mirror. How tacky, I thought. Then I remembered the better strippers I'd seen, and paraded around the room in various poses, batting my eyelids and taking ages to roll down my stockings.

I'd be better than Buxom Maximus any day, I thought, admiring the sway of my hips in the mirror. *And I've got a better proportioned body. I don't look like I'm about to topple over.*

At the end of April, I received a note from Maman telling me that she'd been moved from the clinic to a special convalescent home on the River Road that Doctor Emory had recommended. I wondered why nobody had consulted me first and went to visit her there straight away.

When I saw the grand driveway leading towards a Greek Revival mansion with mammoth fluted columns, I was dumbfounded. I could only imagine what it cost to stay there! Doctor Monfort had obviously not explained clearly enough to Doctor Emory that we were struggling for money. I'd barely been making the payments for the clinic as it was.

A nurse led me through to an entrance hall decorated with giltwood furniture and crystal chandeliers, then out into the garden. Maman was sitting near a pond bordered with roses and hydrangeas. Despite having had a lung removed, she looked better than she had in years. She had colour in her cheeks and her eyes sparkled when she smiled at me.

'Ruby, darling! Isn't this the most wonderful place? I've met so many interesting people here. There's an opera singer from Boston and a scientist from Germany. I have a charming room that overlooks the avenue of oaks, and every afternoon a pianist comes to play Chopin and Rachmaninov and other wonderful composers. The library is magnificent too. I've started reading again.'

The garden was certainly beautiful with its green lawns and elegant fountains. It reminded me of our own plantation home where we'd spent summers before it was sold from under our feet to pay my father's debts. The memory of that sent a shiver down my spine.

I sat next to Maman and took her hand. The trembling she'd suffered for so long had vanished and she'd put on weight in a becoming way. Seeing her well after so many years of watching her deteriorate gave me my first inkling of hope. Maybe Maman would see her fiftieth birthday, after all.

I beamed a smile back at her. 'Maman, I'm pleased to see you looking so vibrant.'

'I feel better than I have in years,' she said. 'A nurse comes every morning to give me a massage, and another helps me take a walk around the garden every afternoon. It's so heavenly beautiful here that I can't help but be happy. Isn't Uncle Rex so kind to have arranged for me to stay here for my recovery?'

The smile froze on my face and I turned away so Maman wouldn't read my expression. I hadn't heard a word from Uncle Rex since Mae had informed him of Maman's dire condition. But I let Maman believe that it was Uncle Rex who was paying for everything because she wouldn't have been able to bear the truth that I was working to keep everything together.

Maman tugged on my sleeve to make me face her again. 'Dear Ruby, how pale you are. You've been worrying about me, haven't you? I insist that you don't. You can see how well I'm cared for here — you mustn't give my welfare another thought!'

A maid came and served us tea from a silver pot, and I admired the blue Wedgwood cups. As I sipped the tea, I realised what was doing Maman so much good. It was the beauty all around her. A stronger person, used to the struggles and harshness of life, would have done fine in Charity Hospital, but I was convinced Maman would have died there. She was fragile and poetic. Perhaps it was the loss of our social standing and having to sell our material possessions that had brought on her illness in the first place.

I rested my head against her shoulder. 'I'm fine, Maman. Don't you worry about me.'

She rubbed my arm. 'Well then, a young girl like you should be thinking of pretty dresses and parties. I'm sure Aunt Elva would be happy to chaperone you along with Eugenie until I'm better.'

I was lost for words. Maman was an intelligent woman, well-read and accomplished in singing and piano. She was also kind and thoughtful towards others. But she had no idea how the real world worked. She'd never had to earn money or manage it. I was convinced that if ever we were lost in the woods, I would find a way out while Maman would sit and wait to be rescued. Only millionaires and movie stars could afford to recuperate in a sanatorium like this one, but Maman was blissfully unaware that the cost was beyond our means.

On the way home in the bus, I rested my head against the seat and closed my eyes. I'd seemed to be just digging us out of the hole we were in and now I had this new worry. I hadn't been able to bring myself to ask the receptionist how much an extended stay at the sanatorium was going to cost, but I guessed it would be around five hundred dollars. If I didn't pay it, Maman would be back at Charity Hospital. The happy expression I'd seen on her face during my visit made the idea unbearable. I couldn't let anything destroy the little ray of hope I now harboured that I wouldn't lose Maman while I was still a young woman.

All right, I thought, *I'm going to have to squeeze more tips out of my customers and put something aside each week towards the account. Maman is too precious to compromise.*

ELEVEN

Ruby

When I turned up for work that night, Rolando was waiting out the front for me. 'Listen, Ruby, the girls don't like you watching their performances. It's causing me grief.'

I stiffened. Was he about to fire me? That was the last thing I needed.

'Don't worry,' he said, 'I've got something for you to do while the girls are on stage. You'll stand behind the curtain and catch their clothes, okay? Don't open the curtain more than a slip. You simply catch their clothes and hang them up.'

I put my hands on my hips. 'I'm not catching their clothes! Do they think I'm their maid?'

'I'll pay you five dollars extra a night to do it,' he said.

I bit my lip and considered my options. Each night there were three strippers: one main act and two 'warm-up' girls. I could turn this in my favour.

'Five dollars a girl,' I said.

Rolando's face scrunched up as if he was about to get mad, then a smile formed on his lips and he scratched his chin, regarding me with respect. 'You know how to take care of yourself. Five dollars a girl. Make sure you don't upset my star acts. If you were ugly they wouldn't care.'

'If I was ugly,' I told him, 'I wouldn't be able to get the customers to drink Dom Pérignon instead of sparkling wine.'

Despite my initial reluctance, I enjoyed working backstage with 'the talent'. The star acts were divas, but the warm-up strippers were usually nice. There was Paige, nicknamed Miss Frigidaire by the other strippers because since she'd married the previous year she only worked when she wanted a new household appliance. Her husband was a foreman in a mattress factory and gave her all his wages to manage, but he didn't make enough to satisfy Paige's desire for modern conveniences.

'He's a good, honest man,' she told me, 'but he's got muscles in his body and muscles in his head. No sense of finances whatsoever. He thinks we live in Lakeview and drive a Chevrolet Bel Air on his wages!'

While some of the girls liked the glamour of burlesque and the adoration they received, everybody was there for the money. Like Bethany, whose husband was in hospital with kidney disease while she had three children to support.

'The back-door johnnies think we must be oversexed because we strip,' I heard one of the star acts, Lola, say to Bethany when I was helping hang up their costumes after the show. 'But I don't have the energy for a romp when I get home. I put on my pyjamas and go straight to bed!'

'What do you think about when you're up there on stage?' Bethany asked her.

Lola grimaced with pain as she pulled off her pasties, which were attached to her nipples with tape. 'Me? I make up shopping lists, or think about what I'm going to eat for supper later.'

Bethany laughed. 'Didn't you prefer working in the theatre, Lola — those big, magnificent productions with chorus girls, acrobats and comedians? That's all gone now, of course. Killed off by television.'

'I'd rather work in a nightclub anytime,' Lola replied, dabbing some baby oil on her irritated nipples. 'When I worked in the theatre, I'd look out at the front row and there'd be some guy jerking off behind his newspaper. The nightclub audiences are classier.'

One night when I was helping Bethany scrub off some gold body paint, she said to me, 'You're pretty, Ruby. Why aren't you stripping? You'd make much more money than you do hostessing.'

I didn't want Bethany to think that I judged her. She was in an awful situation with her husband and children and I sympathised. But as desperate as I was about my own family problems, there was a line I couldn't cross. 'I couldn't. My mother would be so ashamed,' I told her.

'My mother-in-law was horrified at first,' Paige piped up from the opposite dressing table. '"What? You take your clothes off!" she hollered at me. But when she realised that I can make two hundred dollars a week while my husband only makes fifty-five with overtime, she shut up. We've got one house paid off and are saving for another. Believe me, my mother-in-law doesn't say a thing now.'

'You can make two hundred dollars a week?' I cried.

Paige was amused by my surprise. 'That's nothing! The big stars make much more. Blaze Starr, Tempest Storm and Lili St Cyr — they can earn anything from a thousand to five thousand dollars a week.'

Five thousand dollars a week for taking off your clothes? Paige could have knocked me down with a feather. With that much money I could keep Maman at the River Road Sanatorium for as long as she wanted.

But Mae's words of warning rang in my ears: *You got nothing left but your reputation. Don't sully that — for your mama's sake.*

Although the acts only gave an illusion of nudity and the strippers stopped short of fully revealing themselves, stripping had a stigma to it. Burlesque performers hung around with other burlesque performers because they weren't acceptable in polite society. And as Bethany had once said, 'Stripping on stage leaves a stain on you.' Whatever you did in the future, it would always be there in your past. That was enough to stop me considering it seriously.

Maman had a favourite facial cleanser called Deep Magic that was only stocked by a pharmacy near the French Market. For a treat, I decided to get her a bottle. As I passed Antoine's on St Louis Street, I stopped for a moment. Before our money troubles and her deteriorating health prevented it, Maman and I used to eat at Antoine's regularly. Each dining room was decorated in a different theme, and our favourite was the Rex room with its green walls and Mardi Gras memorabilia. I closed my eyes and drank in the memory of the sweet café brûlot, a coffee flavoured with orange liqueur, cinnamon, cloves and lemon peel, and served flaming with dessert. Then I realised that if I stayed there a moment longer I'd start to feel defeated, knowing I could never take Maman there now. Even the facial cleanser was a luxury on the money I was making.

I was about to move on when Clifford Lalande stepped out of the restaurant with an older gentleman. He was wearing a plaid jacket and tan pants and looked as dashing as the first time I'd seen him.

'Ruby!' he exclaimed when he saw me. 'I was beginning to think you'd left town. I hope we didn't scare you away from Prytania Street?'

I'd not forgotten Clifford Lalande. How could I? But with Maman's illness and working each night, I never thought I'd see him again.

'I had to give up my tours,' I told him. 'My mother became seriously ill the day that I saw you.'

His face filled with such compassion that it caused a little explosion in my heart. 'I'm very sorry to hear that, Ruby. How is she now?'

'She had a major operation, but she's recovering well in the River Road Sanatorium.'

'That's the best sanatorium in the South,' said Clifford's companion. 'A colleague of mine had stomach cancer and I'm sure he's alive today because of the care he received there. Your mother is in the best hands.'

'My apologies, Ruby, for not introducing you to my father,' said Clifford, turning from me to the man. 'Father, this is Miss Vivienne de Villeray, the fascinating young lady Mother and Kitty told you about.'

'It's a pleasure to meet you, Miss de Villeray,' Mr Lalande said, taking my hand. With his twinkling eyes and soft voice, he exuded the special charm of a mature Southern gentleman. I imagined that in another thirty years, Clifford would be exactly the same.

I pointed to the door of Antoine's. 'I see you've been dining at the Quarter's finest restaurant. I hope your meal was delicious?'

'Indeed it was very good,' said Clifford. 'We've been celebrating.'

'Is it your birthday?'

'Not quite,' replied Mr Lalande. 'Clifford and I have been following the Brown versus Board of Education case in the Supreme Court. Yesterday, the plaintiffs were victorious.'

The Brown versus Board of Education case was so controversial that even the strippers at the club were discussing it. A group of coloured parents had challenged segregation in schools, claiming that it was unconstitutional. Their victory was a step forward for the Civil Rights Movement. If segregation of schools was unconstitutional, then the desegregation of other public facilities would have to follow.

'New Orleans could be a great city,' continued Mr Lalande, 'but segregation is costing us, not only economically but psychologically. It's time for all of us to move forward, coloured and white equally.'

I could tell where Clifford had gotten his intrepid optimism from. The Lalandes seemed convinced that every problem had a solution. It uplifted me. Perhaps my problems had solutions too.

'I hope so, Mr Lalande,' I said, remembering what had happened to Mae's father, 'I truly do. But I fear for the coloured folks. People can be resistant to change, even when it would benefit them.'

Mr Lalande regarded me with approval in his eyes. 'That's very true, Miss de Villeray, but I believe in the people of this city. There will be resistance, but in the end what is right must prevail.'

He was about to say more when Kitty came out of the restaurant on the arm of a red-haired young man. 'Ruby!' she cried when she saw me. 'Where have you been?'

Clifford gallantly stepped in to explain about my mother.

'Ah,' Kitty said, as if understanding something that had puzzled her. She touched my arm sympathetically. 'She'll be all right, Ruby. Especially with such a lovely daughter to take care of her.'

She introduced me to Eddie, her husband.

'I hope your wedding was lovely,' I said to them.

Kitty started giving me the details of her grandmother's pearls, the nervous priest, the lilac rose bouquet and the three-tiered wedding cake, when more people came out of the restaurant and it became too crowded on the banquette. We were going to have to move.

'Look,' said Kitty, glancing at her brother and taking out a pen and notepad from her handbag, 'we mustn't lose you again. Write down your telephone number for me. Clifford's tennis partner broke her wrist horse-riding and can't play. Won't you come and fill in for her?' She looked at me in a meaningful way. 'Eddie and I are dying for a game.'

Clifford leaned towards me and covered his mouth with his hand. 'I have to warn you,' he said softly, 'Kitty's personality changes on the court. She becomes very ... competitive.'

Eddie laughed knowingly and Kitty playfully pinched his arm.

I thought about what Maman had said; that I needed to get out and have fun.

'Well, I haven't played for a few years,' I told them. 'But I'd be willing to give it a try.'

A date was decided for the game and we parted company, heading in opposite directions. Before the group disappeared around the corner, Clifford and I both turned simultaneously and looked straight at each other. He made no effort to hide the smile that broke out on his face.

On the walk to the market there was a bounce in my stride. I knew the meaning of the look Clifford had given me. The fact that he was older than me only increased his allure. I thought it would be thrilling to have a more mature beau. Then I remembered what I was doing for a living. Clifford might not have smiled at me like that if he knew about the Havana Club.

I lifted my chin and carried on. There was no need to worry about that yet. I'd tell Clifford when the time was right. I was sure once he got to know me better, he would understand.

The morning of the tennis game, I took pains with my appearance, asking Mae to re-iron my white dress several times. As I took my hair out of curlers and lightly powdered my face, I imagined how the day would go and pictured it ending with me and Clifford embracing in the sunset.

'Where's your head this morning, Miss Ruby?' Mae asked, looking in the door. 'It's already half past nine and you've got to be at City Park at ten thirty. How are you intending to play tennis on four hours' sleep anyways?'

I'd told Mae that I was working the more lucrative night shift at the telephone exchange, which was why I didn't come home until the early hours of the morning.

'If all goes well,' I said, dabbing perfume behind my ears, 'I won't be working nights much longer.'

City Park was beautiful in the spring. The magnolias were in full bloom and I stopped for a moment to breathe in the air. The scent of magnolias was the perfect perfume — clean and fresh like lemons but sweet like vanilla too. I continued on with a skip in my step, filled with optimism that something wonderful was about to happen. I hadn't felt that way since my debut.

When I approached the courts, Clifford and Eddie were already there tightening the net. Kitty was warming up in the corner, swinging her racquet and bending her knees. She looked very modern in her tailored shorts and cap-sleeved shirt. I'd gone for a more traditional pleated skirt with a belted tunic top and a wide tulle hairband. I didn't have any choice: it was the only tennis dress I had.

Clifford was the first to spot me. His beaming smile brought the heat to my face. I opened the court gate and he walked towards me, unzipping the cover of a racquet and handing it to me.

'I thought you might like this one,' he said, a playful glint in his eye. 'It's my lucky racquet. I was using it the one and only time I ever won a match against my sister.'

'Well, you did say that Kitty liked to win.'

He looked dashing in his immaculate shorts and a V-neck knitted vest over his shirt; the pure white of his outfit flattered his tanned skin and emphasised his good shape. I had to be careful not to stare. The broody French Creole men were regarded as a handsome breed, but I liked this clean-cut American's *joie de vivre*.

'Hey, Ruby's here,' I heard Eddie say. He ran to greet me, with Kitty prancing after him.

'How are you feeling, Ruby?' he asked, wrapping his arm around Kitty's shoulders. 'Up for a tough game against the champ?'

'I'll do my best,' I said cheerfully.

Usually I liked to win at anything I did but around Clifford I didn't care about any of that. All I wanted from the day was to have fun.

'You can't be any worse than Cliff,' Kitty replied. There was a competitive edge in her voice although she was smiling.

Clifford raised his hands as if surrendering. 'Well, I did warn you that I'm only good at boxing. I'm simply here to make a foursome.'

We spun a racquet. Kitty and Eddie won and chose to serve. Clifford and I took our positions on the court, with me on the forehand side, receiving first, and Clifford up at the net. I was expecting a social game with long rallies and good sportsmanship, and was shocked when Kitty delivered a scorching serve that whizzed straight past me before I even had a chance to see it.

'All right,' said Clifford, grinning at me. 'I think this game is going to be over pretty quickly and we can have an early lunch.'

By the time Kitty served to me again it was already apparent she was by far the superior player. She volleyed and smashed fiercely, made a killer drop shot, and soon had me and Clifford running all over the court as she and Eddie quickly won the first game to love. A short match it was going to be indeed!

Kitty raised her arms triumphantly. 'When you said you were out of practice, Ruby, you weren't kidding, were you? How could you have missed that last shot?'

A prickle of annoyance roused me. Creole women competed on their beauty not their athletic prowess. I turned to Clifford but he only chuckled.

'Don't take it personally,' he said, patting my shoulder. 'Kitty wants to win at any cost. Psyching out her opponents is one of her tactics.'

My shoulders tensed up and I rolled them back, trying to relax. I didn't intend to be 'psyched out' by anyone. After being so friendly towards me in the beginning, Kitty's attitude stung but I wasn't the only one she had her fangs out for.

Eddie played solid strokes and demonstrated a natural eye for the ball, but Kitty didn't give him an ounce of credit. 'Get to the net! Get to the net!' she shouted at him. When he failed to reach a return from Clifford, and she got to it but then sent it flying over the baseline, she pouted and stamped her foot. 'You sure messed that one up, Eddie!'

I wasn't sure if my jaw dropped or not, but it felt like it did. Maman had told me the worst thing a woman could do to a man was to publicly humiliate him. But Eddie nimbly toe-danced on the baseline as if he hadn't heard the comment. Americans were certainly different. A Creole man would have been livid.

It came as no surprise that Clifford and I lost the first set six–love.

When we took a short break to dry off and sip water, he whispered to me, 'Kitty is playing pretty hard, I hope you don't mind. She wants to go into the amateur championships this summer and needs the practice.'

'She's a very good player indeed,' I confided. 'We'd better lift our game.'

He laughed and pushed his hair away from his face, and I noticed his hands. They were smooth but large and strong. Perfect hands for boxing. I imagined slipping my hand into his and the idea of it thrilled me.

'When Kitty asked you to join us for tennis, I did try to warn you,' he said. 'I thought, "Oh no, if Ruby plays with us we will definitely never see her again." Jackie, our usual fourth player, has known Kitty since we were children, and she rather enjoys a fight herself.'

I wasn't exactly enjoying the game, but I did like the way Clifford looked at me. For that, I could put up with anything.

In the second set, Clifford and I got into a better rhythm. I managed to kick some of the rust off my forehand and I hit a perfect cross-court shot into the far corner, which won us the first game.

'Great shot!' said Clifford with a smirk.

Gradually we played better and our coordination improved. Clifford finally had a chance to show off his athletic prowess with some skilful play at the net, and I enjoyed the feeling of us working together. We fought as a team for every point and I sensed Clifford was having fun beating Kitty for once.

We pulled ahead and soon won the second set six–three. The deciding set went with serve to six–five in our favour. Then after several gruelling rallies, we managed to break Eddie's serve — and win the match!

'Well, I'll be darned,' said Kitty, relaxing her posture and grinning from ear to ear. 'Clifford should partner with Ruby more often. She lifts his game and makes me work hard!' When Clifford wasn't looking, she winked at me and I realised that she'd let us win.

'Well, I'll be darned too,' I said, smiling and shaking my head at her. What was she up to?

I sat next to Clifford and helped Kitty unpack the wicker picnic basket and cooler. She'd brought a feast of sandwiches with the crusts cut off, potato salad, coleslaw and even chocolate fudge cake. I found myself warming to her again. On the court, she was a fierce competitor, but off it she was a charming hostess. She was thoroughly modern.

Because we were sitting close to each other, whenever Clifford reached for something, his arm would brush against mine and my skin would tingle. When he passed me the platter with the curried egg sandwiches and looked straight into my eyes, I was as happy as a puppy with two tails.

'Who's your favourite tennis player, Ruby?' Eddie asked.

'Oh, that's easy,' I replied, accepting a cup of lemonade from Kitty. 'Althea Gibson. Not only is she the first coloured woman to play at Wimbledon but she has impeccable manners.'

I'd been sincere in my answer, but was pleased to see Clifford's eyes light up in response.

'She is grace under fire,' he agreed. 'She and her family weren't allowed on the tennis court until after it closed and she had to play in the dark, yet despite all the obstacles thrown at her she's gone on to be a champion.'

'Unfortunately, despite being a champion she still has to enter clubs through the back door and can't use the white dressing rooms here in the South,' Kitty added. 'Segregation is so ludicrous.'

Clifford was about to say something when a car horn sounded. We looked up to see a Cadillac convertible with two women in it pull up near the courts. They waved when they spotted us. Kitty frowned.

The women stepped from the car. One was blonde and full-figured, with her right arm in a sling; the other, dark-haired and slender, was wearing a fashionable tulip dress. I guessed the woman with the sling was Clifford's usual tennis partner who'd broken her wrist horse-riding.

'Well, hello there,' she said brightly as they approached us. 'I thought you were supposed to be playing tennis, not lounging around and having a picnic!'

'We played a good game,' said Clifford, rearranging the picnic items to make room for the women to sit down. 'Ruby and I won!'

'Heavens forbid!' said the blonde. 'Now I wish I'd seen that.' She plunked herself between Clifford and me so I had no choice but to move away, then she draped her uninjured arm possessively over his shoulder.

'What brings you two here?' he asked, shifting away from her. 'I thought you were helping your mothers with the fundraiser?'

'It was too boring with all those old ladies drinking tea,' said the blonde. 'We thought we'd scoot over here and see what you were up to.'

She reached up and stroked Clifford's cheek. A prickly feeling overcame me. It was an intimate gesture but this time he didn't move away, despite the fact she was engaged. The diamond in the white-gold ring on her left hand was so big I couldn't miss it.

'Let me introduce you to Vivienne de Villeray,' Clifford said to the women.

The dark-haired woman reached for my hand and shook it. 'I'm Laura Simos,' she said. Her skin was cool and scented with a spicy oriental fragrance.

Because of her injury, the blonde girl couldn't shake my hand and instead flashed a set of perfect white teeth at me. 'And I'm Jackie Fausey.'

Everything about them exuded wealth, from their Tiffany earrings to their perfectly coiffed hair. I felt self-conscious. My clothes were presentable, but they were old. And the only jewellery I hadn't pawned was a set of pearl earrings and a cameo necklace.

'So how did you find playing against Kitty, Miss de Villeray?' Jackie asked. 'She acts like a man on the court, doesn't she?'

'You can call me Ruby,' I told her, although I felt anything but friendly towards her. If she kept flirting with Clifford, she was going to regret it.

Jackie was no natural beauty — she had premature wrinkles around her eyes, and although her features were even they were plain — yet she radiated self-assurance from every pore of her well-upholstered body and I had to admit it gave her a peculiar charm.

The scowl on Kitty's face made it clear that she didn't appreciate Jackie's comment, and I decided my loyalty lay with her.

'The game was spirited,' I replied. 'I can see why Kitty is a champion.'

Jackie stared at me, her nostrils flaring, and then laughed uproariously. 'Well played, Ruby! Your Creole tact is adorable. If only I could be so generous towards my future sister-in-law.'

The whole world turned upside down. My head went woozy. Did Clifford and Kitty have a brother I didn't know about? One to whom Jackie might be engaged? I looked at Clifford, hoping he would set everything straight again but he stared at his sandwich as if it was the most interesting thing on the planet.

Jackie's injured hand started bothering her and she leaned with her full weight against Clifford and rested her head on his shoulder. As brash as she was, I was pretty sure she wouldn't be doing that if she was engaged to Clifford's brother. The beautiful spring day turned a couple of shades darker. I coughed as if something was crawling in my throat. Clifford and Jackie were engaged? Then what had all those smiles and looks he'd given me been about? I barely heard the others when they started a discussion about the baseball season. I'd thought I could tell everything I had to know about Clifford Lalande just by looking at him. Now I realised how foolish I'd been. We had seemed so close a few minutes earlier but it had been an illusion. 'Men see nothing in their flirtations, and women see everything,' Maman had once warned me. As awkward as it would have been for me to leave the picnic then, every inch of me wanted to flee. *Clifford's tennis partner broke her wrist horse-riding and can't play*, Kitty had told me when she'd invited me to join them. Why hadn't she said *fiancée*?

'Do you follow baseball, Ruby?' Clifford asked me.

The friendly expression on his face stung like a slap.

I shook my head, wishing I could get my jumbled thoughts back together.

'What about football?' asked Eddie.

He and Clifford were making an effort to include me in the conversation. Through pride alone I managed to rally enough to answer, 'Why, yes, I saw the Sugar Bowl last year and screamed my lungs out for the Saints.'

It wasn't true, of course. I had no interest in football. But I had to say something to avoid making an even bigger fool of myself by withdrawing.

Jackie lit a cigarette and blew a stream of smoke into the air. No, she wasn't beautiful, but she had the self-possession that came from belonging to a family that had been rich for generations and would be rich for generations to come. She hadn't descended from a line of flighty French romantics who'd tossed away their fortune so now the youngest of them had to entice men in a club to drink expensive liquor. I felt as humiliated as I had the day in the hairdressing salon on Canal Street when all the women had laughed at me.

Laura glanced at her watch and announced she had another social engagement. That got everyone else thinking about what they had to do that evening and brought the picnic to an end. I stood up faster than anyone. All I wanted to do was get home and cry into my pillow.

Kitty linked arms with me. 'I'll walk with you to the streetcar stop.'

I lingered a moment, hoping against hope that Clifford might offer to come with us, and on the way say something that revealed I'd misunderstood the situation. Perhaps it was a joke between him and Jackie to pretend they were engaged. We would laugh about it and things would go back to how they were before. But when, after saying goodbye to me, Clifford and Jackie put their arms around each other, I knew there had been no misunderstanding.

The afternoon was turning cloudy and threatening rain. The magnolia blooms that had smelled so magical that morning were closing up under the overcast sky.

'I'm so glad you came today,' said Kitty when we reached the streetcar stop. 'Jackie's a strong player, but you're much better company.'

I squeezed my fists so hard my nails pierced the skin of my palms. Kitty had wanted me to come today, not Clifford — I should have realised that. She was the one who had invited me.

'But Jackie is Clifford's fiancée,' I said wearily. 'You have to like her because he's going to marry her.'

'It's impossible to like her!' Kitty whined. 'She's got a degree from Newcomb College but she's as shallow as a puddle.' She squeezed my arm and grinned. 'Anyways, today was such fun I hope Jackie's wrist stays broken forever! We'll get together for another match soon, won't we?'

I was relieved when the streetcar arrived at that moment and I had an excuse not to answer her question. I would not be playing tennis with the Lalandes again; those rich, happy-go-lucky Americans had toyed with me enough.

I sat in the dining room of our apartment in the Quarter in the fading twilight. The scratched mahogany dining table and the musty smelling velvet-upholstered chairs, which I'd managed to buy back from the pawn shop, were a world away from the Lalandes' immaculate house in the Garden District. I stared at the portraits of my ancestors on the walls, with their fine French features and their elaborate nineteenth-century clothes. The decadence of the de Villerays was a thing of the past now and I was the one who had to deal with the harsh reality of it.

Mae came in and served me a vegetable stew with rice. 'Are you all right, Miss Ruby? You're a little peaky in the face. I don't see how you can play tennis all day, then expect to work tonight.'

She was right, of course. But I couldn't afford not to work.

'I'll be all right after I've eaten,' I told her, blinking hard to keep the tears from my eyes.

Mae went back to the kitchen, and I let the tears fall down my cheeks. I was trying to live too many different lives. There was Ruby the B-girl, Ruby the fallen Creole aristocrat, and Ruby the young woman who was in love with someone who didn't want her.

I picked up the threadbare table napkin and wiped my face, then turned my attention to the stew. Mae had made it the way I liked it — smoky and spicy with a liberal amount of cayenne pepper and paprika. I could hear her moving about in the kitchen, washing saucepans and getting ready to sit down for her own meal.

'This sure is good okra, Mae,' I called. 'Where'd you find it?'

'Down at the French Market as usual,' she called back. 'But now you're bringing in money from your job at the telephone exchange, I don't have to get the scraggly bits no more. "Only the freshest," I tell Mr Goines.'

I savoured a few mouthfuls of the stew. It was the kind of comforting food I needed, as if Mae had sensed my melancholic mood and made the right meal to remedy it.

'Mae,' I said, 'why don't you come sit with me?'

In the kitchen, she didn't make a sound, like a little mouse that was afraid of being discovered.

'Mae?'

'I can't do that, Miss Ruby,' she said finally. 'You know that. That's not my place.'

I leaned back in my chair and closed my eyes. It was too absurd. Here I was sitting in this grand dining room by myself while Mae sat by herself in the kitchen, with only a door between us. I opened my eyes again and discovered Mae looking at me from the threshold.

'You sure you're all right, Miss Ruby? Did something unpleasant happen today?'

Unpleasant? Well, that was one way to describe having my heart snapped into two.

Mae was wearing her black uniform and starched apron as usual. Why did she continue to dress so formally? Couldn't she see that all those rituals had collapsed around us?

I longed to unburden myself to her, to confess what I'd really been doing for work and to confide in her about Clifford. But as she couldn't bring herself to eat with me in the dining room, I couldn't bring myself to share anything with her that might cause her concern. Yet if there was one good thing that had come out of my association with the Lalandes, it was a better understanding of what coloured people had to put up with.

'Mae, please come sit with me,' I said. 'I feel lonely, and this is a far more pleasant place to eat than the kitchen.'

She wavered, then went back into the kitchen to return a few moments later with her stew in a plain white bowl. She would have eaten it standing up in the corner of the room if I hadn't gotten up and pulled out a chair for her. I took some silver cutlery from the sideboard and she obediently allowed me to place a linen napkin on her lap, the whole time looking as uncomfortable as a cat in a Mardi Gras outfit.

'You know the city of New Orleans is going to desegregate soon,' I told her. 'You're going to have to get used to it.'

'Who's desegregating?' she asked, keeping her eyes fixed on her food. 'I don't see how that can happen with so many folks against it.'

'Well, Loyola Law School desegregated and they have some coloured students going there now.'

'Hmph!' she said, taking hurried spoonfuls of her food as if she couldn't wait to finish and get out of the room. 'All that will happen is the white students and professors will leave to go to other universities, so the coloured students may as well have stayed at a coloured college anyway. Then after all that studying, the white students will work for fancy law firms, while the coloured ones are going to end up clerks at the post office.'

Mae had accurately described how things were and I was pleased she could express herself with me. If Maman was home, she would have pretended everything was wonderful as it was.

'But it won't stay that way,' I told her. 'Change takes time, that's all. Sometimes you've got to start with little things. Like us now, sitting here together, no longer segregated.'

She looked at me and narrowed her eyes. 'What nonsense you're talking tonight, Miss Ruby! This ain't a bus. I hope you don't expect me to eat with you every night? I'm a maid, and a maid's got a place.'

'You're not a maid,' I told her. 'Maids get a wage. I know you've been using what I've been paying you to buy me new underwear, and those rosewater soaps in the bathroom didn't come from nowhere.'

'Figure you deserve it,' she said, turning back to her food, 'the way you've been helping your mama.'

'Well, don't you see, Mae? If you won't take a wage from me, then we aren't a maid and a mistress.'

She took a mouthful of stew. 'What are we then?'

'We're family.'

'Hmph,' she responded, stirring her stew.

'That's right, Mae,' I said, sitting back in my chair. 'You're my aunt.'

Mae turned to me incredulously. Then the grooves around her mouth tightened and her eyes crinkled. She slapped her knee and let out a laugh that was half a yelp. 'Your aunt! Oh Lord Almighty, Miss Ruby, you kill me sometimes! You going to tell people that this Negro lady is your aunt?'

I nodded. 'That's exactly what I'm going to tell them.'

She laughed harder and used her napkin to dry her eyes. ''Cause you and me, Miss Ruby, we look so much alike!' She laughed a while longer, then calmed herself and told me, 'You'll do no such thing. People will either think you've got some colour in you and they'll shun you, or they'll think you've got a hole in your bag of marbles and put you in the nuthouse.'

I reached over and touched her arm. Her skin was warm and dry and smelled of oatmeal. She could indeed be my aunt if I closed my eyes — she was so familiar to me. 'Aunt Mae,' I said, leaning in close, 'truth be known, I'm a little tired of worrying about what other people might think.'

TWELVE

Ruby

A good entertainer gives her audience exactly what they want, Clifford had said when he caught me making up stories as a tour guide. That evening at the Havana Club, I put on a smile and attended to my customers with as much charm as I could muster for a young woman who couldn't see a promising future for herself.

A stripped named Melody was on stage doing her mermaid number, blowing bubbles seductively at the audience while shimmying and wiggling her costume tail like a siren of the sea.

'Why don't you perform on stage?' my customer, Earl, asked me. He was a regular at the club and always good to me. With his hooded eyes, grey sideburns and well-cut suits I imagined he was a banker who lived Uptown with a blonde wife who looked like Grace Kelly.

'Me?' I asked, taking the bottle of champagne from the ice bucket and pouring him another glass.

'Yes, you, Miss Ruby! You're the prettiest girl I've ever seen and you've got class. You'd make a lot more money dancing than you do being a hostess.'

I looked at Melody. Out of all the dancers, she fascinated me the most. Not only did she have the most beautiful costumes, which she sewed herself; when she showed up backstage, she was the proverbial wallflower, with thick-rimmed glasses, a checked shirt-dress and plain brown court shoes. Watching her dress for her act was like watching a caterpillar morph into a butterfly. I was mesmerised by the way she painted a beautiful face onto her plain one: creating arched eyebrows above her natural ones; expanding her thin lips into a seductive pout; and winging out her eyeliner to turn herself into a goddess. The addition of a blonde wig over her mousy hair and she went from being Melody, who no-one would notice in the street, to the luminescent Golden Delilah before us on stage.

'Earl, tell me honestly, do you look down on dancers like Golden Delilah?' I asked.

His eyebrows shot up with surprise. 'Look down on her? That lady up there is an artist!'

'An artist? Now that is a new way of seeing things.'

The music changed tempo and Melody wiggled her hips as she unzipped her tail and revealed her green fishnet-stockinged legs. The audience cheered her on.

'Ruby, look around the room.' Earl waved his arm at the men who were gazing at Melody with rapture on their faces. 'Those ladies on stage inspire us. Most of us have given up on our dreams — to be adventurers, famous sports heroes, even just to be admired by our wives. For the short time we come here, we can watch the dancers and forget our quotidian existence. You don't look down on a lady who can do that; you revere her!'

I considered what he was telling me. I knew Melody had the same mundane problems as the other strippers who performed at the club: lack of money, a husband who'd shot through, young children and elderly parents to support. The other night, Lola had been hauled off stage and arrested for bills she hadn't paid. Her undignified exit had sent chills down my spine. As for the men in the audience, who knew what was going on in their lives? It was as if they and Melody were participating in a moment of magic, where life was fun, beautiful, cheeky and carefree. The magic was an illusion, of course. Burlesque had its erotic element, but the nudity was a trick of the eye, created by net bras and body suits. Although I'd heard that in other, bawdier clubs the girls 'flashed', sticking pieces of fur or wool onto their net panties to make the men think they were catching a glimpse of something more.

'Tell me you'll think about it?' Earl said to me. 'It's a pity that a beautiful girl like you doesn't get her full due.'

'I'll think about it,' I replied to humour him. Even though things were tamer at the Havana Club than they were at Poodle's Patio and the Hotsy Totsy, if I did any sort of suggestive or scantily clothed dancing and my mother found out, she would die of shame. In fact, I was sure that would kill her faster than her diabetes would.

'Miss Ruby, a letter came for you yesterday,' Mae told me, leaving the envelope next to my bowl of cornmeal, which I was eating at my new breakfast time of two in the afternoon.

The sender's address and logo were printed in the top left-hand corner: *The River Road Sanatorium*. I'd been expecting the bill, and was proud of myself for having put aside five hundred dollars for the exact purpose of paying it.

'I told you I'd look after you, Maman, and I have,' I said quietly.

As our fancy bronze letter-opener had been pawned years ago, I used a butter knife to open the envelope, took out the bill and unfolded it.

'Holy Mother of Mercy!' I cried when I saw the amount. Stars floated up around me as if I'd received a blow to the head. Rather than the five hundred dollars I'd been expecting, the bill totalled two thousand, five hundred dollars. That was more than half the average American family's total yearly income! Even a five-star hotel wouldn't have charged that.

The cornmeal I'd eaten burned in my throat. I covered my mouth and tried to stand, but instead found myself sinking to my knees. There was no way I was going to be able to pay that amount. There were no more days left in the week that I could work, and there weren't enough customers at the Havana Club who spent big bucks on champagne. I'd milked that job for every cent I could already.

An image of Maman being dragged from her toile de Jouy–wallpapered room at the sanatorium and deposited unceremoniously at Charity Hospital stabbed at my mind. Then I pictured myself being hauled off by the police like Lola for not paying the bill.

My thoughts raced to find a solution. I could ask Doctor Monfort to use his persuasive powers to let me pay the amount in instalments, as he had with Doctor

Emory for Maman's operation. But even if I did pay in instalments, I'd still have to find the money somewhere. I returned to my seat and gulped my coffee, trying to slow down my thoughts. We had one thing left to sell: the apartment. It was the final piece of de Villeray property that we owned, but what else was to be done? I'd sell it, find somewhere else for us to live, and then bring Maman home so Mae could take care of her.

Having come to that decision, I calmed down. I imagined us renting a charming Creole cottage by the river and living a simpler life. All I had to do now was find the deed to the apartment and get Maman to sign the title over to me so I could sell it.

Maman kept her important papers in the locked drawer of the escritoire, and the key in her jewellery box. There was only one piece of jewellery left in the box — a green Peking-glass necklace that wasn't worth much — so it was easy for me to find the key. The deed was the first document I spotted after my parents' marriage certificate, but there was an attachment to it. I sat on Maman's bed and read the document carefully. Twelve months after the death of my father, Maman had transferred the title of the apartment over to Uncle Rex. Why had she done that? I'd have to see her to find out.

When I arrived at the River Road Sanatorium, Maman was in the library, reading Faulkner's *Light in August*. Her hair had been set and although the navy silk jacquard afternoon dress she wore was one she'd had for years, it still fitted her girlish figure perfectly. All those elements, along with her smooth hands and the soft afternoon light through the window that gave her a rosy glow, made her a vision of loveliness. I prayed my asking about the deed wouldn't upset her equilibrium.

'Ruby,' she said, smiling at me. 'Go and smell those roses by the window.'

I did as she told me, leaning out the open window and breathing in the air.

'The scent was even stronger this morning,' she said, 'but you can still smell them. Doesn't the fragrance remind you of apple blossoms?'

Dear Maman, every little piece of beauty gave her delight. I had no time to smell roses, or appreciate wine, or feel the texture of different fruits in my hands. I'd been working so hard that all my senses were dead. But I couldn't let her know that; I couldn't let her worry.

'Maman, I've been getting our affairs in order before you come home. I wanted to check all our documents were together, and I noticed the deed to our apartment was signed over to Uncle Rex after Papa's death. I was wondering why you did that.'

There, I thought, *I've said it calmly*; and without a tense note in my voice betraying the panic that was making my heart race. For why, if Maman had entrusted him with a valuable piece of property, had Uncle Rex been unwilling to help her when she'd had her life-threatening operation?

'Precisely because of that look on your face,' she said, taking off her reading glasses and reaching out her hands to take mine.

'What look?' I asked, lowering myself into the seat next to her.

She touched her finger to my forehead. 'So I'd never have to see that frown there. So you would never have to worry about money. I handed over our property to Uncle Rex because it's not right for women to concern themselves with such things. It taxes our systems. And hasn't he done a fine job, Ruby, putting me in such a lovely place until my health is restored?'

Not tax our systems? Surely my mother couldn't be serious? A faint buzzing noise started up in my head.

'What was Uncle Rex supposed to do in exchange for the title?' I asked as casually as I could.

'Exactly what he has been doing,' she said firmly. 'Paying our expenses. I gave him the apartment on the agreement that he was to support us until the time of your marriage.'

I stood up and walked slowly to the window, pretending to smell the roses again so Maman wouldn't see my face twitching. All this time I'd thought Uncle Rex was being generous leaving that housekeeping money in the jar on the mantelpiece, when all he'd been doing was meagrely doling out our own money to us while we were selling things left and right to keep food on the table! What right had Aunt Elva to stop him? Surely she knew the money was ours — or did she?

'Maman, one more question,' I said, picking a rose and bringing it to her. 'Did you make the agreement with Uncle Rex in writing? I don't mean the transfer of title, but what he was supposed to do in return for it?'

'Of course not,' she said indignantly, straightening her spine. 'You don't need written documents between family.'

My stomach tightened. Could Maman really believe that? Could she be so naive?

Working as a bar girl had knocked all the Creole-belle naivety out of me. When the haughtier strippers called me a B-girl, they meant it as a put-down, but I told myself it meant 'business girl'. And when it concerned money these days, I meant business.

A puzzled look came to Maman's face. 'Is everything all right, Ruby?'

I smiled brightly. 'Of course it is, Maman,' and I put my arm around her shoulders. 'It's as I said: I wanted to make sure that everything's in order before you come home.'

'But why the rush for me to come home?' she asked, patting my hand. 'I'd only be a burden to you and Mae, and here they give me physiotherapy twice a day to strengthen my remaining lung. I'm more than happy to stay until the end of the year.'

Clifford's father had said his friend had survived stomach cancer because of the care at the sanatorium. How I wished I could afford the best care for Maman too. But if I didn't find a solution quickly, she was going to be out of there faster than a hot knife through butter. How could I tell her that?

Instead, I squeezed her tighter and said, 'Maman, you know you could never be a burden to me.'

Uncle Rex and Aunt Elva lived in a 1920s Mediterranean mansion with a sweeping front lawn and a fountain garden. The house had been a wedding gift from Aunt Elva's father, who had made his money on the river. With determination tinged by a sense of uneasiness, I pressed the doorbell.

Melodious chimes rang through the air. A maid in a crisp uniform and with her hair oiled back into a tight bun answered the door. I recognised her straight away as Aunt Elva's housekeeper, Millie. She was thicker around the hips than I remembered, but her skin was still smooth and tight.

'Hello, Miss Ruby,' she said, beckoning me into the semicircular entrance hall. The winding staircase I remembered, but was the Jacobean-striped linen wallpaper new? 'It's a long time since I've seen you! You were only a girl then; now you're a lovely young woman.'

Indeed, the last time I'd been in this house was before my papa died. Aunt Elva had never invited us here after that.

'Your aunt is out at a meeting, but your uncle's home,' Millie said, leading me to the parlour. 'I'll go tell him you're here.'

I was relieved to learn that Aunt Elva wasn't around, but surprised to hear that she was attending a meeting. Aunt Elva was the least civic-minded person I knew.

Like the entrance hall, the parlour had been redecorated since I'd last been in the house. The wallpaper and fabrics were French silk. I sat down on a sofa and rubbed my hand over the cherub-print slipcover. Uncle Rex had been prepared to let Maman die while he lived in luxury! My blood boiled.

It took a long time for Millie to return to take me to Uncle Rex's study. One look at my uncle's tense expression and I could tell he knew why I'd come.

'Ah, Ruby, please take a seat,' he said, pulling an armchair away from the wall for me, but averting his eyes. 'What have you been up to?'

I'd intended to stay calm. I'd promised myself to stay calm. But his cheery tone, false as it was, made me bristle. 'Aren't you going to ask how Maman is?'

He paused for a moment, then moved back to sit at his desk, as if creating a barrier between us would protect him.

'She had to have a lung removed, and has had a long — and expensive — convalescence.'

His face reddened but he still couldn't bring himself to meet my eyes. 'Ruby, as I explained to Mae, I've done all I can to help.'

'Have you?' I said, noticing the way he stiffened at my tone. 'Well, it seems there is one more thing for you to explain.' I opened my purse and pulled out the deed to the apartment. 'It seems Maman passed the title to you on the understanding that you would take care of us until I married.' He opened his mouth to say something, but I spoke over the top of him. 'Don't tell me that you've given even an eighth of what you owe to Maman! We desperately need the rest of the money and we need it now!'

Uncle Rex's head dropped lower and he fiddled with the top button of his shirt. When he finally managed to look up, his eyes entreated me to understand. 'I can't give it to you,' he said, then added in a strange voice, 'forgive me.'

'You can't give it to me?' I waved my hand at the French carved-wood table lamp and the English mahogany and bronze stationery set on his desk. 'We've been forced to pawn or sell almost everything. We need that money!'

He stood up, agitated. 'This is all Elva's money,' he said, indicating his luxuriously appointed office. 'She's kept her inheritance in her name. I'm only paid an allowance.'

His revelation surprised me. It was certainly an unusual arrangement between husband and wife. All my life I'd assumed that Uncle Rex had a fortune of his own.

'Then we need to see a lawyer together and get the apartment title returned to us,' I said. 'I will sell it and pay you the amount you've given us. Aunt Elva doesn't even need to know.'

I felt that I'd found the most rational solution to the problem, but Uncle Rex sank back into his chair. 'You can't sell it,' he said. 'It's mortgaged to the bank.'

It took me a moment to comprehend what he'd said.

'Mortgaged for what?' I asked, panic cutting short my words.

Uncle Rex didn't answer me. He picked up the pencil tray from his desk, then pushed it aside.

'Well,' I said, 'you're going to have to sell whatever you mortgaged the apartment for and give the money to us.'

A feeble smile came to his face and I knew something was terribly wrong. This nervous and shifty man in front of me wasn't the Uncle Rex I knew; the man I'd held up in my mind as the only responsible de Villeray male. The world was changing around me: things I'd assumed to be true weren't true at all.

'What the money has been spent on can't be sold,' he said, resting his head in his hands.

The blood drained from my face as fast as if I'd been shot in the heart. I stared at my uncle, at his thinning hair and freckled, pasty hands. He was nothing like my father in looks or charm, but now it was dawning on me that they were exactly alike in character. They were both cheats. Then I remembered the day I'd seen him looking dishevelled in Jefferson Parish. Weren't there several casinos on South Carrolltown Avenue? The full horror of the situation hit me.

'You've lost it gambling, haven't you?' I cried.

For a few seconds, neither of us moved. Then Uncle Rex moaned with shame.

I stared at him in disbelief. The man who Maman had trusted had squandered our final means of support. Now, not only did I have the bill from the sanatorium to pay but I'd have to pay the bank myself if I wanted to get Maman's apartment back. My heartbeat tripled.

'I don't care what you have to do, you need to get that money back for us!' I shouted. 'Or I'll tell Aunt Elva that you've been gambling!'

'She knows,' he said, without lifting his eyes. 'She knows.'

So Aunt Elva had been happy for him to gamble away our money as long as he didn't touch hers. It was a good thing she wasn't home when I realised that, for I surely would have strangled her. It seemed that the problem was insurmountable and that every avenue was closed to me.

'You were our last hope,' I told Uncle Rex. 'Our last hope!'

He finally lifted his head. 'You can still marry well.'

The remark was like a slap in the face. How could I 'marry well' without a dowry? I stared at the pathetic excuse for a man that was my uncle.

'I will get us out of this mess,' I told him, 'but it won't be by marrying. I will never, ever rely on a man for anything again!'

As I caught the streetcar home, my mind churned over the only apparent way open to me for saving us. Maybe it wouldn't be so bad. The burlesque dancers at the club seemed happy enough, and they were making good money. I'd never be able to be part of Creole society again, but would that be such a bad thing?

I stopped at Saint Louis Cathedral and lit a candle. 'Dear God,' I prayed, 'if me becoming a stripper is the only way to help Maman, then give me a sign.'

Folks say God moves in mysterious ways. I'd say he has one big sense of humour too, if what happened that night is anything to go by.

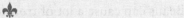

Rolando was distracted that evening, running around the club like a maniac, shouting at the chef and ordering the waiters to straighten each tablecloth. The barman told me that Joe Grimaldi, one of New Orleans' infamous crime bosses, had booked out the club on the spur of the moment for him and his mob to celebrate his sixtieth birthday. In a way, I was relieved that I probably wouldn't be able to talk to Rolando about becoming a stripper at the club that night; but in another way, it drew out the agony because I was going to have to do it sooner or later.

'You'll have to help Melody,' Rolando told me. 'She's the only stripper act for the night. Grimaldi doesn't like hostesses selling his men drinks, so I don't need anybody but myself, the Master of Ceremonies and the waiters on the floor.'

I went to the dressing room, where I found Melody sitting before her mirror, plucking her eyebrows.

'Rolando's working up a sweat,' I said.

'I don't blame him,' she replied, pressing a fingertip to her browline to calm the redness. 'Grimaldi can make or break a club. If he doesn't like you, you're done.'

I laid out her costume while she put on her stage make-up.

'You know, Ruby,' she said, pinning up her hair, 'you look a lot like Elizabeth Taylor.'

'So I've been told. But I don't have any beaus, and she's already got a second husband and she's only a few years older than me!'

Melody laughed. 'Don't be too distressed about it. Beaus can cause a lot of trouble.'

Her costume was a flamenco-style dress with an embroidered bodice and lace bolero jacket. As I removed the jacket from its hanger I wondered about Melody's comment. She might be right about beaus. I had thought Clifford was different from other men, but he'd caused me heartache just the same.

I was about to help her into her outfit when she let out a gasp. I turned to see a man in a suit watching us from the doorway. His eyes were red with drink and he staggered on his feet. I didn't like the look of him. The strippers attracted their fair share of backstage johnnies, but the bouncers were vigilant that they didn't get near the dressing room. They must have been distracted by the preparations.

'Huey, what are you doing here?' Melody asked.

I relaxed when I realised that she knew him and wondered who he was. A boyfriend? A fiancé? Was he the beau causing her trouble?

Huey squinted at her. 'You slut!' he said, scowling and moving towards her unsteadily. 'You said you were staying with your sister!'

The hairs on the back of my neck stood on end. This guy was trouble for sure. I reached to pick up the internal phone and call the front desk, but before I could dial, Huey yanked a gun from his jacket. I screamed as he pointed it at Melody's head and fired.

By the Grace of God, Huey staggered the second before the gun discharged and the bullet missed its aim and hit Melody in the arm instead of the face. The impact knocked her to the floor. She clutched her arm and stared at Huey in disbelief. 'Why?' she screamed, trying to staunch the blood that was seeping through her fingers. 'Why?' Huey's face was blank but all the veins in his neck were raised and I could see his pulse beating in his throat. He raised his arm to fire again but the gun jammed. Footsteps and shouts rang through the corridor and the next moment the room was filled with people. The bouncers wrestled Huey to the floor while Rolando grabbed a towel to bind Melody's wound.

'Call an ambulance!' he screamed at me.

With the ambulance came the police, creating the kind of scene that would turn Grimaldi and his men away. Rolando paced the floor, tearing at his hair. 'Tonight of all nights!' he cursed.

Even when Melody was safely on her way to the hospital and the police had taken Huey to gaol, Rolando still didn't settle down. After Grimaldi and his men arrived, the waiters and the Master of Ceremonies did their best to look after them while the club singer performed all the Italian favourites and encouraged the mobsters to sing along with 'Ba-ba-baciami Piccina'.

Rolando disappeared into his office for a while, but returned to the dressing room looking dishevelled and anxious. 'I can't get a dancer at this late notice.'

Grimaldi's men were growing restless. We could hear them complaining to the Master of Ceremonies: 'Where is the beautiful woman? We were promised a beautiful woman!'

Rolando's forehead beaded with sweat. 'They are going to turn me into alligator chum!' he said, a tremor in his voice. I had cleaned up the blood from the floor but

Melody's robe was ruined. Not knowing what I could do to help Rolando, I went to throw it in the garbage when he suddenly let out a sharp cry and grabbed my arm.

'You'll do it, Ruby, won't you? You'll get me out of this spot? You've seen enough acts to know what to do.'

I had already decided to strip but I had not intended my start to be in front of a rowdy group of mobsters! Rolando noticed my hesitation. 'I'll pay you a hundred and fifty dollars to do it.'

I was so desperate for money, I didn't have much choice. But shrewdness stopped me from agreeing immediately. Rolando looked fraught. If I refused, he was in real trouble. I knew exactly what Baroness de Pontalba would have done in the same situation.

'Three hundred for tonight,' I said. 'Then we'll negotiate my weekly salary tomorrow.'

'Geez, Ruby!' He paced the floor again. 'That's more than we pay the star acts!'

'Three hundred and I'll do it,' I said firmly. 'Take it or leave it.'

He shook his head and threw up his arms. 'All right! But get ready quickly!'

He turned to leave but I called him back. 'I need a stage name. I can't perform as Ruby.'

He mulled it over for a moment. 'I like Ruby, but if you don't want to use it then why not change your name to Jewel? That still sounds classy.'

After Rolando had left, I ran my hands through my hair, trying to calm my nerves.

I sat down at Melody's dressing table and began to put on stage make-up as I'd seen her do dozens of times, but my head throbbed and I felt as if I was splitting into two different people. Then I remembered Maman's favourite saying: *If you must do a thing, then do it graciously.*

I stared at my reflection in the mirror. 'Jewel, if you are going to be a stripper, then be a good one!'

I knew the order in which Melody put on her clothes for a performance, but in my excitable state I overdid it. As well as the net panties with a satin modesty patch at the crotch, the nipple pasties, the see-through net bra and the full bra, I added a corset, fishnet stockings, panel skirt, fascinator and feather boa.

The stage manager called my name and I made my way to the wings. The band played my introduction and the Master of Ceremonies announced me as 'The glittering, sparkling, dazzling Jewel of New Orleans'. Grimaldi's men clapped and cat-called. I waited in the wings a moment, then sucked in a gulp of air before gliding onto the stage. I froze as soon as I found myself in the spotlight. Every table was filled with men. It was as if the entire Louisiana mob had come to the club that night.

I caught a glimpse of Rolando at the bar. He gestured for me to do something. Although I felt like a human coat stand with all the clothes I had on, I sashayed across the stage as I'd seen the other girls do.

You're Jewel now, I said to myself. *Not Ruby.*

My legs quivered and I'd developed a nervous twitch around my mouth.

'Take something off,' the stage manager whispered from behind the curtain.

I moved towards the dark corner of the stage, but the spotlight followed me. I undid the pin of my fascinator, flung it to the side and let down my hair. A shift occurred in the atmosphere of the room. I felt the ripple of excitement that ran through the audience.

I slipped the bolero jacket from my shoulders and rubbed the feather boa across my chest. The men whistled and cheered. The more they egged me on, the more I began to enjoy myself. Their adoration electrified me.

I moved my hands over the shape of every item of clothing, as if to suggest the loveliness that lay underneath it, before removing it. Rolando nodded his approval at my teasing, but also pointed to his watch as a signal to speed things up. I'd put on so many items of clothing, it was taking much longer than the usual ten minutes to get them all off. The band had to play the same piece of music over twice, but the audience didn't seem to mind that my act was spinning out to a full show.

My nervousness returned once I'd taken my corset off and it came time for me to remove my outer bra. My breasts would be revealed then, except for the net bra and pasties. I almost fled the stage at that point, but somehow I summoned the courage. *Here goes!* I thought.

My heart pounded as I fumbled with the front clasp of the bra. I flung it aside, not realising that I'd undone the net bra as well and all I had on were my pasties with no support. I shimmied awkwardly and one of the pasties flew off and landed in someone's drink. The men roared with laughter and cheered. Well, that was as good a finale as I could hope for!

I demurely placed my fingers over my bare nipple and waved to the audience with my other hand. I expected the spotlight to go off then so I could exit the stage without having to show my near-naked bottom, but it remained on. All I could do was keep waving.

But it was all right: I'd earned three hundred dollars and a standing ovation for doing nothing but wiggling about a bit and taking off my clothes. I couldn't understand why it had taken me so long to finally become a stripper. I was hooked.

THIRTEEN

Amanda

My head was spinning. Whatever I'd expected my elegant New Orleans grandmother to tell me, it wasn't that she'd been a stripper.

'Are you shocked?' she asked, studying my face.

I recovered my composure and shook my head. I could imagine Aunt Louise being upset by her mother's past, but I thought it was fabulous. It made me feel less of a misfit. I had taken burlesque classes when Dita Von Teese came on the scene and what Grandma Ruby had described was tame compared to what went on in Kings Cross these days. Yet a very important question remained.

'I'm surprised but not shocked,' I told her. 'I am curious to know what you being a stripper has to do with me and the back porch?'

She looked horrified at my question and shook her finger at me. 'Amandine, you are impatient!' she scolded. 'In New Orleans patience is a way of life. That dish

Louise made the other night wasn't something whipped up in a microwave. Gumbo is a blend of traditions from Africa, France and the Native Americans. It's got the taste of centuries in it. Louise has added her own present-day spirit to it by making it with chickpeas and kidney beans. When you make Creole food, you've got to add each of the ingredients with feeling and a sense of order. You don't slap anything together. Then it would merely be a stew. Likewise, you don't rush a storyteller with her story. You've got to trust that things are leading somewhere. So be patient, Amandine. I'll get to that part when I'm ready.' With that she blew out the candles which had burned low and turned on the light. 'Now to bed.'

I watched her walk up the stairs with the same disbelief the sultan of Arabian Nights must have felt when Scheherazade left him hanging on for the rest of her tale each night.

I woke up the next morning to the sound of Flambeau crowing so loudly that I thought he must be under my bed. When I realised he wasn't, I tugged on a skirt and tank top and crept downstairs.

I'd assumed that Grandma Ruby kept Flambeau in the potting shed at night so I was surprised to see him standing in a dog bed near the back door. He clucked when he saw me and strutted as if he wanted to go outside. I opened the door, and the first thing he did on greeting the morning air was an enormous poop on the lawn. He appeared to be toilet-trained. Was that even possible?

I followed him outside and re-examined the woodwork on the porch. What had seemed only yesterday to be deterioration now took on a mysterious meaning. The maidenhair ferns that sprouted around the lattice hid a secret. But what was it? What did this porch have to do with me?

'Good morning!' The deep voice made me snap to attention. I turned to see a man wearing khaki overalls and a wide-brimmed hat standing behind me.

'You must be Amandine. I'm sorry, I didn't mean to give you a fright,' he said, extending a friendly hand. 'I'm Oliver. I do the garden here.'

He looked to be a few years older than me, but with his strong bone structure and ebony skin it was hard to tell. He could have been forty and only looked young.

My heart slowed to its normal rhythm again. 'The garden is beautiful,' I said.

'Thank you. I'm following a family tradition working here. My great-uncle Ned was the gardener when your grandmother first moved here, and I took over from my father ten years ago.'

I glanced back at the rotten lattice. Ten years? Maybe he knew something about the porch?

Oliver noticed where I was looking. 'I've been telling Ruby for years that we need to replace that wood. Fortunately there's no evidence of termites, but the damp is causing it to rot. I want to remove the floorboards and dig a perimeter trench to deal with the moisture, but every time I mention it, she avoids the topic.'

I had to tread carefully now. The porch needed to be fixed but I wanted to find out what the secret was first. 'I think this place has a sad memory for her,' I said. 'When the time is right, I'd like to convince her to fix the porch too.'

'A sad memory? There may be something to that,' said Oliver, with a curious look in his eye. 'But my father and great-uncle came from a tradition where employees never talked about their employer's business, so I don't know. My father tried to instil the same values in me: "You see nothing, and you say nothing." That's the way the old folks did things.'

He nodded towards the garden path. 'Have you had a chance to look around the garden? Lorena said you studied restoration architecture.'

'I know a lot about buildings and furniture from my studies, but I did learn something about plants from my nan who loved to garden.'

'Well, the first thing to know about Victorian gardens,' he said as we walked side by side on the path, 'is that they're romantic.' He pointed to a lattice arch that perfectly framed a flowerbed brimming with petunias and pansies. 'This garden was landscaped according to a Victorian ideal of elegance, but the plants and trees had to be suitable for the climate and soil of New Orleans.'

'The Victorians had a taste for the exotic oriental too,' I said, noticing the red geraniums and azaleas.

Next to the gardener's cottage was a cutting garden blooming with white and pink roses, formosa lilies, zinnias and watsonias. Oliver pulled a pair of secateurs from his pocket and cut some white tuberoses. Their scent was rich and sultry.

'Give those to Lorena for your grandmother's breakfast tray,' he said. 'They're her favourite cut flowers. It was nice to meet you, Amandine. If you've got any questions about the garden, I'd be happy to answer them.'

I passed the rear porch on my way back to the house. A shiver ran down my spine and I stopped in my tracks. The image of Grandma Ruby dancing for Joe Grimaldi and his mobsters flashed into my mind. Aunt Louise had said that the New Orleans mafia used to hide bodies under the houses of respectable citizens. Then I thought of Uncle Jonathan's family finding skeletons buried in their garden and recalled Grandma Ruby's ghost tour story about a man who was supposed to have been murdered by his wife and buried under the porch. A sick feeling pinched my stomach. Could there be more to that story than Grandma Ruby was letting on? I pushed the thought from my mind. The last thing I needed now I had reunited with my New Orleans family was to discover something gruesome in their past.

When I entered the house, Lorena had arrived and was busy making breakfast. It was going to be difficult to talk to Grandma Ruby about family secrets with her in the house. An hour later, Uncle Jonathan and Aunt Louise turned up carrying their laptops and a box full of binder folders.

'We decided to take you up on your offer to look after Momma, Amandine, and go on the trip to Arizona,' Aunt Louise said, plonking her laptop on the kitchen table. 'We hoped to work today to get everything up to speed before we go away but we forgot that the maintenance management had arranged to fumigate our office building this weekend. I had some drycleaning of Momma's to bring over so we thought we may as well work from here today.'

Uncle Jonathan patted me on the shoulder. 'Louise told me about your offer to look after Ruby so we can go on our trip. That's very kind of you, Amandine. It's something we've been looking forward to for a long time.'

'Of course,' I said. 'Your trip sounds exciting!'

I was tempted to ask Aunt Louise if I could use the internet on her laptop for a moment. I hadn't brought mine with me, and apart from the console television in the sitting room, the portable one in the kitchen and the CD player in my room, the house seemed devoid of electronic devices. I was curious to see if I could find any mention of a burlesque dancer named Jewel who had performed in New Orleans in the 1950s. That way I could be sure Grandma Ruby hadn't made the whole thing up to stir me the way she used to stir the tourists she took on ghost tours. But I decided against it. I didn't want to raise Aunt Louise's suspicion about anything to do with Grandma Ruby's past. I'd find the public library instead and use the internet there.

I went upstairs and grabbed my mini backpack, and tossed my digital camera into it along with a map of New Orleans. Then I filled my stainless-steel flask from the water cooler in the kitchen before attaching it to the strap of my bag.

'What are you planning to do today?' Uncle Jonathan asked. He was sorting papers into piles on the table.

'I was thinking of walking around the French Quarter, and maybe taking an architectural tour.'

'You'll love it!' said Aunt Louise. 'But come home by seven. I'll cook dinner for us tonight.'

I glanced up the staircase, hoping Grandma Ruby might make an appearance before I set off.

'Oh, don't expect to see her downstairs anytime soon,' said Aunt Louise, giving me a peck on the cheek. 'Ever since Daddy passed away Momma's been a late riser.'

I caught the streetcar to Poydras Street. On the map it didn't look too far to walk to Loyola Avenue from there.

But after ten minutes I began to wonder if I should fork out the money for a taxi. The humidity was making my clothes stick to me — and the business district was the least charming of all the places I'd seen in New Orleans. The wide blocks and the square buildings with tiny windows were too stark for my taste, although fans of modernist architecture would have loved them. I hated buildings that were eyesores but considered brilliant simply because they broke with convention. They would be torn down eventually to be replaced by buildings with better aesthetics. It was wasteful.

The area didn't seem all that safe either. I passed a bus stop, but the people squatted around it weren't waiting for a bus, they were smoking crack.

With grim determination, sweat and a blister on my heel, I made it to the post office but couldn't see the library. A postal truck driver told me it was located at City Hall on Perdido Street a few blocks down. 'Be careful crossing the streets here,' he warned me. 'People drive like maniacs.'

As if to illustrate his point, I nearly got wiped out on a pedestrian crossing by a mother with three children driving a Chevrolet Suburban. Gone were the genteel manners of the Garden District.

There wasn't a taxi in sight, so I gritted my teeth, finished my water and headed in the direction the postal driver had indicated. I found City Hall — a cement block with blue windows that wouldn't have been out of place in the former Soviet Union — but there was no sign of the library.

'Could you tell me where the public library is?' I asked a woman waiting on the steps outside City Hall.

'I have no idea,' she replied.

Exhausted and thirsty, I sat down under a tree in the park across the road. Then I noticed a young man sitting on the park's low wall and holding a hardcover book with a plastic cover. A library book!

'Hey!' I called, rushing towards him. He grabbed his bag and held it to his body, eyeing me suspiciously. 'Sorry to scare you,' I said. 'I only want to know where to find the public library.'

My accent seemed to reassure him that I wasn't deranged. He pointed to a building at the edge of the park.

'Thanks,' I told him with a smile, but he didn't return to his reading until I was a safe distance away.

The public library had been built in the same era as City Hall judging by the bronze-anodised sunscreen around the top two floors. As I'd gone to so much trouble to find it, I thought I may as well take a picture. I pulled my camera out of my bag, but spotted a security guard glaring at me. A security guard outside a library nobody could locate? What was that about? Then I noticed the airport-style metal detectors as I walked into the building and the sign that read: *No weapons*. This was insane!

I'd once been scolded by a student inside Sydney University's library because she thought my new Doc Martens squeaked too loudly. What would she have said if I'd pulled out a Glock pistol and started a shoot-out right there between *Architectural Materials* and *Buildings for Religious Purposes*?

I bought myself a time card at the front desk, and sat down in front of a computer to search for a New Orleans burlesque dancer named Jewel. I found plenty of information about Evangeline the Oyster Girl who emerged from a giant shell on stage, and who became so jealous of a rival act, Divena, who stripped underwater, that on stage one night she attacked Divena's water tank with a sledgehammer. There was also Lilly Christine, the Cat Girl, famous for a stalking dance that the chief inspector for the district attorney described as 'the most filthy, most lewd and indecent performance I had ever witnessed in my life'. Then there was Wild Cherry who danced to Afro-Cuban jazz, and Linda Brigette who had an act that featured a baboon, a python and fire-eating.

I looked up the famous New Orleans clubs of the day — the Hotsy Totsy, the Flamingo, Poodle's Patio and the 500 Club — and used up all the keywords I could think of, but couldn't find one mention of a stripper named Jewel. Perhaps Grandma Ruby had made the whole thing up after all. I sat back and chewed on my nail. That was the confusing thing: for somebody who supposedly kept so many secrets, Grandma Ruby came across as authentic.

I decided to give the old-fashioned way a try and switched over to the library's catalogue. Perhaps I'd find what I was looking for on the shelf. I located a book in the New Orleans entertainment section titled *Bourbon Street Babes: A history of burlesque dancers in New Orleans*, and sat down in a vinyl armchair to read it.

In the introduction I discovered that Christian evangelist Billy Graham described the French Quarter as the 'middle of hell' on a visit to the city in 1954, but as I studied the pictures of the Bourbon Street nightclubs and their patrons, I thought it seemed much classier than it did now. The men were wearing suits, and the women were dressed to the nines with tiaras and silk gloves. The dancers who'd performed there in the 1950s — Tempest Storm, Tiger Lily, Fatima, Reddi Flame — looked like goddesses in their feathers and sequins.

I scanned the pages, still searching for Jewel but not holding out much hope, until I came across a black and white picture of a dancer on stage, taken from the side view. It was captioned: *The dancer Jewel, one of the most popular acts in New Orleans, who disappeared mysteriously in 1955.* I read the copy, but there was no further mention of her.

I stared at the picture. It showed a woman wearing a figure-hugging, black lace fishtail dress. Her soft curls hid most of her face, but the audience's expressions ranged from adoration to rapture. I tried to see Grandma Ruby in the woman, but the angle of the photograph made it impossible to discern her facial features. All I could deduce was that Jewel had been beautiful.

I put the book back and accepted I'd reached a dead end — for now anyway.

On my way to the French Quarter I stopped at a Walgreens to buy a couple of bottles of water. As I waited in line for the cashier I eyed a dumpbin full of baby alligator heads. The sign above it read: *On Special: $7.99.* Were they real or plastic?

'In case you were wondering, yes, I'm afraid they're real, Amandine. They're preserved after slaughter to sell to tourists.'

I turned to see Elliot Davenport, the jazz history professor I'd met at Estée's funeral. He wasn't wearing a gaudy outfit this time, but a grey fitted shirt that showed off his toned body. In his shopping basket were some potatoes, flour and several packets of Fig Newtons biscuits.

'They're a weakness of mine,' he said. 'I like to munch on them when I'm marking student papers.'

'They're called Spicy Fruit Rolls in Australia,' I told him. 'They were my favourite biscuits when I was a child.'

'Biscuits?' he said, grinning. 'That sounds very posh. We call them cookies here.'

After finishing at the cashier, we stepped out into the street together.

'What have you been up to this morning?' he asked me.

I wasn't about to reveal that I was trying to find out if my grandmother had been a stripper or not, so I told him I was exploring the area.

'Well, would you like to come back to my place for a "biscuit"? My apartment building is a former Creole mansion constructed in 1820 — it's still got the original windows and transoms. I think you'll like it.'

I laughed. 'Okay, that sounds good. I was planning on doing an architectural tour anyway.'

We walked along Bourbon Street, past a rowdy group of male tourists with plastic cups of beer in their hands. One of them was wearing a tank top with a silhouette of a pole dancer and a slogan that read *I support single moms*. I thought of the pictures I'd seen of well-dressed patrons watching strippers in the 1950s. Things had certainly changed in the Quarter.

'White trash!' Elliot whispered to me.

'Bogans!' I whispered back.

'"Biscuits", "bogans" — I'm going to Australia to learn the language!'

Further on, a crowd had gathered around a gangly girl with curly hair who was playing a piano accordion and singing. Elliot and I sat on the kerb to listen to her. She had a crystal-clear contralto voice that reminded me of the 1930s jazz singer Connee Boswell, but with a modern element to it. She was singing Louis Armstrong's 'Skeleton in the Closet'. When she finished the piece, the audience applauded enthusiastically and dropped notes into her accordion case. She moved on to other jazz numbers, and the crowd was joined by more people.

'She's unique,' I said to Elliot. 'I'd pay to see her perform. Why is she out on the street?'

'In New Orleans we don't snub street artists or think of them as buskers,' he explained. 'You'll see some of the best music out here on the street. Even our famous musicians are just part of the scene. I saw Dr John at the laundromat on Esplanade the other day, washing his shorts like any other regular guy.'

We dropped some dollar bills in the girl's case and continued on.

'Jazz is considered a sophisticated taste now, but it didn't start out that way,' Elliot told me. 'It had its birth in the bordellos of the Storyville district of New Orleans and is a blend of musical influences from everything, from the old slave chants to ragtime and the blues, brass bands and a primitive African beat. It was considered the right kind of music to put men in the mood to spend money on women and liquor. A lot of people don't know that Jelly Roll Morton got his start playing in brothels, or that Louis Armstrong's mother was a prostitute.'

'Wow! I had no idea.'

'Boston, New York and Philadelphia might have museums and opera houses sponsored by honourable philanthropists and businessmen, but many of the charitable institutions and public works in New Orleans were paid for by the madams of brothels. This is a city built on sin.'

I remembered Grandma Ruby's story and was about to ask him about burlesque and jazz, but before I had a chance we reached his apartment building. The courtyard was accessed through an arched passageway that I assumed had once been used for horse-drawn carriages, and was a dizzying riot of banana trees, bamboo, fan palms and ferns in hanging pots. A fountain in the middle tumbled water into a pond brimming with lilies and goldfish. Looking around the courtyard helped me understand Grandma Ruby better. She loved the house in the Garden District because that's where she had lived with her husband and children, but she was definitely a product of the French Quarter: dark and sultry.

'Our resident ghost walks straight across this courtyard, humming an old French song, "Sur le Pont d'Avignon",' Elliot said. 'She then goes through this wall into my apartment before disappearing. 'But she looks content and doesn't cause any trouble so nobody has ever called in the ghost-busters.'

'Seriously? You've seen her?'

He grinned. 'Not yet. I've only heard about her from my neighbours. But a few more drinks on Friday night on Bourbon Street and I might.'

I followed him through the front door and was immediately charmed by the quirky and cramped apartment. The kitchen, dining room and living room were all one space, with roughly hewn floorboards, oriental rugs and more CDs on the custom-made shelves than there were books in my parents' bedroom. A saxophone was propped on a stand in the corner, and a wrought-iron spiral staircase led to an upper floor. Three of the walls were the original exposed brick while the fourth had been painted vintage green, which worked well with the lush vegetation of the courtyard. But it was the kitchen corner that intrigued me. It was the most minimalist kitchen I'd ever seen, consisting of only a narrow fridge, a square ceramic sink, a medicine cupboard and a freestanding cooker. But judging by the well-used saucepans and the crowded spice rack that hung along the wall, Elliot must love to cook.

'Come meet Duke,' he said, placing his shopping in the medicine cupboard before turning to an armoire whose doors had been removed and replaced with chicken wire. Inside was an arrangement of branches, water containers and a kitty litter tray on the bottom. Elliot reached in and brought out a grey squirrel, perching him on his sleeve to show him to me. The squirrel climbed up and down Elliot's arm and playfully swiped at his face.

'He's so cute,' I said, patting the animal.

Duke leaped from Elliot's shoulder onto the curtain rod and began grooming himself.

'Is he happy in his cage?' I asked. 'Doesn't he want to go outside?'

'I only put him in the cage to keep him out of trouble when I'm not home. Otherwise he's got free use of the room, and I take him out for a run around the courtyard at least once a day. I don't believe in keeping wild animals as pets, but he came to me in an unusual way. I discovered him on the back seat of my car when I was returning from a teachers' conference in Oregon. He was a baby, and I couldn't reunite him with his family as I didn't know where he'd come from — I might have acquired him at any number of stops I'd made along the way. I took him to a vet who showed me how to feed him. She noticed he was blind in one eye, and for that reason he'll never be able to be rehabilitated back into the wild.'

'He's lucky he found you then,' I said.

He plucked Duke from the curtain rod and rubbed cheeks with him. 'No, I'm lucky to have found him. He's good company for me. My apartment's too small for a dog or a cat and I love animals.'

The more I discovered about Elliot, the more I liked him. Being able to cook and being kind to animals were big pluses.

'Do you mind if I use your bathroom?' I asked.

'No problem. It's upstairs.'

The bathroom was as quirky as the rest of the apartment, with low exposed beams and unfinished walls that contrasted sharply with the sparkling white bathtub and sink. In the corner was a slim bathroom cupboard. Although I tried not to, I couldn't resist looking inside for 'girlfriend evidence' — lipstick, perfume, scented bath salts — among the guy stuff. But there wasn't any.

On my way back downstairs I caught a glimpse of the tidy bedroom with its pale blue colours and canopied bed. *Very nice*, I thought. I was getting a good feeling about Elliot.

He had made coffee and set out some Fig Newtons on a plate.

'I appreciate you sharing your stash with me,' I told him.

'My pleasure. I'll share my biscuits with you anytime, Amandine.'

I blushed so deeply I felt like a fourteen-year-old girl again.

He looked at me curiously, then took a sip of coffee. 'I was thinking that I should introduce you to a friend of mine. He's a jazz aficionado in his seventies. You can quiz him on the A–Z of New Orleans music and he knows all the answers. There's a good chance he could have met your father. We can go see him now if you like?'

'You bet!' I said. 'I know it might be hard to believe, but I only discovered recently that my father was a musician. Learning about him through his music is like a gift to me.'

We finished our coffee, then walked to St Peter Street where Elliot had parked his Ford Taurus. He opened the passenger door for me before getting into the driver's seat. 'I'm taking you to the Lower Ninth Ward. Have you heard of it?'

'No.'

'It's a neighbourhood of New Orleans where tourists don't go,' he said, putting on his seat belt and turning the key in the ignition. 'It's got a lot of trouble with gangs and drug dealers. But don't worry, you'll be safe with me.'

I bit my lip and braced myself inwardly. Between going to a funeral where the deceased participated in her own wake and discovering Grandma Ruby had been a stripper, I was ready for anything.

'I don't think it's as bad as people make out,' he said, as we crossed the Industrial Canal into the Lower Ninth Ward. 'The area has a sense of community. Many of the residents have lived here for generations, but unfortunately it's the riff-raff that give it a bad name. Now you're in New Orleans you might hear the joke, "I'm from the Ninth and I don't mind dying."'

The district had a rural feel about it with its chain-link fences, dirt roads, and grassy vacant lots. Many of the older houses were wooden rectangular-style dwellings known as 'shotguns' because of their design. The rooms followed one behind the other, with the front and back doors in line, so theoretically a bullet could be fired from one end straight through to the other. Some of the houses and lawns were neatly kept, but many showed the tired neglect of poverty. An elderly couple sat in beach chairs on their lawn. A group of boys with their jeans hanging halfway down their buttocks and their caps turned backwards did skateboard tricks in a driveway.

'The area was once a plantation, but then it was subdivided into cheap land for poor European immigrants and former slaves who were working in nearby industries,' Elliot told me. 'Their descendants lived together in harmony until the schools were desegregated in the 1960s. Then a lot of the white people moved out.'

He pulled up in front of a blond-brick house with a bright yellow roof and the initials *F.D.* painted on it. 'Do you know who F.D. is?'

I shook my head. 'No.'

He started humming 'Blueberry Hill'.

'Fats Domino!' I cried. 'Did he used to live in the Lower Ninth Ward?'

'He still does, right there in that house, though most people don't even know he's still alive. Everyone remembers Elvis Presley, but Fats Domino is almost forgotten. Well, if the Lower Ninth is good enough for a founding father of rock'n'roll, then it's all right by me. This place has soul.'

Elliot drove on a few more streets before pulling up in front of a house that stood out from the others around it. It was freshly painted in a caramel colour with maroon shutters and trimmings. There was a camel-back extension in the rear, and the tidy garden was bordered by a heritage green metal fence. Gardenias lined the path to the front door, and a Chinese fan palm shaded the front porch.

We got out of the car and I expected Elliot to knock on the door, but he pushed it open and called out, 'Terence! I've brought someone to see you!'

'Elliot! Come in,' a sonorous voice called from inside.

I followed Elliot into a wood-panelled front room. A couch and armchair upholstered in orange cotton plaid faced a Rhodes electric piano. I knew those pianos had been built in the 1970s and used hammers like an acoustic piano, but the only one I'd seen until now had been in an exhibition at the Sydney Conservatorium of Music.

The doorway to the kitchen had been converted into an arch. A man sitting at a Formica table with a newspaper in front of him waved to us.

'Come in, kids,' he said, standing up.

He was over six foot and straightbacked and carried himself with such regal dignity that he could have been welcoming us in a tuxedo rather than the shorts, singlet and massage sandals he was wearing. The combination of his velvety voice, sable-toned skin and intelligent brown eyes mesmerised me.

'Hey, Terence,' said Elliot, giving him a man hug. He turned back to me. 'This is Amandine from Australia.'

'Australia?' said Terence, shaking my hand firmly. 'Well, nice to meet you, Amandine. You're a long way from home.' He pulled out the vinyl seats around his kitchen table for us to sit on, then opened his kitchen cupboard, which was so methodically organised it could have been a pharmacist's cabinet.

'Can I get you something to drink?' he asked. 'Tea, coffee, a root beer?' He took out a box from the cupboard and stared at the label dubiously. 'Or I've got this funny smelling green tea my neighbour Wanda left the other day. She said it would be good for my liver.'

'Is there something wrong with your liver?' Elliot asked.

'Not that I know of.'

'Then don't drink it.'

Terence laughed heartily. He had a nice laugh: warm and rich, like hot chocolate.

I drank green tea all the time, but I'd never tried root beer so when Elliot accepted Terence's offer I asked for one too. I'd thought it was a soft drink so was surprised when Terence took an unlabelled bottle filled with a coffee-coloured liquid from the refrigerator.

'Terence brews his own root beer,' Elliot explained, while his friend poured the thick liquid into glasses.

'That's right,' said Terence, sitting down and raising his glass to toast us. 'From my grandfather's old recipe. Not that stuff they sell in the stores. Real liquorice, ginger and dandelion roots, along with wild cherry tree bark, juniper berries and a cinnamon stick.'

I took a sip. It was delicious ... and very alcoholic!

'I thought root beer was a soft drink,' I said, coughing.

My statement made Terence laugh. 'In New Orleans, this is a soft drink.'

'I brought Amandine to meet you because her father was a New Orleans jazz musician and we wondered if you might have known him?' Elliot said to him.

The old man leaned back in his chair and looked at me. 'Well, if your father was a jazz musician in New Orleans I most certainly would have known him. There are only six degrees of separation at most in this city. What was his name?'

'Dale Lalande.'

Terence's face froze for a moment. 'But … how? Dale Lalande died so young. Too young.'

'I was two years old when my parents were killed. I grew up in Australia.'

Terence took a while to digest this information. 'I didn't know Dale had a child. Well then, that's even more of a tragedy,' he said finally. 'You see, Dale Lalande was one of the finest musicians I've ever heard. He played New Orleans jazz like New Orleans jazz should be played: refined but also down to earth. I heard him play piano, saxophone and clarinet. He was a strong musician and a precise one.' He took a sip of his root beer, and thought deeply about something before continuing. 'He was not only an exceptional musician but a special young man. I treasure the conversations I had with him about music. People like Dale don't come along every day and he was taken away from us way too soon.'

It was uncanny — and a bit eerie — to hear someone talk about my father, especially in such glowing terms. It reminded me of how I'd felt when Aunt Louise and Grandma Ruby spoke about him.

'I met your mother on a couple of occasions too,' continued Terence, then smiled to himself. 'She was a wild child. I think Dale's solid temperament calmed her down while she stirred him up. They were quite a pair, but they were obviously deeply in love.' He nodded towards the front room. 'Come with me a moment.'

We followed him to the front room. He sat down at the piano and turned it on.

'This was one of your father's,' he said, placing his hands on the keys. 'I remember it well.'

His left hand produced a powerful swing bass pattern while his right moved nimbly over the keys. The music pulled at something inside of me. The piece was complex yet playful, intense yet cheeky.

Terence stopped playing and turned to me. 'Do you want to have a go?' He stood up to make way for me. 'Try it. I'll show you how the left hand goes.'

I sat down and gingerly touched the piano. 'I don't know if I can. I stopped playing after I left school, and I've only studied classical music.'

He grinned at me. 'Of course you can. You're the daughter of a jazz genius — you've got it inside of you. Your daddy could play Ravel and Debussy and street music too. He never limited himself, and you shouldn't either.'

He showed me the hand positions and chords, and to my surprise I picked things up faster than I'd expected, even though I was out of practice.

Elliot applauded.

'Not bad at all,' Terence said. 'Why don't you come to me for lessons, Amandine? I'd be happy to teach you more of your daddy's stuff.'

He looked at me with such compassion that tears pricked my eyes, but I managed to calm myself. Tamara's partner, Leanne, was into crystals and was always talking about serendipity. I'd often ribbed her about her new age beliefs, but now I found the fortune I'd had in meeting someone who had known my father and his music almost too much to bear. It was enough to make me believe in magic myself.

'That would be awesome!' I told him.

'Good,' he said, with genuine enthusiasm. 'You've got a nice touch. You're not a heavy-handed player, you move gracefully.'

'You play very well yourself,' I told him. 'Were you a professional musician too?'

'Hell, no! I was a carpenter. I left being professional to the guys who were really good. I enjoy playing myself, of course, but I enjoy listening to the best even more.'

We finished our root beers and talked more about jazz in New Orleans. Before I knew it, time had got away and it was almost six o'clock. I looked at Elliot apologetically.

'Have to go?' he asked, then nodded.

I thanked Terence again for introducing me to my father's music.

'Why don't you come again tomorrow morning?' he offered. 'That will give us more time. I know Elliot goes to see his sister and her family on Sundays but you can catch the bus and I'll meet you at the stop.'

As he walked us to the gate, it occurred to me that he might have seen Jewel perform too.

'I'm interested in the New Orleans burlesque scene as well,' I told him. 'Have you ever heard of a performer called Jewel?'

Terence stopped in his tracks. 'Wow! Where did you hear that name? She was a performer like no other, but nobody knows her name these days. When she came on stage the whole world stopped. She was mesmerising. She danced at the Vieux Carré nightclub, a classy place on Bourbon Street. It's gone now, of course. How'd you hear about her all the way from Australia?'

His reaction confirmed that Jewel had actually existed, but I wasn't about to reveal that my grandmother claimed to be her, so I answered that I'd come across her picture in a book about New Orleans entertainers and it said that she'd suddenly disappeared. The story sounded intriguing.

'Well,' said Terence, 'I can tell you that she was the best burlesque dancer by far. You could feel the electricity in the air when she performed.'

I wanted to hear more, but didn't want to upset Aunt Louise by being late for dinner. 'Till tomorrow,' I told him.

He waved to us from his gate as we drove off.

'Terence has so much charisma,' I said to Elliot.

'I know. It's that voice. It's like talking to God.'

We laughed, then drove in silence for a while before he said, 'I didn't realise you'd lost your mother as well in the accident. That's really tough. But how come you grew up in Australia if you still have family in New Orleans?'

'That's a difficult story. I don't know all the details, but apparently there was a legal dispute. My nan in Australia got custody of me.'

'But she didn't let you visit New Orleans?'

'No.'

He bit his lip. 'I'm sorry, I didn't mean to pry.'

'You didn't.' I was surprised at how calm I felt. Usually, talking about my family situation jangled my nerves. But I didn't feel that way with Elliot. It was easy to be with him.

He sighed. 'Few of us get the *Brady Bunch* ideal happy family. My dad shot through when I was a kid. My sister and I were raised by my mother and aunt. We both turned out all right though. My sister's happily married with three kids in Baton Rouge, and I'm very close to them all. Not having a father made me feel like a freak at school, but in the end we all decide for ourselves what kind of person we want to be.'

What Elliot said was true, but I was struggling with only now coming to terms with the man who had been my father. I was forced to reassess so much of my life as I learned each new thing about him.

When we reached the Garden District, Elliot glanced at me. 'I'm going to look for your father's recordings on Monday morning so call me anytime after that.'

I was tempted to invite him in to meet the family, but stopped myself. I didn't want to create any diversion to Grandma Ruby finishing her story. 'Thank you for everything. I enjoyed myself today,' I said.

'My pleasure,' he replied with a good-natured smile, before driving away. I watched the car disappear down the street and then walked up the path to the front door with a spring in my stride.

When I stepped inside the house, Uncle Jonathan was speaking on his mobile phone while Aunt Louise was cooking in the kitchen. The mouth-watering fragrances of roasting garlic and melting cheese filled the air and reminded me of evenings at home with Nan. It made me both happy and sad. Grandma Ruby was in the laundry, giving Flambeau a bath. I'd never seen anybody give a rooster a bath before, but then Elliot's squirrel had a litter tray.

Grandma Ruby winked when I greeted her, as if we were co-conspirators.

'Did you have a good day sightseeing?' Aunt Louise asked, turning from the oven.

I gave her a kiss on the cheek. 'It was great.'

I wasn't ready to tell anyone about Terence yet. He'd shown me a new aspect of my father that I wanted to keep to myself without anyone else putting a spin on it. Besides, I wasn't sure how pleased Aunt Louise would be that Elliot had taken me to the Lower Ninth Ward. I glanced at Grandma Ruby, now drying Flambeau in the bonnet of a 1970s hairdryer. Maybe I'd get to be as good at keeping secrets as she seemed to be.

Uncle Jonathan cleared the breakfast table of papers. 'Let's eat in the kitchen,' he said. 'I feel too stitched up in the dining room.'

Aunt Louise had made eggplant lasagne with a chopped Italian salad. As we ate, Uncle Jonathan told us about a difficult property settlement he and Aunt Louise were negotiating, while Grandma Ruby fed pieces of a banana to Flambeau, who was sitting in the chair next to her. By the time we had enjoyed a dessert of grilled peaches, and cleaned up the kitchen, it was eleven o'clock.

After Aunt Louise and Uncle Jonathan left, I was afraid Grandma Ruby was going to turn in for the night and not continue her story. But to my relief, she lit new candles in the dining room, settled Flambeau on her lap and beckoned for me to join her.

'I'll tell you about Leroy tonight,' she said, her lips trembling. 'He is the most important part of the story.'

'Who was Leroy and where did he sit?' I asked, looking at the place settings.

Grandma Ruby brushed her hand over Flambeau's feathers. 'No, this is quite a different story,' she said softly. 'Quite a different story indeed.'

FOURTEEN

Ruby

Deceit is not a desirable thing, but here is the reality of it: sometimes you have to keep secrets. If I was going to strip for a living without humiliating my mother, I was going to have to do it in disguise.

I'd seen enough of the other strippers on stage to know that red or blonde hair was more striking under the lavender stage lights than brunette tones. After spotting a poster of Rita Hayworth in a barber shop on Bourbon Street, I bought a wig to imitate her lustrous copper waves.

'Changing your appearance isn't enough to avoid being recognised,' Melody advised me when I went to visit her. After the shooting, she'd decided to retire from stripping and move back to Baltimore. She was selling me her costumes for a fraction of the price it would have cost me to have my own made.

The shotgun house she'd been renting in the Seventh Ward, with its porcelain Bambi ornaments and lace doilies, suggested nothing of Golden Delilah, but suited homely Melody to a tee. She was a master of illusion and I'd do well to listen to her.

'What should I do?' I asked, trying on the headdress of her mermaid outfit — a massive crown of starfish, pearls and sea shells.

'You've got to develop different gestures, a different style of walking, even a different way of thinking.' She helped me to step into the fishtail skirt, using the arm that wasn't bandaged up. 'Every time you pass a restaurant, observe how alluring women hold their glasses in their fingertips, reapply their lipstick ever so slowly, and touch their throats when they're flattered, as if they are beckoning to be kissed there.'

I'd been fascinated by Melody's transformation into her stage persona. Now I was learning that it was no accident: deliberate thought had gone into every move. Earl had called her 'an artist' and he'd been right.

I flicked my hair back and exposed the skin on the inside of my wrist as if I were enticing someone to kiss it. 'Like this?' I asked, studying my reflection in the mirror.

Melody turned my body to an angle where the sea shell bra of the costume accentuated my curves. My eyes seemed to darken and my jaw set more firmly, making me appear worldlier. Who was that sassy stranger looking back at me? I marvelled at how a single pose and gesture could transform me from a pretty young girl to a seductress.

'Jewel,' I said, pouting my peaked red lips. 'Expensive, brilliant, shimmering, radiant, enticing.'

I was in awe of my metamorphosis and scared too. It was as if a different person had slipped inside me.

'Excellent,' Melody said, zipping me up. 'I wasn't born attractive; I was a knock-kneed, shy thing. But I decided to be beautiful, and when I was on stage people believed it. Never underestimate the power of belief or a trick of the eye — magicians use them all the time. You must become a magician of sorts, creating an illusion.'

Excitement thrummed through me. I was determined to master my transformation as convincingly as Melody had hers.

As well as the mermaid outfit, I bought a gold chiffon Cleopatra dress that Melody had never had a chance to wear, along with a snake-charm headdress and arm cuffs; and an elegant strapless dress of black satin with a side split, and matching gloves that reached my shoulders.

'I'll drive you to the club so you can store your costumes there,' Melody offered. 'They aren't the sort of thing you carry on the bus.'

'Indeed,' I said, but then realised I had another problem. 'Now I'm stripping, I can't walk into the club as Ruby and leave as Ruby in case someone recognises me. I'll have to find somewhere between home and the club to switch!'

'Good idea!' Melody said, holding up her bandaged arm. 'That was my mistake with Huey. He followed me. You'd best hire a room somewhere near the club. Lola used to have a pied-à-terre in Chartres Street. Why don't you go and see if it's still available for rent?'

The address Melody gave me was for an apartment building down the quiet end of Chartres Street, away from the nightclubs and restaurants. It wasn't decrepit but it was far from pristine. The shutters were crooked and in need of paint, and a side balcony sagged so woefully it looked as though it wouldn't withstand the weight of a child. At the front of the building, a gallery trimmed by a cast-iron railing with an oak leaf motif was the last remaining hint of the mansion's bygone glory. The front entrance was too conspicuous, but I was pleased to see an overgrown walled garden with a gate to the street and a side entrance next to the building. I'd be able to enter and leave discreetly through that.

'Everybody minds their own business, that's the rule of the house,' said the proprietor, an elderly woman with bandy legs and frizzy hair. 'We've got two painters here who like things quiet, and one veteran who keeps to himself.' She led me to a ground-floor apartment at the rear of the building. 'Pay your rent every Saturday and I won't cause you any trouble.'

Before opening the door, she stopped to appraise me. I tried to look composed, but my lack of complete assurance didn't escape her keen eyes. I was too well-dressed to be looking for a cheap flat for noble purposes and she knew it.

'The former tenant left the apartment in better condition than she found it so I'm going to have to charge you extra,' she said as she opened the door.

I was pleased to discover that the apartment was indeed in better condition than the rest of the building. While the tan paint on the walls was peeling and the chandelier that hung from the ceiling looked like it hadn't been functional for years, the room was clean and held a wrought-iron bed and mosquito net, two large wardrobes, a dressing table and a red velvet chaise longue. The door to a combined kitchenette and bathroom was hidden behind an oriental screen. A French painting of a young woman in *déshabillé* added to the boudoir style of the room. It was the perfect place to transform into Jewel.

'Yes, I'll take it,' I told the woman.

'When do you want to move in?'

'Right away ... and I'd like a key to the garden gate.'

A knowing look came into her eyes and I blushed. I could imagine what she was thinking.

'Come at seven,' she said. 'I'll have a spare key ready for you then.'

As I prepared for my act that evening, it occurred to me that my desire to transform myself went deeper than to avoid being recognised. I wanted to keep Ruby for my life with Maman, so Jewel would have to be an alter ego. It was the only way I could live with myself and what I was doing.

Rolando and I had agreed on a sum of one hundred and eighty dollars a week, which was good for a beginner. But I wanted to be more than an average stripper; I wanted people to be wild for me the way they were wild for Tempest Storm, Dixie Evans and Blaze Starr — and to pay big bucks to see me.

I studied attractive women assiduously — not only other strippers but women out on the street — for that special *je ne sais quoi*. My favourite place was the glittering lobby of the Roosevelt Hotel. There, a world of beautiful, exotic women paraded before me: visiting Hollywood stars, and the wives — and mistresses — of business tycoons. I scrutinised their hair, their make-up, their mannerisms and the way they walked. Jewel was becoming a composite of the most beautiful women in America.

But I still had a major challenge: my voice. What if someone recognised me from the way I spoke? The Southern accent was sultry by nature, and even strippers from the West Coast swapped their rising inflections for the more melodious tones of the South. But I needed to differentiate myself.

My answer came one day in the Roosevelt's lobby when I saw a woman walk out of the elevator, as regally as if she were Cleopatra herself. Her navy blue dress was cut on the bias and unadorned, creating the perfect contrast for her silk turban with a diamond-encrusted jaguar brooch at the centre of it. The effect was dazzling. Every eye turned to her. She was aristocratic, extravagant, mysterious. Then when she spoke to the concierge to collect her mail and arrange for a car, I knew I had found my voice.

'Thank you, Mr Wiltz,' she said in a tone rich with elegance. 'That is most kind of you and I am truly, truly grateful.'

She spoke slowly and deliberately in an upper-class accent that was halfway between British and North American. It was hypnotic. I tried to put my finger on the quality that made her voice so different. Then I realised it was elevated. Her voice was not noise, but music.

The blissful look on the concierge's face showed he was under her spell.

In my little room in Chartres Street, I practised the woman's gilded voice and added my own hint of Southern seductiveness to it until it became my own. 'I am so truly, truly grateful,' I said over and over again to the mirror.

When it came time for Melody and her children to leave for Baltimore, I helped her pack her car. I was losing the first friend I'd had in years. But that was the price I was going to pay for being Jewel: I couldn't associate with anyone too closely or get to know anyone too intimately, in case my secret life should be discovered. *Gracious but guarded; be friendly to everyone but confide in no-one*, I wrote in the notebook I kept in the Chartres Street apartment to record my thoughts on Jewel's personality.

When Melody was ready to leave, she hugged me, then looked me up and down. 'I can't believe the transformation — I can barely recognise you at all. But remember, the real test will be if you can pull it off with someone who has known you for years.'

Melody dispelled some of my self-doubt, and I knew she was right: the only way to test if my alter ego was convincing was to try her on someone. But I couldn't take the risk with Maman or Mae. I thought about who else I could try, then smiled when the answer came to me.

Doctor Monfort's eyes nearly popped out of his head when he saw me in the waiting room, and not because he recognised me. His usual patient wasn't a femme fatale decked out in a scarlet pencil dress, nude stilettos and smelling of Femme Rochas perfume.

'Good morning, Miss Charrette,' he said, inviting me to take a seat in his consulting room.

The place was familiar to me, with its eye chart and scales and smell of Clorox bleach. There was a jar of candies on Doctor Monfort's desk and I remembered fondly how he used to offer them to me as a child, after I'd let him examine my ears or throat without a fuss.

'What can I do for you today?' he asked.

I'd entered his rooms with the intention of saying I had a sore throat, but the expression of delight on his face brought out the mischief in me. I lifted the skirt of my dress to expose my right knee. 'I have a pain here,' I said, running my finger over my kneecap, 'when I walk.'

Doctor Monfort must have seen a lot of legs in his lifetime but the sight of mine seemed to interest him significantly. He bent down and pushed his glasses further up his nose to take a look.

I wriggled when he felt around my calf and kneecap. 'That tickles.'

'Oh,' he said, his face all aglow. 'Could you ... perhaps take off your stockings and sit on the bench so I can get a better look?'

Taking off my stockings was something Melody had taught me to do to perfection. I stood up and paused a moment in a three-quarter stance before I stepped out of my shoes. Then I stroked my hands up my leg until they reached my garter belt clips. Doctor Monfort loosened his collar and attempted to look away, but he was smiling as if he were thinking about something pleasant. It was terrible to tease a professional man — and a family friend at that — but my penchant for cheekiness took over. I slowly rolled down my stocking and the temperature in the room seemed to go up a few degrees. Then I leaned forward to keep my balance as I lifted my leg behind me and pulled off my stocking with a flourish.

Doctor Monfort gave a little cry as he followed the movement, then looked flustered. 'Very good. Now take a seat on the bench, please.'

I kept my eyes on his face, so that every time he looked up from examining my knee with his trembling fingers I was ready to smile at him. Our faces were in close proximity, and if he hadn't recognised me as Ruby by now I was confident he wouldn't.

'I can't feel any abnormalities or swelling,' he said. 'You might have strained the tendon, that's all. Do you wear high heels like that all the time?' He pointed at my stilettos.

I tilted my head and peered deeply into his eyes. 'I usually do ... except when I'm naked, although sometimes I do then as well!'

He chuckled, then remembered himself. 'Well, you get dressed now, Miss Charrette,' he said, moving to his desk as briskly as if he were stepping away from a hungry alligator, 'and I'll give you a prescription for a liniment. Try not to wear those shoes all the time, and if your knee isn't better in two weeks come back and see me.'

'Oh, I will,' I said, as he passed me the prescription and showed me to the door.

'Well, you can come back anytime,' he added, 'sore knee or not.'

Next to Doctor Monfort's office was a store that sold bathroom accessories. As I passed the shop window I caught sight of my reflection in one of the cabinet mirrors. I stopped and gave myself a wink. Fooling Doctor Monfort had given me courage. Now I was ready for anything!

For my next performance as Jewel, I wore the black strapless dress and gloves I'd bought from Melody and teamed them with a silk turban and lace corset. The music I chose was Duke Ellington's 'The Mooche': its languorous, haunting beat enhanced my sinewy movements. Every time the clarinet and muted trumpet slipped down the scale, I slithered with them.

The men in the room seemed to hold their breath for my entire number, and then let out a collective sigh when I'd finished. But none of them would be able to get close to me. I'd stipulated in my new agreement with Rolando that I wouldn't entertain customers off stage. It was necessary for me to remain aloof to maintain my Jewel persona.

Rolando congratulated me on my new stage presence. 'That was incredible, Ruby. It was class all the way.'

'Jewel,' I reminded him. 'There is no Ruby in this club. Only Jewel.'

Back in my room in Chartres Street, while I was changing into my Ruby clothes, I suffered a splitting headache and had to lie down. The squeezing pain at my temples was so severe it almost blinded me. I thought of the racking pangs and nausea that Dr Jekyll suffered when he drank the potion that turned him into Mr Hyde. 'What's happening to me?' I cried.

Then I calmed myself. Jewel was not an aberration of nature. She was a creation that allowed me to do what was unthinkable as Ruby in order to help Maman — or so I thought.

'What's up with you?' Mae asked, when she brought the camomile tea I'd requested to my bedroom. 'You've always been the healthy one. These strange hours you're keeping ain't doing you no good! What's going to happen if you get sick?'

'Shh!' I said. Maman was asleep down the hall. Doctor Monfort had convinced her to return home. 'I never see my patients do so well as when they're in the bosom of their family,' he'd told her. While it was easier on me financially now Mae had taken over nursing Maman, I was always on high alert because the need for secrecy was even greater. Mae knew that I worked at night, but not what I really did. Maman, on the other hand, had to be kept in the dark that I worked at all.

'How long do you think we can keep this up?' Mae asked. 'I got to pretend you're sleeping, or you're at Mrs de Pauger's home having a piano lesson. What are you going to do if your mama invites Mrs Pélissier to visit and requests you to play something?'

I bit my lip and tried to shut out the image of me performing a shaky rendition of 'Moonlight Sonata' for Maman and Babette. Like Mae, I feared that at any moment things could come undone. 'We've got to keep going,' I told her. 'We have to be like soldiers in a war doing our duty. If I don't keep working, we're going to be out on the street with nothing but the clothes on our backs!'

She drew a breath and rubbed her forehead. 'You sure got some spirit in you, Miss Ruby. You're a fighter, that's for certain. All right then, I'll fight alongside you, seeing we don't have much of a choice.'

'I'm making good money, and we're saving more now Maman is back home. As soon as we pay the sanatorium bill and the mortgage, I'll stop working so hard. Life will be better then.'

Mae looked at me sceptically. She didn't excel at arithmetic or know exactly how much I was making, but she must have been able to figure out that the money we owed wasn't going to be paid back anytime soon. Some days I couldn't even bring myself to think about how long it was going to take to pay it all off.

'When you find yourself a nice man and get married, then life will be easier,' she said emphatically.

I smiled sweetly, but the irony of her comment was like a kick in the stomach. Now I was a burlesque dancer, no nice man would want me.

One night after I'd been performing as Jewel for a couple of months, one of the warm-up strippers told me there was someone in the club who wanted to see me.

'I don't mix with the customers any more,' I told her.

'Oh, you don't say no to this one,' she said. 'It's Sam Coppola. He's got links with the Mancuso gambling family. His speciality is making people disappear without a trace. Rumour has it one of his suppliers got on the wrong side of him and ended up dissolved in a tub of lye and emptied into a swamp.'

Half of the entertainment business in New Orleans was run by the mob and I couldn't afford to get on the wrong side of them. I dressed, reapplied my lipstick and fixed my hair.

A waiter showed me to the table where Sam Coppola was sitting. I'd been expecting a stocky Sicilian with bad table manners and was surprised to see a good-looking Italian man in a white tuxedo and black bow tie beckoning to me and pointing to a bottle of Bollinger in a champagne bucket.

'Won't you join me, Miss Jewel?' he asked, standing. He had slicked-back hair and a tanned face. There was a slight lisp in his speech that might have been annoying in another man, but coming from his full lips was strangely sensual.

'Thank you,' I said, placing myself in the chair he'd pulled out for me.

'Do you want something to eat?' he asked. 'I wouldn't trust the food in this joint, but I can send for something from Antoine's?'

One thing that was clear in the first few minutes of meeting Sam Coppola was that he wasn't of peasant stock. His tastes were expensive.

I shook my head. 'No, I'm fine, thank you.'

He stared at me for a long time, as if sizing me up.

'Did you enjoy the show, Mr Coppola?' I asked, to break the ice.

'Call me Sam,' he said. 'And to answer your question, yes, I did enjoy the show. But I expected I would. I've been hearing a lot about Jewel at the Havana Club, so I decided to come see what all the fuss is about.'

I was aware of something he wanted to say beneath the polite chit-chat. The way he looked me over made my stomach pitch. It was a fall to become a burlesque dancer, but I didn't intend to sink further and end up a gangster's moll, even for a man as debonair as Sam Coppola. If he made any sort of suggestion like that, I'd tell him I was engaged. Surely the mob had its own code of honour in that regard. I didn't want to end up in a tub of lye.

'How much money do you make here?' he asked.

Why did he want to know? Was he going to offer me a role as a courier or drug runner? I shifted uneasily in my seat and he noticed. Sam Coppola never missed a thing.

'The reason I'm asking is because whatever it is, I'll double it. I'm opening a new club on Bourbon Street and I want it to be class all the way. I'm looking for a local dancer to be the main act, rather than a string of out-of-towners. The act has to be pure glamour and not cheap striptease. I'm creating the sort of place that men would feel comfortable bringing their wives and girlfriends for dinner and a show. You interested?'

His offer was a good one. Rolando liked to change his acts around and that was going to be a problem for me. The other girls toured the country to perform at different venues, but I couldn't do that because of Maman. A permanent spot in New Orleans was what I needed, and what Sam was talking about was exactly the sort of burlesque dancer I wanted to be.

'I make five hundred dollars a week,' I told him, poker-faced. 'So it'll be one thousand dollars a week for me to come work for you.'

The frown lines on his forehead deepened. 'One thousand! Isn't that a little steep?'

'No, I don't think so,' I said, managing not to fidget or avert my gaze. 'You said you wanted class and class doesn't come cheap.'

It was a risk to tell someone like Sam Coppola a lie, but I'd gone to see Tempest Storm perform at the 500 Club. It annoyed me she was making so much more money than me. She was very pretty and had an eye-popping figure, but she couldn't keep time to the music. When the drummer gave her a beat, she'd miss it. Her dancing was uncoordinated and her act — well, her act was a little tacky. One thousand dollars wasn't even half of what she earned.

'Now, Miss Jewel, don't you get smart with me,' Sam said. 'I know you make one eighty a week and I'm willing to pay you five hundred — and provide your costumes.'

'Then why'd you ask me if you already know?' I said indignantly.

He rubbed his chin. 'To see how good you are at lying. Anyone who works for me has to be like a box with the lid shut tight. You focus on the job I'm paying you to do and nothing else. Anything you see and hear you keep to yourself. You don't even raise an eyebrow. You simply erase it from your mind like you never noticed it to begin with. As we say here in Louisiana, three can keep a secret if two are dead.'

My blood turned to ice. Was I prepared to work in a club owned by the mob? What if I accidentally witnessed something I wasn't supposed to see? But five hundred dollars a week and a long contract was too good to refuse. With that amount of money, I had a chance of getting our debts paid off faster than I'd ever dreamed.

I lifted my chin proudly. 'Well, how did I do? Did I meet your criteria as a good liar, Sam?'

He grinned, and I noticed for the first time the scar on the inside of his lower lip that must have been the cause of the lisp. 'You did pretty good. But get rid of that phoney transatlantic accent, will you. You're slipping in and out of it like a faulty radio. You're Creole, right? Well, speak with a French accent if you want to sound haughty. It will be a hundred times more convincing. And remember the most important point of disguising your voice: err on the safe side — talk low, talk slow, and don't say too much.'

'How come you know so much about changing your voice?'

He chuckled but didn't answer the question. 'Now come see me on Monday and we'll sign the contract.'

He poured the champagne and we clinked glasses. I had a feeling I was going to like Sam Coppola. As long as I stayed on the right side of him.

When I told Rolando I was leaving to work for Sam, he was pleased for me. 'That you were once Vivienne "Ruby" de Villeray is a secret I'll take to my grave,' he said, with his hand dramatically over his heart. 'But I hope if I ever need it, you'll put in a good word for Rolando.'

Before returning home that afternoon, I had some errands to run for Maman. When I passed Jackson Square I found a crowd had gathered there, and stopped to see what was happening. The faces of the people in the crowd were grim and I could feel their anger simmering in the atmosphere like heat. A man with a bald head and trimmed beard was standing on a wooden stage, surrounded by reporters and an audience of men and women holding placards urging citizens to *Say No to the Desegregation of Schools*.

'Do you want your daughters associating with niggers?' the speaker asked the crowd. 'Do you want mongrels for grandchildren?'

The murmurs from his audience made it clear that they didn't.

'The purity of the white race is threatened by desegregation,' the speaker continued, beads of sweat popping up on his hairless pate. 'We must protect white womanhood against the predatory instincts of the coloured man, who has only recently emerged from the darkness of Africa.'

The man in front of me turned to his companion and sneered, 'Some of those darkies are hung like thoroughbreds. They should be sent to the knackery like finished up racehorses before they can cause any trouble, or be castrated at birth!'

His companion sniggered, then looked around him with fierce eyes. 'If a daughter of mine associated with any nigger, I'd lynch both of them myself.'

My heart beat hard in my chest and my hands turned clammy. I remembered what had happened to Mae's father and wanted to be sick. For the first time in a long while, I thought of Clifford Lalande and his family. This was the kind of hatred they were up against in trying to improve society. These people in the square looked ordinary, the sort of people you'd see in a department store or holding their children on their shoulders at the Mardi Gras parades. But something evil lurked in their minds and it made them volatile and dangerous.

I pushed through the crowd and headed home. Something was happening in New Orleans. Something terrible. I could feel it.

FIFTEEN

Ruby

My first impression of Sam Coppola had been right: everything he did was ritzy and lavish, and the Vieux Carré Club was no different. When I went to sign my contract, I gaped in awe at the white marble floors, the gold damask-papered walls and the recessed lights. Builders were working on the revolving glass podium I was to perform on.

My contract had a strict code of rules including: *No bumps and grinds, no flashing and no hanging on the curtains.* None of those things were my style, but when I read that Sam Coppola also had the final say in what I wore off stage, I protested. Until the lawyer showed me a rack of Balenciaga and Dior dresses.

'Any objections to these?' he asked.

I shook my head.

My stage costumes were to be made by an Australian designer named Orry-Kelly, who had dressed Hollywood stars like Bette Davis and Marilyn Monroe. I was nervous when I went to see him at his suite at the Roosevelt Hotel, but when the maid showed me into the room I was surprised to find an unassuming man with grey streaks in his hair and a pair of horn-rimmed glasses perched on his droopy nose. He looked more like a bank manager than a haughty clothes designer.

'Well,' he said, 'you're younger than I was expecting. As I'm getting older, I enjoy being around young people more.'

He opened a desk drawer and took out a measuring tape. I noticed an antique figurine of a white cat sitting on a notebook on the desk. Pansies and vines were painted on her coat, as if she was peering out of a garden.

Orry saw me looking at it. 'Do you like it? I collect cat figurines, and I picked up this beauty in a pawn shop down on Royal Street would you believe?'

I could believe it. It was one of the family heirlooms I'd pawned months ago and hadn't had a chance to buy back. It seemed strange for it to have ended up in Orry's hands. Was it a good omen?

I handed my clothes to his maid, and Orry took measurements where I'd never had measurements taken before: from my navel to my crotch, and my crotch to my ankle.

'Burlesque costuming is still high couture but it's also an engineering feat,' he explained. 'The zippers have to be durable, and the snaps placed in exactly the right positions. The costumes must stand up to the rigours of performance.'

The creation of my costumes was a performance in itself, with numerous sketches and fittings.

'Normally I prefer simple, unadorned elegance on a petite woman like you,' he said, pinning me into a beautiful gown with a gold satin base, pale gold for the chiffon overlay, and bronze flower motifs running from shoulder to hip. 'But on the stage you need a bit of glitz to catch the light.'

As well as the gold dress, he designed a pink and silver silk-jersey ensemble consisting of a corset, jacket, skirt and headdress. The outfit was embellished with bugle beads, pearls and rhinestones sewn on in feathered lines. The skirt wrapped around to produce a draped effect and was secured with a large hook and eye.

As he worked, Orry liked to gossip about the stars he'd dressed for Hollywood. 'Marilyn might act sweet, but she's a devil to please. I enjoyed dressing Jack Lemmon and Tony Curtis as women far more for *Some Like It Hot*.'

The day before he flew back to Los Angeles, he invited me to his office and handed me a silver box tied with a bow. Inside I found the white ceramic cat.

'I don't know why, but every time I looked at it, something told me you should have it,' he said.

I thanked him, and he kissed my cheek and said, 'Work hard and persist, persist, persist. That's the only route to stardom. I know: I've been watching starlets come and go for years.'

Guilt stabbed my conscience and I clenched my hands. Although Orry meant well, his remark drove home that many of the other performers at the Havana Club had dreamed of stardom all their lives. I was only performing for the money, but it seemed I was getting what they'd wanted without having sought it. I knew I'd have to put everything into my act now — or else be exposed as a fraud.

I met my choreographer, Miss Hanley, the following week in the club's rehearsal studio on Dumaine Street. The Quarter was deluged in light, and as I made my way there I squinted at the brightness. It was unusual for me to be out at this time of day; I had become a creature of the night.

Miss Hanley was a slight woman of a certain age, wearing a black blouse, piped pants and black dance shoes that gave her an unbroken line. I was in a grey skirt and off-the-shoulder fire-orange blouse that flattered my assets in a ladylike way.

She looked me up and down and smiled. 'I see Sam has been dressing you. Very elegant. Now show me some arabesques and entrechats so I can get an idea of your style.'

I stared at her blankly. My 'style' was a conglomeration of what I had seen other strippers do and some moves I'd worked out in my room in Chartres Street.

'I'm sorry, Miss Hanley, but I haven't done ballet since I was a child. You see ... I'm a stripper, not a dancer.'

Her hand flew up to stop me. 'No, you're a dancer,' she replied firmly. 'Sam told me so. An exotic dancer is a dancer nonetheless.'

I understood: I wasn't to call myself a stripper in Miss Hanley's presence.

'Why don't you show me one of your routines,' she said, folding her arms. 'We'll start from there.'

We were interrupted by a knock at the door, and Miss Hanley went to open it. She looked over her shoulder and asked me, 'Did you bring your sheet music?'

I shook my head, feeling out of my depth.

'Never mind. Your accompanist, Leroy, can play anything. If you hum a few bars, he'll recognise it.'

She opened the door and beckoned in a young coloured man a couple of years older than me. Despite the heat he was sharply dressed in a blazer, tie, flannel trousers and a crisp white shirt.

'This is Jewel,' she said to him. 'She's the star dancer at the club.'

'It's a pleasure to meet you, Jewel,' he said, taking my hand in his cool one and squeezing it gently.

A jolt ran through me and I pulled away. Coloured men did not touch white women's hands. Nor did they look directly into their eyes or call them Jewel instead of Miss Jewel. Then I remembered myself and was ashamed of my reaction. Of course he could shake my hand the same as any white man would do. He'd merely caught me unawares, that's all. I liked the fact that there was nothing of the shuffling, obsequious stereotype of a coloured musician about him.

I reached for his hand and clasped it. 'It's a pleasure to meet you too, Mr ...?'

If Leroy was offended by my initial reaction he didn't show it. He smiled wider and revealed a row of straight white teeth. 'My last name is Thezan, but you can call me Leroy. Everybody does.'

He was handsome, that was for sure, with chiselled cheekbones and a nose like an Indian chief. I was mesmerised by the amber shade of his skin, smooth and glowing like the complexion of a healthy child. He contemplated me with a spark of amusement dancing in his honey-gold eyes and I realised it was because I was still staring at him.

'Jewel is going to tell us what music she'd like to dance to,' Miss Hanley explained.

The routines I'd been performing at the Havana Club

were too quirky for the Vieux Carré. My 'Mooche' routine was the most sophisticated, but I was sick of it. 'I've been developing a routine to a piece of music I bought at the record store on Chartres Street,' I told them.

'What's the name of the song?' asked Leroy, opening the lid of the piano and taking a seat. He rubbed his hands vigorously, then played a blues riff to warm up.

His manner was so relaxed it should have put me at ease, but for some reason my heart started pounding in my chest like a bongo drum.

He looked at me again, waiting patiently. A rush of warmth heated my skin.

'Jewel?' said Miss Hanley.

The name of the song had gone out of my head. I couldn't even recall the melody.

'It's about a man searching for his lover,' I said.

Leroy chuckled. 'Well, that's a little thin to go on, Jewel. Every man is looking for his lover.'

'She's lost.' My face twitched in that foolish way it always did when I was nervous. I had to remind myself that I was sophisticated Jewel now, and Jewel did not lose her composure.

'Hmm.' He rubbed his chin thoughtfully. 'What colour is it?'

'Excuse me? Colour?'

'Yes. What colour does the song make you feel?'

Describing a song by its colour was an unusual way of doing things. How was he ever going to pick a song from knowing only that? I let out a breath and thought about it. The music was rich and expressive, but it wasn't red. It was tragic, but not black.

'Blue,' I said, recalling the song's haunting atmosphere. 'Dark blue.'

'Like night?' he asked, grinning.

A sense of playfulness bubbled up in me and I loosened up. It was as though Leroy was leading me on an adventure.

'Like night,' I agreed.

He tried out a few notes on the piano before turning back to me. 'Night in the city, or out in the bayou where it's dark and quiet except for the creatures of the night?'

'Dark as in the swampland,' I said, enjoying the game. 'But with flashes of gold.'

'What's the gold? When I imagine gold in the dark it always makes me think of hope.'

I'd been picturing torches, but hope sounded more romantic. I nodded.

He turned back to the keyboard. 'Is this it?' He played the first few bars of the song 'Chloe'.

'How did you pick out a song by its colour?' I cried. 'Are you a mind reader?'

His lips formed into a wry smile and he swung his legs over the stool so he faced me. 'Earlier this afternoon, I was having a soda at the drugstore on Esplanade Avenue when a fashionably dressed lady walked past. I didn't know who you were then, but I distinctly heard you humming "Chloe".'

Miss Hanley laughed, and after a moment's surprise I did too.

'He's a sneaky one,' Miss Hanley said. 'You watch out for him.' Then she clapped her hands. 'All right, we've got the song now. Show us what you've been working on, Jewel.'

Leroy began to play. I wasn't in costume, so I mimed the parts where I took off items of clothing. Several times I caught Leroy watching me. The band leader at the Havana Club had done that too, to see where I was up to in the routine, but something in Leroy's scrutiny was different. I'd been taking my clothes off in front of men for some months now and yet I'd never felt so shy as I did in front of him. A man was a man as far as I was concerned, but white strippers never undressed in front of coloured men. Not in the South at least.

I finished my dance, expecting Miss Hanley to be contemptuous, but she was tactful.

'You never stop moving, Jewel, but I want you to think of yourself as a sculpture. You have to stop at certain points and let the audience drink you in.' She held herself in a pose with her chin up and a haughty expression in her eyes. It was a convincing transformation from choreographer to stripper. She turned back to me and was herself again. 'With Orry-Kelly designing your costumes for one thousand dollars apiece, you'd better make sure the audience has time to appreciate them or Sam will have a fit.'

She turned to Leroy. 'What do you think?'

'Yes, Jewel should stop still so people can admire her,' he agreed, tugging at his collar as if he was too warm.

Miss Hanley indicated for Leroy to play the piece again and we spent nearly an hour on my walk alone. 'Regal, but leading ever so slightly with the pelvis,' she instructed me.

She had me stand in poses for minutes at a time. 'Everything you do must convey flirtation that eventually becomes seduction: the way you breathe, the blinking of your eyes, the slightest movement of your fingers ...'

I did everything that Miss Hanley asked me to, but my pulse was racing. It was as though I was directing every gesture and movement at Leroy instead of an imaginary audience. 'What a pity you didn't continue with ballet,' Miss Hanley said when we'd finished for the day. 'You could have been great. You have the quality a good dancer needs: the ability to convey energy even when you are still. We'll meet again the same time tomorrow.'

'Tomorrow?' I asked, surprised. 'We're going to do all this again tomorrow?'

Miss Hanley huffed. 'Why, yes, my dear. Sam has requested a new routine a week. We had better get cracking! And don't forget you'll have to do the final rehearsals with Leroy and his band.'

Leroy led the way down the stairs. I kept my eyes fixed on his square shoulders and tried to think of ways to start a conversation. 'There is no way I could have been a ballet dancer,' I finally managed to say when we were out on the street. 'I don't have the discipline and I don't like pain. My calves are aching enough just from the past few hours.'

'Well, rest up before tomorrow,' he said, putting on his hat. 'Miss Hanley was being gentle on you today. She's a taskmaster.'

I watched Leroy walk down the street with a self-assured gait. His sudden coolness stabbed me but I was grateful for it at the same time. Wherever my imagination had started to wander during the rehearsal was too dangerous to follow.

That night, I sat in our dining room eating dinner with Maman, Ruby again. Maman looked well in the lilac dress I'd bought her. Mae had been doing as good a job with her rehabilitation as the nurses at the sanatorium, walking her up and down the apartment stairs every day and around the courtyard to strengthen her remaining lung.

I turned my attention to the table and the new Wood and Sons dinnerware I'd bought to replace the dishes we'd had to pawn over the years. The set wasn't as fancy as the Haviland Limoges china we'd had in our family for decades, but it was pretty nonetheless. And the food on the table was of the best quality, from the cornbread to the maque choux. *I did this*, I thought. *I provided all this through my hard work.*

'Ruby, there's a light in your eyes I haven't seen for a long time,' Maman said. 'Those tennis lessons Mac tells me you're taking in the afternoons are doing you the world of good.'

I glanced at Mae, who was standing in the doorway in her new tailored uniform. She didn't blink and it took all the theatrical control I'd learned from Miss Hanley not to burst out laughing.

Mae had covered for me superbly, but I longed to tell Maman about the Vieux Carré Club. I would be a star there — desirable, exotic and sought after. But here at home, Jewel was someone to be ashamed of and kept secret. Becoming Ruby again after being Jewel was like returning to earth after a balloon ride.

'Is there a young man?' Maman asked with a smile. 'You've got the glow of a young woman with a beau on her mind.'

'No, Maman,' I said, taking a piece of cornbread and buttering it. 'There isn't any young man.'

'Not yet,' she said, slicing into a stuffed bell pepper and lifting her fork to her mouth. 'Not yet. But there will be soon. I can feel it. Love is going to come calling for you, Ruby. Very soon!'

❖

The next day, after I'd changed into Jewel in my room on Chartres Street, I passed the drugstore on Esplanade Avenue that Leroy had mentioned and peered in the window. Some young Negro men were sitting at the coloured end of the counter, but Leroy wasn't among them. I went in anyway and ordered a vanilla flavoured soda. While the soda jerk poured it for me, I perched on a stool up the white end of the counter.

The soda jerk placed the glass on a paper doily in front of me and I'd just taken a sip when I heard an imperious voice behind me. 'Excuse me, young lady.'

I turned to find myself face to face with Aunt Elva. She had put on weight since I'd last seen her, but she was still expensively outfitted in a slate grey dress teamed with a cropped jacket and a clamper-style floral hat. She blinked at me and I froze, sure that she'd recognised me. But then she smiled and I knew she hadn't. Aunt Elva wouldn't smile at me. The closest I'd ever gotten from her was a pained grimace.

'I hope you don't mind me asking,' she said, in the sugary voice she reserved for people who weren't members of her family, 'but what shade of lipstick are you wearing? We have a similar skin tone. I think it would quite suit me.'

What would suit Aunt Elva most would be a bag over her head, but I kept my mouth shut. I saw my life as Jewel going down the drain with one false move. Then I decided it was a test. If I could fool shrewd Aunt Elva, I could fool anybody.

I fixed my gaze on a point above her head and said, 'Bessette's Cherry Red,' in my stilted French accent.

Her eyes narrowed and my pulse raced again. My toes clenched in my shoes.

'Oh,' she said, with a little laugh. 'Well, thank you. You have a fine day.'

I nodded and let my breath go. A giddy feeling came over me as Aunt Elva went to the cosmetics clerk and told her she wanted a tube of Bessette's Cherry Red. I watched the clerk package the purchase and Aunt Elva leave the store.

I turned back to the counter and contemplated the red smudge at the top of the straw in my soda. I wasn't wearing Bessette's Cherry Red; I was wearing Revlon's Fire and Ice. But I'd heard the coat-check girl at the club say that Bessette's Cherry Red had given her a painful skin rash that had lasted a week. *Lord, I've got the devil in me*, I giggled as I finished my soda. Maybe this would all catch up with me one day, but I was sure enjoying the thought of Aunt Elva's lips swelling up like she'd stuck her head in a beehive.

I arrived at the rehearsal studio half an hour early. Miss Hanley, who was doing some stretches at the barre, was surprised to see me.

'Enthusiasm — now that's what I like!' she said.

I stopped listening to what she was telling me about the beauty of long, lyrical movements when I heard footsteps coming up the stairs. Light, buoyant steps and yet distinctly male.

Leroy stepped into the room. 'Good afternoon,' he said.

He was wearing a slim-fitting pearl-grey suit with padded shoulders. He looked smart and there wasn't a drop of sweat on his forehead despite the New Orleans humidity.

'Lord, it is hot!' Miss Hanley said, moving to open the window facing the street.

'Have you been practising your queenly walk?' Leroy whispered to me. His aloofness at our parting the previous day had dissipated and he was smiling warmly at me.

'I have,' I replied. 'All the way here.'

'That must have made many a man's day!'

My heart fluttered. I stepped away from him so he couldn't see me blush.

Miss Hanley returned to her position and rehearsal began. But I found it more difficult to concentrate than I had the day before. Every time Miss Hanley told me to turn right, I'd go left instead. When she marked the spot where I should remove my dress, I overshot it.

'You do realise you're standing in the orchestra pit right now, don't you?' she said, looking as flummoxed as I felt.

After two hours of rehearsal, Leroy apologised that he had to rush off to practise with this band. 'I shall see you the same time tomorrow, ladies.' He said it to both of us, but I felt his eyes linger on me.

I sighed, disappointed that he'd gone. Rehearsing was going to be a bore without him.

'He's a nice young man,' Miss Hanley said. 'Now let's get back to that walk of yours, Jewel. I want you to enter stage left.'

She cleared her throat. 'Jewel?'

'Oh yes, I'm sorry,' I said, taking my position.

She cocked her head. 'Are you all right? Is the heat getting to you?'

'I'm not used to rehearsing so much,' I confided in her. 'Where I used to dance we only got to practise our routines a couple of times with the band before we had to perform.'

Miss Hanley's face softened and she patted my shoulder. 'You're in the big league now, Jewel,' she said. 'You're going to be a star. Mr Coppola doesn't have patience for amateurs. You've got to be perfect and it's my job to make you so. Now, let's get back to your entrance.'

After the rehearsal I had a meeting with Sam Coppola. As I walked to the club, I thought about Leroy and wondered about his life. Where did he live and what was his family like? There was something about him that I related to and I wanted to know more about him. I would have spent the whole day with him if I could have.

The club had come a long way since the last time I'd seen it. All the tables and velvet-upholstered booths were installed, and crystal chandeliers hung from the ceiling. There was an orchestra pit to the right of the podium with buttressed urns around it.

'Is this where Leroy and his band will play?' I asked Sam.

He shook his head and beckoned for me to follow him down the stairs to the dressing rooms.

'Can't have a coloured band playing for a white performer. That pit is for the club's main orchestra. Leroy and his band will play behind a curtain backstage.'

'Then why did you get a coloured band for me,' I asked, 'if you can't put them on show?'

He opened a door at the bottom of the stairs. 'Because I wanted the best jazz musicians for my star act and Leroy and his band are the best. But this is the South and I can't afford to get this place shut down.'

I followed him into a dressing room, where a blonde woman was laying out the pink and silver ensemble Orry-Kelly had designed for me.

'I'll leave Annie here to help you get dressed,' Sam said. 'A photographer is coming in an hour to take some publicity shots. After that I have an interview lined up with a reporter from the *Times-Picayune*.'

Publicity shots were one thing, but an interview with a reporter? What if he discovered who I really was?

Sam saw the fear in my face and led me to one side. 'Is something wrong?'

I lowered my eyes. It seemed a beautiful dream was about to be ripped from me. 'Jewel isn't my real name. I'm stripping to support my mother.'

'I know that,' he said. 'What's the problem?'

I looked up at him, surprised, and blushed.

'Don't you think I get everyone thoroughly checked out before I hire them?' he said. 'You're Vivienne de Villeray, and your family has a name but not a dime. I understand the whole picture. Do you think my family is proud of me and what I do?'

I'd assumed that Sam's family was part of the mob too, but apparently not.

'Listen,' he said, 'I'll make sure you're only interviewed by journalists who owe me a favour and won't be nosey. They'll write what I tell them to, you understand? Now let's get Annie to help you into your costume, and let me do the worrying.'

He led me back to Annie, who was taking a pair of beaded shoes out of a box.

'And, Jewel,' Sam added, 'if your family isn't proud of you, you should at least be proud of yourself. Some people have star quality and others — no matter how talented — just don't. You've got oodles of it. Your personality bursts out right past the floodlights. That's not common, and it's why I hired you. Remember that.'

By the following week, the club was finished and I was called in for my dress rehearsal with Leroy's band. The stage was opposite the bar, and the barman was already in, stocking the shelves.

'Good afternoon,' I said as I passed him.

He turned, but didn't reply. He was short and wiry, and the expression of disdain on his face made it clear that he looked down on me. *Never mind*, I thought, ignoring the snub. *I bet he doesn't make five hundred dollars a week doing what he's doing.*

Leroy was to keep track of where I was in the routine by a strategically placed mirror and a slit in the curtains at the side of the stage. When I took my position, and Annie did some last-minute adjusting of my costume, I noticed him soaking his hands in a bowl of steaming water and wondered why.

He saw me watching and flashed his winsome smile.

'You won't improvise on me?' I asked, stepping through the curtains. 'I know you jazz musicians get carried away, but Miss Hanley has blocked out everything perfectly and I've got to make a good impression on Sam.'

'I'd never do such an ungentlemanly thing,' he answered in a soothing tone. 'You and me, we're a team.'

He dried his hands with a towel and leaned towards me. 'I'll let you into a little secret, Jewel. You will be fine out there. You know why? Because you're the best. But if you do make a mistake, don't worry — I'll cover for you. That's my job.'

My heart swelled. He'd seen through my bravado and guessed how nervous I was about performing. I wanted to hug him, but of course I couldn't.

'Thank you,' I replied instead, lowering my gaze before returning to the stage.

Sam and the others took their seats, and the stagehands dimmed the lights before turning on the spotlight. My stomach ached because I'd been holding my breath so long before the band started playing. I glanced at Leroy and he winked. The gesture gave me a surge of confidence and I stepped out on stage, my head held high like a queen. I used Miss Hanley's technique of 'self-possessed stillness', not moving a muscle until I had the onlookers in a high state of tension. Only then did I begin to dance. True to his word, Leroy had the band punctuating my shimmies, hip-rolls and drops with perfectly timed drum accents and trombone slurs. The embellishments brought my routine to life and made it sultry and sexy.

When the number was over, the onlookers broke into applause. Sam and Miss Hanley stepped onto the stage to congratulate me.

Miss Hanley embraced me. 'Bravo, Jewel! Bravo!'

'Well, congratulations to you too, Miss Hanley,' Sam said. 'And to the band.'

I willed for Leroy to come out on stage too, but he kept his eyes averted from me as he and the band packed up.

Annie and I went to the dressing room, where she helped me out of my costume. When I returned to the bar in my street clothes and looked around for Leroy, he seemed to have already left. I noticed the barman glaring at me. It was a hate stare if ever there was one. What the hell was his problem?

'Who are you looking for?' asked Sam, when he saw me rushing into the foyer.

I stopped and pasted on a smile for him. 'Why, you of course! So how did you like my act?'

'I told you already. It was good. Now hurry on home and get some rest. It's seven days until opening time and we'll be going over everything again tomorrow.'

When I reached the room in Chartres Street, I soaked my aching feet in a basin of hot water and Epsom salts. Strutting around in stilettos on and off the stage while being elegant was no walk in the park — and it was going to be a full dress rehearsal tomorrow again too. I closed my eyes and relaxed my shoulders. I thought of Leroy again and the kind words he'd said to me that afternoon. I could bear the pain as long as he was there.

In my opening-night performance at the Vieux Carré Club, I did everything Miss Hanley had instructed me to do. As long as Leroy was leading the band, I didn't have a care in the world. When I appeared on the podium, a hush fell over the crowd, sparkling in their tuxedos and evening dresses. Even the waiters stopped in their tracks to see what I was going to do.

Leroy led the band into the first bars of 'Chloe' and I moved slowly and deliberately, lingering over each step.

I executed every gesture — the removal of my jacket, the unfastening of my skirt — with elegance and style, and the audience went from being transfixed, to being aroused, to being dazzled. I had them in my hands, and left the stage to loud applause and a standing ovation. It was exhilarating and I realised that I was no longer a woman trying to make a quick buck. I was a performer.

After the crowd went home in the early hours of the morning, Sam shouted to the barman, 'Champagne for all the performers and crew, Jimmy!'

The satisfying pop of the cork of a bottle of Dom Pérignon sounded and champagne glasses were filled. The barman handed me a glass and I lifted it, toasting the stage manager and production assistants, the lighting men and Sam in turn. Then I turned to the band and stopped short. The barman was pouring their champagne into paper cups.

The blood rushed to my head.

'What do you think you're doing?' I shouted at him. 'You don't treat my band like that! You give them glasses now, you hear!'

The barman spun to face me, his eyes red with fury and his mouth twisted into a sneer. 'I don't serve Negroes.'

A tense silence fell over the room. The drummer, Abe, looked at me with pleading eyes, as if begging me not to make matters worse. Annie fidgeted with her bracelet. Leroy was sitting with his back to me so I couldn't tell what he was thinking.

But I was so mad at that idiot for humiliating Leroy and the band that I couldn't stop myself. 'Good!' I said, swiping the bottle from him. 'Because I don't eat them!'

Everybody's mouth gaped open. Leroy whipped his head around and stared at me like he couldn't believe what I'd said. Then Sam's throaty laugh rang out. The others exchanged glances, unsure what to do, but Sam only laughed harder and eventually smiles broke out on their faces too.

'Give the band glasses, for God's sake, Jimmy,' said Sam. 'Where do you think we are? The sticks?'

But Jimmy didn't move an inch and it was Annie who went to the bar and put the glasses on a tray for me to pour champagne into for the band. I could feel him staring daggers at us, but I didn't care. I handed Leroy his glass and our fingers touched. He didn't look at me but he didn't move his hand either.

I turned away and raised the champagne bottle again. 'Bravo!' I said. 'Bravo, everyone!'

My face burned as though I was coming down with a fever but I knew there was no inoculation against what was flaming through me. Until then, my only salvation had been the possibility that Leroy had the sense not to feel the same way about me as I did about him. But now, even without looking at him, I knew that last stay was gone.

SIXTEEN

Ruby

When I arrived at the rehearsal room to start work on my next routine, I found Leroy there alone. He was straddling a chair by the piano and immersed in reading Charles Dickens' *Our Mutual Friend*. He'd cut his hair, and the neat edges of his hairline accentuated his chiselled cheekbones and strong jaw. He grew more handsome each time I saw him.

I had been longing to find myself alone with him, and now I was terrified of the moment. I cleared my throat and asked, 'Do you like Charles Dickens?'

He looked up and his lips drew into a smile. 'Well, this story of a double life is fascinating. One life is demanding enough. A double one would be exhausting!' He stood up and placed the book on top of the piano. 'You could never be open with anyone.'

If only he knew! Living a double life, I'd discovered, required nerves of steel and constant vigilance to keep your stories straight. The switches from Ruby to Jewel and then back again were playing havoc with my mind, but being Jewel was the only way I could help Maman and Mae.

I quickly changed the subject. 'Did you always want to be a pianist?'

He stepped towards me, his gaze skimming over me as if he was paying more attention to the red dress I was wearing than my question.

'I'm not a pianist, Jewel. I'm a piano player.'

'Is there a difference?' I asked, my face growing hot.

'A pianist is serious. I'm not serious,' he said with a chuckle. 'I wanted to be an athlete like Jesse Owens, but I learned from watching older boys that playing the piano was the fastest way to get a pretty girl interested in you. So I gave my dreams of gold medals a miss and concentrated on music.'

A pang of jealousy struck me. It was like I'd seen a whole lot of goodies in the five-and-dime store window but had banged my head on the glass when I'd leaned towards them. Maybe Leroy looked at plenty of girls the way he was looking at me now.

'Well,' I said, more sharply than I'd intended, 'if you wanted to be around attractive women, you chose the right profession!'

A teasing smile twitched at the corners of his lips. 'One pretty girl is enough. Especially if she's fiery.'

The anger rushed out of me so fast I felt lightheaded. Leroy stood on the spot as if he was waiting for something. He was so close that I could smell the minty scent of soap on his skin.

I remained awkwardly where I was, not sure what it was he wanted me to do. The silence between us was like a loaded gun about to go off. Who would make the first move? I lost my nerve and glanced towards the door. 'I wonder where Miss Hanley is?' I said. 'She's normally so punctual.'

Leroy sighed and moved back to the piano. I was trapped somewhere between relief and disappointment. I wanted him to stand close to me again but I was scared of what might happen if he did.

'I'll play your new piece,' he said, rubbing his hands together vigorously. 'It's "Egyptian Fantasy" by Sidney Bechet.'

His hand-rubbing worried me. Maman's diabetes meant her extremities were always cold. I hoped Leroy wasn't sick too.

'Do you have trouble with your circulation?' I asked him.

'Cold hands run in the family,' he replied, stretching his fingers backwards one at a time. 'I've been to see all the specialists. One says it's because I'm anxious, but that isn't true. Another specialist said I don't breathe deeply enough, but I can run a hundred-yard sprint and not get out of breath, so that can't be right either. I've settled on my mother's explanation: *Cold hands, warm heart.*'

'Is it true?' I asked, my voice catching in my throat.

He tilted his head to one side and gave me an intense look. 'Touch them.'

I hesitated, knowing we were venturing close to that forbidden line again. Despite all the jangling nerves in my body warning me to resist, I moved towards the piano and placed my palms on top of Leroy's outstretched ones. He closed his fingers over my right hand and pulled it towards him, placing it over his heart. His chest was so warm it burned my skin.

'It's true, you see,' he said, staring up at me. 'Isn't it? Cold hands, warm heart.'

He rose and pulled me closer, drawing his face to mine. Our lips brushed, but at that moment Miss Hanley burst in the door. Leroy pushed me away and hastily sat down at the piano.

Miss Hanley missed catching us by seconds. If she'd seen us kiss she would have told Sam, and Leroy and I would have been out of the Vieux Carré in the blink of an eye. Fortunately she was too preoccupied with her swollen cheek to notice the tension in the room.

'I'm sorry I'm late!' she wailed. 'I've had a toothache all night and I've come straight from the dentist.'

'Do you want to take a break for the day?' I asked, helping her into a chair. I was too scared to look at Leroy's face.

'No, no!' she said. 'The costume for this act is the most elaborate one yet, and I've got to teach you how to use the fans. We have to perfect this routine by next week!'

When I finally built up the courage to look at Leroy again, he was shuffling sheet music around on the piano. All the tendons in his neck were standing out like the roots of a fig tree.

If a daughter of mine associated with any nigger, I'd lynch both of them myself — that's what the man at the anti-integration rally had said. New Orleans was not a city where a coloured man and a white woman could even contemplate being together. White families put their daughters into mental asylums for falling in love with coloured men. The anti-miscegenation laws made it impossible to marry. Even religious leaders argued that God had created separate races and intended them to remain separate. Leroy and I had to stop this dangerous game. Nearly getting caught by Miss Hanley was a warning.

For the rest of the week, I avoided being alone with Leroy. I sensed that he was avoiding me too. We never looked directly into each other's face, but stared at our feet or over each other's shoulder when we had to discuss some point of music.

Miss Hanley was right about my new costume. It was an iridescent gold and sapphire chain, bead and coin G-string and bra, and I was to dance the number using two large black feather fans. 'Egyptian Fantasy' was heavy on the drums, and Leroy took the saxophone part during the dress rehearsal while another band member, Virgil, filled in at the piano. I knew Leroy had put Virgil in charge of watching me on purpose but when Leroy blew that saxophone and I danced, the music did something to me. It took me somewhere deep, dark and erotic.

I was supposed to hide and reveal myself with the fans in a way that would tease the audience to glimpse something more than I was giving. But the whole time I danced, all I could think about was Leroy and what it would be like to touch his smooth skin. I lost concentration, and while I was leaning over I accidentally dropped one of the fans. Sam Coppola was treated to a full view of my derriere.

'*Dio buono!*' he said, standing up from his seat. 'Don't make that mistake on the first night. The district attorney is my special guest and I don't need us closed up for a month.'

I glanced over to Leroy who'd put down his saxophone and was laughing. I grinned. But one look at Miss Hanley's tense face and I controlled myself. The fans made my dance alluring, but they also required fancy footwork and intricate movements of the fingers and wrists. She had worked for hours with me to get the technique right and I couldn't let her down.

'I'm sorry,' I said, before nodding to Virgil. 'Can we begin again?'

The weather was sultry the evening I did the dance with the district attorney in the audience. I worked the fans like a professional. One minute you saw me, and then I disappeared again behind my feathers, revealing and hiding myself like an exotic bird.

When I returned to my dressing room, I heard a loud thunderstorm snapping across the sky. By the time I was ready to leave, the rain was coming down hard. I searched for a cab on Bourbon Street, but they'd already taken the streams of patrons home and had retired for the night. I had no alternative but to borrow an umbrella from the coat-check and make a run for it.

I was hurrying down the street, cursing the overflowing gutters that were ruining my shoes, when I became aware of someone following me. I began to walk faster and they did too. Then I ran and the steps picked up behind me. I turned to face my pursuer, but couldn't see clearly through the lashing rain.

'Jewel, is that you?' It was Leroy's voice. He appeared from the dark. 'Why are you running off in the rain like that? Why didn't you ask Sam's driver to take you home?'

'I didn't think of it,' I said, feeling the water squelch in my shoes.

He chuckled. The streets were empty, which was unusual for the Quarter even in the early hours of the morning. Leroy must have sensed the opportunity it offered him. 'Here, let me walk you home,' he said.

I lifted the umbrella to his height and he put his arm around me to shield me from the rain.

We reached the house on Chartres Street. The other residents had closed their shutters against the weather. It was as if the house was squeezing its eyes shut and nobody could see us. I opened the gate to the garden, and Leroy noticed the overgrown ferns and palms and the cracked footpath.

'You live here?' he asked.

The rain suddenly came down so forcefully it was like someone had overturned a bathtub on us.

'You're soaking,' I told him. 'Come inside and I'll make you some coffee.'

He hesitated a moment before nodding.

We went in the side entrance, and I opened the door to my room and turned on a lamp on the side table. The umbrella was dripping so I put it in the bathroom. Leroy's gaze travelled from the armoire where I kept my Ruby clothes to the one where I hung my Jewel outfits. It occurred to me that he was standing on the bridge between my two worlds.

'You seriously live here?' he asked again, frowning.

I looked around the room and tried to see it as he would. It wasn't really an apartment; it was more like a cramped dressing room.

'What did you expect?' I asked with a smile. 'A palace?'

'Why ... yes! Or at least something ...'

I let him leave the sentence unfinished. I'd brought

him inside on impulse, without any thought about how I was going to explain this place to him.

'There are towels in that cupboard there,' I said, pointing to the small linen press near the door. 'Dry yourself off. I don't want my band leader getting a cold. I can't turn on the heat in summer, but you can roll your shirt and jacket in a towel if you like, then put them on a hanger.'

I smiled at him and disappeared into the bathroom. 'What a mess,' I muttered when I saw myself in the mirror. My wig had been protected by the umbrella but it was damp. I took it off and placed it on the wig stand. I peeled off my wet dress and underwear and wrapped myself in a robe. My make-up was smudged so I rubbed cold cream onto my face and wiped it off with tissues before removing my wig cap and fluffing out my hair.

When I stepped out of the bathroom, Leroy had taken off his shirt and jacket as I'd told him to do and was wearing only his undershirt and trousers. It was the first time I'd seen his broad bare shoulders and the well-defined muscles of his arms.

'Lord, is that you, Jewel?' he asked, looking surprised and amused at the same time. 'You sure look different without your war paint. It's like one woman went into the bathroom and another came out. Are you certain Jewel didn't climb out the window?'

I put the coffee on to brew and heated some cream on the stovetop. I'd been pretending and lying so much; I didn't want to lie to Leroy as well.

'Which version do you like better?' I asked, dipping two teaspoons of molasses into each cup of coffee and handing him his.

He took the cup and looked me over with a pleased expression. 'Well, I like both, but this brunette version seems a little younger.'

I laughed. 'Did you fancy Jewel was an "older woman"?'

'Something along those lines,' he said with a grin. He took a sip of the coffee. 'You make coffee like a Creole, you know that?'

'I am a Creole,' I told him. 'My name is Vivienne de Villeray but everyone calls me "Ruby". My family used to own several plantations and my forebears were favourites of the French king.'

Leroy's eyes twinkled and he laughed. 'You kill me, Jewel! One minute you're Jewel the dancer and now you're a dark-haired Creole aristocrat. What else you got up those pretty sleeves of yours?'

In other circumstances I might have been hurt by his mocking tone: I was making an effort to come clean with him, but he didn't believe me. But I wasn't going to argue the case with him. Not tonight, anyway. Instead, I found myself thinking about the way he was looking at me, as if he was eating me up with his eyes.

He finished his coffee and put the cup in the kitchen sink, then reached for his jacket and shirt. 'I better get going. It won't do you any good if someone finds out you've had a coloured man with you. Thank you for the coffee.'

'Stay,' I said.

He frowned and shook his head. 'You know I can't.'

'I don't care,' I said, moving towards him and putting my hand on his arm.

He turned and we gazed into each other's eyes. His lips trembled and I could see he was wrestling with his feelings, trying to resist them. Then he reached up to my cheek and brushed it with the backs of his fingers.

'I've been wondering what it would feel like,' he said. 'Like satin.'

He pulled me to his chest and wrapped his arms around me. I nuzzled my face against his shoulder.

'I've wondered too,' I said, pressing my lips to his warm flesh.

He took my face in his hands and kissed me down my neck and along my collarbone. His warm breath sent tingles through me.

'Are you sure, Jewel?' he whispered, opening the front of my robe.

His fingers lingered over my breasts and I took his hands and put them to my flesh. He caressed me and a desire I could not have imagined rushed through me. I swooned with it. It was nothing like the wedding-night stories I'd heard from the older Creole girls about feeling ashamed and wanting everything over with. I felt like I was floating down a bubbling river.

Leroy picked me up in his arms and carried me to the chaise longue. He slipped my robe from me, before stroking his strong hands down my body and along my stomach and thighs.

'You're beautiful,' he said with reverence. 'Even more beautiful now than when you're on stage.'

His touch was so tender that any fear I had about what we were about to do faded away. The outside world might have its views, but we were cocooned from it in the room on Chartres Street and everything felt right and natural between us.

⚜

Who would have thought that a simple thing like watching Leroy shave could make me so happy? I loved to lie on the chaise longue and see him moving the blade down the contours of his face before dipping it again in a bowl of sudsy water. A thousand butterflies took flight in my stomach. Perhaps it was the same excitement men felt when I rolled down my stockings on stage.

The room on Chartres Street had become our haven. We would meet there after the show and before we went back to our respective homes. I would arrive first, and then Leroy would sneak through the garden and climb in the window I'd left open for him. Like Jewel — no, even more than Jewel — he had to remain hidden. The joy of what we shared depended on secrecy. It would be destroyed — we would be destroyed — if anyone found out.

'I love listening to your heartbeat,' I told him one morning after we'd made love and I was resting my cheek against his chest. 'I don't need to go anywhere else in the world to be happy. All I need is to be near enough so I can hear your heart.'

'I'll remember those words forever, Jewel,' he said, kissing the top of my head. 'I don't need to be anywhere else either, as long as I can see you.'

'Now you know my name is Ruby,' I said. 'Jewel is my stage name. I don't want to be fooling you along with the rest of the world.'

'Yeah, I know. Vivienne de Villeray, the Creole aristocrat. You're dancing to support your mother and maid. But when I'm with you, you're Jewel: my beautiful, mysterious girl.' Then he noticed something in the open armoire and got up, treating me to the sight of his smooth toned buttocks. 'Didn't you see this shelf is lopsided?'

'No,' I told him, leaning on my elbow. 'I don't care about things like that.'

The next morning, I woke to loud banging: Leroy was fixing the shelf with a hammer and nails. I giggled. He couldn't stand untidiness. Even at the club, he couldn't pass a painting without making sure it was perfectly straight.

'It's like we're a married couple,' I told him, 'you fixing things for me.'

He turned to me with some nails held between his lips and nodded, pleased by the thought. He took the nails out and hammered them into place.

'I like doing things for you, Jewel. I like taking care of you.'

'I like it too.'

I'd never known a man like Leroy: someone who wanted to take care of me. My father had only cared about himself, and Uncle Rex was no better. I'd gotten used to taking care of myself.

I watched Leroy check the shelf was secure and wondered how he felt about having to sneak around. He never spoke about it. Perhaps, like me, he didn't bring it up for fear of breaking the beautiful spell we were both under.

'Well,' he said, taking his shirt from the hanger and putting it on, 'time to go. I'll see you at rehearsal.'

I stood up and put my arms around him, kissing his luscious mouth. I hated this routine. It hurt me every time I had to extricate myself from him.

After Leroy left, I rushed about the room dressing myself as Ruby. Despite the minimum sleep I was getting, my cheeks were rosy and my eyes shone. Passion for Leroy was the only thing that gave me the stamina to continue with this frenetic life. I was terrified that somehow it would all unravel when I least expected it.

SEVENTEEN

Amanda

The quiet of the night was broken by the squeal of tyres. I hadn't expected hoons in the Garden District but it seemed every place had them after all. 'Idiots!' I said under my breath.

The sound disturbed Grandma Ruby more than it did me. She blew out the candles before going to the window to investigate, peering into the night and not moving until the car sped off again, leaving behind it the smell of petrol and burning rubber.

'A scalded cat fears the fire,' she said. 'For a long time we had to be afraid of sounds like that.'

I waited for her to say something more, but she only shivered and turned towards the door. With a sinking feeling in my heart and stomach, I realised that after beginning that scorching tale of forbidden love she was going to leave me in suspense again.

As we went up the stairs, Grandma Ruby's breathing became laboured. I linked my arm with hers to give her support. When we reached the door to her bedroom, she deliberated a moment then looked at me.

'Life is half spent, Amandine, before we even know what life is. Make the most of every day and be happy.'

The following morning, Grandma Ruby wasn't up when I went to the kitchen, and Lorena didn't work on Sundays, so the house was quiet except for Flambeau noisily pecking at his plate of corn.

I left Grandma Ruby a note to say I was going to the French Quarter, although what I really did was to get off the streetcar at Canal Street and catch a bus from South Rampart Street to the Lower Ninth Ward. I was the only white person on the bus. Most of the other passengers were elderly, or housewives with shopping bags full of groceries. One woman, in a pair of denim micro-shorts and with dyed orange hair, sported a monitoring anklet without the slightest hint of self-consciousness. I stared out the window and thought about what Grandma Ruby had told me about segregation in New Orleans. The city was still segregated in a way, not so much by white and black facilities but by where people lived.

I rang Terence on my mobile and he met me at the bus stop.

'Well, hello, Amandine,' he said, smiling broadly. 'You're getting around like a local.'

'Yeah, I'm getting to know the city pretty quickly,' I said, falling into step with him as we headed off in the direction of his house.

In truth, even though I'd been in New Orleans only six days, it was as though a lifetime had passed. I wasn't the same girl who had arrived at the airport with holes in her history. Grandma Ruby's stories about my New Orleans family were creating a foundation I'd never had before. But how could I even begin to explain all that?

'Hey, Terence!' a man standing on a ladder and fixing a wonky gutter called out as we passed. 'Hot and humid as hell, ain't it? Real hurricane weather!'

Terence waved and replied, 'Sure is,' before we walked on.

'I read an article in *NOLA Life News* about a possible superstorm,' I said.

Terence surveyed the sky. 'Yes, a lot of folks are getting worked up about that possibility.'

Two women were drinking beer on their front porch and watching a boy play with a dog. A man was painting his letterbox lid, while another was trimming a plant by his front door. Nobody here looked too worked up about anything.

'You'll get out if it comes, won't you?' I asked. 'According to Elliot, the low-lying areas like here are in the greatest danger of flooding.'

Terence opened the gate to his garden and ushered me through it. 'We get storms every year, Amandine. Sometimes we're without electricity, or a couple of windows get broken. I lived through the flooding after Betsy. People forget that when they get all excited about the "Big One".' He took his key from his pocket and pushed it into the door lock. 'It's too expensive for most folks here to get up and go each time the weatherman decides to up ratings by warning us about a superstorm. You got to pay for your gas, and unless you got family somewhere else, you got to pay for a hotel room in Lafayette or Jackson. And what about your pets? You going to subject your cat or dog to eight hours in a hot car in slow-moving traffic? You can't leave them behind all on their own either, can you?'

He paused on the porch and indicated the neighbouring houses with a nod. 'Mr and Mrs Williams across the road, they're too elderly to go anywhere. The woman two doors down has five kids and no car; and Augusta next door, she's got no legs and is in a wheelchair. Who's going to look after them if I go? No, if a hurricane is coming, I'll be staying to look after these folks.'

I followed him inside the house. Maybe worrying about hurricanes was a luxury of the rich. From Terence's description of his neighbours, it seemed they had more to worry about in their daily lives than some high-powered winds.

'Sit yourself down,' he said, then raising his eyebrow comically asked, 'Shall I get you a "soft drink" before we start?'

I nodded, knowing he meant one of his potent root beers. 'When in Rome do as the Romans do is my motto.'

While Terence got the drinks, I looked about his front room and tried to discern something about him. There were no family photographs or mementos anywhere. Was he a bachelor? An orphan? A widower? Did he care so much about his neighbours because he had no family of his own? I found myself intrigued by him. But I didn't want to go prying into his business ... not yet anyway.

He brought the root beers, and we drank them with relish then sat down to play. I liked his teaching style. It was hands-on with no mucking about with scales and theory.

'This is a composition of your father's that I remember well,' he said, playing a phrase that was colourful and vigorous, then waiting for me to copy it.

We continued through the piece that way, phrase by phrase.

'You've got a great sense of rhythm,' he said with genuine appreciation. 'You sure you haven't got any colour in you?'

I laughed. 'No, not at all. I'd love it if I did, though.'

His eyes opened wide. 'Really? How's that?'

'Black is beautiful! And all those cool moves.' I did my version of a hip-hop body wave.

He shook his head. 'Well, the world has changed. Nobody would have said that back in the days of segregation. Well, almost nobody. To be black then was considered some sort of curse. Even black folks discriminated against each other by gradations of colour. The fairer you were, the better. That caused a whole lot of trouble for the Civil Rights Movement. Whites beat on blacks, and blacks beat on other blacks because they were darker.'

I thought back to what Grandma Ruby had told me about the white supremacist rallies against desegregation. 'You've seen a lot of things in your lifetime, haven't you?'

'Yes, I have,' he said thoughtfully.

We both fell into silence for a minute. I didn't know what he was thinking about, but I was remembering Grandma Ruby and Leroy and how they'd had to hide their love out of fear for their lives. The world certainly had changed. Elliot and I could hang around with Blaine and nobody batted an eyelid. I was here alone with a black man for a piano lesson, and the reason I hadn't told my family wasn't because of his colour but because he lived in the Lower Ninth Ward and I didn't want them to worry.

We continued with the lesson and Terence showed me how to embellish the piece, then played a clarinet along with me, sometimes harmonising with the melody and other times playing a rhythmic arpeggio. It was strange and otherworldly, but somehow I felt my father coming to me through the music. I looked at my hands, and for a moment they seemed to be his hands gliding across the keys.

'You got the storytelling gene in you,' Terence told me. 'Your father really conveyed a story when he played. The effect was as electrifying as reading a piece of great literature. His music moved me.'

'My Grandma Ruby is quite a storyteller,' I said. 'It must be in the genes.'

He smiled as if enjoying a private joke. 'Good storytellers are as highly valued as musicians in Louisiana. They add spice to life by embellishing it.'

He picked up his clarinet and began to play a piece that was soulful, dark and passionate. Even at his age he was an attractive man. There was something about him: a gentleness of spirit and yet an underlying strength too. He didn't talk a lot, but every word he said had value. I looked around his house again. It was tidy and organised but had no feminine touches anywhere. Surely a man like Terence couldn't have been a bachelor all his life?

'My parents met at Preservation Hall,' I said, when he'd finished his piece. 'My father was playing there. It's a big deal to perform there, isn't it?'

He looked at me compassionately. 'Your father was a big deal, Amandine. A really big deal. I'm sorry for you that you never got to grow up with your parents. It's an honour for me to teach you jazz piano. It makes me think that somehow I'm paying respect to your father for all the pleasure his music gave people.'

We finished our lesson and Terence turned off the electric piano. 'Why don't you come again on Wednesday? You learn fast and there's a lot more I can teach you.'

As he walked me back to the bus stop, a toothless man shouted to him from a rundown weatherboard house. 'Hey, Terence, you got yourself a nice girlfriend there!'

Terence laughed and waved back to the man. 'Don't mind him,' he said to me. 'He hasn't got all his marbles. He lost them in Vietnam.'

My bus arrived and the driver opened the doors.

'So we'll get together again on Wednesday,' Terence said.

'If a hurricane hasn't hit,' I quipped.

He chuckled and helped me onto the bus step. 'You're developing a real dark New Orleanian sense of humour, Amandine. You could be one of us.'

I ate black-eyed pea fritters and baked sweet potato in the French Quarter, before wandering down Royal Street humming the pieces Terence had taught me. I stopped to look in the window of an antique jewellery store and admired a rose-gold ring with a large ruby setting — a true power ring! I thought of Grandma Ruby, but it was far too big for her delicate hands.

I held my own hand up and studied it. It was uncanny how I'd felt my father through my fingers when

I'd played his composition. The bass chords required playing tenths — two keys longer than an octave. My large hands had always mystified me, but now I saw they contained hidden talents.

I remembered what Grandma Ruby had said about Clifford having perfect-sized hands for boxing. My father and I must have inherited our hands from him. At last my physical characteristics were starting to make sense and I was thrilled by the idea of having a place on a distinguished family tree.

I continued along the street before catching the streetcar back to the Garden District. I wanted to hear what happened next in Grandma Ruby's story.

However, when I reached the house I found Blaine and Grandma Ruby taking tea in the garden.

'I'm glad you're back early, Amandine,' said Grandma Ruby, standing up to kiss me. 'Blaine wants to take you for a romantic drive along the River Road.'

Blaine, who was dressed in a fitted white shirt, beige pants and boat shoes, grinned at me. 'Some of the most beautiful antebellum plantation homes are along there. It will give you a feel for Southern history; and afterwards, I have a friend who's invited us for a meal in her swamp cabin.'

Although I wanted to hear the rest of Grandma Ruby's story, she seemed keen for me to go with Blaine and the drive did sound intriguing. The sanatorium where Maman, my great-grandmother, had stayed and which had caused Grandma Ruby such trouble was along the River Road. It would be interesting to see it.

I went inside the house and grabbed a shawl for the evening and changed into a pair of flat sandals. When I came out again I was surprised to see Blaine waiting for me in the driveway in a blue Chevrolet Corvette with the roof down.

'I borrowed it from a friend especially for today,' he said. 'I told him I needed to impress a stylish girl.'

Grandma Ruby kissed me again. 'Enjoy yourself,' she said with a whimsical smile. 'You know the swamp around there is supposed to be haunted ... and you'd better watch out for the alligators.'

I glanced at Blaine, who winked. 'You take me to all the best places,' I told him.

The view of endless fields of sugar cane along the Mississippi River was exactly what I needed to clear my head and absorb everything I'd been learning about my family since coming to New Orleans. The breeze on my face was soothing, and the hum of the Corvette's engine put me in a meditative state. I was in the mood to take stock of my life in a way that I hadn't been before; as if I was moving towards something for which I'd been searching for years. But what that something was exactly, I couldn't say.

I'd asked Blaine to point out which antebellum mansion had been the River Road Sanatorium, and after we'd been driving for about forty-five minutes he pulled up outside the gates of a massive plantation home. We climbed out of the car to take a look.

The sight of the place brought back all the thrills I'd experienced as a teenager watching *Gone with the Wind*. I tried to drink it in all at once but it was impossible. I had to focus on one wing at a time. The central portico accentuated the majestic height of the building, while the ironwork railings on the galleries gave it a sense of elegance. The live oaks that Grandma Ruby had described were still there, along with the rose and hedge gardens. A small herd of deer was grazing on the lawn alongside the drive. The lush, rich beauty of the place reminded me of 'Amandine', only on a much grander scale.

'Do you know why there are two sets of stairs leading to the front door?' Blaine asked.

I shook my head.

'The left side was intended for the ladies, while the right was for the gentlemen, so when the ladies lifted their skirts to take the stairs the men wouldn't glimpse their petticoats.'

'How quaint!' I giggled.

Blaine rested his hand on the gate. 'It's a private home now, owned by an oil company executive. After the Civil War it was near impossible for plantations to stay profitable without the use of slave labour. A lot of these places fell into disrepair, which would explain how this one ended up being a hospital. But after the Second World War, when the economy was peaches again and the tourist trade had kicked off, these old homes started coming back to life.'

'Well,' I said, shading my eyes and letting my gaze travel the full length of the massive white columns, 'my dream of restoring a historic home has hit epic proportions. If I'm ever commissioned to do one of these plantation homes, I'll call on you to help with the interiors.'

Blaine beamed. 'Oh, my! Just the doorknobs and keyholes would keep me busy for a year! Not to mention the fireplaces and mirrors and chandeliers. I'd probably die of ecstasy doing the chandeliers, but it would be a wonderful way to go, I assure you.'

'I wish we could see inside it,' I said, eyeing the *Keep Out* sign on the gate. 'Maybe if I wrote to the owners they would let me?'

Blaine shook his head. 'They're probably sick of treasure hunters. When the Union soldiers stormed the South, raping and pillaging, many plantation families buried their money and jewels in the ground but never returned to reclaim them. There's always talk of millions to be made if those treasures are found.'

He nodded down the road. 'If you'd like to see an old plantation home on the inside, Oak Alley is only a few miles along. We've got time to take a tour before we head out to Zeline's place.'

We drove on a while further before Blaine brought the car to a stop at the front gate of Oak Alley plantation. I stared down a tunnel of ancient oak trees whose gnarled branches created a canopied arch. The greenery perfectly framed the Greek Revival mansion with its French windows and grand colonnade of Doric columns. Softened by the trees, the house was more beautiful than imposing.

'Does it seem familiar to you?' Blaine asked.

I peered at the wide galleries and dark green shutters. 'Yes, it does.' Then it suddenly came to me. 'It's Louis de Pointe du Lac's house in *Interview with the Vampire*!'

Blaine nodded and swung the car back towards the road. 'The visitors' entrance is at the rear. I thought you might like this plantation house because it's —'

'Let me guess!' I interrupted. 'It's haunted? Is there anywhere in the whole of Louisiana that isn't?'

He laughed. 'You're catching on quick!'

We went into the gift shop to buy our tickets. As well as the ubiquitous postcards, tee-shirts and cookbooks there was a display of historical material, including a framed advertisement from *Le Courrier de la Louisiane* in 1837 offering a reward for an 'escaped Negress': *she is very tall and walks very fast,* the ad said. There was a warning at the end: *All persons are cautioned against harboring a runaway Negress or aiding her escape to another state. The law will be rigorously enforced.*

I shivered. I couldn't imagine what it would be like to be a fugitive and have your freedom taken from you when you weren't guilty of any crime.

'There's a tour of the house in fifteen minutes,' the woman at the counter said. 'You can join them if you'd like.'

We thanked her, bought some vanilla gelato and ate it as we made our way through the garden towards the house. We passed a row of small wooden cabins — the slave quarters — and looked inside at the bare walls and roughly hewn furniture. According to the plaque, each tiny cabin could house up to ten people. The difference between the plantation house and these barely adequate buildings was palpable. As breathtaking as Oak Alley was, it had been built on the suffering of slaves.

'It's a dark part of Southern history,' Blaine said. 'Even though my family were free people of colour, some of my ancestors owned slaves. Your ancestors did too.'

He was right, of course: Grandma Ruby had come from a plantation family, but I'd never considered that I was part of that legacy of cruelty too. It seemed that as well as the good things I was discovering about my family, I would have to accept some unpleasant realities.

'The idea of people being sold into slavery horrifies me,' I said. 'I only hope as a species we are improving and will eventually do away with all forms of cruelty.'

The tour guide, dressed as a Southern belle in a cotton dress with a scooped neckline and three-tiered skirt, was waiting at the front door with a group of visitors.

We gave her our tickets, and she ushered the group through the central hall and into a parlour with blue velour-upholstered chairs and a large fireplace that she explained was faux marbre — wood painted to look like black marble — as the doors were faux bois, artificially grained to look like oak.

As she led us through the house, Blaine gushed over details like the convex courting mirror that allowed a chaperone to keep an eye on a young couple even when they left the room; and a candle holder that lengthened or shortened the duration a candle could burn, used by the master of the house to limit the visit of a guest he didn't like. Meanwhile, I admired how well the house, built in the 1830s, had been constructed for the climate. The hip roof acted like a parasol against the sun, while the dormer windows let out heat that built up under the roof. The wraparound galleries and double French doors all facilitated air ventilation, and the rooms could be closed off to keep them warm in winter. The tree-lined drive had a cooling effect too, practically and psychologically. Once again I found myself lamenting Sydney's treeless suburbs, where houses baked under the hot sun and the inhabitants racked up the electricity bills in order to keep their homes cool.

'It's a crime against the environment and public health,' I muttered under my breath.

I felt Blaine's hand on my shoulder. 'You talking to yourself, Mademoiselle Amandine? The Southern sun will do that to you. It's hotter than a billy goat's ass in a pepper patch today!' He led me to a bedroom on the second floor. 'Look at this. Isn't it fabulous?'

I stared into a room with two canopied beds and a lavender-pink chaise longue and matching armchair. 'It's pretty, but the furniture doesn't match the period of the house.'

'It was the bedroom of Josephine Stewart, the lady responsible for saving the house and opening it to the public. It's been turned into a shrine. All the clocks in the house are stopped at 6.30 am, the time of her death. She's buried on the property, along with her husband and the family dog. They say her spirit still hangs around, checking on everything.'

The tour ended in the central hall, where the guide told us about the ghost of Louise Roman, the daughter of the plantation's original French Creole owners.

'A drunk suitor tried to kiss Louise and, as she fled him in anger, she tripped and cut her leg on the iron frame of her hoop skirt. She lost her leg to gangrene. Sure that no man would want to marry her, she joined a convent, but returned to the plantation in her later years.' The guide pointed to the staircase. 'Sometimes, when all the guests are gone for the day and we're closing up, we catch a glimpse of Louise coming down the stairs or pacing the galleries.'

I glanced at Blaine, who grinned back at me. It seemed nothing enhanced one's experience of a historic Louisiana property more than a good ghost story.

'I wonder what the takeaway lesson is there?' he asked as we made our way back to the car. 'Should you let your drunk lover kiss you — or not?'

'Maybe the lesson is to not wear ridiculous hoop skirts.'

We nudged each other, enjoying our shared sense of humour.

Before returning to the parking lot, we stopped off at the gift store again to use the bathrooms. When I reached the car, I found Blaine already waiting.

As I slipped into the passenger seat, he handed me a book. 'I bought it for you at the gift store. It's about the restoration of Oak Alley, starting in the 1920s and continuing to today.'

I flipped through the pages and found a picture of the mansion in 1923 after it had been abandoned for many years. It was covered in vines and the columns were cracked. The majestic oaks were being choked by an overgrowth of Spanish moss.

'Thank you!' I cried, giving Blaine a hug. 'This is like cocaine for restoration buffs.'

Once we were back on the main road, Blaine said, 'I know a lot of restoration architects in New Orleans. I can introduce you to them ... if you're thinking about staying?'

'It sounds like Grandma Ruby's been in your ear,' I said with a smile. 'I know she wants me to stay in New Orleans for good.'

Blaine turned down a tree-lined road that led past more plantations. 'When you walked into the shop with your grandma, my heart lifted like a hot-air balloon,' he said. 'I haven't seen Ruby look so happy in years. She had three big blows in succession: Clifford's death; the tragedy of your parents' accident; and then you being taken away. She'd always been a character, but after that it was like the life went out of her.'

I hadn't expected such a personal observation from Blaine. He was fun and I liked him, but he'd struck me as superficial. Now I could see that wasn't the case.

'It's only six days since I reunited with Grandma Ruby,' I told him, 'but they've been life-changing for me too. I didn't even know of her existence until Nan's death, and yet I feel like I've always known her.'

Blaine listened with interest, but my private nature got the better of me and I deflected the conversation back to him. 'Grandma Ruby said that your families go back a long way?'

'Yes, that's right. I remember you as a baby in your cot but your diaper stinkers and milk vomits were a turn off to getting to know you better,' he said with a grin before turning serious again. 'I looked up to your daddy — he was so cool. He was gifted, but always content to let others shine. I was fourteen when your parents were killed and I felt like I'd lost a brother and a sister. It was your daddy who inspired me to become an antique dealer.'

I closed my eyes and took a deep breath. While I enjoyed discovering things about my parents, a sense of loss welled up in me. I was listening to people who had known them intimately, while I couldn't remember a thing about them.

'How did he inspire you?' I asked.

'My mother's side of the family came from the land, but my father's side had been furniture makers. It was a big thing for my grandfather and father to obtain law degrees and practise in New Orleans. I was expected to follow in their footsteps, but I had no heart for the law. I've always loved beautiful things. Your daddy going his own way to be a musician gave me the courage to pursue my passion too.'

The sun was starting to set, bathing the scenery around in tones of pink. I breathed in the woody, sweet-scented air.

'So do you think you will stay?' Blaine asked.

It was something I'd been thinking about since I'd arrived in New Orleans, but again my loyalty to Nan confused me.

'I'm not sure yet. It's too soon to tell. I feel so at home here, but I was brought up in Australia. That's a big part of me too.'

Blaine tittered. 'Your Grandma Ruby isn't the only one keen to convince you to stay. There's a certain professor in the French Quarter who I believe would like to know your intentions.'

Despite my best effort to stop myself, I blushed. 'Elliot? Really?'

'Say aha! I could see by the way he looked at you at Estée's funeral that he was taken.'

'What's he like?' I asked.

'Hmm, that question sounds like you're interested?' said Blaine, changing gears.

'Well ... yes ...' I was interested, all right.

He was thoughtful for a moment. 'To tell you the truth, he reminds me of your father. He's got the same down-to-earth manner. And like your father, I think he's attracted to women who are non-conformist. Your mother was a real livewire.'

'I'm not a livewire,' I said.

He pulled a mock-serious face. 'You underestimate yourself, Amandine. You're calm and considered like your father, but I think deep down you're a maverick like your mother. Every so often an impish smile comes to your face and I say to myself: "Oh, there you are, Paula!"'

Blaine's words struck a chord with me. I'd often suspected that there was another person in me trying to get out. I remembered my mother's letter about the woman hula-hooping in the French Quarter and how the image had appealed to me for its sense of freedom and pure joy. I'd never experienced those things. I'd always been so restrained in Sydney. Maybe that was why my mother had fallen in love with New Orleans: perhaps she'd been able to be herself here. 'I feel like I'm coming alive,' I said. 'If you're a passionate person, New Orleans is the place to be.'

EIGHTEEN

Amanda

The scenery changed from sugar-cane fields to gnarled cypress trees covered in Spanish moss. They cast sharp, pointed fingers of shade across the road. The chirping of crickets was thick in the air.

A few miles along, the road dwindled to a track. Blaine stopped the car and pulled the roof over. Then he wound up the windows. 'You'll be right at home here, Crocodile Amandine. They've got it all in the swampland — alligators, poisonous snakes and spiders ... even Bigfoot.'

'Is that why you put the roof up?' I asked, smiling ironically. 'Because of Bigfoot?'

'Well,' he said, easing the car down the track, 'mostly I'm afraid of the swamp people. Those fur-trapping, gator-eating rednecks are barely human!'

'Are you kidding me?' I started to feel uneasy. I had no fear of supernatural beings, but gun-toting, drunk, antisocial humans were another matter.

Blaine glanced at me and laughed. 'Yes, I'm kidding.'

He opened the glove box and handed me a can of insect repellent. 'It's the mosquitoes I'm trying to avoid. They're relentless out here.'

A short while later we came upon a wooden cabin on the edge of a green lily-covered bayou. Twilight had fallen and long-legged water birds searched for food along the water's edge while fish sporadically jumped above its surface. Several other cars were parked at the end of the drive.

'Zeline is a white witch,' Blaine explained, as he opened the door for me. 'Every August she invites her non-Wiccan friends to her cabin for a special wish-making ceremony. I thought you might like an insight into the superstitious side of Louisiana.'

'Thanks,' I whispered, getting out of the car. 'When Grandma Ruby said you'd show me around, she wasn't kidding!'

I knew of Wiccans and Pagans back in Sydney, but they lived in terraces in Newtown and Enmore and had jobs in advertising and fashion. This roughly hewn cabin out in the sticks was plain eerie. I wrapped my shawl tightly around me and followed Blaine down the grassy path towards the cabin. Before we reached the stairs, a strange, prehistoric growl broke the air, followed by a gurgling sound like an outboard motor struggling to start.

Blaine stopped to listen. 'Well, I'll be! Zeline must have called him up especially for you. Do you know what it is?'

I shook my head.

'It's an alligator — a big one. He's somewhere nearby. Well, actually if he's growling there's probably another one around too.'

It wasn't something I wanted to hear when I was surrounded by foot-high grass. 'Just get up the stairs, will you,' I said, prodding Blaine in the back.

A murmur of voices came from inside the cabin, and the porch screen door was unlocked. We wiped our feet on the doormat which had written on it *Blessed Be* instead of *Welcome*.

The inside of the cabin was cosier than I'd been expecting from the exterior. A potbelly stove stood in one corner with an ironwork pentacle above it, the walls were sage green, and the upholstered furniture looked like it had come straight from a 1960s yard sale. My nose twitched at the strong scents of pine, lemon ... and wax. Drippy candles covered every available surface from the hall table to the bookshelves, turning the cabin into what my health and safety lecturer at Sydney University would have termed a 'quaint fire hazard'.

A dozen smiling faces turned in our direction. Zeline's guests had come from all walks of life judging from the variety of ages. Most were wearing normal street clothes, but a couple of black women wore traditional African dress, and one Caucasian woman had donned a sari and an Indian nose chain.

'Blaine, you're here!' a woman called out.

She was about fifty years of age with wild salt-and-pepper hair and gypsy black eyes. One look at her burgundy velvet dress with crisscross front lacing and I knew she had to be Zeline.

'So nice to see you too!' said Blaine, kissing her hand. 'This is my friend Amandine, from Australia.'

Zeline took my hands firmly and peered into my eyes. 'A pleasure to meet you, Amandine.' Leaning in closer, her gaze became more intense and her grip tighter. 'I hope tonight will be fruitful for you.'

A meal was set out on a wooden trestle table on a screened porch facing the bayou. We filled our plates with rice pilaf, spicy butternut pumpkin and sweet potato fritters, before sitting down on tie-dyed cushions to eat.

'Who is the swamp supposed to be haunted by?' I asked Blaine.

'Ghosts of escaped slaves,' he said, taking a bite of a fritter. 'They were known as maroons. If they were found, they were whipped or made gruesome public examples of in Jackson Square. So they used their voodoo to make themselves invisible, create curses and terrify their white masters from pursuing them.'

I thought of the advertisement I'd seen in the Oak Alley gift shop calling for the return of an escaped slave. I wondered if she'd ever been recaptured and what happened to her.

Once the meal was finished, Zeline called us back into the living room where she'd set up an altar of white candles. Sandalwood incense wafted in the air. She rang a tiny bell and the chatter in the room fell silent.

'The temple is about to be erected,' she said. 'The circle is about to be cast. May all who are gathered be here of their own free will.' She lit the candles and blessed the four directions of the room — north, east, south and west. 'I evoke the God and Goddess and invite you all to participate in peace and love in this ritual for the non-initiated.'

I glanced at Blaine whose shining eyes were fixed on Zeline in rapt attention. For one nervous moment I thought she was going to ask us all to take our clothes off and dance in the moonlight. Instead she passed around a basket with pieces of paper and pencils in it.

'We are going to use the natural energy of the moon to assist our own powers of manifestation to help us on our path. I want each of you to take a few moments to write down what it is that you most long for in your life.'

When everyone had a piece of paper, Zeline turned on a CD player and Celtic music filled the air. I watched the others scribbling down their desires while I couldn't think what it was that I most wanted in my life. I'd never asked myself that question so directly before. Up until her death, what I'd most wanted was to please Nan. I'd enjoyed my architectural studies, but wasn't convinced that architecture was what I most wanted to do with my life. Would I like to be a musician like my father? Would I like to fall madly in love — perhaps with Elliot — and stay in New Orleans?

I noticed Zeline watching me. She pressed her palms together and closed her eyes as if she was trying to help me. As corny as I thought the whole exercise to be, I closed my eyes too. Slowly an idea appeared like the sun rising on the horizon. Gradually the form gained clarity. The words had been there for years, buried in my heart, but I'd never articulated them.

I picked up the pencil and wrote: *I want to truly belong somewhere.*

When everyone had completed the task, Zeline opened the kitchen door and revealed a path into the woods lit by hurricane lamps and fairy lights.

'Each of you will follow the trail one at a time,' she explained. 'As you travel, I want you to think about your desire and what its granting would mean to you. Along the trail is a clearing with a cauldron. I want you to read your wish out loud then drop it into the cauldron and let it go. Trust the energies to bring your desire to you. Then continue along the trail and it will eventually bring you back to the front door of the cabin.'

I stared down the path. It was pretty but unearthly. We must have all taken leave of our senses if we were each going to walk out into the swampland alone.

Because Blaine and I were at the back of the room we were the last to go. As each person set out on the path, I strained my ears, waiting for a blood-curdling scream. But when they returned to the house, the guests' faces were calm and thoughtful.

Zeline selected Blaine to go before me. When he'd set off on the path, I tugged Zeline's arm and asked: 'Does this wish-making thing really work?'

'It sure does,' she said, resting her sage-like gaze on me. 'But be aware that your desire will come to you in a way you never could have anticipated.'

When Blaine returned, he sat in a corner by himself with his eyes closed and a blissful smile on his face. I wondered what he had asked for, but I guessed part of the exercise was to keep our wishes to ourselves.

When it was my time to walk the path, my stomach tightened and I wavered. Zeline sensed my fear, linked her arm with mine and guided me towards the path.

'Walk calmly and slowly,' she said. 'Don't rush. The spirits will keep you safe, but whatever you do, don't touch the trees.' Don't touch the trees? I wondered why she had instructed that so adamantly, but before I could ask she whispered in my ear, 'Be brave. You are a young woman on the verge of a breakthrough,' and gave me a gentle shove onto the path.

The moon was bright in the sky and the trees loomed overhead like dark phantoms. The owls hooting added to the spookiness of the atmosphere. Every rock and tree root jabbed through the thin soles of my sandals. A pair of yellow eyes glinted at me from the darkness, then disappeared. Had they been real or a figment of my imagination? I stopped and glanced over my shoulder. I was tempted to turn back, but as nobody else had chickened out, including Blaine, pride overcame my fear and I stumbled onwards.

I saw something move in a cypress tree ahead of me. The hairs on the nape of my neck stood on end. A speckled snake was coiling itself around a branch. Was that why Zeline had instructed me not to touch the trees? Because they were infested with snakes? I wrapped my arms around me and walked gingerly on until I reached the clearing where the cauldron was burning.

I read my wish out loud as Zeline had said to do: 'I want to truly belong somewhere.' A shiver ran through me as I dropped the piece of paper into the cauldron and the flames flared.

A chirping behind me made me spin around. I found myself exchanging stares with a fuzzy creature, about the size of a small dog, with a black band marking across its eyes: a racoon. I'd never seen one for real before, only in books and movies. His bright eyes glistened as if he was trying to tell me something. Then he sniffed the air and scampered away. The animal's appearance had been special somehow. I returned to the house buoyed by the hope that perhaps my wish really could come true.

As I was the last of the guests to have made a wish, the chatter in the room had resumed.

Blaine beamed at me. 'Honeybun, I was starting to worry about you! I wasn't kidding about Bigfoot — there have been several sightings of him this year.'

Zeline approached me. 'Did you like your journey into the swampland?'

'I saw a racoon,' I told her. 'In the clearing where the cauldron was.'

'Ah,' she said thoughtfully. 'Racoons are magical creatures to the Native Americans. They symbolise secrets. His appearance could be foretelling that something very important is about to be revealed to you.'

Blaine and I didn't say much on the trip home because he needed to concentrate on the dark road. When we reached the Garden District it was well after midnight, but I wasn't tired.

'Thank you for taking me out today,' I told him. 'It was fun!'

The light in the dining room was off and Grandma Ruby had already gone to bed. She'd left a lamp lit in the entrance hall for me, and the sconces that led to my bedroom were on, guiding me like the fairy lights and hurricane lamps had on the path through the swampland.

I climbed into bed and thought about all the things that had happened that afternoon. Zeline had said that I was a young woman on the verge of a breakthrough. Then I thought about her prediction that my desire would be fulfilled in ways I could not anticipate. 'Good ways, I hope,' I said before drifting off to sleep. 'I'm not a fan of surprises.'

I slept heavily and probably would have dozed most of the following day if I hadn't been woken by the beeping of my mobile phone to alert me that I'd received a text. I saw the message was from Elliot: *I found some of your father's recordings. Would you like to meet at my place this afternoon?*

I looked out the window: the sun was high. Then I glanced at the time. It was nearly one o'clock. I dressed and went downstairs to find Lorena dusting the parlour.

'I overslept,' I told her.

She smiled and sprayed some vinegar solution on a cleaning cloth and began wiping the mirror. 'Your grandmother has gone to a doctor's appointment Uptown. She didn't want to wake you because you came in late last night.'

I was torn between wanting to hear my father's music and waiting for Grandma Ruby to return so I could listen to the rest of her story. 'Do you know what time she'll be back?'

'Usually when she goes Uptown she visits some of her friends and returns around five o'clock.'

I rang Elliot and agreed to meet him in an hour. I sat on the edge of my seat all the way in the streetcar, barely able to keep still. When I rang the doorbell to Elliot's apartment, I jiggled from foot to foot and tugged at the owl charm necklace around my neck. I hadn't felt comfortable wearing Nan's pendant for this occasion.

'Hello,' said Elliot when he opened the door. 'Come in.'

His smile and the sight of Duke the squirrel perched on his shoulder helped to calm me. I let out a breath and followed him into the living area.

'I called your house last night to see if you wanted to listen to a band at Snug Harbor,' he said, moving some magazines so I could sit down on the couch. He placed Duke on the windowsill. 'But your grandmother said you were out for the evening.'

I looked at my lap and straightened my skirt so he wouldn't see the beaming smile on my face. He'd wanted to go out with me?

'I was with Blaine. We took a drive along the River Road and then went to a Wiccan magic ceremony in the swampland.'

Elliot clapped his hands and laughed. 'Blaine is a character! — when he invites you on one of his adventures, you can be sure it'll be interesting. I've been to a frog festival with him, and visited the ambush site of Bonnie and Clyde with a male psychic friend of his who'd dressed as Bonnie for the occasion!'

It was my turn to laugh. 'I like Blaine too. He's quirky.'

'Do you want an iced tea?' Elliot asked, standing up and moving towards the refrigerator. 'It's non-alcoholic, I promise.'

Despite the ceiling fans that rotated the air, it was hot inside the apartment. Beads of sweat had formed on Elliot's lip, and I was glad that I'd given up wearing heavy eye make-up since coming to New Orleans, otherwise I would have looked like the racoon I'd seen the previous night. I nodded, and he took out a jug of cold tea with pieces of lemon, pineapple, peaches and mint in it. Homemade: I liked that. He poured the tea into highball glasses and placed one on a coaster in front of me. I took a sip. The tea was tangy and refreshing and not overly sweetened.

'Perfect!' I said, taking another sip before placing my glass back on the coaster. If I'd been more forward I might have added, 'Just like you!'

Elliot indicated two CDs on the coffee table. 'I made you a compilation of the recordings I found of your father playing in various clubs. The other CD is an interview he did with WTUL radio in 1978. I thought you might like for us to listen to that together?'

I nodded and he inserted the CD in his player. After the announcer had introduced my father as 'a trailblazer in leading a revival of jazz in New Orleans', he asked how he was enjoying his new fame.

'I'm not interested in being a star,' my father replied in a low-key, softly spoken tone. 'What I'm passionate about is music and being able to share it with others. In fact, I think stardom can spoil the art. It can make you mediocre and common, and I don't want that to happen.'

I took a sharp breath. My father spoke with the charming lilt of a Southern gentleman. I didn't know why, but I hadn't been prepared for that. He sounded like I'd imagined Clifford Lalande had sounded. He was humble in his manner too. I was aware that Elliot was watching me and in spite of myself I started to cry.

'Are you all right, Amandine?' He reached over and turned off the CD player.

I stood up and moved to the window. 'His voice!' I gasped. 'His voice! It's as if he's here in the room!'

After Nan died, I'd kept her answering-machine tape and played it over and over so that I'd never forget the sound of her. But I'd been familiar with her voice. Hearing my father for the first time was a shock.

'It's more intense than looking at photographs or examining objects that belonged to him,' I told Elliot, wiping my face. 'He seems alive in real time ... but he can't hear me. I can't ask him all the questions I have.'

Elliot stood and grasped my hands in his. 'It's all right, Amandine. I thought the interview might be difficult. That's why I suggested we listen to it together, so you wouldn't be alone.'

Something about the word 'alone' made me cry harder. 'Alone' was what I'd felt for years. The only time I'd had any relief from it was when I was with Nan ... and now that I was here with my New Orleans family.

Elliot guided me back to the couch and cradled me in his arms. His embrace made me feel protected, like I was enclosed in a suit of armour. I nodded to let him know I was ready to listen to the rest of the interview. He pushed the play button.

Now that the initial shock had dissipated, I listened to my father's every word with a deep ache in my chest.

When the interviewer asked him about his highly advanced technique, he replied: 'I loved to play music. Nobody had to tell me to practise. I was up early before school, and raced home straight afterwards to sit at the piano. Perfecting my technique was a way of respecting the music, of allowing something greater than myself to move through me.'

He finished the interview by saying: 'I give thanks every day that I was born in New Orleans. I've had the finest teachers. Some of them paid for by my parents; others were the great old men of jazz who I met in bars and clubs and who wanted to impart their knowledge to me. I've been living a charmed life. I owe it to the city to honour its traditions.'

After the interview ended, I rested my head against Elliot's chest. He stroked my hair with the tips of his fingers. The only sounds in the room were the whirling fans, our breathing and Duke crunching on some peanuts. The peace gave me a chance to reflect on the things my father had said and to further build my picture of him.

'When the interviewer said my father was leading the way for a revival of jazz in New Orleans, what did he mean?' I asked. 'Hasn't New Orleans always been the jazz capital?'

'It is the birthplace of jazz, but the city's segregation policy exacted a high price,' he answered. 'Many of the greats moved north to get away from the oppression. Places like Chicago, New York and San Francisco benefited from the influx of skilled jazz musicians, while New Orleans grew staid. Your father studied, adapted and modernised traditional New Orleans jazz, as well as creating his own compositions. He laid the foundations for the sweeping revival of the 1980s and 1990s, but unfortunately he died before he could see it.'

I relished the feeling of Elliot's warm chest against my cheek. Somehow we were together naturally. I remembered Blaine saying that my father and Elliot had similar personalities. Was that one of the reasons he was so easy for me to be with?

When he turned my face towards him with his hand and kissed me, a bubbly sensation filled my heart. His lips were warm and tasted fruity from the iced tea. When he pressed me harder to him, I wanted to stay, but my father's interview had brought up feelings that were overwhelming. I needed to clear my head before returning to Grandma Ruby.

'I've got to go,' I told him, breaking away. 'I've got to sort myself out.'

He nodded and didn't try to convince me to stay. 'I'll take you to Preservation Hall tomorrow night,' he said. 'Your father first played there when he was fourteen years old. I think you'll like it.'

We kissed again when we parted in the courtyard of his apartment building.

'After Preservation Hall, I'll take you to Pat O'Brien's,' he added. 'We'll make a New Orleans night of it.'

'Okay,' I said, not afraid to let my beaming smile show now. 'I'll look forward to it.'

After I left Elliot, I had an urge to visit my parents' tomb again. I bought a bunch of pink dahlias, then caught a bus from North Rampart Street to Saint Louis Cemetery Number 3, but when I arrived at the gate I couldn't remember exactly where the Lalande tomb was located. Had Aunt Louise and I turned left or right? I took a guess on right. I recalled us making a detour from the main path but couldn't remember where.

Despite the orderly layout of the cemetery, I was lost. I was pondering the problem when I saw a familiar figure walking towards me. It was his straight posture and relaxed gait that gave him away, otherwise I wouldn't have recognised him in his pressed shirt and tie, with a trilby hat perched jauntily on his head. I'd only seen him in casual clothes.

'Terence!' I called.

'Well, hello, Amandine,' he said, lifting his hat. 'You're looking a little flustered. Is everything all right?'

'I came to visit my parents' tomb but I can't remember where it is.'

He turned towards the section to the left of us and rubbed his chin. 'I'm sure I've passed the Lalande family tomb a few times and I have a feeling it's over there. Let's go take a look.'

I thanked him, and a short while later we were standing in front of the tomb. The flowers Aunt Louise and I had left were gone — they would have dried out in the heat by now — but there was a bunch of lavender in one of the urns. It touched me to think my father might have a fan who hadn't forgotten him. I put the dahlias I'd brought in the opposite urn, then Terence and I sat down on a stone bench.

'Elliot played me a recording of my father being interviewed on local radio,' I told him. 'I feel confused. I loved my nan, but I'm angry at her for never letting me know anything about my father while I was growing up. I'm twenty-five and everything I learn about him hits me like a tidal wave. I'd like to talk with her, and I'd like to talk to him, and I can't talk to anybody!'

He squeezed my arm but didn't speak for a while. Then he said, 'Sometimes the people who love us do things we don't understand because they love us so much. Even though they know what they're doing will hurt us, they do it to protect us from greater harm.'

I thought about what he said, but I still felt mad at Nan. I didn't know how I was ever going to regain my peace of mind. Still, it wasn't Terence's problem so I changed the subject.

'How come you're at the cemetery today?' I asked him.

'My grandparents are buried here. I try to come a few times a year.'

'Just your grandparents?'

'That's right,' he said.

After Blaine's detailed explanation of New Orleans burial customs and how many family members could fit into one tomb, I found it unusual that only Terence's grandparents were buried in the cemetery, but he didn't elaborate and I didn't pry.

'So the cemetery wasn't segregated then?' I asked instead.

He shook his head. 'Most cemeteries in New Orleans aren't. In light of the fact that we're all equal in death, it seems a pity we spend so much of our earthly lives squabbling with each other, don't it?'

I thought of the stories Grandma Ruby had told me about segregation, and remembered the slave quarters at Oak Alley plantation.

'Do you feel angry about the way black people were treated?' I asked.

He stared at the tomb and said quietly, 'What's the use of being angry about times gone by? Can't change it. I'm thankful for the people who laid down their lives for the advancement of other black people. I try to show them respect by being the best man I can be. That's the only way I can repay them.'

A breeze scattered the dahlias I'd placed in the vase. I stood up and fixed them more securely. When I turned around I was surprised to see Terence weeping.

'Your father was too vibrant and special,' he said, dabbing at his eyes. 'A person like that shouldn't die so young.'

I was moved that my father's death had affected him so deeply. I thought about the interview Elliot had played for me earlier. My father wasn't in any way the selfish, thoughtless man Nan had brought me up to believe him to be.

I returned to the bench. 'You were one of the musicians who taught my father how to play traditional jazz, weren't you? In the interview he said there were men in New Orleans who he'd met in bars and clubs who taught him the true style of New Orleans jazz.'

Terence's eyes opened in surprise. 'Yes, Amandine, I was. I met him at Preservation Hall. He used to sneak to my place in the Lower Ninth Ward without telling his family, just like you're doing now.'

'What makes you think I'm sneaking?' I asked.

'I know what those fancy folks in the Garden District think about where I live. If they knew, they wouldn't let you come.'

A twinge of guilt pricked me. I was sneaking around for exactly the reason he'd described. I linked my arm through his. 'I'm glad I found you. It feels like magic. You'll be my special secret, okay? I want to surprise Grandma Ruby by playing her something of my father's.'

He stared at his hands and smiled. 'There are no secrets in life, Amandine. Just hidden truths that lie beneath the surface.'

When I returned to the house in the Garden District, I was surprised to see Uncle Jonathan's Mustang parked in the drive. Then I remembered that he and Aunt Louise were leaving for their Native American retreat later that evening.

In the kitchen, Aunt Louise had already started on dinner. I kissed her, then kissed Uncle Jonathan, who was sitting at the breakfast counter reading a book on the Sedona desert.

Aunt Louise removed the frying pan from the stove and spooned the potato, mushroom and onion mix onto some plates. 'I usually don't make such hearty meals in summer, but as Johnny and I are going to be eating a lot of cactus for the next week, I thought we'd better fill up.'

'Where's Grandma Ruby?' I asked.

'She's having a rest before dinner,' Aunt Louise replied, taking four placemats from a drawer and setting the table.

I folded the napkins for her. 'Is everything okay?'

'I usually take her to her medical appointments, but today she wanted to meet with some Uptown friends — women she knows from the civil rights days. Instead of catching a cab home like she promised, she got on the streetcar. I think the heat has worn her out.'

Once the table was laid, Grandma Ruby appeared. Her hair was coiffed into a bouffant updo and she smelled of Lily of the Valley perfume. But there was a pallor to her skin that her pink blush and lipstick couldn't mask, which worried me. Then I watched her smile radiantly and tuck into her food and wondered if I was overreacting.

'What did Doctor Wilson say?' Aunt Louise asked her. 'Was your blood test all right?'

Grandma Ruby lifted her glass of wine and tossed her head back. 'He told me to drink less coffee and have more sex,' she replied with a cheeky grin. 'Apparently sex is good for one's heart despite the old wives' tales.'

Aunt Louise grimaced, but Uncle Jonathan laughed out loud and winked at Grandma Ruby. 'Well, hopefully Louise and I will be having a cardiovascular workout this week,' he said. 'It's a long time since we took a holiday together.'

'Johnny, please!' Aunt Louise scolded, nodding in my direction. 'Mind your manners. We're going to be staying in tents most of the time anyhow. How much hanky-panky can you get up to when the walls are that thin?'

I was happy that the three of them were relaxed enough around me now to let their genteel manners go a bit and be risqué. I was also glad that my presence was allowing my aunt and uncle to enjoy some time away.

After dinner, Aunt Louise ran through Grandma Ruby's medicines with me. 'She knows how to take them,' she explained. 'I'm just showing you so you know what's what. The main thing to notice is if she gets prolonged shortness of breath, extreme tiredness, or complains of headaches or chest discomfort. But honestly, Momma hasn't shown any symptoms of her illness for years. Lorena knows what she can and can't eat with the warfarin, although every now and then Momma sneaks something on the restricted list like kiwi-fruit or mint. Small amounts of those foods won't hurt her.'

When it was time to leave for the airport in the Mustang, Aunt Louise handed me her car keys. 'I've parked the Prius in the garage. It's yours to use. Our spare house keys and the alarm code are in the top drawer of the desk in the study.'

'Just remember we drive on the right side here,' added Uncle Jonathan with a grin.

Aunt Louise gave me a hug before she got in the car. 'I can't tell you how happy I am you're here to keep an eye on Momma. I wouldn't feel safe leaving her with anybody else.'

'Don't worry,' I told her. 'I'll take good care of her.'

I returned to the house to find Grandma Ruby

downing a glass of water and some tablets. Despite our hearty meal, the colour hadn't returned to her face.

'Are you all right?' I asked. 'Did your doctor really say everything was okay? You weren't putting on an act for Aunt Louise and Uncle Jonathan?'

She grimaced as she put the glass in the dishwasher. 'Oh, Amandine, don't take on Louise's role while she's away! I'm looking forward to spending time with you. Of course I'm all right. My blood was a little thick so they changed my medication, which always unsettles me for a few days.'

'Would you like me to put the kettle on?' I asked, hopeful that now we were alone she might be in the mood to continue her story.

She shook her head. 'Let's get up early and spend the day in the summerhouse. I have so much to tell you.'

My disappointment was tempered by my concern for her. After I'd accompanied her to her room, I sat in the wing-back chair in my room and stared at the moonlit garden, trying to guess the answer to the question that had been bothering me. If Grandma Ruby had been so in love with Leroy, how had she ended up marrying Clifford Lalande?

The following morning, I was pleased to find Grandma Ruby up earlier than usual and waiting for me in the summerhouse. A mini-feast of freshly squeezed orange juice, grilled tomatoes, baked sweet potato, cornbread and mango tapioca pudding was spread out on the table.

'Did you make all this?' I asked her, sitting down in a wicker chair. 'You must have been up early.'

'Because of the change in medication, I didn't sleep well,' she said, then looking down at the food she added: 'I haven't prepared a meal like this for anybody for years. I'd forgotten what a pleasure it is.'

I studied her face. There was tension in her jaw and her cheeks were flushed. When she stared into the distance and her hands clenched into fists in her lap, I wondered if it was what she was about to tell me, rather than her change of medication, that had made her sleepless.

NINETEEN

Ruby

One morning, as Leroy was getting ready to leave the room in Chartres Street, he turned to me and said, 'I'd like you to meet my family this Sunday.'

A thrill ran through me. If Leroy was asking that, then he must be serious about me. 'Of course, I would love to,' I told him. 'But will they be all right with you bringing home a white girl?'

'They'll love you,' he said, straightening his jacket. 'There's nothing to worry about with them, you'll see. They don't care so much about the things other people get wound up about.'

'Are you going to explain that?'

Leroy's grin stretched from ear to ear. 'No, I'll let you discover why for yourself.'

It was only when he had kissed me goodbye and snuck out the window into the garden that I saw the dilemma. What would it be like once he and I stepped out of this room together? It had been a cocoon to us, a place of safety from the world outside.

Then there was the question of my identity. Did I go as Ruby or Jewel? Would I have to deceive Leroy's family the way I did everyone else? I opened the door of the armoire that held Ruby's clothes then immediately shut it again. Of course I would have to go as Jewel, albeit a toned-down version. Not only was that how Leroy thought of me but Jewel belonged to the demimonde of New Orleans society, along with the musicians, magicians, transvestites, comedians and members of the mob. It was still a leap for her to be with a coloured man but for Vivienne de Villeray, the Creole aristocrat, it was impossible.

Leroy lived with his family in Tremé, an area famous for its jazz and racial mix of African and Creole cultures and everything in between. It wasn't far from the Quarter, and when I was a child my father sometimes took Maman and me there to see the Mardi Gras Indians show off their splendid feathered parade outfits. But it was a long time since I'd crossed over Esplanade Avenue into that part of town. The November sun shone gently down on the mix of shotguns, double-shotguns, Creole cottages, Craftsman-style homes and Italianate mansions that created a kind of gumbo architecture in the area.

I was wearing a jade green dress and matching sweater, and had pinned my wig into a respectable beehive. But I was still conspicuous among the old folk and families out strolling to see the turning autumn leaves. A group of young Italians sitting on a stoop whistled at me and one man was scolded by his wife for rubbernecking me when I passed them on the banquette.

Leroy's street was bordered by evergreen camphor trees, but the leaves from the crepe myrtles had fallen and they crunched under my feet. I checked the house number Leroy had written down for me and found myself standing opposite a stately white house with black shutters and ironwork. A sign in Gothic script out the front read: *Thezan Family Funeral Home*. I heard a babble of voices and someone playing the banjo.

I walked down the gravel drive that led to the back of the building and found myself in a garden of palmettos and arches covered in ivy. The lawn was occupied by a group of coloured children: three girls in braids skipping rope, and two smaller ones playing pitty-pat. A boy no more than five years old was picking up the nuts that had been dropped by a pecan tree and placing them in a pail. Another boy was twisting himself around on a swing attached to an oak tree. The girls skipping rope noticed me first and stopped to stare. Then one of them, in a starched cotton dress, covered her mouth to hide her smile before walking towards me. She took my hand and without a word led me down a walkway bordered by cannas towards a raised cottage with dormer windows and a front porch.

The house was old but meticulously kept, with a freshly painted front door and stark white columns. The four full-length windows that looked over the porch were open and inside the room a fire blazed in the grate. Leroy looked out of one of the windows and smiled like a sunburst when he saw me.

'Well, Darlene,' he said to the little girl, 'looks like you found me a fine lady.'

The girl covered her smile again with her fingers and nodded before running away to rejoin the other children.

Leroy laughed and walked down the steps towards me. 'Come meet the family,' he said, taking my arm.

I flinched. We'd never made physical contact out in the open like this. But before I could express my unease, Leroy had guided me into the room with the fire, which was occupied by four men dressed in their Sunday best. They stood when they saw me.

'So this is the famous Jewel we've heard so much about,' said the oldest of the men, stepping forward to clasp my hand cordially. 'I'm Joseph, Leroy's pa.'

Joseph spoke in the same rich tenor voice that Leroy did. He wasn't as tall as Leroy, but he was handsome, with chiselled features and a neat close-cropped moustache.

Leroy introduced me to his uncle Milton, his cousin Dwight and brother-in-law Gerald. All the men smiled genuinely and didn't seem put out by my presence. If I'd walked into Maman's bridge club with Leroy on my arm, we would have been met by deathly silence and horrified stares.

'Come meet the womenfolk,' said Leroy, guiding me into a yellow-painted kitchen where the air was steamy with the smell of frying garlic.

The women looked up and greeted me with the same friendly smiles the men had.

'Well, look at you!' said a stocky woman with her grey hair braided into a bun. 'Ain't you a pretty one!' She took both my hands in hers. 'I'm Alma, Leroy's grandma.' She turned to two other women who could have been twins with their neatly curled hair and full plum-coloured lips. They were dipping chicken pieces into egg batter, then rolling them in flour and breadcrumbs. 'And this is Leroy's mother, Pearl, and my other daughter, Eleanor. That skinny one by the sink is Bunny, Leroy's sister, and that one cutting up the tomatoes is Dora, Eleanor's daughter-in-law.'

Apart from Dora, whose skin was dark, the women had what was called 'teasing' complexions: lightly tanned. Bunny, with her height and long, straight hair, could have passed as a Spaniard. I wondered if there was some white blood in the family.

Pearl pushed Leroy back into the main room. 'Now you stay with the men, you hear? It's bad luck to have a man in the kitchen. We'll take care of your little Jewel.'

Leroy and I exchanged a smile before he disappeared. Pearl took my purse and placed it on a chair. Then she handed me an apron.

'The mains are almost done and I'm fixing to start on the sweet potato pudding,' she told me. 'You can help. There's no use assisting Eleanor with her creamed turnips. She guards her secret ingredients as closely as I do my embalming ones.'

Bunny giggled. 'The families always say Mama makes their dearly departed look better in death than they did in life.'

Pearl nodded. 'I know how to fill them out just right and give them a healthy glow.' She handed me some eggs, a bowl and a whisk, clearly intending for me to do something with them. 'Even the mob sometimes secretly bring their boys to me, then transfer the body back to their Italian funeral homes when I'm done. I've fixed up gunshot wounds and put back together a man who was cut to shreds. It was like working on a jigsaw puzzle! I'm the best in New Orleans.'

I wasn't squeamish and Pearl's story didn't faze me. What was bothering me was the bowl and whisk. This was uncharted territory for me. In our home, our guests didn't see the kitchen; the food mysteriously appeared on a trolley pushed by Mae. I couldn't recall Maman even making herself a cup of coffee, and I'd never so much as stirred a saucepan.

'What's the matter, honey?' asked Pearl, stepping back and studying me with her twinkling eyes. 'You don't cook?'

She was about fifty years of age, and Alma looked to be seventy. Alma had been born after the Civil War, but her parents could have been slaves. I wasn't going to say that we had a coloured maid at home who did everything for us. Luckily Dora chimed in and saved me from having to explain anything.

'You gotta learn how to cook, Jewel!' she said emphatically. 'I know you entertainers live on Chinese takeaway, but those pretty looks of yours ain't going to last forever. You got to come up with something else to please your man.'

'Hey!' said Eleanor, grinding her hips at the stove. 'I might be an old married lady but I can cook *and* please my man. It don't have to be one or the other.'

The women burst into laughter. From the living room came the sound of ragtime — the men were jamming.

'Well, Jewel, I'm going to teach you how to make a pudding,' said Pearl. 'Then next time you come, we'll work on a main.'

I was eighteen years old and it was the first time I'd ever beaten eggs. But I learned a lot more that day than how to make sweet potato pudding, garlic spinach and spicy tomato salad. As we cooked, Pearl and Eleanor took me through the entire process of conducting a funeral, including collecting the body.

'We went to collect good old Florence Lewis who lived on the top floor of a townhouse. But she weighed over five hundred pounds! We had to get her down the stairs while the family waited in the foyer, weeping and grieving. We tried to be dignified, with Milton carrying the stretcher at the head and Joseph and Dwight at the feet, and me walking slowly in front with a rose in my hands. But Milton stumbled on the narrow stairway and Florence's body slipped off the stretcher. Those of us in front had to run like crazy down the stairs or else get crushed. Thankfully, one of Florence's legs got wedged in the balustrade and she came to a halt, otherwise there would have been more than one funeral to arrange!'

This story, which had obviously been told before, sent the women into peals of merriment.

'Of course, Leroy don't work in the family business,' Pearl told me. 'Goes faint at the sight of a corpse. He became a musician instead. But I always remind him he got his start playing in funeral parades.'

Bunny, who had been sneaking admiring looks at me, asked, 'Jewel, do you really take your clothes off on stage?'

In Ruby's social circle that question would have been the end of the conversation. I was surprised Leroy had told them what I did. But the women considered me with curiosity rather than disdain.

'Well, I don't take everything off,' I explained. 'Men appreciate a little mystery. In fact, you can get a room of men excited just by slipping off your sweater if you do it the right way.'

'Show us something,' said Eleanor, putting down her spatula. 'Show us one of your moves.'

I'd never performed for a group of women before, and certainly not in a kitchen, but I slid my hands up along my body and flicked back my hair before slowly untying the apron strings at my neck and waist. I tugged the apron away and held it out for a moment before letting it drop to the floor. Then, one by one, I undid the buttons of my sweater before slipping it deliberately over my shoulders and wriggling free of it.

The women clapped and cheered.

'Woo hoo!' said Alma, fanning her face. 'You keep that up, young lady, and I reckon you could turn me into a lesbian!'

Dora and Bunny had to hold their stomachs they were laughing so hard.

'Hey, ladies,' called Joseph from the living room. 'What's all this monkeying around? Your men are hungry.'

I'd never known such camaraderie between women before. Even the charity lunches Maman used to take me to were highly competitive. I wondered why Leroy's family was so accepting of me, apparentlty not at all bothered by my race or what I did for a living. Maybe it was because their own profession — and the horror people associated with death — put them on the edge of society too. Or maybe dealing with death had made them realise what was truly important in life.

The food was laid out on the dining table on a fruit-patterned tablecloth that matched the curtains in the front room. The adults sat around it, while the children were delegated to their own table in the kitchen. I took a moment to admire my surroundings. Bunny had made a centrepiece from a carved-out pumpkin filled with sunflowers, which bloomed until autumn in New Orleans. The plates were simple Pyrex trimmed in green, and the serving dishes were ceramic. There was nothing showy about Leroy's family home. Nothing was there to impress. Rather, every item — from the overstuffed armchairs to the pictures of waterbirds on the walls — seemed to have been chosen to create a welcoming atmosphere.

Leroy, seated opposite, winked at me. I couldn't have been happier in that informal setting, where people passed dishes to each other instead of waiting for a maid to do it. I'd never known family life like this — everyone talking at once about everything from baseball to the neighbour's new baby and yet seemingly able to understand each other. It made me wish I really was Jewel and not Ruby. If I could become Jewel forever and live like this, I'd do it.

Then I thought about Maman and Mae. I doubted they could adapt to this life, even if it would do them the world of good. Maman was a kind person who'd always treated her servants with respect, but she'd only ever seen coloured people as domestics. And Mae couldn't seem to picture herself any other way.

There were eleven adults squeezed around a table designed for eight, but there was one place left empty. Who was it for? A deceased loved one? I received my answer a few minutes later when a young coloured man dressed in a grey flannel suit stepped into the room and everyone's eyes lit up like the Lord himself had walked in the door.

'Ti-Jean!' cried Pearl, standing up and embracing him. 'I didn't know if you were going to make it. I got a plate warming in the oven for you, but you sit down and help yourself to what's on the table.'

Everyone else greeted Ti-Jean, then Joseph directed him towards me. 'This is Jewel, Leroy's lady friend,' he said, then said to me, 'Ti-Jean is my eldest son.'

The flicker of surprise that had initially crossed Ti-Jean's face now became a frown. He flashed a look at Leroy as if to say, *What are you doing bringing a white woman into this house?* Although it deflated me after the warm welcome I'd received from the rest of the family, I understood it. As soon as Ti-Jean had arrived, I'd recognised him. He'd been the leader of the three men who'd sat in the 'Whites Only' section at Avery's Ice Cream Parlor. Although he wouldn't have recognised me, dressed as I was as Jewel, his disapproval was understandable after the treatment he'd received from the white people at the parlour.

The conversation for the remainder of the meal was civilised, despite the hostile glances Ti-Jean sent in my direction. Bunny filled me in on some of Leroy's childhood pranks, including climbing to the highest branch in the pecan tree and getting stuck; and Alma talked about how she stole out of the house with her late husband when they were engaged to listen to jazz in Storyville. It was only when the table was cleared and we'd retired to the garden for some coffee and coconut cake that Ti-Jean finally exploded.

'You trying to raise yourself in society by bringing a white girl home?' he said to Leroy. 'Isn't a coloured girl good enough for you?'

Leroy bristled. 'Mind yourself, Ti-Jean!' he said, a growl of warning in his tone.

'Your brother's right, Ti-Jean,' said Joseph sternly.

'Jewel is a guest in our home and you'd better treat her with respect.'

My face twitched and I wanted to cry. I'd been feeling so welcomed by Leroy's family and I wanted to be liked and accepted by them. Despite his attitude towards me, I could see why the family looked up to Ti-Jean: something in his manner commanded attention. I didn't want him to turn the rest of the family against me.

'There's nothing wrong with having white blood,' piped up Bunny. 'Plenty of advantages if you do. Sometimes, for the fun of it, I ride in the white section of the streetcar and drink from the 'Whites Only' fountains. People aren't sure whether to tell me off or not because I look more Mediterranean than coloured. I'm often mistaken for a Spanish Creole.'

Alma nodded to me. 'This family's got white blood in it anyhow. My daddy was a plantation owner. My mama was a housemaid. You get the picture.'

Yes, I did and I hated it. The liberties plantation owners took with their servants, even the married ones, were horrific. Even more so because once the coloured servant was discovered to be pregnant, the plantation owner's wife would send her off, often to a place with worse conditions.

'Bunny,' Ti-Jean said, 'wouldn't it be better if you could sit wherever you wished and drink from whatever fountain you wanted to? Wouldn't it be better if in order to do those things you didn't have to pass yourself as white?'

The awkwardness the others had tried to dissipate returned. Leroy clenched his fists. I would have hated to be the cause of a fight. I could have told the truth then and there about my privileged background and let the Thezans decide for themselves what they wanted to about me, but I desired so much to be loved and approved of by them. Maman always said that the best way to break tension was to tell a good story and my propensity for telling stories got the better of me.

'I know all about passing,' I said to Ti-Jean. 'I live as a white, but my great-grandmother was a quadroon.'

A hush fell over the gathering and all eyes turned to me.

'That's right,' I said. 'Like Alma, she was born to a French plantation owner and a mulatto servant. But the servant died in childbirth, and little Claudine was so pretty and fair that the childless plantation owner's wife took her as her own. The only reason we know about it was that when Claudine was grown, her birth mother's sister urged her to remember her mother and her heritage, even when passing as white.'

'Lord have mercy!' said Alma, rubbing her knees. 'I thought you did have a little colour in you. I can usually tell.'

Leroy regarded me with a curious expression, no doubt wondering why I hadn't told him this story before.

Eleanor pointed her finger at Ti-Jean. 'That's what you get for making assumptions. Of course Jewel's got to pass herself as lily white to work in that exclusive club. How else is she going to make a living?'

Ti-Jean tugged at his earlobe and looked contrite. I felt ashamed but tried not to show it. There I was, Vivienne de Villeray, descended from a line of French aristocrats, passing myself off to these good people as the great-granddaughter of a quadroon maid.

'You got to excuse our Ti-Jean,' said Pearl, patting my hand. 'He didn't mean to be rude. He's active in the National Association for the Advancement of Colored People and he takes things more seriously than the rest of us. I don't want the schools to desegregate. I don't want coloured children to learn white people's ways.'

'Oh, I do,' said Bunny, 'I want the schools to desegregate. Each time Darlene gets a secondhand book at school with a white child's name written in the front, she cries and wants to know why God didn't make her good enough to get new books too.'

I recalled what Mrs Lalande had said about how giving coloured people inferior facilities was a hindrance to them getting the same level of education as white people. That day at the house in the Garden District felt like centuries ago. I hadn't thought about the Lalande family for a long time. Kitty had called a few times to see if I wanted to play tennis again, but I'd always found an excuse not to. She'd eventually stopped calling.

The sun faded and the air turned cold. It was time for me to go home to have dinner with Maman before I left for the club. Leroy walked me to the gate; it was still too light for him to accompany me all the way back to Chartres Street.

'My family likes you,' he said.

I grimaced. 'Not Ti-Jean.'

Leroy shoved his hands into his pockets and lowered his voice. 'Oh, don't worry about him. He's mad at the world because he came top in his class at law school but he can't get a job. Still, under that stony exterior lies a warm heart. When you get to know him, you'll see.'

'I admire him joining the NAACP,' I said. 'He doesn't want things to be different; he wants to *make* them different. What about you, Leroy? Don't you want things to change too?'

'Of course I do, but I got another way of going about it. I'm proud of who I am and what I do. When I meet a white man I look him straight in the eye, not to intimidate him, but to say, I believe you're a good man and I'm a good man too. We should respect each other. I believe each white man I encounter goes away thinking a little differently about coloured men because of the way I act. Mama always says you catch more flies with honey than you do with vinegar.'

Leroy's gentle strength was one of the many things I loved about him. I wished I had his patience but I didn't.

'Don't you wish things would change faster ... for us? So we don't always have to hide?'

He looked at me hopefully. 'Is it true you've got coloured blood in you?'

By law, only one drop of Negro blood would make me coloured, no matter how white I appeared to be. If I was 'coloured', nobody could stop me and Leroy from getting married, although we'd still suffer harassment because I looked pure white.

I shook my head. 'I only said that because I thought it would make it easier on your family. Every time I see the happy couples who come to the club, to dance and dine together, it stings me that you and I can't do that. Don't you think about our future, Leroy?'

He looked at me tenderly and brushed his fingers against my cheek. 'I love you and you love me and that's all that matters for now. Let's be as we are and let life give us the answer.'

By the time winter arrived, I'd earned enough from dancing at the Vieux Carré to pay the River Road

Sanatorium in full. I set my mind to getting our apartment back, and asked Sam for his advice.

'That low-down scum,' he said, after he'd listened to my story. 'I can get your title deed back and I can fix that uncle of yours.'

I was touched that Sam had protective feelings towards me, but I declined his offer. 'All I want is the title deed back — and in my name this time. Then if you can help me speak to the bank about paying the mortgage in monthly instalments, I'd appreciate it.'

He nodded approvingly. 'You've got a practical head on your shoulders, Jewel. If you weren't a woman, I'd have you as one of my associates.'

'Thank you,' I said, rising from the chair. 'But I think I'll stick to dancing.'

He laughed. 'You need anything, you see me, all right? You've been good to me, Jewel, and I'll be good to you. Remember that.'

When I rose the next day, I found Maman out on the gallery watering the ferns. A bone-chilling damp hung in the air.

'Maman, you've got to stay inside over the winter,' I told her, guiding her back into the sitting room. 'You can't afford to get a respiratory infection.'

'But I get bored,' she protested. 'You're young and out and about. I miss you.'

Apart from the elaborate breakfast we shared on Sunday mornings before I set off to visit Leroy's family on the pretence that I was visiting Adalie de Pauger, I had been neglecting her. It wasn't that I didn't want to be with her, but all the to-ing and fro-ing from the club to home left me exhausted. Although it was going to mean less time for napping at Chartres Street, I committed myself to reading to Maman for an hour every day before I left.

We started then and there with Mark Twain's *Adventures of Huckleberry Finn*, which had been one of my childhood favourites. But now as I read it, I saw things as an adult that I hadn't before, like the hypocrisy of slavery. Maman, however, was riveted.

'Thank you, my darling,' she said when we'd finished for the day. 'That was the most enjoyable hour I've spent in a long time.'

'I'm sorry I've been busy,' I told her.

She smiled and took my hand. 'It pleases me that you're enjoying your life, Ruby. You are doing exactly what I would want you to do. But tell me, do you have any beaus?'

Her question had me squirming in my seat. How was I going to answer?

Fortunately, Mae came into the room to remind Maman that it was time for her massage. She helped her up from her chair and the way Maman wobbled on her feet made my heart ache. Although she had improved, she was not strong and never would be.

Maman's greatest wish was to see me married and happy before she died. But how could I ever reconcile the two worlds I now lived in? My life was a fantasy, but I knew reality wouldn't leave me alone for long. It had a way of seeking a person out and wresting her from her dreams.

After we'd worked our way through the books we had in the apartment, Maman said she'd like a mystery novel for a change. On my way to Chartres Street I stopped by a bookstore on Canal Street. I was studying the bestsellers in the store window when something in the reflection caught my eye. I turned to see a coloured girl about six years old standing behind me. She was smartly dressed in a checked cape-collar dress and Mary Jane shoes.

She pointed to the sign in the shop window and read aloud, 'No col-o-reds.' She tilted her head and considered me with curious eyes. 'What does that mean? *No col-o-reds?*'

My stomach flipped. The street was full of signs like that, telling coloured folks that they could look at but not try on clothes or hats, couldn't use the toilets, or couldn't eat at the same end of the lunch counter as white people. All those instructions conspired to send the message that Negroes were inferior. The girl folded her hands in front of her and waited politely for my answer. I bit my lip. How could I tell this innocent child, beginning to find her place in the world, that 'col-o-reds' meant her? Before I had a chance to think what to say, the girl's mother arrived and grabbed her hand.

'Lakisha, why did you wander off like that? You nearly gave me a heart attack!' The woman glanced at me nervously. 'I hope she wasn't bothering you?'

'Not at all,' I said. 'She's charming.'

The woman hoisted Lakisha onto her hip and I watched the two of them hurry down the street.

The bookstore clerk came out and asked if I was interested in anything in the window. I shook my head and walked away. The man I loved and his family suffered the indignity of being treated as inferior every day of their lives. If they weren't welcome in that store, I wasn't going to give them my money. It was then that I noticed Lakisha's mother had dropped a piece of paper. It was a pamphlet. I picked it up and read: *Urban League of New Orleans. Meeting Tomorrow.* That was the organisation that had been formed to better the lives of coloured people. The meeting was to take place in Ursulines Avenue. Out of curiosity, I decided to go after I'd finished reading to Maman.

The next day, I turned up at the meeting and was surprised to see nearly a hundred people gathered there. From the conversations taking place around me, I discovered they were an eclectic mix: priests, rabbis, coloured teachers and social reformers, university students, Jewish housewives, and a few Uptown ladies. While it wasn't illegal for coloured and white to be under the same roof as long as they were segregated, it was highly subversive for everyone to be sitting mingled like this, looking for all the world like a bag of mixed marbles instead of a well-ordered chess game.

I noticed Lakisha's mother and approached her. 'I'm Vivienne de Villeray,' I said, holding out my hand. 'Your little girl stopped to speak to me yesterday on Canal Street.'

The woman took my hand. 'And I'm Renette Fabre. It's a pleasure to make your acquaintance, Miss de Villeray. Lakisha's at that age when she's curious about the world. She wants to know how everything works and why certain things are so.'

'My mother often says that I never grew out of that stage.'

Renette laughed. 'Well, maybe that's not such a bad thing. I guess that's why we're here, aren't we? We're the people who haven't stopped asking why.'

Renette and I took seats next to each other and I recalled the night I'd forced Mae to join me in the dining room and how uncomfortable she'd been. It was going to take a lot of us to be willing to make ourselves uncomfortable before anything could change.

I glanced over my shoulder at the other people who were arriving for the meeting and my heart dropped when Clifford Lalande walked in with his mother and sister. Kitty waved wildly when she spotted me, and nudged Clifford in the ribs. His eyebrows rose in surprise and then he beamed at me. I returned the smile but his appearance meant my anticipation of the meeting was now tempered by the awkwardness of the situation. Clifford and Jackie would be married already, although there was no sign of her. I couldn't forget the humiliation of that day at the tennis court when I'd realised Clifford was not interested in me.

The seats in the section where I was sitting were all taken so the Lalandes made their way to the opposite row. Mrs Lalande mouthed a 'hello' to me before sitting down.

The first speaker was Joan Fischer, the daughter of a well-to-do businessman. She stood at the podium and explained how she'd become involved in the Civil Rights Movement.

'My husband fought in Europe and returned with stories of the genocide there. That furthered my own belief that racism is the greatest threat to human progress,' she said in her lilting society accent. 'Those of us living Uptown think we know coloured people and what they want, but we don't. If you talk only to your cook or your gardener, do you truly think those who rely on your goodwill are going to tell you about their real troubles and aspirations? Coloured people are not content with their lot and nor should they be. The median income for a coloured family is half that of a white family in this city, and it's near impossible to improve oneself when you are forced to attend inferior, segregated schools. The only way to even begin to start knowing each other is to mix with each other in all areas of life. Let's start with the new generation, our children. Let them grow up side by side as equals, knowing each other for the fellow human beings they are. That is where our hope for the future lies.'

The audience responded with applause. The coloured chairman announced that the next speaker would be Clifford Lalande. 'But before Mr Lalande comes to the podium,' the chairman said, 'on behalf of the committee, I would like to express our condolences to the Lalande family. Their much loved patriarch, Stanton Lalande, passed away after a short illness six weeks ago. Stanton Lalande helped to organise this chapter of the Urban League. He was a great civic leader and a loyal friend, and he will be sorely missed. We are grateful that his son has joined us today to take his place.'

I glanced at the Lalandes and felt sorry for their loss. I thought of the lovely Southern gentleman I had met outside Antoine's Restaurant with Clifford, and how he had kindly comforted me regarding Maman's illness.

Clifford adjusted his tie and cleared his throat before stepping up to the podium. After thanking the chairman and the committee for their words regarding his father, he began his speech.

'Mrs Fischer is correct when she says that change must begin within our school system and that is the hard road ahead for us,' he said, looking around the audience. 'Ever since the Brown versus Board of Education case, the Orleans Parish School Board has done everything in its power — by legal or quasi-legal activities — to prevent the desegregation of schools. The State of Louisiana, going against Federal rulings, has voted to cut off funding to schools that desegregate and to deny admission to State universities to those students who have attended desegregated schools. Newspaper men and community leaders who have taken a stand for desegregation, including myself, Mrs Fischer and Rabbi Feibelman, have found ourselves branded communists and have received threatening letters and telephone calls.

'As we work together to win the hearts and minds of our fellow New Orleanians, I believe it is necessary for us to combat the Orleans Parish School Board with legal action, including class actions by parents. The NAACP has been successful in legal actions such as achieving the desegregation of the law school, graduate school and nursing schools at Louisiana State University. It is my belief that we also must use legal means to force change.'

Along with the questions from the audience, the meeting ran for nearly an hour. When it finished, I realised I'd have to rush to Chartres Street to get any sleep before Leroy arrived. I was torn between approaching the Lalandes to express my sympathy for their loss and my need to hurry. Then the awkwardness of speaking to them at all overcame me, and I decided to leave and send them a condolence card later. I was making my way to the door when I felt a tap on my arm. I turned around to see Clifford standing next to me. 'Ruby, what a pleasant surprise to see you here.'

'Your speech was very moving,' I told him. 'Your father would have been proud.'

'Thank you,' he said, pausing for a moment before continuing. 'My father was always active; I never would have thought he could catch pneumonia and pass away so quickly. But his final request to Mother, Kitty and myself was to carry on, and that's what we are trying to do.'

It must have taken some courage for Clifford to deliver that speech in his father's place. Given the circumstances, it seemed odd that Jackie had not come to the meeting to support him. But that wasn't the only strange thing. It was the way Clifford was looking at me so intensely. A married man should not be gazing at another woman as if she was the only person in the room.

'Would you like to join my family for lunch at our house?' Clifford asked, his amiable smile returning to his face. 'I'm curious to know all about what you've been up to.'

Perhaps it would have been kind of me to go, but I felt too uneasy. It was possible Clifford was simply being polite, but a gnawing feeling told me otherwise.

'I'm sorry,' I said, 'I'm in a hurry to get home. I read to my mother every afternoon and she'll be waiting for me.'

It was a lie, of course. I'd already read to Maman for that day. I'd forgotten that he wasn't easily deterred.

'Well, let me walk you home,' he said. 'It will give me a chance to catch up with you and hear your thoughts about desegregation.'

'But don't you have to join your family for lunch?'

He shrugged. 'Oh, it's a very casual affair. Anyone who has attended the meeting is welcome to drop in to our place afterwards for a buffet luncheon.'

I couldn't let him walk me to Chartres Street. I decided I would hold a cordial conversation with him for the walk back to our apartment in Royal Street and then leave it at that. I could go on to Chartres Street from there.

'All right,' I said.

A cold wind was blowing up from the river and we tugged our coat collars up around our mouths and ears. It made conversation difficult, which I was thankful for, because the reason I was interested in desegregation was because I wanted to be with Leroy. Clifford kept bumping into me on the narrow banquette, so he stepped behind me and put his hand gently on my back to steady me.

'Here it is,' I said, when we reached my apartment building.

'It must be exciting living in the Quarter,' he said, looking around. 'The Garden District is so quiet. You hardly see anybody on the street — except for the occasional pretty tour guide.'

I swallowed. It was obvious he was looking for an excuse to prolong our conversation but I had to get away. Why had a man who was married insisted on walking me home? It felt cruel, considering his recent bereavement, but if he was entertaining any idea that we could have more than a friendly acquaintance, it needed to be stopped.

I was about to wish him well and go inside when Maman stepped out onto the gallery with only a shawl around her shoulders. She looked down and her eyes widened.

'Ruby!' she cried, lifting her hand to her throat in a gesture of guilt. 'I expected you back —'

I knew she was going to say 'later', but Clifford interrupted before she had a chance to finish. 'I'm the reason she's late back, ma'am. I insisted that she chat with me.'

'It's cold today. Why don't you come up for some coffee?' she said, all aflutter at the sight of her unmarried daughter standing next to an attractive man. I could only imagine how Clifford appeared to Maman with his clean-cut features, his fine clothes and his charismatic smile.

I wondered what he must have been thinking when I led him up the stairs to our apartment. I'd made improvements with the money I'd earned at the club, but the cobblestones were slimy, the garden overgrown and the brickwork needed painting. It was all tumbledown compared to his orderly house in the Garden District. 'Do come in,' said Maman, who, in the short interim between me and Clifford making our way from the street to the apartment, had managed to spray rose perfume in the air and pull her hair into a fetching chignon. The quiet atmosphere of our apartment was transformed, with Beethoven playing on the record player and the smell of baking coming from the kitchen.

'Maman, this is Clifford Lalande,' I told her.

'I'm very pleased to meet you, Mr Lalande,' said Maman, inviting him to take the best seat in the parlour: a French oak carver chair that I'd only managed to buy back from the pawn shop the previous week, along with the faded Aubusson sofa that Maman and I sat on together.

'What is it you do with yourself, Mr Lalande, when you are not accompanying my daughter home?' Maman asked him.

Our French ancestors had been petite people and the carver chair was too low for Clifford's long legs. He crossed them and then uncrossed them in an effort to get comfortable. But nothing could erase his affable smile. 'I'm a lawyer. I work in my family's firm.'

'So you must have graduated from Louisiana State University?'

'That's right. Like my daddy and granddaddy before me.'

Maman emitted a gasp of delight. 'Was your grandfather Judge Lalande by any chance? I believe I met him once, a long time ago when I was a young woman.'

'Indeed he was,' answered Clifford.

She smoothed her dress in a way that indicated she was impressed. Southern people didn't feel comfortable with a new acquaintance until they'd uncovered at least one person they knew in common. Seeing Maman in action reminded me how much she enjoyed social nuances and connections, and how much her illness and my father's extravagant lifestyle had taken from her.

'He spoke perfect French,' Clifford said. 'I bet he wanted to speak only French with you? He was very proud of it.'

'Yes, I believe he did!' said Maman with a girlish smile. 'And do you speak French too?'

'I wish,' he replied, glancing in my direction. 'But I guess there's always time to learn ... if I can find the right person to teach me.'

I fidgeted with my sleeve cuff. If he'd dropped a hint like that when I'd first met him, I would have been walking on air. But now, under the current circumstances, I only wanted to flee from the room and hide.

Mae entered pushing a trolley with a coffee pot and cups and almond madeleines fresh from the oven. While Mae served Clifford, Maman flashed a look at me. Despite her outward appearance of graceful calm, I knew her mind was ticking over. Her eyes shifted to Clifford's left hand and she smiled to herself when she saw he wasn't wearing a wedding band. I was curious about the lack of a ring too. Jackie Fausey hadn't struck me as the kind of woman who would wait.

'And what will you be doing with yourself this winter, Mr Lalande?' Maman asked after Mae had left.

'Well, of course there are all the activities around Mardi Gras. My mother always organises charity events and my sister was the Queen of Carnival a few years ago.'

Maman's eyes almost popped out of her head. 'Oh, Ruby loves Mardi Gras! You must promise you'll take her to see the parade with your dear sister. I've always loved it too, but unfortunately due to my health I can't stay out in the cold.'

'It would be our pleasure,' said Clifford, glancing at me. 'My sister is very fond of Ruby.'

Maman described the Mardi Gras balls of her youth, the parades of the king, queen and court, the dance call-outs and the elaborate midnight suppers. I glanced at the clock on the mantelpiece. There would be no time for sleep now. Leroy would be waiting for me at Chartres Street.

Fortunately, Clifford himself realised the time. 'I'm sorry but I'm going to have to leave your charming company, Mrs de Villeray,' he said. 'I have an appointment Uptown with a client.'

Maman rose with him to show him to the door. 'I receive visitors every Tuesday morning,' she said. 'Please do come and see us again.'

We hadn't 'received' visitors for years, and not with any regularity on a Tuesday and certainly not without a formal invitation first. I knew exactly what Maman was hinting at.

After Clifford had left, she turned to me, her face glowing. 'Ruby, you sly girl,' she said in a teasing tone.

'So you do have a beau!' She touched my cheek tenderly. 'Is it because he's American and not a Creole that you were afraid to tell me?' She put her arms around me. 'You shouldn't have been worried. Times have changed and we must change with them. Those sorts of delineations don't mean so much any more. I only want someone for you who will make you happy and take good care of you. He's a lovely well-mannered man and he couldn't tear his eyes away from you. And he is the grandson of Judge Lalande.'

'Maman,' I said, breaking away, 'I'm keeping Adalie waiting. I have to go.'

She gave me a fond look, then kissed me lightly on top of my head. 'All right, Ruby, I know you don't want to be late for your friend.'

I thought of Leroy waiting for me at Chartres Street, wondering where I was. I rushed down the stairs and into the street, all my insides quivering. I had a terrible feeling that things were about to get complicated.

TWENTY

Ruby

The following Tuesday, after we'd finished our reading for the day, Maman and I sat in the parlour together taking turns to furtively glance at the clock. She was hoping that Clifford Lalande would come calling, while I, my jaw clenched tight and guilt coursing through me, hoped that he wouldn't. Mae had been sent to the exclusive French patisserie across the street for some petits choux with Chantilly cream.

It was impossible for me to leave for Chartres Street now, not even using Adalie as an excuse. Maman was a gentle soul until she heard the sound of wedding bells; then she developed an iron will. In her mind, a female friend would understand being kept waiting if a beau had come to call.

An hour passed and I was about to get up to leave when a knock at the door had both of us nearly leaping out of our skins. Mae went to answer it and I heard Clifford greeting her. I didn't dare look at Maman. If he'd come a second time, then he was here because he was interested in me. Our shabby apartment and reduced circumstances hadn't deterred him. Being pursued by Clifford was a dream for Ruby, but a nightmare for Jewel. My compartmentalised life only worked as long as everybody stayed in their place.

Clifford sent me an adoring smile when Mae showed him into the parlour. He was carrying a table arrangement of fuchsia pink camellias, which he handed to Maman. 'My sister picked them,' he explained. 'I think camellias look striking in a winter garden — and in the hair of Southern beauties.'

Maman brought her hand to her face. 'I'm positively charmed. What a thoughtful gesture.'

She placed the arrangement on the bureau and the three of us sat down. Mae discreetly left a coffee tray on the table in front of us and left. I did my best to remain composed, but so many worries were rushing through my mind I was sure I was about to suffer a seizure. Now it was certain that Clifford was coming courting, how could I discourage him in a way that wouldn't arouse suspicion in Maman? It would be inexplicable if I turned down an eligible young man when no-one else was pursuing me. I was also terrified that Clifford would mention the Urban League meeting. Maman would then suspect I'd been going to all the meetings and hadn't been visiting Adalie at all. One telephone call to Adalie and all would come undone. I was like a rudderless boat bobbing hopelessly towards a plunging waterfall.

Clifford noticed my discomfort and when Maman excused herself to take a telephone call from Doctor Monfort, he seized the opportunity to confide in me.

'Ruby, I would like to explain to you what happened between me and Miss Jackie Fausey that resulted in the breaking of our engagement.'

He may as well have stuck me with a prod I got up from my seat so fast. I busied myself pouring the coffee. 'Oh, there's no need,' I said. Of course I was dying of curiosity about what had happened with Jackie, but I also knew that intimacies shared would only increase his sense of a bond with me.

'I don't want there to be things weighing between us,' he said, looking at me in an enamoured way that caused me to swallow hard. 'Jackie and I have been friends since childhood. She was a tomboy and we climbed trees and flew kites together, and it seemed the most natural thing in the world that we would grow up and marry each other. But as we got older, we changed and wanted different things. In the end, my beliefs were something we could never agree upon and we felt it was best to part ways.'

I passed him a cup of coffee and sat back down, resigned to the fact that there was no way to escape this awkward situation. 'You mean your beliefs about equal rights for Negroes?' I asked.

'Indeed,' sighed Clifford, rubbing his knees. 'I don't blame her, of course. We were starting to be left off invitation lists. No young woman wants to be the wife of a social pariah. Besides that, her father and I clashed. When the Federal Government ordered New Orleans to desegregate its schools, Judge Fausey urged white parents to fight the order by moving their children to private schools.'

I looked directly at him for the first time that visit. He was a good man who wanted to help coloured people. I thought of Leroy and his family and I couldn't help but be grateful that there were some white people who viewed them as deserving of the same dignity as everyone else.

'The ones I find most disgusting are not the ignorant rednecks — they don't know any better,' Clifford continued. 'It's the legal men who use their education and social advantages to create legislative proposals to keep the coloured people down. It's those men I want to fight. The rednecks will go in whatever direction the wind is blowing.' He paused and rubbed his hands. 'It's a special woman who can admire a man for his beliefs and not only his social standing.'

I knew what he was hinting at. Since I had attended the Urban League meeting, he assumed that I was as passionate about civil rights as he was.

I stared at my hands. The men in my family had been so unreliable it was impossible to trust them. Clifford was a courageous man and a principled one. If when I had met him earlier he'd been free, I wouldn't be working as a stripper. But falling in love with Leroy had changed everything.

'From what you describe it sounds like the race situation in New Orleans is getting worse,' I said.

'Things are worse all right,' he replied grimly. 'New Orleans has always had the reputation of being tolerant, but the Brown versus Board of Education ruling has stirred things up. Normally reasonable people have been convinced that coloured men think of nothing else but impregnating white women. Instead of focussing on equality of education and moving both races forward, the debate has been hijacked into a panic about the survival of the white race. Even the more liberal-minded citizens abhor the idea of miscegenation.'

'They only abhor it one way,' I said bitterly. 'White men have been impregnating coloured women for centuries.'

Maman returned, and Clifford and I exchanged a glance. Politics was not a topic for her and I was touched when he understood that and turned the conversation to the more pleasant subject of the upcoming carnival season.

'When I was young I loved the floats and the magnificent costumes, but most of all I loved the masquerade balls,' Maman said. 'How delicious to hide your identity for one magical night!'

Clifford smiled. 'Well, you are braver than I am, Mrs de Villeray. As a child I found the costumes and masks terrifying. One year my parents hosted a party at our home. I was supposed to be in bed, but I snuck out and screamed when I saw the people in masks. When they took off their disguises to try and comfort me it made my fear even worse. I couldn't understand why my parents and their friends would pretend to be other people.'

Clifford and Maman laughed, but I was stung. Hiding my true self had become a way of life for me.

'Well, seeing as you can't go out in the damp air, Mrs de Villeray,' Clifford said, 'I propose that I provide the King Cake on January sixth and we have our own celebration here.'

Maman's eyes lit up. 'Oh, that would be wonderful!' she said, clapping her hands. 'How thoughtful you are. Yes, you bring the cake and Ruby and I will do the decorations.'

Clifford and Maman made their plans while I listened with apprehension. The more Maman became enchanted by Clifford, the less I'd ever be able to speak up.

After he'd left, Maman frowned at me. 'Ruby, you do like Clifford Lalande, don't you? Because he is very taken with you. The fact that he came here today is a sign of that.'

'Yes, of course I like him,' I said, unable to meet her gaze.

She lifted my chin until I was looking directly into her eyes. 'What is it, Ruby? Lately I feel like you've become a stranger. It's as if there is someone else living inside your head.'

'Don't say that, Maman!' I told her, frightened by her observation. 'You know I'm your Ruby.'

'But why are you so indifferent towards Clifford? Tell me the truth: is there someone you like better?'

Guilt ate at my bones. There shouldn't be secrets between Maman and me. I wanted everything to go back to how it had been the previous week, before I went to the meeting. I'd had everything in balance then — or so I'd thought. A longing to confess everything took me by surprise. But how could I? The truth would destroy Maman, and it would destroy me.

'I don't want to get hurt,' I told her instead, biting my lip.

The tense expression on her face dissolved into a smile. 'Well, that's natural enough. But Clifford is an honourable man. I don't think he's playing with your feelings. By all means go slowly, but don't be so cold you put him off.'

'Why don't I go after him now?' I said, walking to the closet to get my coat. 'He couldn't have gotten very far. I'll make as if I couldn't wait to tell him some detail about the party we're planning. He'll feel special that way.'

'Oh, yes,' she said. 'Go do that, Ruby.'

I hummed a cheerful tune as I went out the door but my insides were churning. I ran along Royal Street and spotted Clifford turning into Canal Street.

'Clifford!' I called. The air was chilly and steam blew from my mouth.

He turned, his face breaking into a delighted grin. 'Ruby!'

'Can I wait for the streetcar with you?' I asked. 'I want to speak to you alone.'

'I'm surprised your mother let you come after me without a chaperone. She's so charmingly old-world Creole.' He chuckled. 'I'd be delighted for you to keep me company — there's something I want to ask you. I've been invited to a ball and I would be honoured if you'd come as my partner.'

My breath caught in my throat. A Mardi Gras ball! That would have been Ruby's big dream. But I couldn't. When Maman had said I was becoming a stranger, she was right. I was less and less Ruby and more and more Jewel. And Jewel loved another man.

'Ruby, what is it?'

'Clifford, I have something to tell you. I'd love to come to the ball with you, but I can't.'

The St Charles Avenue streetcar arrived but Clifford ignored it. He stared at me with a confused expression. 'You can't?'

My intention had been to come clean with him. I still cared for him and I didn't want to lead him on. But how could I explain everything about my double life while standing in line for the streetcar? Instead, I gave him a partial version.

'You see, I work at night. Maman doesn't know. She thinks we're living off family money. But there is no family money. I work to keep the roof over our heads and to pay Maman's medical bills.'

If the situation wasn't so awful, the astonished expression on Clifford's face would have been comical.

'Where do you work?' he asked.

I lowered my gaze. 'At the telephone exchange.'

'At night?'

'It has to be at night,' I said, rubbing my hands against the cold. 'I have to sneak out after Maman's gone to bed. She doesn't think a lady should work — but I had no choice. She would have died if I didn't find the money for her operation.'

I raised my eyes. At first my confession rendered Clifford speechless. Then a smile slowly appeared on his face. 'Ruby, are you ever going to stop amazing me? What you're doing for your mother ... well, it's wonderful!'

I wondered if Clifford was ever going to stop amazing me! 'You think so?' I asked doubtfully.

'Yes, it's courageous to take matters into your own hands!' he said, touching my shoulder. 'And the exchange won't give you even one night off during Mardi Gras?'

'It's the busiest time of the year. The town is full to the brim with tourists.'

My explanation was technically true, if you transferred it from the telephone exchange to the Vieux Carré Club. Mardi Gras *was* our busiest time of the year and I was expected to do several routines a night.

'Well, I understand your position,' he said in a reassuring tone. 'But if you can't come to the ball, then please come to my family's open house on parade day and bring your mother. My mother and Kitty are always asking after you.'

Clifford's understanding about everything made it difficult to refuse. 'I'll come,' I said, 'but I can't bring Maman. She mustn't go out in the cold at all. Thank you for the offer of the King Cake celebration. That made her very happy.'

Another streetcar arrived and Clifford squeezed my arm. 'Everything I learn about you makes me admire you more,' he said. Then he leaned closer and whispered in my ear, 'I knew the moment I met you that I could never marry Jackie. But out of respect for her feelings, I can't be too open until an appropriate amount of time has passed. But soon, you won't have to work at the telephone exchange any more. You and your mother will be well taken care of.'

He stepped onto the streetcar and waved to me before taking a seat. I waved back numbly, too surprised to think of any other response. The meaning of Clifford's words had been clear: he intended to propose. I'd attempted to dig myself out of a hole and had only dug myself in deeper.

New Orleans buzzed with anticipation as tourists joined the locals for the most exciting event of the year. Sam had the club decorated in the traditional colours of green, gold and purple. Pennant banners hung from the ceiling, and the tables were adorned with fleur-de-lis runners. I laughed when I saw the waiters dressed in harlequin outfits.

Miss Hanley put me through my paces. 'This has to be the best show yet,' she told me and Leroy during rehearsals. 'We have to exceed everything else we've done so far.'

The regular velvet curtain was replaced with one fashioned out of silver Mardi Gras beads, and I would be dancing to classics like 'Wild Cat', 'Heebie Jeebies' and 'New Orleans Blues'. My costumes were magnificent. My favourite was a red ball gown with a ruffled organza skirt and beaded bodice. Underneath I wore a matching strapless bra and rhinestone G-string.

The stagehands applauded me when I stepped out under the lights for the dress rehearsal.

'It's brilliant!' said Sam, approaching the stage. 'Jewel, you are more splendid than the Queen of Carnival herself!'

Indeed, the costumes, the decorations and the music all combined to give me a sense of arrival that I'd never felt as Vivienne de Villeray the debutante. It was as if I was finally who I was truly meant to be: Jewel.

Because of the weight of the fabric, the fastenings were more complicated and I had to practise getting out of the gown several times.

I wasn't bothered by the lighting men and stagehands seeing me dance, but more frequently Jimmy the barman came in early during the rehearsals. He was supposedly checking stocks, but he never seemed to be doing so when I performed. He'd stand in front of the bar, arms crossed, and stare at me with eyes that were cold and flat. It made my blood turn to ice.

'Jimmy gives me the creeps,' I confided in Annie as she helped me change costumes in the dressing room. 'He glares at me like he's thinking about killing me.'

'I've noticed the way he looks at you too,' she said. 'He tried to tell me once that you shouldn't be talking to Leroy the way you do.'

My skin prickled. Leroy and I were constantly on guard to avoid suspicion at the club. We made eye contact but not too much eye contact; we never touched each other; and we never allowed ourselves to be alone together for more than a minute. It took discipline and a good memory, but we did it because the cost of discovery was too high.

I turned to face Annie. 'What did he mean by that?'

'With respect,' she said innocently, laying out my jewellery for the next routine, 'it's obvious Jimmy doesn't approve of a white dancer being accompanied by a coloured band.'

I turned back to the dressing table so she wouldn't see the relief on my face. 'Who cares what he thinks? If Sam approves, it's got nothing to do with him.'

She placed her hand on my shoulder. 'I'll speak to Sam if you like,' she said. 'If that jerk's turning you off your performance, he'll get rid of him. Plenty of barmen in this town. Only one Jewel!'

Later, after the show, when Leroy met me in the room in Chartres Street, I pushed him into a chair and then strutted around him, modelling the red strapless bra and G-string.

'I thought I'd do away with the superfluous dress,' I said, swinging my hips, 'and just get down to business.'

He watched me, grinning widely, before he grabbed my hips and brought me to a stop in front of him. 'You might dance in front of other men,' he said, kissing my stomach and pulling me onto his lap, 'but only think of me, all right?'

I rubbed my cheek against his forehead. 'I always think only of you.' I curled up against him and looked around the room. 'The best days of my life are the ones I've spent here.'

'The best days *so far*, you mean,' he said, caressing my face.

'The best days *so far*,' I repeated, running my hands through his hair and pulling him into a long kiss.

After we'd made love, I lay in Leroy's arms while he dozed and watched the dawn appear through the window. I traced my finger along his firm chest and fantasised about what it would be like to have a normal relationship, where we could hold hands without fear, or go grocery shopping or walk in the park as if it was a natural thing for a coloured man and a white woman to be doing. I thought about Jimmy, and how he didn't even know Leroy; he simply hated him because of his colour.

Reluctantly I removed myself from Leroy's embrace and dressed. There was always a sweet joy when we met and a nagging torment when we had to part.

Leroy opened his eyes and smiled sleepily at me. 'Is it that time already?'

'We're like vampires,' I said. 'We disappear with the sunrise.'

He sat up and looked at me tentatively. 'I heard that Jimmy got fired last night. He wasn't too happy about it.'

'I'm glad,' I said, slipping into my shoes. 'He's not right in the head.'

Leroy stood and tugged on his pants. 'Be careful, Jewel. When he left he said he was going to get even. Sam didn't give you as the reason for firing him, but I think it's pretty obvious. Everybody's noticed the odd way he's been staring at you.'

'Why didn't you mention it last night?' I asked, slipping on my coat.

'I didn't want to spoil the evening. And I needed to think about what to do. When you finish at the club, don't leave too far ahead of me. I'll walk a distance behind you where I can still see you. All right?'

'You really think he's dangerous?'

Leroy nodded. 'He's like one of those white supremacist hicks that are always threatening Ti-Jean. You never know what they might do.'

'All right,' I said, moving to his side and kissing him. 'You always look out for me, don't you, Leroy?'

He took me in his arms. 'And I always will. You're my precious Jewel.'

The following Sunday when I went to visit Leroy's family, I found the Tremé alive with jazz. From the houses came the sounds of trumpets, clarinets and trombones. People gathered on their stoops to listen. A brass band paraded down Claiborne Avenue with old ladies, housewives and children dancing after it.

I entered the Thezans' garden and a skeleton jumped out of the bushes and growled at me. I screamed and leaped back. Laughter bubbled up from behind a hedge and Bunny and her children bobbed their heads up. I realised the skeleton was a man in a black suit with white bones painted on it. He removed his mask and revealed himself as Gerald, Leroy's brother-in-law.

'Give you a fright?' he asked, grinning at me.

'Heavens!' I said. 'You nearly stopped my heart! You're not supposed to do that until Mardi Gras morning!'

He chuckled. 'We're practising. Come up to the house. The women are cooking up a storm.'

I found Alma, Pearl, Eleanor and Dora in the kitchen enveloped in the bay-leaf-scented steam from pots boiling on the stove. Every bench and table was set up for food preparation. I cast my eyes over the chopped celery and onion, rice, cooked shrimp, corn cobs, bunches of fresh parsley and dried thyme. We were going to have one big feast.

'Leroy's out watching the band. He'll be here in a minute,' Pearl said, kissing me on the cheek. 'Now, Jewel, do you think you can manage the remoulade sauce like I showed you?'

'I'm certain I can,' I assured her.

'Good!' she said with a twinkle of approval in her eyes. ''Cause I'm not having any daughter-in-law who can't even make mayonnaise! Leroy's too skinny as it is.'

My heart sang. I knew that Pearl liked me, but now I understood how much.

I made the sauce, and helped with the corn maque choux too, with a sense of contentment. But as we laid out the table for the meal, a pain pinched my heart. It was only because Pearl believed I was part coloured that she even considered the idea that I might marry Leroy.

I stared out the window at Bunny and the children playing in the garden. If Leroy and I had children they'd be mulatto, and get called anything from mongrels to jiggaboos. It would be humiliating for them. If we were to stay in New Orleans, the only way for me to be with him would be to pass as coloured. It was common knowledge that light-skinned Negroes passed themselves off as white all the time in order to gain privileges and better-paid work. I'd never heard of anyone white passing themselves as coloured. But I'd do it for love. I'd do it for Leroy. But then there was Maman and Mae to consider.

372 • BELINDA ALEXANDRA

My thoughts were interrupted when Leroy arrived with Ti-Jean. I hadn't seen Leroy's brother for a few weeks now. Leroy said he'd been in the country, encouraging coloured people to vote. All of us sat down, and Leroy reached under the table and squeezed my leg. He must have sensed I was downhearted because he kept complimenting everything I'd had some hand in making.

'Mama says you do the seasoning just right for the fried rice,' he whispered to me. 'She says she's got competition! It's not easy to get a compliment out of Mama in regards to food.'

I smiled, touched by his desire to cheer me up.

Usually Ti-Jean ignored me at family lunches but today he was particularly interested in me. 'So what have you been up to lately, Jewel?'

Ti-Jean was university educated. I didn't want him to think of me as some ding-a-ling stripper.

'Well, I went to a meeting of the Urban League,' I replied.

'The lady who supplies our flowers has been going too,' said Alma. 'She says the white folks who attend are real nice.'

'That is a *nice* organisation,' said Ti-Jean. 'Nice white folks and philanthropists trying to help raise us Negroes up in society.'

The sarcasm in his voice stung me like a slap in the face.

Leroy frowned. 'Why are you being so hard on Jewel? She went to a meeting with the idea of making life better for coloured people. You should be happy about that.'

'Well, it's good that some white folks are trying to be helpful,' said Pearl, dishing out the red beans and rice.

'We're all God's children and we should be acting that way. No man higher or lower than another.'

I was grateful to Leroy and Pearl for defending me. It seemed that no matter what I did or said it would never be the right thing by Ti-Jean. Still, I wasn't going to let him get away with being contemptuous of people like Clifford Lalande and his family simply because of *their* colour. They were making personal sacrifices in the name of justice when they could have been gallivanting around and enjoying all their white privileges.

'The leaders are very committed,' I said. 'One of them is a lawyer, Clifford Lalande —'

'I know Clifford Lalande,' interrupted Ti-Jean, mopping up his jambalaya with a piece of bread. 'A nice white boy from a good family.'

I ate a spoonful of rice to hide my surprise and burned my tongue. 'How do you know him?' I asked.

'When I got out of law school he tried to find me a job with an Uptown firm.' Ti-Jean's lip curled with anger. 'The best he could do was a clerk in the mail room. "It will be a foot in the door," he told me. "You can prove your worth once you're in." Funny how a coloured man who excelled with honours has to "prove his worth" whereas a white boy who barely passed can waltz in the door and get his own office.'

I pursed my lips. The favour Ti-Jean was quick to dismiss had most likely cost Clifford a few opportunities of his own. I wanted to defend him, but I was always walking on eggshells with Ti-Jean so I kept quiet. I hadn't explained to Leroy yet that Clifford was coming every Tuesday to visit and I didn't know how to stop him without raising Maman's suspicions.

'Well, you can't hate the man for trying, Ti-Jean,' said Joseph. 'He was doing his best to help you. It's not his fault Louisiana is how it is.'

'You might think Lalande and his colleagues have pure motives, Pa,' retorted Ti-Jean, 'but they're looking out for themselves. They know segregation is costing New Orleans economically and hurting their interests.'

'Well, whatever their motives, the Urban League is nothing like that dreadful White Citizens' Council,' said Eleanor, twisting the head off a crawfish and sucking the flesh from it. 'They're trying to make it impossible for any Negro who tries to vote to hold a job or run a business.'

Milton leaned back in his chair and nodded. 'They got all the aims of the Ku Klux Klan with the veneer of respectability of a church picnic. Yes, I give credit to the Urban League for convincing one hundred white people to sign a petition for the desegregation of schools. But the Citizens' Council got fifteen thousand to sign one against it without even breaking a sweat.'

'It's worse in Mississippi,' said Joseph. 'The planters are forcing their labourers to tear up their poll tax receipts or find themselves off the land.'

'That's white people for you,' said Ti-Jean, sending a nod in my direction. 'They can hang us, burn us, castrate us, shoot us and rape our women and children, but we've got to take it yessing and grinning and shining shoes for a living.'

'Well, you be careful, Ti-Jean,' said Pearl. 'They're collecting the names of NAACP members and putting you all on a watch list along with the communists.'

Leroy frowned. 'Be careful too, Jewel. They'll probably do the same with the Urban League members. You could find yourself on a blacklist.'

I ate a mouthful of the corn maque choux. It was flavourful and seasoned just right, but it left a bitter taste in my mouth that had nothing to do with the food. I understood Leroy's fear. If I ended up on a blacklist, I'd be closely watched and it wouldn't be so easy to slip between being Ruby and Jewel.

Clifford had told me that things were growing worse in New Orleans, and I discovered it for myself a few days later when I was on Canal Street. I heard shouts and chants and thought it might be a parade practice, but then I noticed the shoeshine men hurriedly pick up their tools and disappear. A Negro maid dropped her shopping and broke into a run. The few stores that catered to coloured clientele hurriedly shut their doors and put up their closed signs. White people began to flee too. I watched a mother herd her four children into her Oldsmobile and speed away. A cold tremor ran down my spine.

A group of people holding placards and banners were marching down the street. When they got closer, I could read what their slogans said.

Keep our schools white!

Race mixing is communism!

The NAACP's real target is the bedroom!

At the front of the demonstration were two men holding an effigy of a Negro with a rope around his neck. Behind them came a man with a sign that said: *Tar and feathers and don't forget the matches!* I recognised Jimmy, the former barman from the Vieux Carré Club. He looked in my direction and I froze, but I was dressed as Ruby, not Jewel, and he didn't recognise me.

While many white people had fled, more had come out onto the banquettes to cheer the protesters on and some even joined them. Racists were crawling out of every nook and cranny like cockroaches.

'Two-four-six-eight!' the demonstrators shouted, using a popular chant. 'We don't want to integrate!'

A gangly boy, no more than eighteen, walked past with a banner that read: *Negroes go back to Africa! Except Fats Domino. He can stay!*

If I had a lick of faith that the carrier of the sign was an intelligent human being, the words might have been taken as an ironic comment. But these protesters were ignorant bigots and that's what made them so dangerous. I couldn't bear to even look at them.

I struggled through the spectators to reach Royal Street, but instead found myself pushed into the path of the protest, and came face to face with a woman holding a placard that read: *Communist Jews are behind school integration.* Oh, God! It was Aunt Elva! I hadn't seen her or Uncle Rex for a long time. She'd been furious that Sam had gotten the title deed to the apartment transferred back in my name. They were no longer our family as far as I was concerned.

She lowered her placard and glared at me, then her gaze fell to my navy overblouse dress and beige clutch coat, which were the first new items of clothing I'd bought for Ruby in over a year.

'You little Jezebel!' she growled, bringing her face so close to mine that every hate-filled line and pore seemed magnified. 'I know what you've been up to! Everyone is talking about it at the women's club. You've brought shame on us all by taking up with *that man*. Every time someone mentions your name, I spit! You're no niece of mine.'

My stomach turned queasy and I gasped. How had she found out about Leroy? If people knew, there was a danger that someone in the Citizens' Council would harm him.

Aunt Elva's nostrils flared. 'Ha! So the rumours are true! You thought I wouldn't find out?'

I tried to bluff, although my hands were trembling. 'Find out what?'

'That you're engaged to that despicable traitor Clifford Lalande! He's been calling on you and your hussy of a mother. Well, good luck! He's rich now, but that won't last. He'll be starved out of town — the Council will see to that!'

It took me a minute to comprehend what she'd said. When I realised she was talking about Clifford and not Leroy, I clasped my hand to my chest and laughed.

'You dried-up old prune!' I told her. 'I can't stand you, nor your no-good gambler of a husband!'

'Why, you!' she screeched, her face turning purple. 'I'll kill you!'

She shoved me, and I shoved her right back. Then she boxed my ears and grabbed my hair, pulling so hard I thought she was going to rip it from my scalp. I brought my hand around her neck and wrestled her to the ground lest she do some real damage. When I saw she was trying to bite my hand, I pinned her arms behind her head and sat on top of her.

The bystanders thought the fight was because I was defending Negroes, and some shouted support for me and others for Aunt Elva. Something flashed and I noticed two newspaper photographers taking pictures of us. I quickly got up and hid my face. The last thing I needed was to end up in the papers.

I was relieved when the *Times-Picayune* didn't run a picture, until Leroy showed me the full-sized photograph on the cover of the *Louisiana Weekly*, the newspaper for coloured people. *Young white woman takes on anti-segregation march!* the caption read.

'It's a pity no-one in my family will recognise you. Even Ti-Jean would have been impressed,' said Leroy with a grin.

'It's lucky Maman and Mae don't read the *Louisiana Weekly*,' I told him, 'because they'd be anything but impressed.'

We were ribbing each other, but then Leroy turned serious. 'Be careful,' he warned. 'If the supremacists go after Ruby, it won't take them long to find Jewel.'

TWENTY-ONE

Ruby

There was no time for sleep the morning of the Mardi Gras parade. I came home from seeing Leroy just in time to get to my room before Maman rose, so that I could pretend I'd been home all night. She always woke earlier than usual on the day of the parade. It would have been impossible for even the heaviest sleeper to continue to doze through the sounds of the bands warming up in the streets and the revelry of the patrons spilling out of the bars. When I heard her walk down the hallway and greet Mae in the dining room, I smoothed down my skirt, opened my bedroom door and went to join her for our traditional Mardi Gras early breakfast of beignets and coffee.

'Good morning, Maman!' I said, with the breezy smile of a young woman who might have had ten hours' uninterrupted sleep.

'Well, you're looking lovely,' she responded, admiring my navy blue dress, which had survived the scuffle with Aunt Elva.

It was fortunate that Aunt Elva no longer contacted us because she would have loved telling the story of our fight to Maman. Whenever Maman asked about my aunt and uncle, I pretended that they'd both contracted shingles or influenza or some other contagious disease and were afraid of infecting her. Maman would write cards to wish them a speedy return to health, but I'd never send them.

After breakfast, I set Maman up in a chair on the gallery rugged up in a coat, hat and scarf. Mae placed a pot of hot coffee beside her. The parade wouldn't pass directly by, but she'd still be able to see plenty of action. Jazz music filled the air, and children dressed as pirates and ballet dancers pranced after their parents. Maman and I watched two girls — one dressed as an angel, the other as a devil — skip along eating cotton candy and chattering excitedly to each other.

'You used to love to dress up when you were a child,' Maman told me. 'One year you wanted to be Alice in Wonderland, and the next, Little Bo-Peep.'

'Is that right?' I said. I had a vague recollection of my childish imagination carrying me away. It had obviously been good practice for my adult life. I tucked a blanket around Maman's legs and chest. 'Are you sure you don't want me to stay with you? It's going to be freezing today.'

She smiled brightly. 'Go and have fun! If it gets too cold for me, Mae will help me inside.' I kissed her on the cheek and she grasped my hand. 'You're good to me, Ruby. A mother couldn't ask for a better daughter than you. You're always thinking of me.'

It was true: I was always thinking of Maman. But that didn't stop me feeling guilty about all the sneaking around I was doing.

The streetcar routes had been redirected and it was impossible to find a cab, so I walked to St Charles Avenue. It took me over an hour but I didn't mind. I loved Mardi Gras. Clowns on stilts entertained children and tourists, charities had erected grandstands and were charging a dollar a seat to raise funds, while the less altruistically minded were renting out ladders for profit. I passed street vendors dressed in antebellum costumes and selling cotton candy, roasted peanuts and toffee apples. I closed my eyes for a moment and breathed in the sugary cold air.

I had arranged with Clifford to go with him to see the Rex Parade pass down Napoleon Avenue into St Charles Avenue. Rex was the King of Mardi Gras and his role was played by a different prominent member of the city each year, his identity kept secret until the morning of the parade.

I reached City Hall, where the Queen of Carnival was waiting with her maids to receive Rex's toast when he passed. A jazz band was playing 'If Ever I Cease to Love'. I thought about Leroy and his family: they would be heading out to watch the Zulu Parade, a parody of the Rex Parade. 'Zulu' was a racial slur, and everything Rex did, the Zulu King mocked. While Rex arrived by yacht up the Mississippi, Zulu came on a tugboat. Whereas Rex held a sceptre, Zulu held a ham bone, and his entourage handed out coconuts instead of beads and trinkets. The Zulu King, although played by a coloured man, wore blackface. The parade was a mockery of white people and how they treated coloured people, but I'd never considered that until now.

I rang the front doorbell of the Lalande home. Instead of a maid, I was greeted by an animated Kitty waving a copy of the *Louisiana Weekly* with me on the cover. Theodore, the Labrador, pranced excitedly around her feet.

'Come in, Ruby,' Kitty said. 'You've been the topic of conversation all morning!'

Philomena appeared and took my coat and gloves before Kitty tugged me into the parlour. Given the social standing of the Lalande family, I had expected their open house to be an elaborate affair with people spilling out of every room. I was surprised to find Clifford in the company of only his mother, Eddie, and a refined-looking coloured man. They were standing around the fireplace and drinking champagne. Their faces lit up when they saw me.

'My, Ruby, that is a very fetching outfit,' said Mrs Lalande, stepping forward to kiss me.

'Oh, thank you,' I said, accepting the glass of champagne that Eddie poured for me.

'We're practically family now,' Kitty whispered, nudging me in the ribs.

I glanced at Clifford, who smiled. How was I ever going to set this right?

Eddie guided Kitty away. Before they left, Clifford took the newspaper from his sister and leaned towards me.

'I told you before and I'll tell you again,' he said, his eyes shining. 'You never stop amazing me.'

'Oh,' I said, patting my hair, 'I'm a bit dishevelled in that photograph.'

He leaned closer. 'You look like Joan of Arc.'

'Indeed she is like the Maid of Orléons,' said the coloured man. 'A noble heroine.'

'Ruby, let me introduce you to my good friend Christophe Galafate,' Clifford said. 'He's a lawyer too and is working on civil rights cases for the Urban League and NAACP.'

'I wouldn't be able to do what I do without the help of the good Lalande family,' Christophe said graciously. He wore a silk cravat like a French aristocrat, and I liked the elegant way he tilted his head when he spoke to me.

There weren't many places in the South where a white family would entertain a coloured man on equal terms. It made me think of Ti-Jean. Maybe if he'd accepted the job in the mail room, he'd be where Christophe Galafate was now, despite the unfair disadvantage. Maman always said it never paid to be bitter.

A young coloured woman dressed in a mauve slim-fitting dress suit with a cape collar walked into the room holding the hands of two equally well-dressed coloured children.

'We should get our coats and set off if we want to see the parade,' she said. Then noticing me, she apologised.

'This is my wife, Clarita,' said Christophe, with pride in his voice. 'And these are our children, Adolphe and Isabelle.'

Isabelle, who looked as adorable as Shirley Temple, stared up at me. 'You're pretty,' she said.

I kneeled down to her. 'Well, you're pretty too. And your brother is very handsome, don't you think?'

She nodded shyly and the adults chuckled.

Philomena helped us all with our coats and scarves. When we reached the garden gate, Isabelle clasped my hand. 'I'm going to walk with you.'

Clarita's eyes darted to mine. I would have liked nothing more than to hold darling Isabelle's hand as we walked, but I knew what her mother was worrying about.

'You'd better hold on tight to your mama's hand too, because we don't want to lose you,' I said to Isabelle.

'No, I always hold Mama's hand. I want to hold yours today,' she insisted, giving me a winsome smile that showed her tiny white teeth. Clarita bit her lip and nodded to me. We set off in the direction of the parade. Until the tension over the integration of schools, New Orleans had been an easy-going city. But in the current mood it didn't surprise me that people glared at me and the Lalandes for walking in the company of coloured people who were clearly not our servants. I hoped they might assume we were out-of-towners from the North who didn't know any better but unfortunately too many people recognised the Lalandes. Even during a wonderful time like Mardi Gras, people couldn't forget their divisions.

A woman bumped into my arm roughly. A foul-smelling man sidled up to me and muttered, 'I'll kill you. Chop you up like a racoon, you nigger-loving bitch!' I shivered. He reminded me of Jimmy.

Isabelle didn't notice their hostility, she was too taken by a group of children who were dressed as pink rabbits, but Clifford did and stepped up to my side, while Christophe walked next to his wife. When Isabelle was distracted by a harlequin, Clarita discreetly took Isabelle's free hand and I let go of her.

'I'm glad most of the white people here won't have seen the *Louisiana Weekly*,' I told Clifford. 'Otherwise I'm going to get myself a reputation for being a troublemaker.'

'You're walking with a group of troublemakers,' he replied. 'It's already guilt by association. Do you mind?'

I shook my head. 'If I did, I wouldn't have come.'

His eyes lit up and he squeezed my arm. 'Thank you, Ruby. I admire your courage.'

The excitement was building as we reached the corner of St Charles and Napoleon avenues. The beat of the marching bands' drums and the roar of police motorcycles got louder, signifying that the parade and its floats were approaching. Christophe lifted Isabelle onto his shoulders. Rex appeared on his throne at the head of the parade, giving the spectators his royal wave. The crowd cheered and as the floats passed, people reached up their hands to receive the trinkets and beads dispensed by the riders. 'Throw me something, mister!' they called, giving the traditional cry.

The theme for this year's Rex Parade was the life of George Washington. The floats illustrated stories from his life, including the one about him cutting down his father's favourite cherry tree, his military victories during the American Revolution, and his inauguration as the first president of the United States. One of the floats carried a banner emblazoned with his famous quote: *Happiness and moral duty are inseparably connected.*

I glanced at Clifford. 'That reminds me of something you said to me when I first met you: "You've got to do what's right even if it hurts you, otherwise the human race is headed for disaster."'

His eyes swept over my face and he parted his lips slightly. For one uneasy moment I thought he was going to kiss me, but instead he shook his head dolefully. 'It used to be full house at our home on Mardi Gras day. Just as well you declined my invitation to the ball because my name has been struck from the guest list. Everything that has happened has taught me about the ugliness of the human race. But I've also seen inner beauty and courage, and that makes me willing to fight on.'

I sensed his loneliness and his desire to have me by his side. I knew then no matter how much I tried to avoid it, I was going to have to set things straight with him soon. I could not mislead this fine human being.

After the parade, we returned to the Lalande home for lunch. Kitty showed me to the powder room upstairs so I could fix my hair and reapply my lipstick.

'Jackie was unbearable,' she confided. 'I'm glad Clifford broke it off with her.'

I put my lipstick back in my purse and snapped it shut. '*He* broke it off with her? I had the impression that it was a mutual parting of the ways.'

'No. Clifford is a gentleman and has done everything to make it appear that way, including being discreet with you. But as patient as he is, I think it got too much for him. Jackie has a college education but she's lame-brained. She talks about nothing but who is going to marry who and the latest scandal. It's near impossible for anyone intelligent to listen to her for more than five minutes.'

'She likes scandals?' I asked, a nervous feeling gnawing at my stomach.

'She eats them for breakfast. Unfortunately, she wields them like a weapon too — she's destroyed a few reputations that way.'

I turned to the mirror and ran my fingers through my hair. 'She wouldn't harm Clifford, would she? They've been friends since they were children.'

'Wouldn't she?' Kitty leaned against the wall. 'She's damn angry about the broken engagement. For a plain-looking girl like her, Clifford was a real catch.

Fortunately, there are no scandals in Clifford's life. He's as honest as they come.'

Mrs Lalande called us downstairs and I followed Kitty to the dining room with my head throbbing. So Jackie was a spiteful person? My not being truthful with Clifford could do him a lot more damage than simply hurting his feelings. It could do irreparable damage to his cause.

The table had been decorated festively for Mardi Gras, with Venetian glass pitchers and goblets, beads, and a centrepiece of a crown and sceptre. While the lunch was buffet style, with tureens of red beans and rice, stuffed peppers, redfish court-bouillon and green beans set out on a side table, the main table had been laid with gold and green plates and the cutlery was wrapped in napkins and tied with purple masks. But even the sight of such a lavish table couldn't cheer me. I made up my mind that I would set things straight with Clifford before Mardi Gras was over.

After we were all seated, Mrs Lalande proposed a toast, again quoting George Washington: 'Be courteous to all, but intimate with a few, and let those few be well tried before you give them your confidence.'

When it was time to leave, Clifford walked me to the gate. I slipped the address of the club into his hand and told him, 'I'm working tonight, but I want to meet you at the Vieux Carré Club afterwards. Eleven o'clock.'

He looked surprised by the location, but nodded. 'All right, Ruby.' The note of trust in his voice pinched my heart. 'I've heard they play excellent jazz there but I've never been.'

As I walked home, I kept bumping into people and taking wrong turns. I knew that tonight would bring things to an end with Clifford for good. Part of me was sorry, but part of me was relieved too. I was proud of Jewel and proud that by my own enterprise I'd taken care of Maman and Mae. Why should I be ashamed of that, or of Leroy, or anything else?

That night's show was an extravaganza, with comedians, singers, magicians and the dance band booked to play until four in the morning. Tickets were five times the normal cost and had been reserved weeks in advance, but the maître d' promised to squeeze in a table for Clifford when he arrived. I wanted him placed near the stage where he could get a good view of my act, but I didn't intend to reveal I was Ruby until after my performance.

My gown for my final routine was silver satin embellished with rhinestones and sequins, with sleeves fashioned like angel wings. The song was a jazzed-up version of 'Angel Eyes'. In the dressing room, I attempted to add more false lashes to my eyelids but my hand shook so much I ended up poking myself in the eye. A vein was pulsing in my temple and I had to breathe in and out slowly to make it disappear. My gaze constantly returned to the clock on the wall. At quarter-hour intervals I found myself imagining what Clifford would be doing at that moment: eating dinner with his family; dressing for the club; stepping into a cab. When the hands reached ten-thirty I couldn't sit still any longer. I opened the door to the hall and called the stage manager. The band was playing 'There'll be a Hot Time in the Old Town Tonight'.

'Is my guest here?' I asked.

'Yes, he arrived about ten minutes ago. Real nice gentleman. He seems to be enjoying the show.'

Not since the first time I'd performed at the Havana Club had I been so jittery before going on stage.

'You want something?' Annie asked when she came in to help me with my headdress. 'Can I get you a drink? Or a Miltown?'

A lot of performers at the club took 'happy pills' to steady their nerves. But I wanted to meet Clifford with a clear head.

'No, I'm fine,' I told her. 'It's the biggest crowd we've ever had, that's all.'

As I climbed the stairs to the wing, my legs trembled as if I were heading towards the gallows rather than the stage.

'Give it your best,' the stage manager told me. It was what he always said.

I swallowed. Was I really going through with this? My throat tightened with panic but I resisted the urge to flee. I glimpsed Leroy waiting with the rest of the band for the cue from the stage manager. He grinned at me. I had to do this for him as well as out of decency to Clifford.

All conversation ceased when I stepped onto the podium. I couldn't bring myself to look in Clifford's direction though I was aware of him in my peripheral vision. My number was sultry, with a lot of slinky struts and shoulder rolls and holding my arms out to simulate flying. Only when I was down to my underwear did I allow myself a glance at Clifford. He was watching me intently but his face was expressionless. I couldn't tell what he was thinking.

When I returned to my dressing room, my heart was pounding and my hands and feet had turned to ice. I removed my wig and stage make-up, before taking off my performance lingerie and changing into a blue silk faille dress so I could reveal myself to Clifford as Ruby. How horrible would those first moments be? Would he get mad and make a scene? Or say nothing and walk away? Or even worse, would he resent being made a fool of and tell Maman?

The last scenario was so terrifying that I nearly backed out of telling the truth at all. I could simply go out the stage door, come in the main entrance and say I was late because I'd been held up at the telephone exchange. A knock at the dressing-room door made me jump. I opened it, expecting the stage manager, but instead I found the nervous-looking maître d' with Clifford standing behind him.

'I'm sorry, Miss Jewel, but your guest insists on seeing you right now.'

I was breathing so rapidly I could hardly get my words out. 'It's all right, Claude.'

Clifford brushed past the maître d' and shut the door behind him. I braced myself for an ugly scene. Somehow, despite my full costume and under the lavender lights in a different setting and doing something nobody would expect Ruby to do, Clifford had recognised me.

His gaze travelled from the costumes hanging on a rack to my dressing table covered in brushes and pots of colour. He picked up a powder puff and examined it before sitting down in a spare chair and squinting at me. 'Explain this to me, Ruby, because I can't get a handle on it. What's going on?'

The calmness in his voice was unnerving. 'How did you recognise me?'

He regarded me for a moment before answering. 'Did you think I wasn't going to? It doesn't matter what a woman does to her hair and clothing, a man will always recognise the woman he loves.'

I sat down at my dressing table. His solicitous tone made me realise that Clifford truly loved me; maybe not passionately, but sincerely. I straightened my shoulders and looked him in the eye.

'I didn't know any other way to show you what I do for a living. Working at the telephone exchange wouldn't have been enough to get us out of the debt we were in. I had to save Maman and Mae from ruin, only I had to ruin Ruby in the process.'

He shook his head as if he were mystified. 'Is that what you believe — that you are "ruined"? What does that mean anyway?'

That the conversation wasn't going in any direction I had expected made my head spin. I struggled to explain what I had always assumed without question. 'It means that I can never marry well.'

'Marry well,' Clifford repeated. He stood up and paced around the room. 'What does that mean?'

I flinched. 'What does that mean? It means marrying someone with standing in society ... from a good family,' I said.

'Is that what you wanted, Ruby? To marry someone with a position in society?' he asked, his voice hardening. 'What about respect and companionship? Aren't those things important to you too?'

I wrung my hands, wrestling with beliefs I had always accepted without question.

'If marrying well was your chief desire in life, I don't think you would have sacrificed it even to save your mother and your maid,' he said. 'I think you're a woman who lives by her heart. You love them and that's why you did what you did. A woman who wants to marry well doesn't risk her place in society by turning up at a meeting supporting integration, does she?'

'I don't know,' I replied, rubbing my forehead. 'I've never thought about it like that. I only did what I felt was the right thing to do.'

Clifford sat down again with his hands on his knees and sucked in a breath. 'Marrying well by New Orleans standards would have tied me to Jackie Fausey and her family forever.' He smiled faintly. 'I don't want that. I want a woman with both passion and compassion, and I've found her in you, Ruby.'

I was so confused that I wanted to cry. I'd thought that revealing myself as Jewel would send him running, but he seemed even more enamoured than before.

'But if anyone finds out what I do for a living, it will ruin you, Clifford. It will destroy your credibility for a cause you care deeply about.'

'That word "ruin" again,' he said with a sigh. 'Would it have been better for the cause if I'd married Jackie? Do you know what she said to me? "I don't care if coloured people are equal to us in intelligence or even in God's eyes. We need people to be our maids and clean our shoes and do all the jobs we don't want to do. That's why we have to keep niggers in their place."'

I stopped wringing my hands and sat back. There was a lot more to Clifford Lalande than met the eye. I wanted to know about what happened with Jackie but I was aware of the whispers in the corridor outside. There was nothing people at the Vieux Carré Club loved more than gossip, and I was sure the maître d' had told everyone that I had a wealthy man in my dressing room, something I'd never done before, and that he was my special guest for the evening. I dreaded to think what Leroy might make of it.

I'd intended to reveal to Clifford what I did for a living but not about Leroy. But he'd opened his heart to me and he deserved the truth. 'Clifford, I couldn't tell you what I do in front of Maman — I hope you understand? She comes from a different world from us. If she knew that I'm dancing for money, it would destroy her. But ...'

'But what, Ruby? There's something else you want to tell me, isn't there?'

I stared at my lap and nodded.

'Is there someone else?'

I looked up at him but I couldn't bring myself to respond, and Clifford took my silence as my answer.

'Well, lucky guy!' he said, blowing out his cheeks and running his hand through his hair. 'At least it explains your attitude to me. Why doesn't your mother know about him?'

I bit my lip before answering, 'He's coloured. That's why Maman doesn't know about him, and that's why I came to the meeting. I love him and his family, and I want a good life for us all.'

Clifford stood up and started pacing again. 'Good God, Ruby! Do you know what you're doing?'

Here it comes, I thought. *All this talk about equality is fine until a white woman actually goes and falls in love with a Negro man.* I was ready to admonish him for his hypocrisy, but when I looked into his face I didn't see anger in his expression, only concern.

'Ruby, you are too many decades ahead of your time,' he said. 'But if you love him, he must be a fine man.'

I had a sudden desire to unburden myself to Clifford.
It was as if he understood things about me that I didn't
understand myself.

'I don't know what to do,' I told him. 'I know we
aren't safe here, but I can't leave Maman. He loves his
family too.'

Clifford shook his head. Although his disappointment
weighed on his features, there was no bitterness in his
voice when he said: 'I wish I could advise you, but I
can't. Be true to your heart, Ruby, that's the best any of
us can do.' He moved to the door and when he opened
it, a burst of music and laughter sounded from the club.
Before stepping into the hallway he turned back to me.
'If ever you need my help, you come to me, Ruby. Do you
understand? I mean what I'm saying. If ever you need
help, come to me.'

After that night at the Vieux Carré Club, I didn't need
any more proof that Clifford was a gentleman, but when
he wrote a note to Maman explaining that he had to
leave town for some time and would call on her when he
got back, I knew that he'd done it so the break between
us wouldn't seem so sudden.

Leroy was astounded when I explained who Clifford
Lalande was and why he'd come to my dressing room.

'You turned away a rich white lawyer to be with me?'
he said, grinning to show he was glad. 'You wouldn't
have had to work any more, and you wouldn't have to
sneak around with me.'

'I like sneaking around with you,' I told him, placing
my hands on his shoulders.

But he didn't take my words as a joke. 'We've got to figure something out,' he said. 'We can't be playing around and pretending any more. I'm serious about you and you're serious about me. We've got to decide what we're going to do.'

Leroy was right. We were going to have to do something, because staying together in New Orleans was impossible. Only a few days earlier, the *Louisiana Weekly* had published a story about a coloured girl whose tongue was cut out after she named her white rapists; and another about a father shot in front of his children for writing to the Governor and requesting better streetlighting in his Negro neighbourhood. In the next few months things continued to deteriorate all over the South. The Reverend George Lee, a NAACP volunteer, was shot for helping coloured people in the Mississippi Delta register to vote. Even though several witnesses saw the white culprits drive away in their car, the police didn't charge anyone and no investigations were made.

'I heard from the funeral director in Belzoni that the Reverend's face was shot off and had to be sewn back on,' Pearl told us one Sunday when we gathered for lunch. 'But the County Sheriff passed off the death as a car accident and the hundreds of shotgun pellets lodged in the Reverend's face and neck as dental fillings!'

My eyes drifted to Ti-Jean, who was sitting with his fists clenched but not saying a word. I remembered what he'd said a few months ago: 'They can hang us, burn us, castrate us, shoot us and rape our women and children, but we've got to take it yessing and grinning and shining shoes for a living.' But the coloured folks of the South were no longer 'yessing' and taking it. The fear and terror had started to wear off. You could only push people so far before they started to push back.

'Ti-Jean's going to Mississippi tomorrow to organise boycotts and marches,' Leroy told me after the lunch. 'He's going to get himself killed.'

I knew Leroy was right to worry.

TWENTY-TWO

Ruby

Although there'd been no sign of Jimmy the barman since Sam fired him, Leroy still walked close behind me when I returned to Chartres Street after the show. Sometimes, to lift our spirits, we played games with each other. I'd speed up and then slow down to make him trip. Other times, when no-one was around, I'd perform a sexy strut with my hips swinging and my heels making clicking sounds on the banquette. Leroy would whistle tunes from the show or tap dance footsteps behind me to make me laugh.

One night when I turned into Chartres Street, I noticed two men lurking in a dimly lit doorway. One was tall and beefy, the other was runty.

'Hey, sweetie! Where you going all by yourself so late at night?' the beefy one called to me.

My scalp prickled. I could hear Leroy's footsteps — he was only a short distance behind me. Should I warn him or continue on? I decided to ignore the men and keep walking, hoping Leroy would see them before they spotted him. A voice inside my head implored me to run, but if these guys were trouble that would only entice them to chase me, like dogs after a squirrel.

Please, Leroy, I prayed, *please see them before they see you*. But it was too late.

'Hey, boy, you following that woman?' asked the same man who had spoken to me. 'Hey, sweetie, stop. You know you got a nigger following you?'

Leroy must have gotten past them because I heard his voice from a few yards behind me. 'Walk faster, Jewel. I'll turn at the next corner and lead them away from you.'

Panic was making it hard to breathe, but I did as Leroy instructed, gradually increasing my pace and not looking back. But then I heard other footsteps and knew the men were following us.

'Hey, Jewel! Leroy! I know it's you,' a different voice said. 'I've been on to you two for a long time.'

The tone was brittle. I knew who that voice belonged to: Jimmy the barman.

Leroy caught up and urged me on, searching for a house with a light on or somewhere to escape to. But who would open their door to a white woman and a coloured man, especially at this time of night? Our best hope was to reach the all-night laundromat on Esplanade Avenue where someone might help us.

'Where you going?' Jimmy taunted. 'There's no place you can hide. May as well save yourselves the effort.'

Leroy turned and faced the two men. 'What do you want? I accompany Miss Jewel home after the show on Sam's orders.'

'Sure you do,' replied Jimmy. His face was devil-like as he moved menacingly towards us.

Leroy stepped between me and Jimmy. 'Run, Jewel! Run!'

I jumped as Jimmy lunged at Leroy, who blocked his punch and countered with one of his own. The uppercut sent Jimmy flying, but the other man grappled with Leroy, wrestling him to the ground. Jimmy got up and rushed in to kick Leroy. I was terrified but I couldn't leave Leroy there to fight on his own.

'I'll kill you!' I screamed, throwing myself at Jimmy.

He grabbed me by the throat and shoved me against a wall. I gasped for air and clawed at his hands, struggling to breathe as his grip grew tighter. 'I'll get to you in a minute,' he grunted as he clamped down hard on my larynx. I blacked out and when I came to both men had set on Leroy again and with each blow his body crumpled further.

Stars swam in front of my eyes before I realised they were headlights. I struggled to my feet, coughing violently, and waved at the approaching car, slamming my hands on the bonnet when it slowed down. 'Help us!' I cried out to the white driver. But he only looked from me to Leroy and accelerated, nearly running me over as he sped away.

Jimmy and his companion continued to viciously attack Leroy. I knew they wouldn't stop until they had killed him. The sound of the blood gurgling in Leroy's throat threw me back into action. I tore at the men, biting and scratching, trying to pull them off him.

Another car approached, but this one stopped. Two men in suits jumped out.

One of the men wrenched the big guy off Leroy. He turned to punch the newcomer, but the other man pulled out a gun and shot him right between the eyes. Leroy's attacker staggered backwards then fell to the ground. Blood seeped out of his mouth and ears and ran into the gutter.

The shooter turned to Jimmy and pointed the gun at him. Jimmy let go of Leroy and scrambled down the street, knocking over garbage cans as bullets whizzed past him.

'That'll scare him,' the man said, lowering his gun.

Everything had happened so quickly it took me a moment to regain my senses. I ran to Leroy who had managed to sit up, and wiped the blood from his face with my hands. He had a nasty gash above his eye but the other wounds were superficial and no lasting damage had been done. I turned back to the men. Did they intend to shoot us too? I clasped Leroy's hands, waiting for the bullet. But a third man now stepped from the car, and I recognised the debonair form of Sam Coppola.

'Get in the car, Jewel,' he said. 'My men will take care of that garbage in the gutter, and get Leroy to the hospital. You come with me.'

I looked at Leroy, who winced when he stood, as if his ribs might be broken. 'No! I can't leave him!'

Sam moved towards me and grabbed my arm. 'Get in the car. This isn't a scene for a lady.'

'Please, go!' Leroy said, with a grimace. 'I'm all right, Jewel. Please go, for my sake.'

Reluctantly, I got in the car. Sam climbed in next to me and the driver took off. I looked back to see another car arrive and two men get out. They lifted the dead man's body off the street, while another man helped Leroy into the passenger seat.

'You all right?' Sam asked me.

'How did you know they were going to attack us?'

'I didn't. I was on my way to visit a lady friend when I saw you getting your heads beaten in.' He took a handkerchief from his pocket and gave it to me to wipe my hands, which were sticky with blood. 'What the hell were you thinking, Jewel? I thought you had more sense! This isn't Paris. You can't go traipsing around with a coloured man. I've turned a blind eye, but I can't afford to get the club shut down. I'm going to fire Leroy and the band. It's too risky.'

The blood rushed to my head. 'No! I won't perform without Leroy!'

'Don't be a fool!' Sam barked. 'Don't you have your mother to think about? You'll do as I tell you!'

My hands shook. It was the first time Sam had ever raised his voice to me. I turned away and stared out the window at the French Quarter. I used to love New Orleans and now I hated it. The world was closing in on me and Leroy, and I didn't know how to stop it.

Before breakfast with Maman the following morning I applied cold compresses to my bruised neck and wrapped a scarf around my throat so she wouldn't see the marks Jimmy had made. It was painful to swallow and I had no appetite but I did my best to plaster a carefree smile on my face.

'You look like the cat that ate the canary,' Maman said to me. 'What are you thinking about with a sly grin on your face like that? Is Clifford Lalande back in town?'

I shook my head. 'No, Maman. He's setting up a law firm in New York. He wrote you that.'

'He's been gone so long,' she said, a puzzled frown wrinkling her face. 'I didn't think he'd be able to stay away from you.'

After breakfast I went to Canal Street and used the pay phone to call the hospital, but the nurse there said that Leroy had been sent home. I walked to the room in Chartres Street, and put my red wig on before heading to Leroy's house.

I turned into his street and immediately sensed something was wrong. Everything was quiet, not a soul anywhere. Then I saw it and stopped in my tracks, a chill running down my spine. A charred cross had been stuck in the front lawn of the funeral home, with a noose lying around its base. Joseph came out with a handsaw and a sack.

I ran towards him. 'Is everyone all right?'

He looked at me with vacant eyes. 'Yeah, we're all right. Just shook up, that's all.'

'Did you call the police?'

He snorted in disgust. 'The police can't do anything about some cowardly bigot.'

I immediately thought of Jimmy: the act reeked of him. But Joseph had other ideas.

'The Ku Klux Klan is banned in New Orleans. I reckon it was somebody from Mississippi who doesn't like what Ti-Jean has been doing. If they can't get him, they'll get us.'

I held the sack open for him while he sawed up the cross and tossed the pieces into it. Milton came out and took the sack from me.

'It won't make things better if somebody sees you helping him,' he whispered.

Joseph nodded. 'He's right. Go inside, Jewel. You'll find everyone in the house.'

The windows were shut, and for the first time since I'd started coming to the Thezan family's home I found the door locked. I knocked softly. Pearl opened it and ushered me inside and towards the front room, where Bunny was sitting with Alma, Eleanor and Dora and two sullen-looking women I didn't recognise. I assumed they were neighbours. They looked me up and down but didn't say anything. I could see Dwight and Gerard in the next room. Their eyes were cast down and they were speaking in low voices. The mood in Leroy's home had always been congenial and festive; now it was morose.

Bunny embraced me. 'It's so awful! How am I going to sleep at night?'

'And nobody saw who did it?' I asked.

'No,' replied Eleanor. 'We heard a loud bang in the early hours and a car driving off. At first we thought the funeral home had been firebombed, then Milton looked out the window and saw the burning cross. Our Italian neighbours put it out but we wouldn't let Milton and Joseph leave the house until now, in case whoever did it was still hanging around.'

'Pa thinks it's because of Ti-Jean being in the NAACP,' said Bunny.

'Can't think what else it would be,' said Eleanor. 'Our family's lived here for generations and it's always been peaceful and nice.'

'Could be because Leroy's got himself a *white* girlfriend,' said one of the neighbours, her face pinched into an expression of dislike.

'Hush now,' Pearl told her. She turned to me. 'Leroy got bashed last night, down in the Quarter. He's all right though. He's in the tool shed. Go and see him. It's at the bottom of the garden.'

I wondered why Leroy hadn't told his family that I'd been with him when he was attacked, but then I remembered the hostile neighbours and understood his reasons for not saying anything.

I rushed past the vegetable garden, and followed a path through some banana trees to the bottom of the garden. I expected the tool shed to be a shack; instead I found myself standing in front of a neatly constructed cabin with a shingled roof and a barn-style door. The strains of a clarinet came from inside.

I opened the door and found Leroy sitting in a rocking chair, with his eyes closed, lost in his music. Despite the beating he'd taken he didn't look too bad. Two black eyes, a grazed chin and a bandage on his forehead. His playing wasn't interfered with by his strapped right wrist either. While I waited for him to notice me, I glanced around the shed. Screwdrivers, hammers and spanners hung in ascending order of size from a tool board while garden implements were arranged in a systematic fashion along shelves. There was even a braided rug on the floor and a comfortable looking upholstered bench on which to sit. The tools reminded me of how Leroy loved to fix things in the room on Chartres Street. That place had been our haven but after Jimmy had said he'd been watching us, it wasn't safe for us to meet there any more.

Leroy gave a start when he saw me. He put the clarinet down and rose from the chair. 'Jewel, I've been so worried about you,' he said, hugging me to his chest. 'Are you all right?'

It was only when he kissed me that I noticed his lip was swollen. 'Doesn't it hurt to play?' I asked.

'Doesn't hurt to play or to kiss. As long as you're safe, I feel no pain at all.'

His shirt felt lumpy and I peeked inside his collar to see that his torso was bandaged. 'You could have been killed!' I said, resisting the urge to embrace him tightly. 'Do you think it was Jimmy who put the cross on the lawn?'

He shook his head. 'I don't know. Maybe, if he had the time.'

We released each other and sat down on the bench together. With the comfortable furnishings, the shed was more a hideaway than a storehouse.

'Sam's going to fire you and the band,' I said.

Leroy nodded. 'He told me that when he picked me up from the hospital this morning. He's paid us for a full month. We'll find something else.'

'I don't want to work with anybody but you.'

He grimaced and rubbed his strapped wrist. 'What happened last night has shaken my folks. For the first time I heard Mama and Pa talking about moving away and starting again somewhere else. Chicago, or maybe even San Francisco.'

My heart sank. I couldn't bear to lose Leroy's family; they had become like my own.

'Things will calm down,' I told him. 'It's the school desegregation issue. When everything settles down, New Orleans will be like it was before.'

He sighed and rested his chin on my head. 'I was so worried about you, Jewel. I told you to run! Why didn't you?'

'I couldn't leave you.'

He took a deep breath and turned me to face him. 'They could have done something terrible to you. I couldn't bear that. I couldn't bear for you to be hurt because of me.'

I had never seen Leroy look so serious. Something had changed in him. Although we were sitting with our bodies pressed together, he suddenly felt far away. The idea that some gap was forming between us made my pulse race with panic.

'Perhaps we should leave New Orleans too,' I said, grabbing his unhurt wrist and squeezing it. 'I've heard there's plenty of work for entertainers in San Francisco.'

He stood up and moved to the window. 'Do you think it will be so different there? What's life going to be like for you? You won't be able to walk around freely with your husband by your side. What's it going to be like pretending you're part coloured? And what about our children? Don't you want to be proud of your children and show them off to everybody?' He frowned. 'You'd be ashamed of them because they'd be mulattos.'

'What are you saying?' I rose to my feet. 'I *do* want to be proud of my children, Leroy, and I will be when I see you in their faces!'

He shook his head. 'You got a nice white man in love with you,' he said, his eyes cast down. 'Clifford Lalande can give you a life that I can't. He can look after you properly. I'll only make you a target.'

Pain sliced me down the middle and split me apart. The gap between us that I'd sensed earlier was now a gaping chasm. Not because we loved each other less, but because the world was tearing us apart.

'Leroy, I love you! Only you! You don't want me to suffer? Well, I'll suffer if I'm separated from you!'

The desperation in my own voice made me cringe but Leroy remained firm.

'What about your mother? You can't leave her behind, and I wouldn't ask you to.'

'I've done everything for Maman and I always will,' I said breathlessly. 'But she's got to face reality too. She can't keep us living in some imaginary past forever. It might turn her world upside down, but I know she'll love you once she gets to know you.' I moved towards him and clasped his arm. 'What's left for Maman and Mae in New Orleans? To waste away in our museum of an apartment? San Francisco might give them both a new lease on life too.'

Leroy stared out the window for a long time before he asked quietly: 'Is that what you want, Jewel? To leave everything and marry me?'

'I'll die without you, Leroy! I'll just die!' I had never cried in front of him before. I resisted crying in front of anybody. My pride wouldn't allow it. But this time the tears got the better of me.

Leroy hesitated, wrestling with something in his mind. Then he took me in his arms and kissed me deeply.

'Don't cry, I'll always look after you,' he said when he pulled back. 'I'll always put you first.'

'Then let me stay with you. I don't care what it costs — I'll pay it. Just let me stay with you.'

He steered me towards the bench, sat down and tugged me to him. He stroked my hair and pressed my head to his chest. 'What we have is too strong to be torn apart by anybody else,' he said.

A rush of warmth and love replaced my fear. I slipped my hands around his neck as he embraced me and lowered me to the rug.

'We'll elope,' he said, gazing into my face. 'We'll go to San Francisco as you said.'

My neck ached from the bruising and the rug was rough against my back and legs but the desire flooding through my body only made those pains exquisite. I moaned with arousal when he undid the buttons at the front of my dress and kissed my throat and breasts.

'Yes, we'll elope together to California,' I whispered, nuzzling into his neck and losing myself to waves of rapture. 'We'll get away from all this madness and always be together.'

That evening before the show I used panstick and layers of powder to hide the bruises on my neck. I slipped on my G-string, and noticed the burn marks on my derriere where I'd rubbed against the rug when Leroy and I had made love. The memory made me smile and reluctantly I disguised them as well.

'A new life,' I told my reflection in the mirror. I was relieved now that Leroy and I had come to a decision about our future. He was going to leave for San Francisco in a few days' time to find work and a place for us to live. Then I would follow him, along with his family. Although I was intoxicated with love for Leroy and excited by the idea of the new freedoms that awaited us in California, I had mixed feelings whenever I thought about Maman and Mae. I had paid off the mortgage on the apartment so they would be financially secure. Once I was established in San Francisco, I would send for them. But would they come? Or would their horror that I loved a coloured man stop them from ever accepting Leroy and his family? None of that I knew and it tainted my happiness with agitation.

I touched the cat figurine Orry-Kelly had given me, which I kept on my dressing table, and steeled myself. I had to believe everything would work out. I had saved us from financial ruin by sheer force of will and my readiness to do something out of the norm. There hadn't been any reason I shouldn't work other than stupid tradition. And there was no reason Leroy and I shouldn't be together other than stupid bigotry.

The stage manager knocked on the door. 'Five minutes to show time, Jewel!'

My routine was one I'd been performing for a week now, yet everything felt jarring when I got out on stage. Marty, the orchestra leader, was at the top of his profession but I didn't feel in sync with him and his musicians. Miss Hanley assured me that things would improve with more rehearsals together but I doubted it. Even though the audience didn't notice it, a spark was missing for me: without Leroy, the magic of performing was gone.

Sam must have noticed I was out of sorts. When I'd finished for the night, he summoned me to his table to share some champagne with him.

'You've got it bad, Jewel,' he said in his familiar lisp. 'You're really stuck on Leroy, aren't you?'

I nodded.

He lit a cigarette and took deep puffs. 'You're a fool, but I can't judge you. I was a fool too when I was your age.'

'Did you fall in love with the wrong woman?' I asked, intrigued.

'I fell in love with the *right* woman, but I married the one my family wanted me to. We haven't had a happy day together since the wedding night. She was the one who drove me to work for the mob — I needed an excuse to get away. My family are all artisans. They aren't even Sicilian; they're glass blowers in Venice.'

I studied Sam with new eyes. 'Your wife is still in Italy? What happened to the woman you were in love with?'

His face turned dark. He inhaled on his cigarette and blew the smoke out through his nose like a dragon. 'She threw herself out of a window.'

I gasped and instinctively put my hand on his arm as if to comfort him. He shrugged, embarrassed at having shared something intimate about himself. His face returned to its normal wary expression.

'I told Leroy this morning not to play around with you unless he's prepared to sacrifice everything for you. Even then, Jewel, you will be shunned by both white and coloured people.'

He looked me directly in the eye. 'Are you prepared to destroy yourself to be with Leroy? You've got a good thing going here. There are a lot of wealthy men who'd be crazy for you. They'd give you everything a woman could possibly ask for.'

There was no point playing games with Sam. I was sure he'd already guessed what Leroy and I were up to.

'We're planning to go to California,' I told him. 'To San Francisco.'

Sam took a last long drag on his cigarette before snuffing it out in the ashtray. Then he sat uncharacteristically silent and still. I wondered if he was going to get mad. I did have a contract with him, after all. But then something shifted in his expression, a subtle softening.

'Go ahead and do it,' he said firmly. 'I'll use my contacts to get you both work. Sometimes you've got to be brave enough to say "Damn it!" and do what you want to do.'

❖

A few days later, as I ate breakfast with Maman, I admired how pretty she looked in the satin dress suit with lace cuffs I'd bought her for her birthday. *It's because of Jewel we have this life*, I thought proudly. *I'm not going to be ashamed of her, and I'm not going to be ashamed of Leroy or our children either. I'm going to make my own path.*

I didn't know how I was going to tell Maman about Leroy. I couldn't tell her beforehand what I was planning to do, because she'd try to stop me. If Mae knew, she'd call the police. I was going to have to present it to them as a *fait accompli*.

Although I thought about Leroy and our new life constantly, I hadn't heard from him since I'd seen him in the tool shed. He'd told me that he'd only get in contact once he was about to leave for San Francisco. 'No news will be good news,' he'd promised.

When I reached the rehearsal studio and saw Miss Hanley had brought in a record player, I choked up. 'I miss Leroy,' I said.

Ever since the attack on me and Leroy my heart felt like it was beating in irregular rhythms. I clutched my head and sat down in a chair, willing the dizziness to go away.

'Goodness me,' Miss Hanley said, pouring me a glass of water, 'what's the matter with you? I miss Leroy too, but Marty is going to come to our studio rehearsals from tomorrow and he's charming. Good musicians move on all the time. You'll have to get used to it.'

Bless Miss Hanley. She hadn't guessed there was something going on between me and Leroy, even though it had started right under her nose. It made her seem foolish but I was fond of her anyway. She'd done so much to shape me into a star and I was grateful. I'd miss her when I went to San Francisco.

We rehearsed together for nearly two hours, using a chair as a prop. It represented a man who was initially impervious to my charms but eventually gave in to them. Then the studio telephone rang and Miss Hanley answered it.

'It's the receptionist from the Vieux Carré Club,' she said, her hand over the receiver. 'She says you have a message from a woman named Bernadine to meet her urgently.'

Bernadine was Bunny's proper name. I realised that Leroy must be about to leave for San Francisco.

'I've got to go,' I told Miss Hanley. 'I'll see you tomorrow.'

I took a cab to Tremé. When it pulled up outside the funeral home, I saw a crowd dressed in black gathered outside. I felt sorry for the mourners and their grief. My life was about to begin and somebody else's had ended. I paid the driver and was heading down the driveway to the Thezan home when I heard Bunny call out to me. Her distressed tone sent a shudder through me.

I turned and saw her walking in my direction. She faltered a couple of times and I wondered if she'd hurt her leg. When she reached me I was horrified by the chalky undertone of her skin. She always looked so healthy.

'What is it?' I asked her. 'Are you ill?'

Her lips quivered and she couldn't bring herself to speak.

'Bunny?'

When she finally looked at me, her eyes were glistening. 'Leroy's dead.'

A sickening numbness spread across my chest. I wavered on my feet. No! Leroy was going to San Francisco. We were going to start a new life together. I closed my eyes as if I could make this nightmare disappear. But when I opened them again Bunny was still standing before me only now she was sobbing.

'We were worried when he didn't come home the day before yesterday,' she said through her tears. 'Then we got a call from the police last night. A fisherman found his body in the river. Someone had shot him multiple times before throwing him in the water.'

Her words hit me like a blow. I staggered and clutched my stomach, struggling to breathe.

'Somebody killed Leroy?' I turned towards the funeral home and the mourners.

'That's for him,' Bunny said. 'Mama laid him out.'

My legs were leaden weights and yet somehow I began to move one step at a time towards the building. I felt as if I'd become a corpse myself. The part of me that had been excited and joyful only a few minutes before had died.

'Don't go in there, Jewel,' Bunny pleaded. 'Please don't, it will only distress you.'

I kept walking. How could I not see him? I loved him. I'd had no chance to say goodbye.

The mourners parted when they saw me coming. Inside the parlour, a woman was singing a hymn in a strange sweet voice. The open casket stood at the end of the room, surrounded by bouquets of gladioli, hydrangeas and lilies. Pearl was sitting at one end of the casket weeping into a lace handkerchief. Joseph and Milton were standing at the other end, their heads bowed. How could my beloved Leroy, so warm and alive a few days before, be lying in that box?

Above the casket was a carving of Jesus carrying his cross. I'd seen that image many times but only now did I understand it. I had a much heavier burden to carry than the one of a secret love.

As I walked towards the casket, the world turned foggy around me. An elderly man looked at Leroy and threw his arms above his head and fell into a faint. He was caught by one of the mourners and helped to a chair.

Bewildered, I regarded the grim faces of Eleanor, Alma, Dora, Dwight and Gerard. They were not the same people I knew. The joy in their eyes was gone.

Dora reached forward and grabbed my arm. 'No, don't look, Jewel,' she said, a note of warning in her voice. 'I don't know why —'

I disentangled myself from her and continued towards the casket. A sickly smell pervaded the space undisguised by the flowers. I reached the casket and looked down. My cry of horror pierced the air of the parlour. There was no jaw, and the top half of the head was missing and so were the hands. The flesh was so bloated that the body barely appeared human. That mangled mess couldn't possibly be Leroy!

I reeled backwards in horror. Milton grabbed me so I wouldn't fall.

'Why didn't you fix him?' he asked Pearl. 'Why did you put him on show like that?'

Pearl lifted her face. The vivacious person I'd cooked with all those Sundays was gone. In her place was a broken old woman. She stared at us with vacant eyes.

'Because nothing was going to fix that! Nothing! I want the world to see what they did to my son!'

Bunny rushed towards me and hugged me, sobbing into my hair. 'I wanted you for my sister-in-law. It's all I've been able to think about for months. And now he's gone. Oh, Jewel, what are we going to do?' she wailed.

I couldn't feel her arms around me. No arms could comfort me after this. Nothing could offer any consolation. My beautiful Leroy was gone.

I turned away from the Thezan family, away from those wonderful times of shared meals and conversations. A strange numbness overtook me entirely as I left Tremé. I couldn't smell the gardenias that bloomed in profusion in the pots on porches, or feel the breeze from the river, or hear the birds in the trees. The cars that rushed by on Esplanade Avenue made no sound, and one of them nearly hit me when I tried to cross.

I didn't care. I staggered back to the Quarter, away from my life as Jewel and back to my life as Ruby, Leroy's destroyed face and desecrated body etched in my memory forever.

TWENTY-THREE

Amanda

Grandma Ruby and I sat in silence in the summerhouse. I heard bees humming in the lavender, and the doves cooing on the lawn, but for us the whole world had come to a standstill. The tears that I'd seen glistening in her eyes while she was telling the story of Leroy's death now rolled down her cheeks. My heart ached for her. While she'd been telling her story, Leroy had come vividly to life for me. I had pictured his warm smile and his handsome face as if he were standing right in front of me. I knew something had happened to break off their relationship, but I had not anticipated such a horrific end.

I looked out over the garden and the dragonflies hovering above the grass. Nan and I had once watched a documentary about Martin Luther King Junior that mentioned the story of the torture and murder of a teenage boy named Emmett Till in Mississippi. His mother displayed his body in an open casket to show the world what had happened to her son, and his death sparked the racial rebellion that led to Rosa Parks refusing to give up her seat to a white man on a bus and the Montgomery bus boycott. But I could not have conceived a similar event had occurred so close to my own family.

Grandma Ruby and I stayed together the whole day, finding comfort in each other's company. We strolled around the garden with Flambeau following us, listened to Beethoven on the CD player, and read together in the sitting room. We both needed to process the past — Grandma Ruby anew, and me for the first time.

At five o'clock I remembered that I'd promised to meet Elliot at Preservation Hall.

'I'll cancel,' I told Grandma Ruby. 'I'm not leaving you alone, especially not tonight.'

'Is Elliot the lovely young man who called here? The jazz professor? We talked a long time.'

I looked at her in surprise. I knew that Elliot had called the house, but not that he and my grandmother had shared a lengthy conversation. 'About what?' I asked.

Grandma Ruby took the telephone from me and put it back in its stand. 'We talked about the city and its music. He was going to take you to Snug Harbor.' With a smile she added, 'He sounded so charming I nearly went with him myself.' She pushed me towards the stairs. 'I don't want you to not go because of me, Amandine. I've been alone in this house many nights with my memories — one more isn't going to kill me.'

I took her hands. 'Are you sure?'

'Of course! Now go and pretty yourself up. Southern men appreciate it when a woman makes the effort.'

Although I thought Grandma Ruby's advice was old-fashioned, I did take time to blowdry my hair straight. Then I dusted my shoulders and legs in shimmer powder.

Having been told that Preservation Hall was the place to hear authentic New Orleans jazz, I expected that the taxi would pull up at the equivalent of the Opera House in Sydney or London's Royal Albert Hall. Instead I found myself alighting in front of a dilapidated townhouse. The weather-beaten exterior hadn't been painted in years and the ironwork was coming apart at the joins. However, the line of people outside stretched a distance down St Peter Street.

Elliot was waiting out the front for me, looking hot in an ethnic-print shirt and white Panama hat. 'Hey, Amandine!' he called, and waved me over. 'You look beautiful,' he said, kissing me and admiring my python-skin-patterned top and pencil skirt. 'You Sydney people sure know how to dress.'

'You look pretty good yourself,' I replied.

He took a bottle of water from the vintage canvas satchel he had hanging on his shoulder and gave it to me. 'No drinks or food are served here. There aren't even bathrooms. Just great jazz.'

Because he'd been able to reserve tickets through a friend, we were placed next to the musicians. Elliot grinned as we squeezed with another couple into an old church pew. The rest of the audience sat on backless benches or cushions on the floor, or stood at the rear.

'Not what you were expecting, is it?' he said.

'Not at all.' I laughed, and gazed over the cracked

soundproofing on the unpainted walls. The wooden floor was rough with gaps in it and the seats set aside for the musicians looked rickety. I sneezed from the dust in the air.

'God bless you!' said the woman sitting next to us.

'We talked the other day about music and segregation,' Elliot said. 'Preservation Hall broke the barrier between black and white. You left your racism at the door when you came here. It was all about the music.'

It was a steamy night and there was no air conditioning in the building, but Elliot and I pressed against each other happily.

He looked into my eyes. 'I'm glad you came to New Orleans, Amandine.'

'I am too,' I told him.

A saxophonist and two trumpeters came out first, and placed their chairs only an arm's length from us. The pianist, bassist and drummer followed. A thrill of excitement ran through me as they began a rousing rendition of 'When the Saints Go Marching In'. I remembered what my mother had written in her letter to Nan about seeing my father at Preservation Hall for the first time: *We locked eyes and I didn't take mine off him until the last note was played. It was like being drunk on a magic potion from the witchcraft store.* I looked out into the audience and imagined my mother there with her pretty face and wild blonde hair, falling in love. Then I looked to the saxophonist and pretended he was my father making eyes in my mother's direction. The picture warmed my heart. I took Elliot's hand and squeezed it.

'Wow! What an amazing coincidence,' he said, nodding in the direction of the pianist: a stocky man in his fifties, with grey sideburns and a white goatee.

'That's Glenn Neville. He played with your father on many occasions.'

Glenn's piano technique was raw and wild. He stomped his black running shoes on the floor as he played and kept his long grey hair out of his eyes by flicking his head. The untucked purple shirt he wore barely hid his beer belly. I tried to picture what he would have looked like in his twenties, when he and my father played together. Then I tried to imagine what my father would have been like now, in his fifties. Would he still be clean-shaven and sharply dressed in a suit? Or would he have adopted Glenn's more modern 'I've just rolled out of bed' style?

The night was magical, with the band playing jazz classics like 'Saint Louis Blues' and 'Sugar Rum Cherry'. When they performed 'Shake That Thing', the audience — as crowded in as we were — got up to dance. When the show was over, I felt that the pieces of the puzzle about my father were coming together faster now.

Elliot and I waited outside on the street, and when Glenn Neville came out, Elliot explained who I was, because I was suddenly too choked with emotion to tell him myself.

'Wow!' Glenn said, grabbing my shoulders. 'Look at you, Amandine! It's like seeing Dale again — only in drag!' He hugged me so fiercely that my feet lifted a few inches off the ground — not a small feat as I was a good deal taller than he was.

'I can't believe you're all grown up!' he said, putting me back on the ground and holding me at arm's length. 'I used to bounce you on my knee and pretend it was a bumpy horse ride. You were a good kid. You only made trouble once when you covered my suede shoes with toothpaste.'

'It sounds like I was a pain!' I told him. I didn't know whether to laugh or cry. It was strange to have had this other life that I couldn't remember. 'No, you were our mascot,' he said, lighting a cigarette. 'The whole band loved you!'

'Listen, would you like to join us at Pat O'Brien's?' suggested Elliot. 'Amandine has come to New Orleans to learn about her father. You knew Dale well, didn't you?'

Glenn's eyes lit up. 'He and I were the best of friends. I'll tell you anything you want to know,' he said to me.

The three of us went to Pat O'Brien's bar, which was crowded with both locals and tourists. Elliot led us straight to the patio to get away from the noise of the duelling pianos.

'Let's take that table by the fountain,' he said. 'It will give you two a chance to chat.'

We sat down, and a waitress took our orders for Hurricane cocktails.

'I can't believe that your father has been dead for twenty-three years,' said Glenn. 'I still talk to him sometimes. I'll always miss him.'

The affection for my father in Glenn's voice touched me. I pressed my hand to my chest. It was as though I was stepping into a new life, one where my father could be a real person to me. In the short time I'd been here, I'd learned more about my him than I'd ever thought possible.

'How did you become friends with my father?' I asked Glenn.

'I met him at a gig — I took to him straight away,' he replied, putting out his cigarette and taking out another one. 'He was smart but very easy-going. Your mother was more of an extrovert. But together they were a dynamic pair. When you came along, it didn't slow them down.

They took you everywhere. Half our van was filled with music gear and the other half was packed with all your baby stuff. The band loved you, and we even took turns at changing you. Though I did get in trouble from Dale once for spiking the juice in your sippy cup!'

Elliot and I laughed.

'It must have been a handful having a small child on tour,' I said. 'I'm surprised my parents didn't leave me with Grandma Ruby or Aunt Louise.'

Glenn shook his head. 'Your father would never have had that. He didn't want to be another musician with a divorce and a broken family. That's why he insisted you all stick together. But he did tell me once that he and Paula were planning another baby and then they'd stop touring. He wanted to open his own jazz club and stay put in New Orleans to give you stability.'

Glenn's revelation stung my heart. My parents had been planning another child. How different would my life have been if I'd had a brother or a sister?

'Was my father ... was he a happy man?' I asked, my pulse racing. I was surprised at myself for asking the question. But I knew why I had, even though it tore me in two. I was ready to know about that night — about the accident.

'Your father didn't have any demons,' Glenn answered emphatically. 'He wasn't a jolly, roll-about-on-the-floor kind of guy. But he was a glass-half-full person. He had the quiet contentment of a man who loved his family.'

The waitress returned with our cocktails. I knew the time had come to ask the question that I'd needed an answer to for so long. But it was agonising because I was afraid it would undo all the good feelings I was starting to have about my father.

'What happened the night my parents died? I was told my father had a blood alcohol reading of 0.21. But everyone who knew him says he was a light drinker.'

Glenn grimaced, then cleared his throat. 'We had a gig to play in Jacksonville, Florida the following evening. We were used to working and travelling at night and sleeping during the day, so we had an early dinner on Canal Street and set off around 7 pm, planning to make a few stops along the way. I remember that your father was different that night. He seemed preoccupied with something, not at all his relaxed self. He usually limited himself to one drink a night, but I noticed over dinner that he knocked back at least four or five. Maybe more, I don't know. The band and I were in the van driving behind your father's car. The accident happened just after Mobile.' Glenn glanced down at his hands. 'I'll never forget the horrible sight of the car swerving across the road and rolling over the embankment.'

Tears pricked my eyes. 'Everyone says my father was a responsible person,' I said, my voice trembling. 'But if he was so responsible, why did he drive drunk with my mother and me in the car?'

Glenn looked confused. 'He wasn't driving, Amandine. When the car left the road, it was your mother at the wheel.'

I couldn't sleep that night. I played the CD of my father's music that Elliot had made for me and tried to lose myself in the passionate and elegant rhythms, but there was no solace there. I'd hoped that coming to New Orleans would give me a sense of belonging and offer me some peace. Now, a gaping hole had opened in my heart. My father hadn't been driving the car when it veered off the road. That was a lie I'd believed all my life.

My mother's blood alcohol reading had put her well under the limit. Glenn said no-one knew why she'd lost control of the car. The cause could have been as simple as a momentary loss of concentration, or lack of experience driving on the right side of the road. He'd explained that usually it was my father who drove, but he hadn't done so that night because he'd had too much to drink.

I got out of bed and paced the floor, unable to think straight. Outside the window, the moon was a huge luminous globe.

There was a soft knock at the door and Grandma Ruby stepped into the room.

'Amandine? What is it, darling? Don't tell me that Elliot hurt your feelings?'

I was touched by the concern on her face. I shook my head. Elliot had been very worried about me and had pulled over several times on the drive home to ask if I was all right. He'd even offered to stay with me so I could talk the shock out. But I'd told him that I needed to be alone, to digest what I'd discovered. He'd only let me get out of the car when I'd promised to call him the next day.

'Then what?' asked Grandma Ruby. 'Tell me what's upset you so much.'

I didn't want to distress her when she was feeling sad herself. But when she sat on the bed and indicated for me to join her, I found myself pouring out my feelings.

'Why did Nan tell me that it was my father who was driving?' I cried. 'Did she make it up? Or was she unable to accept that my mother caused the accident?'

Grandma Ruby shook her head. 'I thought you knew it was your mother who was driving.' We were silent for a long time before she spoke again. 'Perhaps Cynthia convinced herself Dale was driving. She was so angry at all of us. When I learned she was taking legal action to gain custody of you and take you away to Australia, I fought her tooth and nail. After the death of your parents, you and Louise were all I had left. Those days were overwhelming and unbearable and I doubted I would survive. I didn't stop to consider that Cynthia was all alone too. Instead of appealing to her compassion and coming up with some kind of compromise, I used my lawyers to make a counter-case against her. But she won custody on some international technicalities. I was supposed to be given rights of visitation, but with the hatred she felt towards me, that never happened.'

Grandma Ruby took my hand. 'We were fools, Cynthia and I — such terrible fools! We argued about our rights and forgot that you had rights too. The hurt that you've endured is unforgivable. Believe me, I would have done things differently now. And I believe Cynthia would have too. She loved you very much, Amandine. Never doubt that. But people do terrible things out of fear — even to the people they love.'

I was moved that Grandma Ruby could be compassionate towards Nan after all my grandmother had done to hurt her. Finally, I was able to feel the calm resignation that I'd been desperately seeking since I'd returned from Preservation Hall. My parents were both gone, and no amount of twisting my mind out of shape about who was or wasn't driving could change it. No matter who Nan had blamed, the facts would still be the same. I'd grown up without my parents. Why my mother had swerved off the road, no-one could answer.

But there was something I still wanted to know, and perhaps Grandma Ruby could tell me.

'My father's friend, Glenn Neville, said he'd seemed upset on the night of the accident and that's why he drank so much. Do you have any idea what had shaken him up?'

Grandma Ruby's shoulders slumped as if all the air had gone out of her.

'Yes, I do,' she said quietly. 'It's what I've been wanting to tell you. But first let me explain to you how close our family was, so you will understand.'

TWENTY-FOUR

Ruby

The pain of losing Leroy was like hundreds of hands clawing at my heart. The colour drained out of my life. My head spun so much I thought I couldn't go on. And yet I had to. There was Maman and Mae to look after, as there always had been.

As soon as I'd discovered that Leroy had been killed, I'd gone to Sam Coppola and told him what had happened. The loss had been so sudden and so shocking that even as I described it to him, I was sure that I must have dreamed it. I had to clench my fists and convince myself that what had happened was real. Leroy was gone. Gone from me forever. That meant Jewel had to die too.

'Jewel needs to disappear,' I told Sam. 'She needs to vanish without a trace.'

He bowed his head. 'I'm sorry, Jewel. I'd hoped things would turn out for you and Leroy. I'll cover your tracks. No-one will be able to trace you. And if you ever find out who did this, I'll settle the score.'

The Ruby who sat down to breakfast with Maman the following day was nothing but a shell.

'My darling,' Maman said, 'I can't bear to see you so pale. Please tell me, has something happened between you and Clifford Lalande? Even if he is busy in New York, surely he could call?'

Poor Maman had put my grief down to lovesickness. She had no idea of the turmoil in my heart.

'I lost my job at the telephone exchange,' I told Mae. 'I told Maman that Adalie de Pauger was ill with the measles so I wouldn't be visiting her for a while.'

Mae nodded. 'Did you backchat your boss?'

Despite my grief, I almost wanted to laugh at her assumption. 'Well, sort of,' I replied.

'A whistling woman and a crowing hen never come to no good end,' she said. 'You are what you are, Miss Ruby. You're meant to marry a gentleman, not wear yourself out working.'

To my surprise, Clifford Lalande appeared a few days after Leroy's death to visit us, bearing charm bracelets from Tiffany & Co. for Maman and me, and a bottle of eau de cologne for Mae. I hadn't seen or heard from him since Mardi Gras night.

'I'm sorry that business has kept me away from your charming company for so long, Mrs de Villeray,' he told Maman. 'But it was unavoidable. I hope I can make it up to you both somehow.'

Maman's hand brushed her throat and her cheeks blushed from her nose to her ears. I could tell she was both delighted and flustered at Clifford's sudden return.

'That's quite all right,' she said, linking arms with him and ushering him quickly into the parlour as if she was afraid he might disappear again. 'There is nothing to apologise for. We could not be more pleased to see you.'

I followed them in and sat down too. Clifford's gaze shifted to me. I sensed from the faint lines between his eyes that he was worried about me. He must have found out somehow what had happened to Leroy.

'Did you have a successful time in New York?' Maman asked him.

I wondered if Clifford had really been there. He was such an honest person that I wouldn't have put it past him to have travelled there and back just so he wouldn't have to lie to Maman. He told her something about a legal case that sounded as if it could be true, but I found the story difficult to follow. My thinking had become slow and muddled.

I didn't realise that Maman and he were talking about me until Clifford said with emphasis, 'I was wondering, with your permission, Mrs de Villeray, if I may take Ruby for a drive this afternoon?'

Maman blushed again. 'Oh, that would be delightful. Some fresh air would do her the world of good. She hasn't been getting out as much since her friend fell ill.'

Normally Maman would have insisted that she or Mae accompany us, but I could tell from the sparkle in her eyes that she was hoping Clifford had bought more than charm bracelets at Tiffany's.

'I thought I might take you for a drive to Lake Pontchartrain, Ruby,' he said once we were out on the street. He opened the door to his Buick for me, then turned and waved to Maman, who was watching us from the gallery, beaming.

'How did you know she would be standing there?' I asked when he slipped into the driver's seat.

He smiled. 'I knew.'

I was grateful to Clifford for coming. I had no-one to talk to about what had happened and he was sensitive enough to have realised that.

We didn't make further conversation as we drove out of the city, nor as the car bumped and shook along the untarred road to the lake. It was only when Clifford had parked outside a fishing shack on piers that he looked at me.

'It's a simple place,' he said. 'But the food is good and it has a nice view of the water.'

The hut, converted into a home-style café, was bare bones with a tiny kitchen and Formica tables. I could see the muddy water of the lake through the holes in the splintery floorboards. But it was quiet and the breeze off the water was pleasant.

Clifford ordered lemonades for us and told the waitress we would eat later. Then he looked into my eyes and said, 'Ruby, I'm so sorry.'

I nodded. 'How did you find out?'

'From some of my contacts in the NAACP. They keep tabs on all racially motivated murders. When I learned that Leroy Thezan was secretly seeing a white dancer called Jewel, I understood immediately who he was.'

'Do they know who did it?'

'No, unfortunately,' he said, slowly stirring the ice in his drink. 'There are a number of white supremacists in the city; they might have killed Leroy to get at his brother.'

'Does the NAACP know that Jewel is me?'

Clifford shook his head. 'Jewel has disappeared without a trace.' He looked at me levelly. 'She might even be dead herself.'

I blinked back my tears and nodded towards the lake. 'I feel like I'm dead. If it wasn't for Maman and Mae, I would have drowned myself in there.'

He reached across the table and squeezed my hand. 'Don't talk like that, Ruby. Leroy would not have wanted that for you.'

There were only four choices on the menu. We ate fried oyster po' boys with sides of corn and potato. I'd had the appetite of a sick bird and it surprised me that I ate so well that afternoon. Perhaps it was the comfort I felt in Clifford's company.

After we'd finished eating and Clifford had paid the bill, he nodded towards the shore. 'Let's go for a walk. There's something I want to talk to you about.'

We took our shoes off and walked along the gritty grey sand, before taking a seat on some rocks. The air smelled of brine.

'Listen, Ruby,' he said, turning to face me, 'my proposal to you still stands. I love you, and I'll take care of you and your mother and Mae. You're grieving now, but I know in time I can make you very happy.'

A proposal from anyone but Clifford so soon after Leroy's death would have been insulting. But I knew it was motivated by genuine love and concern. My refusal was as genuine.

'You can't marry me,' I told him. 'I'm a woman with a past. I was a burlesque dancer — and I loved a coloured man. If anyone finds out, you'll be the laughing stock of New Orleans.'

'A dancer in a club — so what?' He picked up a stone and sent it skipping across the water. 'You were beautiful and classy. The fact that you could see a coloured man as an equal human being makes me admire you more.' He looked at me again. 'Ruby, the loss you have suffered must be unbearable. I don't expect you to be the blushing bride. But I do want you to think long term. You can't go back to dancing, and you have to secure your future. Maybe you don't love me in a silly romantic way, but perhaps that's even better. What we've got is true companionship. I'm a man who loves you for exactly who you are, and I believe you feel the same way about me.'

For a moment it was as if the world stood still. Everything Clifford had said was true. I stared out at the lake and wondered what Leroy would tell me to do if he were here. I knew the answer. There was an inherent goodness in Clifford that made me confident that whatever difficulties life brought us, our union would be strong.

Weariness swept over me and my body felt as heavy as the anchors that kept the fishing trawlers securely moored on the lake. It was the exhaustion of having carried Maman and Mae for so long and not having had anyone to share my burdens with. What a relief it would be to spend my life with someone I could speak to sensibly and practically like an equal. Someone who truly understood me. What was the point of resisting when that person stood there in front of me, offering his comfort to help me bear the unbearable?

'Ruby?'

I looked up. Clifford had perceived the shift in my attitude and was holding his hand out to me. I stood up and pressed myself into his embrace, feeling his fingers stroke my hair. It was as if the mist that had enveloped me was lifted by his love.

'So will you marry me, Ruby?' he asked.

I embraced him more fiercely but didn't speak for a few minutes. When I did, I said, 'Yes, Clifford, I'll marry you. But I'll never deserve you.'

Clifford insisted that we get married straight away, for my sake.

'You're too alone, and you've carried far too much for too long,' he told me. 'Let me take up the mantle. I won't make any demands of you. All I want you to do is concentrate on restoring your peace of mind.'

Maman, Kitty and Mrs Lalande — Helen — delighted in the matrimonial preparations and I was happy to leave them to organise everything. I watched in a trance as Maman and Mae spent hours beading my wedding dress, and Kitty directed their gardener, Ned, to decorate the summerhouse with pots of white azaleas, roses and chrysanthemums. Even when the baker delivered the cake, trimmed with silver leaves and hearts, I stared at the bride and groom on top and couldn't believe that I was actually getting married.

On the day of the ceremony, Maman, Kitty and Helen, along with Mae, helped me prepare in the bedroom that Clifford and I were to share in the Lalande home. Their excited chatter was like a hundred bells ringing in my head.

'The guests are already arriving — we'd better hurry,' said Helen. 'Even people who haven't spoken to us for years are showing up. All the tongues are wagging and everyone is keen to see the beautiful French Creole Clifford is marrying!'

'Your dress is divine!' gushed Kitty, taking the organza cover off the white tulle and satin gown. Indeed, the dress was stunning with its princess-style bodice and pearl-beaded flowers. It made me think of the magnificent dresses Orry-Kelly had made for me as Jewel and I had to turn away from it.

I glanced at Maman, who was looking as radiantly happy as if she were the bride and this was her wedding day. Her champagne-pink silk dress flattered her complexion and her eyes danced with joy. She truly believed that Clifford and I had created the perfect Cinderella story, with no idea of all the torment that was behind it. But perhaps it was better that she had been spared any anguish.

'Look at these beautiful lilies the Galafates sent you,' said Helen, placing the bouquet in a crystal vase and putting it on the dressing table, where I was sitting while Mae styled my hair.

The honey-like sweetness of the blooms conjured up a memory of Leroy's casket surrounded by flowers. I tried to apply my powder to calm myself, but I saw Jewel's despairing reflection staring back at me. Tears ran down my cheeks.

'Time to get into your dress, Miss Ruby,' said Mae, taking the gown from its hanger. 'Unless you want to get married in your petticoat.'

She caught sight of my face and gasped. The other women gathered around me.

'Ruby!' cried Kitty. 'What's the matter?'

I couldn't answer them. My heart was beating erratically and I found it difficult to breathe. I thought I might black out so I got up from the chair and stumbled to the bed, sobbing as I lay down on it.

'My heavenly days!' exclaimed Helen. 'Are you all right, sweetheart?'

Maman sat down next to me and stroked my back. 'It's bride's nerves, that's all. I had them on my wedding day.'

'I've never seen her like this,' said Mae, squinting. 'She's normally got nerves of steel.'

Maman dispatched Mae to the kitchen to ask Philomena to make some camomile tea for me. Kitty doused a handkerchief in lavender water and placed it on my burning forehead.

'Good Lord, she needs something stronger than that,' said Helen. She left the room and returned a minute later with a decanter of brandy and a glass. 'Here, take a sip of this,' she said.

The liquor burned my throat. I coughed and doubled over. It was as if everything was caving inwards and my mind had shattered into a million pieces.

Someone knocked at the door.

'Is everything all right?' I heard Eddie ask. 'The priest is here and the guests are starting to whisper.'

'You'll only make matters worse saying things like that!' Kitty scolded him. 'Ruby's had a dizzy spell, that's all. She'll be all right in a minute.'

I was in a haze. It was as though I was floating around the room watching myself and thinking, *That can't be me.* It was my wedding day, but I was the saddest I'd ever been.

There was another knock at the door and it opened a crack. 'May I see her?' I heard Clifford ask.

'No!' Kitty cried. 'It's bad luck!'

But Helen acquiesced. 'Let's give them a few moments together. Nothing we've done has made things any better.'

Maman covered me with a blanket and, along with the other women, reluctantly left the room.

Clifford came and sat next to me. 'Ruby?'

I turned to him. He looked handsome in his pale grey suit with his hair combed back from his face. Any other woman would have been blissfully happy to be marrying him. I tried to say something but ended up crying harder. He took my hand and rested my palm against his cheek.

'Ruby, I don't expect you to forget Leroy Thezan. I don't expect you to never speak of him. You loved him. We are going to be husband and wife, and we are going to be best friends and confidants. You can talk to me about him anytime, Ruby. Anytime! But the past is gone and you can't bring it back. Life must be lived now if it is to be lived at all. I know you are strong enough to understand that.'

His words had a calming effect on me. I remembered the day he'd proposed to me at Lake Pontchartrain and how I'd felt so confident then that our marriage would be strong. I looked into his kind eyes and knew that he understood things about me that nobody else did.

I slipped my hand down his shoulder and grasped his fingers in mine. 'I've kept too much to myself in my life and all the secrets have caught up with me.'

He nodded. 'We'll have no secrets between us from now on, Ruby. We'll tell each other everything.' He slipped his hand from mine and stood up. 'Now, go get dressed and come down. I'll be waiting for you. Never mind about anybody else. Just think about me. I'm the one you are marrying.'

His smile gave me confidence. When he'd left the room, I swung my legs to the floor and stood up, still unsteady on my feet. I picked up my purse and took out a key, then opened the wardrobe to find the trunk I had stowed away there. I unlocked it and brushed my hand over the red beaded gown that I'd worn on stage for one of my Mardi Gras numbers. I picked up the strapless bra and G-string that I had modelled for Leroy.

'Goodbye, my love,' I whispered. 'I'm glad we made each other happy. But I have to go on living now. I will never forget you.'

I closed the trunk, and put on my wedding gown and veil, powdered my face and reapplied my lipstick. Then I picked up my bouquet of orchids and opened the door to the hall.

Before leaving the room, I turned back for one more glimpse in the mirror. But it was Ruby in her bridal gown who looked back at me this time. Jewel was gone.

Not long after our honeymoon, I discovered I was pregnant. The excitement in the Lalande house was palpable when Clifford and I told the family one evening after dinner.

'I'm to become a grandmother!' Helen cried, regarding us fondly. 'Oh, Ruby, what happiness you bring to our family! You and Clifford will be wonderful parents.'

'Of course we will,' said Clifford, grinning. 'We've been given the best examples to follow.'

My gaze shifted to Kitty. She had confided in me only a few days before that she couldn't have children because of a malformation of her womb. Eddie and I were the only ones she had told. I'd wanted to downplay the announcement of my pregnancy, but she wouldn't hear of it. Now, she reached over to me and squeezed my hand. 'I'm so excited I'm going to be an aunt,' she said sincerely. 'I want to be known as "Crazy Aunt Kitty"!'

Maman and Mae had come to live with us now that Kitty and Eddie had moved into their own home. After hearing the news, Maman sat lost in a happy dream, her eyes glistening.

'Maman, are you glad that you are going to be a grandmother?' I asked.

A radiant glow came to her face. 'Oh, yes, Ruby, I couldn't be happier or prouder.'

Her words should have been a joy to hear, but they stirred an uneasy feeling in me. Perhaps it was because I could never forget that I had a secret past and that if Maman ever found out about it, it would grieve her deeply. No matter what happiness I enjoyed in the present, that secret would always be my cross to bear.

Maman and Helen set about turning one of the upstairs bedrooms into a nursery. Each day they called me up there to see a new detail that had been added: the nursery-rhyme wallpaper and matching curtains; the folding change table with a quilted cover; the bassinette with a skirt decorated with ruffles and flounces made from leftover material from my wedding dress. It should have been the happiest time in my life, yet the uneasiness I'd felt at the announcement of my pregnancy continued to plague me.

❧

One morning I woke up convinced that the baby had died in my womb overnight.

'Clifford,' I cried, shaking him awake. 'The baby's not moving. I can't feel it!'

Clifford sat up, a distressed look on his face. He pressed his ear to my stomach. 'Darling, I'm sure there is a little flutter in there. But I'll take you to Doctor Monfort this morning anyway.'

Our family doctor was quick to reassure me. 'It's natural that you are anxious with your first baby, but all is well and your pregnancy is progressing normally.'

Despite his assurances, from that day onwards a cold fear dampened my joy. I was haunted by the possibility of losing my child. Anytime the baby was quiet for a long period of time, I panicked. A repetitive nightmare disturbed my dreams: I was walking towards the baby's bassinette, but when I looked inside it there was Leroy's mangled body.

Doctor Monfort could do little to help my nerves, and Clifford enlisted the aid of an Uptown obstetrician, Doctor Delcambre, who specialised in high risk pregnancies and was the brother of one of the white lawyers he'd worked with in the Urban League.

'Maman,' I said one afternoon when we were in the sitting room together knitting booties, 'I hope you don't mind that I won't be having the baby at home with Doctor Monfort. I know you would like that, but Doctor Delcambre feels it best that I go to his private clinic ahead of my confinement.'

Maman put down her knitting and slipped her hand into mine. 'My darling, the most important consideration is you and the baby. That's all. Nothing else matters.'

Helen gave me a book about an abolitionist named Dale Thomas Owen to take my mind off my worries. I read it religiously in bed every night before going to sleep.

One night, when Clifford was getting into bed beside me, he glanced at the book. 'Is it interesting?'

I nodded. 'Dale Thomas Owen reminds me of you. Despite all the setbacks he suffered, including being shunned by his social circle and threatened by those who were making money out of the misery of slavery, he never let fear or loneliness sway him from his cause.'

He took the book from me. 'Dale is a good name for a boy, don't you think? It sounds fresh and new. If the baby is a boy, I want him to be fearless, brave and confident. The world needs men with characteristics like that.'

Our eyes met and we smiled.

'I want him to be like that too,' I said. 'That's exactly the kind of man I would want him to grow up to be. Someone like you.'

On the day I went into labour, I barely registered the pain in my body because the racking anguish in my mind was so great. All I could think about was the child. Was he or she alive?

It was only after several excruciating pushes, when I heard a cry sing out from a healthy set of lungs and the nurse showed me a rosy baby boy, that the darkness I'd felt during my pregnancy lifted and I cried with joy.

'He's so handsome,' I said. 'So very handsome. My darling baby boy!'

Indeed to me, Dale was the most charming child ever born. From the time we took him home, I couldn't stop looking at him. Even when he didn't need to be fed, I'd go to his bassinette to gaze at him. He had a full head of curls, and followed my every movement with his big curious eyes.

If I was enamoured, then Clifford was smitten. When I saw him cradle Dale in his arms and coo to him softly, I fell in love with my husband and knew I had been right to marry him, despite all the grief that had besieged me at the time.

Dale seemed equally captivated by Clifford. When his father danced around him, making monkey faces, Dale would point at him and gurgle with delight.

'I can't wait until he can ride a bike,' said Clifford one evening as we were having supper. 'I'll take him riding in Audubon Park.'

I looked over my teacup at him. 'He hasn't started walking yet ... and you might have some competition from our mothers. I hardly get to see Dale now the weather is warming. His grandmothers make several trips a day around the neighbourhood with him in his pram simply to show him off.'

'All right,' Clifford said, picking up our dishes to take them to the kitchen, 'I'll try to be patient. But let's not wait too long before we have another one. I like being a father and motherhood becomes you.'

TWENTY-FIVE

Ruby

Shortly after Dale's third birthday, I discovered that I was pregnant again. I waited until the following day to tell Clifford the news. He was a morning person and I wasn't, but I made an effort to get up early so we could spend some time together before he left for his office. I watched him pour maple syrup over his waffles, and admired his freshly shaven face and neatly combed hair. From the back porch came the clackety-clack sound of Helen at her typewriter, writing articles for the Urban League newsletter, and the smell of smoke from her cigarette. I'd asked Mae and Philomena to mind Dale in the kitchen because I had something important to discuss with my husband.

As I looked at Clifford, I was filled with a triumphant joy. It had taken longer than anticipated for me to get pregnant again and I knew my announcement would make him happy. A rush of excitement ran through me and suddenly the words came bubbling out as if I could no longer contain them. 'Darling, I'm expecting!'

Clifford looked up, his fork paused mid-air. He stared at me with an expression of awe before a smile broke out over his face. 'Ruby! Really?' He sprang up from his chair and embraced me. 'How long have you known?'

'Doctor Delcambre confirmed it yesterday afternoon, but you looked tired last night so I decided to wait and tell you this morning.'

'Oh, Ruby! This is such good news!' he said, squeezing me harder. 'I should have guessed it. You've been glowing.'

'What would you like?' I asked him. 'Another boy or a girl?'

He shook his head. 'I don't care. Either is great as far as I'm concerned. When do you want to tell the others?'

It seemed strange to me, looking back on it, how I noticed at that precise moment that the sound of the typewriter had ceased. Then I heard Mae scream. The grin slipped from Clifford's face.

My first thought was that Dale had fallen from his chair. I leaped up and rushed to the kitchen. The maids weren't there but my little boy was sitting securely at the table with jam on his cheeks and a bewildered expression in his eyes. Why had they left him by himself? It wasn't like Mae or Philomena to be so careless.

Through the open door I could see Mae standing on the back porch with her hand over her mouth. Philomena was calling for Clifford to come. He ran past me and out to the porch. 'Mother!' he shouted.

I followed and my heart stopped when I saw Helen lying on the porch floor cradled in Philomena's arms. Her eyelids were flickering and a trickle of blood seeped from her mouth. Had she fallen and hit her head? She was mumbling, struggling to tell Clifford something.

Whatever was happening, she was in pain and that snapped me back to attention.

'Call an ambulance!' I told Mae. 'Then go get Maman and ask her to look after Dale.'

The ambulance arrived, and Clifford and I followed it in the car to the hospital. Eddie and Kitty arrived soon after.

The doctor came out with a grave look on his face and ushered us into a private room. I heard Kitty gasp, 'Oh no!' as he shut the door behind us.

'I'm very sorry. Mrs Lalande passed away a few minutes ago,' he told us. 'It appears she suffered a sudden and devastating stroke.'

I grasped Clifford's hand. His face had turned ashen. It was hard to believe that he'd been looking radiantly happy only a short time before.

I placed my other hand on my stomach, sorry that the announcement of my pregnancy would forever be associated with that terrible day.

The loss of his mother was a terrible blow to Clifford. I tried to help him the way he had helped me grieve for Leroy — with patience, respect and unconditional love — but I felt helpless before the world-weary eyes that had once shone and the grim line of his mouth that had replaced his ever-ready smile.

Maman, too, keenly felt the loss of her friend. She put Helen's picture on a shelf in her room and collected fresh flowers every day from the garden to place in a vase next to it.

Kitty and Eddie joined us each evening for dinner, looking for solace in family. It seemed inconceivable that the matriarch of the house, always so energetic and vital, was no longer there to play a part in our lives. How could she have died so suddenly when she still had so much life ahead of her? Her empty chair and table on the back porch filled me with sadness and I asked Ned to move them to the attic. We never used the porch again after that.

One day as Maman and I walked in the garden, she said, 'The house is so quiet without Helen. It will be good when the little one arrives. What we need is some noise!'

I squeezed her arm, grateful for her encouragement. But the truth was, the happiness my pregnancy had brought had been so fleeting it felt like a mere drop in an ocean of grief.

In the end, it was Dale who brought us solace.

Clifford and I were dressing for breakfast one morning when we heard the music to 'When the Saints Go Marching In' playing downstairs. At first I thought Mae or Philomena had turned the radio on early. Then we realised the sound was coming from the music room. Someone was playing the piano. But who?

We went downstairs to investigate and to our surprise found Dale, still in his pyjamas, sitting on the stool and moving his hands over the keys. I gasped. He wasn't picking at the keyboard as if the instrument was a toy. His face was scrunched with intense concentration and his tiny hands moved nimbly. The early morning sunshine bathed him in a soft light that gave him a halo. He looked like an angel sweetening the air with music.

'Good Lord,' I whispered to Clifford, 'I can't play as well as that and I've had lessons.'

'It's no surprise that our son is gifted,' he replied. 'There's an old soul behind those bright-as-a-button eyes.'

When I told Maman what had happened, she showed Dale some easy classical pieces and he picked them up straight away.

'My grandson barely talks,' she told me proudly, 'but he can play Bach!'

Clifford consulted with a music professor at Tulane University, who advised us to wait until Dale was five before giving him formal lessons, but to expose him to all types of music in the meantime and let him explore the keyboard himself.

The exercise became an enjoyable diversion for us all. Maman would sit with him at the piano for an hour a day, playing simple duets, while Clifford and I took him to concerts and to see street parades.

One Sunday, when we were in City Park listening to a Dixieland band, I was momentarily distracted by an ice cream vendor. I asked Clifford for some change, and it was only when I went to pass the ice cream cone to Dale that I realised I'd let go of his hand.

'No!' I cried, frantically looking around.

To my great surprise, I saw Dale mounting the stairs to the stage. Clifford quickly grabbed him, kissed him on the cheek so he wouldn't cry, and brought him back to me.

'He definitely favours jazz,' he said, laughing.

'Of course he does,' I replied. 'After all, he was born in the month of Mardi Gras. He heard all the street bands while still in my womb!'

❖

Shortly after the day in City Park, Maman and Dale were having a piano lesson together when Maman stumbled as she got up from the stool. I thought she must have tripped on the skirt of her dress and felt around her ankle to make sure she hadn't sprained it. When I looked up at her, I could see she was distressed but trying not to show it.

'What's the matter, Maman?' I asked. 'Do your feet hurt?'

She shook her head bravely. 'They feel a little numb.'

'Since when? Did you tell Doctor Monfort?'

'It's nothing,' she said, looking away. 'I'm just getting old.'

'Maman, you're hardly old!'

Doctor Monfort dropped the bombshell when he came to see me after carrying out some tests on Maman.

'There's protein in her urine,' he said with a pained expression. 'That means her kidneys are beginning to fail.'

My heart splintered at his words. 'Is there a medication or a treatment?'

Doctor Monfort grimaced. 'I'm afraid it's irreversible. I will give her some medicines for now, but as the kidneys worsen the only thing that will keep her going is dialysis at the hospital. But that is an ordeal and will only hold off the inevitable for a while. I'd recommend you let nature take its course. She could go on for another six months, or maybe even another six years. Only God knows. Make the most of the time you have left together.'

'Does she know about her kidneys?' I asked.

He nodded. 'She took it well, Ruby — although I didn't elaborate too much on how much time she might have left.' Placing his hand on my shoulder he added, 'You have looked after your mother devotedly. I was amazed that she recovered from having her lung removed, and that's a credit to you. Her disease is like water. You and I have done everything we can to hold it back, but eventually the water will wear down the rock and something will give. It looks like her kidneys have taken the brunt.'

After Doctor Monfort left, I sank down on a chair in the parlour and rested my head in my hands. How could I lose Maman when another child was coming along? I needed her. She was everything to me.

I became aware of someone else in the room and looked up to see Mae. Her eyes were glistening with tears and her lips were trembling.

'You heard what Doctor Monfort said?' I asked.

She nodded and sniffed. 'It ain't right,' she whispered. 'It ain't right. God takes the good ones too early.'

I stood up and clasped her hands. 'It's to your credit, Mae, that Maman has lived this long. It's you who has been watching her diet, monitoring her sugar levels and administering her medicines. You're the one who's slept with one eye open and checked on her several times each night to make sure she's breathing. I owe you everything, Mae. I owe Maman's life to you.'

Mae cried harder and I could no longer hold back my own tears.

'You give yourself credit too, Mrs Ruby,' she said, gripping my hands tighter. 'You created a good life for your mama. You've given her a wonderful home and a lot of happiness, and you worked hard for it. If it wasn't for you, we'd have all ended up in the street.'

I hugged her, my heart filled with both sorrow and gratitude. She had always been there for me and I knew that whatever happened in the future I would always take care of her.

After I'd composed myself, I went to see Maman. She was sitting in the armchair in her room and gazing out of the window. Her feet were propped up on an ottoman. She looked serene, not at all like someone who had been given a death sentence. Perhaps Doctor Monfort had been wrong. As he'd said, after Maman's lung was removed he was surprised that she had survived. Maybe she would defy the odds again.

She smiled at me and showed me a picture from the sewing magazine she had on her lap. 'Look at this beautiful baby quilt,' she said, her cheeks glowing. 'The kittens and puppies on it are just darling. I bet I'll have time to finish one like it before your little one is born.'

My heart felt like it had been tied into knots, but I smiled and sat down beside her. 'That is the most adorable quilt I've ever seen. Tell me what you need and I'll ask Mae to go get it for you.'

She took my hand. I could see she wanted to say something about her illness, and I did too, but we were both too full for words. So we simply sat together and talked about what colours would be best for the quilt like nothing bad was happening at all.

Clifford stayed up with me all night as I poured out my grief and fears to him. 'Oh, God, I hope she won't suffer,' I told him. 'If she suffers, I don't think I could bear it.'

He held me and kissed my forehead. 'Ruby, you are going to have to calm yourself for the sake of the baby. It won't do the little one any good for you to wring yourself out like this. Take it one day at a time. Enjoy your mother while she is still here. You know the people we love can leave us at any time without warning.'

Our eyes met. I took his hands and pressed them to my chest. 'Yes, that's true. You and I should know that as well as anybody.'

The following morning, Clifford kissed me before he left for his office and told me he'd be back at noon to check on us all. I strolled around the garden to ease my grief. The baby was moving around a lot now and I walked slowly. The roses Ned had planted the year Clifford and I married were in their full raspberry bloom and smelled intoxicating. I went to the potting shed for some secateurs to cut a few blooms for Maman.

I returned inside and set her place at the dining table with fine porcelain plates with a gold scroll pattern around their rims.

Since Maman had come to live with us in the Garden District, we hadn't talked very much about the past. When Clifford and I announced our engagement, she'd asked me if I was going to invite Uncle Rex and Aunt Elva to the wedding. I'd had no choice then but to confess to her that I'd broken ties with them because Uncle Rex had been stealing money from us. But I changed the story so that it was Clifford who had rescued us from our debts.

Maman had turned pale at the revelation. 'I should never have believed it if the news hadn't come from you,' she said. And she never mentioned them again.

Since that time Uncle Rex had died, and I'd heard that Eugenie had married and moved to Vermont because her new husband couldn't stand her mother. What Aunt Elva was doing with herself these days, I didn't know. I didn't care to know either.

Mae came into the dining room and saw me setting the table for Maman. 'I checked on her earlier this morning,' she told me. 'She was sleeping like a baby.'

While waiting for Maman to get up, I went to the nursery to see Dale. Philomena was watching him draw a picture of a face with crayons.

'That's Daddy!' he said proudly.

'He loves his daddy, doesn't he?' said Philomena, smiling. 'He's his father's shadow. He's got his daddy's hands and he even walks a little like him.'

I'd heard of some women getting jealous when their child favoured their husband, but it delighted me to know Dale and Clifford were so close. I'd hardly seen my father when I was growing up. I was glad Dale had a good role model.

Maman usually came down for breakfast around ten o'clock. I waited until half past before I became concerned. Was she upset about the news she'd received the day before? Were her feet bothering her and that was why she hadn't come down?

I put her breakfast on a tray and Mae carried it up the stairs while I followed with the roses in a vase. I knocked gently on Maman's door but there was no answer. My hand trembled as I pushed it open. *Please, God*, I prayed. *Please don't let anything have happened.*

Maman was lying in bed. I moved towards her and saw that her eyes were closed and her face was waxy. I reached out and touched her shoulder. 'Maman?'

Her eyes flickered open but the light had gone out of them.

'What's the matter, Maman? Aren't you feeling well?'

I took her hand and flinched when I felt how cold it was. Her lips seemed to be turning blue before my eyes. What was happening? Yesterday she'd had sore feet and some protein in her urine, but Doctor Monfort had said there were months, even years, before she declined. Was Maman upset about what he'd told her? I'd have to rally her somehow. I'd heard of people willing themselves to death after getting a bad prognosis.

'Doctors are wrong sometimes,' I whispered to her. 'You know that. Now what about you have some breakfast and get started on that quilt you were talking about?'

I nodded to Mae, who placed the tray on the bedside table. I put the roses next to it. Maman ignored the food but reached out to touch the flowers.

'They're so beautiful,' she said. 'I've always loved flowers.'

I tugged back the bedclothes so I could help her sit up against her pillows. Her body looked sunken, as if all the air had gone from it overnight. Was something else failing other than her kidneys? *Please, God, not now. Please give us more time.*

Maman smiled weakly. 'I'm so proud of you, Ruby. So very proud. I'm sorry, but I don't think I'm going to be able to make the quilt like I promised.'

'She's talking gibberish,' said Mae. 'I'll go get her insulin. It looks like she's having a turn.'

I sighed, relieved. That's what it was. Only a turn.

'Maman, you'll be all right,' I assured her. 'Mae's getting your insulin now.' I kissed her cheek. 'I'll open the window and let some fresh air in. That's what you need.'

The window took a bit of pushing to open it because the sash was old, but I eventually succeeded. Warm air scented with jasmine wafted into the room. The smell of it calmed my thumping heart. Philomena was playing ball in the garden with Dale, who was trying to catch it but missing every time and laughing just the same. I smiled. He was the light of my life.

I turned back to Maman and saw that she'd sunk down on her pillows. I thought at first she must have fainted, then I noticed the room had turned quiet. It wasn't a tranquil silence, but one that signified absence. I stared at her chest. It wasn't moving at all. Doctor Monfort had always warned me that people with my mother's condition could slip away very quickly from a sudden cardiac arrest. That was why Mae always checked on her several times a night. But that simply could not have happened. Not now!

'Maman?'

But even as I gently shook her to revive her, I knew it was hopeless. My dear, sweet Maman, my reason for so many of the things I had done in my life, was gone.

A month after Maman's funeral, I went into labour. I didn't feel like someone strong enough to give birth; I was as fragile as an eggshell. During the contractions I called out for Maman and grabbed the sides of the hospital bed until my knuckles turned white. Unlike Dale's birth, I didn't worry about the baby. All I could think about was that the woman who had brought me into the world was dead.

After six hours of a labour I barely registered, Louise was born. She was as pink as a blossom and turned to me with a puckered mouth as if waiting for a kiss. But while the nurse fussed over her and Doctor Delcambre said she was one of the prettiest babies he'd ever seen, all I felt was numb.

When I came home from hospital, Kitty came to visit me bringing a bouquet of Chantilly roses.

'Where's Dale?' she asked, taking a vase from the bureau and filling it with water. 'He usually bolts down the stairs to see me.'

'Clifford took him to the park. Poor thing. Louise wouldn't settle and I don't think anybody within a mile got any sleep last night. Dale was as quiet as a mouse when he was a baby.'

Kitty looked at me steadily. 'And where is my little niece? Aren't you keen to show her off to her aunt?'

'Of course,' I said, leading the way upstairs to the nursery. 'I've just fed her so she's probably asleep.'

'She's taking after you then. Every time Eddie and I came to visit you at the hospital, you were sleeping like a log. We decided we'd best come pay our respects when you got home.'

What Kitty said was true: I had slept a lot at the hospital. It was my way of disappearing into my grief. I knew the nurses would wake me when Louise needed to be fed.

We walked into the nursery and peered into the bassinette. Louise was awake, staring around at the world with her shiny eyes. *Lord!* I thought. *Does this child never get tired?*

Without a moment's hesitation, Kitty picked Louise up and cradled her. 'Oh my,' she said, kissing Louise's chubby cheek, 'she is a pretty little thing!'

I rubbed my arms. I loved Louise, of course I did. She was my daughter. But I didn't feel the same overwhelming love for her that I had for Dale. Perhaps I was too upset about Maman to properly bond with her.

Kitty pressed Louise to her chest. There was a strong resemblance between them around the jawline and chin: Louise could easily have been Kitty's child. Kitty would have been a wonderful mother and adored all her children equally. Life was unfair sometimes.

'It's nice that you gave her Mother's middle name,' Kitty said. 'She would have liked that.'

'I hope so,' I said, turning away and straightening the cover on the change table. Perhaps Kitty was wondering why I hadn't named my daughter Desiree after Maman? But I wasn't ready for that. Every time I looked at Louise I would have been reminded of the day Maman died.

'My mother sure loved your mother,' I said to change the subject. 'Even though they were like chalk and cheese. I remember the day Maman, who'd always been so traditional, said to me, "I think us white folks should do more to help the coloured ones, don't you?"'

Kitty laughed. 'Mother had a way with persuasion. You didn't even know she was getting you on board until you were standing there with a pen and a clipboard and challenging people to sign petitions.'

'We could say the same thing about her daughter!'

Kitty smiled. 'Well, you must have read my mind. I do have something I want to discuss with you. The Urban League is holding a fundraising dinner next Mardi Gras and I need someone to help me sell the tickets.' She winked. 'I might be persuasive, but you have real charm. I reckon you could sell ice to an Eskimo.'

I supported all that Clifford and Kitty were doing to better the lives of coloured people, but I'd never gotten involved myself. I was afraid that if I stirred up too many of the wrong people, they might start nosing about and find out things about me that would do more damage than good to the cause.

'Well,' I said, 'I'm going to be a little busy with the new baby and all ...'

Kitty placed her hand on my arm and looked at me sternly. 'It's only selling tickets, Ruby. You could do that over the telephone.'

I shrugged. 'All right, I'll help. But if you think I could sell ice to an Eskimo, I reckon you could sell religion to the Pope!'

Things were changing quickly in the Civil Rights Movement. The protests were no longer ad hoc actions like when I'd first encountered Ti-Jean but a highly organised program of sit-ins at restaurants, 'wade-ins' at beaches, 'kneel-ins' at churches and 'study-ins' at libraries that were still segregated.

In the spring of 1960, Kitty and I went to visit the picket lines on Dryades Street to offer moral support to the protesters. We had spent the morning making brown-bag lunches to give to them. We left Dale and Louise in the care of Mae and Philomena. Although the protest was supposed to be peaceful, there was no telling what could happen.

'Most of the people who shop here are coloured, yet the stores refuse to hire Negroes for anything other than menial work,' Kitty explained to me. 'The Urban League has been trying to convince the store managers for years to hire coloured people as sales clerks. Now all these young kids from the local colleges are taking matters into their own hands. They want customers to boycott the stores until they change their policies.'

Louisiana law allowed for only two pickets per block. Most of the students worked in pairs, but I noticed one young white man on his own outside a supermarket, holding a sign that read *Don't buy from a store that won't employ you.* He shifted his weight from foot to foot and glanced around nervously. I couldn't blame him for being wary. If he had conservative parents, he could be kicked out of home if they found out; and if he had liberal ones, they could lose their jobs over his actions. To add to his woes, white hecklers had turned up to harass the students. They knew they could do it with impunity. If anything happened, the police and the law would be on their side.

'Let's go speak to that boy,' said Kitty. 'He looks like he could do with some encouragement.'

Before we crossed the street, another woman from the Urban League recognised Kitty and stopped to greet her. While they chatted, I noticed a little white girl, no more than three years of age, approach the picketer. She was carrying a pail and a paintbrush.

'I'm going to paint you black, mister,' she said to the young man, dipping her brush into the black paint and aiming it for his pants.

The student tried to ignore her and dodge her at the same time. Where had she gotten the paint from, I wondered. Had one of the storekeepers given it to her? That was a cheap trick.

'Excuse me a minute,' I said to Kitty and her companion. I crossed the street and approached the girl. 'Darling, that's not a very nice thing to be doing, is it?'

The girl stopped mid-action and looked at me with wide eyes. She lowered her head and shook it. 'No.'

She was a cute girl with clean curly hair tied in a bow and her red shoes looked expensive. 'Who told you to do such a thing?' I asked her, scanning around for a mischievous older sibling.

'Don't you tell my daughter what she can and can't do!'

I looked up to see a stout woman in a shirtwaist dress and a mushroom hat rushing towards me. She looked vaguely familiar and I realised it was Jackie Fausey, Clifford's former fiancée. She had obviously gotten married since I'd seen her last and had this little girl, but matrimony had done nothing to improve her looks. With her heavily powdered face and harshly drawn lips, she exuded the same dolled-up frumpiness of Aunt Elva. And the similarities didn't end there.

She pointed at the student. 'If he wants to be a darkie, then Patty is only trying to help him achieve his aim!'

'He's not trying to be coloured,' I told her. 'He's trying to create a fair society.'

'Well, aren't you a Lalande through and through,' she sneered. 'I made a lucky escape from that crazy family. I heard Cliff's mother kicked the bucket, so I guess you've decided to take up the mantle.'

For an Uptown girl and a judge's daughter, Jackie was as common as a bowl of grits. I wanted to give her a good shove for insulting my family, but then I remembered the scuffle I'd gotten into with Aunt Elva, and I knew the hecklers would revel in any excuse to break up the otherwise peaceful protest.

At that moment Kitty came up to us and Jackie's face twisted in contempt and her nostrils flared.

'It's a real pity that my sister-in-law has to teach your little girl about being decent, Jackie,' Kitty said. 'I'd hoped she might learn those kinds of things from you. But I guess not.'

Jackie glowered at us. 'You do-gooders don't understand the situation. Coloured people don't want to think for themselves. Without white people telling them what to do, they'd all regress into savages.'

My blood boiled and I wanted to slap Jackie's fat arrogant face, but Kitty pulled me away in time.

'Don't waste your breath on her,' she said. 'But you can see why Clifford couldn't marry her! Lord, can you imagine that woman in our family?' She giggled and slipped her arm through mine. 'I'm glad he made a much better choice with you, Ruby.'

Kitty and I handed out the brown-bag lunches, then prepared to leave. As we passed a store, a woman came out and blocked our path. I braced myself for some verbal abuse, but she pointed to a crate of apples near the door.

'I noticed you giving food to the young people,' she whispered in a thick European accent. 'Do you think they'd like some apples as well?'

'Yes, ma'am,' said Kitty. 'I'm sure they would appreciate them very much.'

The woman nodded. 'It's not right the way we treat coloured people. I lost my family in Germany. They treated Jews the same way there.'

As we walked back to Kitty's car, she said to me, 'People are so frightened, it's hard to tell who's on our side and who's an enemy.' Then she smiled. 'Clifford said he could tell in an instant that you were one of us.'

'One of us?' I asked, curious.

'You're colourblind, metaphorically speaking. You don't speak to a person differently depending on whether they're coloured or white. It isn't the first thing you notice about a human being.'

The following Sunday when the Galafate family joined us for lunch along with Kitty and Eddie, Kitty told them what we'd seen at the picket protests.

'I admire this generation of kids,' Christophe said. 'They have a strong moral sense of what's right and they're prepared to make a stand for it.'

'It doesn't stop them being arrested, beaten and put in gaol though,' said Clarita. 'They lose their jobs and so do their parents.'

'But their courage and their peaceful protests are gaining attention,' offered Clifford in his usual optimistic way. 'They are disciplined and organised. I've heard they practise by having their fellow students shout at them, slap their faces and punch them, so they learn to conquer their urge to retaliate. Their exemplary behaviour shows their oppressors for the fools they are.'

My gaze wandered to the children, who were playing together on the lawn under the supervision of Philomena and Mae. Adolphe and Dale were flying a toy plane, taking turns at the controls, while Isabelle played with Louise on a rug, brushing her sparse hair gently and holding up different dolls for her to admire. I remembered what Joan Fischer had said at that first meeting of the Urban League that I'd attended: the only way coloured and white people could really know each other was to mix together and for children to grow up alongside each other.

I'd always felt terrible about running away from the Thezan family after Leroy's death. They had been good to me, but Leroy's murder and the abrupt end of my life as Jewel had blown me flat like a house in a hurricane. A couple of months after Dale was born, I'd ventured into Tremé with a letter of gratitude for the Thezans that I'd composed over and over again in my head before committing it to paper. My intention was to slip it into their mailbox, but when I arrived at the funeral home I found its windows boarded up and a *For Rent* sign on the door. From the condition of the lawn and the dust on the windows, it looked like the house had been empty for some time too.

'You looking for the Thezan family?' a woman called to me from her porch across the street. I turned and nodded. 'They all cleared out and went to San Francisco after their son was killed,' she said. 'They didn't leave no forwarding address.'

I stepped closer and recognised the woman. She returned my gaze with some curious scrutiny of her own. It was the neighbour I'd seen in the Thezans' home after the burning cross had been set on their lawn: the woman who hadn't been too happy about Leroy having a white girlfriend. I didn't want to get into conversation with her, so I thanked her and hurried away.

I never returned to Tremé after that, or made any investigations into the Thezan family. I was sorry that they'd had to leave the city they'd lived in all their lives.

I turned back to Dale and Adolphe. If children could see beyond colour, why couldn't adults? I felt I had some role to play in New Orleans, but I had no idea what it was yet.

TWENTY-SIX

Ruby

That year proved a difficult one for the Civil Rights Movement. The NAACP had been banned on a legal technicality in Louisiana, and Clifford and Christophe were now giving pro bono assistance to the students who were arrested for sit-ins or picketing. They spent many hours together working on cases, sometimes through the night.

Kitty and some other women from the Urban League formed an organisation called Save our Schools. The Federal Government was fed up with the State of Louisiana constantly delaying the desegregation of its public schools and finally it ordered the school board to begin desegregation on 14 November 1960. The State hit back by threatening to close public schools altogether.

'If they close the public schools, the city of New Orleans is going to sink back into the dark ages,' Kitty argued.

Education was a subject close to my heart. After seeing how well our children played with Adolphe and

Isabelle, Clifford and I had decided to send Dale to a public school when he turned five.

'He'll learn to mix with children from all walks of life,' Clifford said enthusiastically. 'I can't imagine a better way to prepare him for the real world than that.'

So it was with interest that we watched what happened with the first two schools in New Orleans selected to integrate their first grades: McDonagh 19, and the William Frantz School. Four coloured girls who had performed exceptionally well on their test scores had been chosen to integrate: three were going to McDonagh 19 together; and one girl, Ruby Nell Bridges, was going to the William Frantz Elementary School on her own. On the television that night, we saw a tiny coloured girl in a starched dress with a bow in her hair being escorted by US Federal marshals into the school, while a mob consisting mostly of white mothers shouted abuse at her. One woman yelled, 'Go home, burrhead! You're not wanted here!'

Another screamed that she was going to lynch Ruby Nell and her family.

I stood up. 'That woman told a child she was going to "lynch" her?'

The images were so disturbing that I had to go into the garden and take gulps of fresh air to calm myself. The mob reminded me of the news reels I'd seen of German citizens cheering for Hitler. I wanted Dale to grow up to be strong and confident and to respect all people regardless of colour. But could I subject him to such abuse for the greater good? Maybe it would be easier if we went to live in Los Angeles, where the schools had desegregated even before the Brown versus Board of Education ruling. But the memory of Ti-Jean being mistreated in the ice cream parlour and how I'd failed even to pass him a napkin flashed before me. Then I thought of Leroy. So few white people were willing to stick their neck out to help coloured people in their fight that they needed every single one of us. Running away wasn't the solution.

'Momma, why are you crying?'

I looked up to see Dale standing next to me in his striped flannelette pyjamas.

'It's nothing, sugar,' I said, hugging him tight.

'Ruby?' Clifford appeared at the back door. When he saw my face, he crouched beside me, concern in his eyes. 'Are you all right?'

I nodded. 'Please, take Dale to bed. I'll be up to say his prayers with him in a minute.'

Clifford kissed me and picked up Dale. He glanced at me again, trying to read my hidden thoughts, before going inside.

Later, I went to see him in his study.

'I can't get the image of Ruby Nell Bridges out of my mind,' I told him. 'She's not much older than Dale. I can't imagine people screaming at our son for attending an integrated school. Maybe I'm too big a coward for it, but I can't help feeling that I've got to do something about what's happening in those schools.'

Clifford pointed to a sampler hanging on his wall. I recognised it as the one his mother used to prop in front of her when she typed her letters: *Let's have faith that right makes might; and in that faith let us, to the end, dare to do our duty as we understand it. Abraham Lincoln.*

'All of us are afraid, Ruby,' he said. 'But all of us are called. If we don't answer, then we will never find the courage that exists deep inside of us. Why don't you telephone Kitty now and see what Save Our Schools are planning to do about the situation? I'm sure they can use as many volunteers as possible.'

'So you saw the news?' asked Kitty, when she came to the telephone.

'Those people are so full of hate they can threaten an innocent child!' I told her. 'What are Save Our Schools planning to do?'

'There's an emergency meeting tomorrow morning,' she said. 'I'll pick you up at nine o'clock.'

The meeting was held in the Italianate neoclassical mansion of an Uptown socialite named Grace. Despite the decadent gold-leaf mouldings and ceiling murals in her home, she was wearing a simple woollen dress and her hair was in a page-boy style. She reminded me of Helen: someone so passionately focussed on a cause that she considered any self-embellishment superfluous.

'This badly organised and token attempt at integration has been a disaster,' she told the women gathered in her parlour. 'When the coloured girls entered their schools, the white mothers rushed in and took their children out. The three girls at McDonagh are now the only students there, and Ruby Nell Bridges is in a class on her own. If we don't do something, the public system will collapse and the segregationists will have won.'

We all murmured our horror at the idea.

'The US Federal marshals are guarding the coloured children and escorting them into the schools,' Grace continued, 'but there is another pressing issue. There are a few white children remaining at William Frantz, the Reverend Foreman's daughter among them, but those families and their children are also being harassed and have received death threats. Some of the fathers have lost their jobs. The only way integration is going to work is to convince white families to continue to send their children to those schools. And believe me, there are willing white families but they have been terrorised by the mob. We, ladies, are in a better position to help because we can't be fired or threatened economically as those children's parents can be. Therefore I propose that we divide into teams to take those children into the schools and any other children who want to join them. We'll need teams of two: one lady to drive and the other to accompany the child.'

Kitty and I were assigned to pick up a young girl in the Lower Ninth Ward named Elsie Matthews. She lived in a simple shotgun house with her parents and five siblings, but was beautifully attired in a yellow pinafore dress.

'I can't afford to send her to a private school,' Mrs Matthews told us, 'but she's as bright as a button and has been doing well at William Frantz. I can't see the problem with white children going to school together with coloured ones. They do it in other States.' She bent down and kissed her daughter on the cheek. 'You study hard today and do everything these nice ladies tell you, all right?'

Elsie nodded, and Mrs Matthews turned to us with concern on her face. 'I can't take her myself because I've got to be at the factory in fifteen minutes, and her grandmother is too old to walk that far. But we can't send her alone because of those mobs. I sure appreciate what you're doing.'

'We'll take good care of Elsie,' I assured Mrs Matthews. 'I've got two small children at home myself. I'll look after her as if she was my own.'

Elsie took my hand and we climbed in the back of Kitty's Cadillac wagon, which had four doors and would allow Elsie and me to get out quickly when we pulled up at the school.

As we approached, I could see that Ruby Nell Bridges had arrived with the US Federal marshals and I felt terrified for her. There were even more people outside the school than there had been on the first day. The police had set up barricades, but people ducked under them. A group of high-school boys were holding up a Confederate flag and singing, 'Glory, glory, segregation, the South will rise again!'

Ruby Nell was taken into the school through its front doors, but the Save Our Schools organisers had arranged to drive the white children to the back of the school so they could enter through a rear door. These children had no protection apart from us and a handful of half-hearted New Orleans policemen.

'It's amazing,' said Kitty, holding up a pass we'd been issued by the Federal Government for a policeman to see, and inching the car towards the rear of the school. 'Clifford is defending college kids who've been sent to gaol for peacefully picketing and yet these people are able to act like this with impunity.'

'I heard that those housewives call themselves "The Cheerleaders",' I said. 'Ugliest bunch of cheerleaders I've ever seen!'

'Good Lord!' moaned Kitty. 'Look at that woman!'

As Ruby Nell passed the crowd, the woman Kitty was referring to held up a baby's funeral casket with a black doll inside it. A shiver passed down my spine, not only because of the horrible implication but because I recognised the woman. It was Aunt Elva. I no longer had to wonder what she might be doing now Uncle Rex was dead and Eugenie had moved away. She was engaged with nasty business, like she'd always been.

To our horror, a mob was waiting at the rear of the school too.

'Traitors!' they shouted at us, pelting the car with tomatoes and eggs and spitting at the windows. 'Uptown bitches! We're going to kill you along with the niggers you love so much!'

They rocked the car violently and I feared for Elsie. I had promised to take care of her and was tempted to tell Kitty we'd better reverse and drive her home.

But then Elsie looked at me with her big blue eyes. 'I hope those angry ladies don't make me late for class. I've missed out on going to school for two days already and I want to say hello to the little coloured girl.'

After I'd told Clifford about Jackie Fausey's behaviour with her daughter on Dryades Street, he'd commented that racism was a disease that adults passed on to their children. Now, little Elsie passed on her courage to me. I took her hand.

'You ready?' I asked her as a policeman opened the door for us. 'You hold on tight to my hand and don't let go!'

The noise as we stepped out of the car was deafening. I shielded Elsie with my arm as people spat at us and threatened to do obscene things to us. It seemed to take forever to reach the school door while the policemen pushed back the crowd that was jostling and trying to grab us.

When we finally got inside, we found the principal of the school waiting for us. I breathed a sigh of relief to be on friendly ground. But if I'd expected her to be pleased by our heroic effort, I was soon set straight.

She pursed her lips and scowled. 'Well, I hope you're satisfied with yourself, you uppity do-gooder. Look at all the trouble you've caused!'

I gripped Elsie's hand tighter. Was I really going to leave her with this hard-lipped poor excuse for an educator?

'We weren't given enough time to prepare for this,' the principal continued.

For one tense moment, I thought she was going to send me and Elsie back out to face the mob. But then I had a sense that I was standing at a significant point in history: a time when some things were going to unravel and fall apart, while other things were going to crystallise. This school principal stood for the past, and Elsie stood for the future. I thought of Leroy and his family and steeled myself. Things were going to change whether the old guard liked it or not.

'You've had plenty of time to prepare,' I told the principal. 'You just didn't want to. Now tell me where Elsie's classroom is and I'll take her there myself.'

Once Elsie was safely in her classroom, I went to leave the building through the rear entrance. But through the glass doors I saw that the crowd had grown larger and more volatile. The women were shouting obscenities worse than I'd heard the most uncouth prostitutes on Bourbon Street use. I spotted Kitty's car. Policemen on motorcycles had surrounded it, but it was covered in smashed eggs and the back window was shattered.

I moved to the building's front entrance, but the crowd was even worse out there. How was I going to make it the short distance from the door to Kitty's car? When I'd entered the school, I'd been focussed on Elsie's safety. Now I had to worry about my own. I could see the principal watching me from her office, a spiteful smile on her lips.

Then, by the grace of the good Lord himself, one of the marshals who had accompanied Ruby Nell Bridges into the building saw my dilemma. He took my arm and told me, 'Look straight ahead. Whatever you do, don't meet anyone's eye. Act as if they aren't there.'

He opened the door and touched the gun in his holster. *Please don't let it come to that*, I thought.

At the sight of the marshal and me emerging from the building, the crowd erupted.

'Kill the bitch!' one woman shrieked.

The policemen surrounded us as the crowd closed in. Although the officers pushed people back with their batons, the marshal and I were shoved and pushed as if we were caught in a riptide. I was terrified that we would become trapped. Someone tugged on my arm and I found myself facing Aunt Elva. She held up that awful casket but said nothing. She looked so demented, I wasn't sure if she'd even recognised me.

The marshal pushed her away and managed to get me to Kitty's car in one piece. He opened the passenger door and shut it firmly after me. 'Accompany these women,' he told the motorcycle police.

As Kitty moved the car forward, I gazed around us at the contorted faces chanting, 'Burn the witches!'

But Kitty was as cool as a cucumber. 'We really stirred this lot up, didn't we?' she said, a triumphant smile on her face.

✤

Back at home in the Garden District, Kitty and I spent the rest of the day playing with Dale and Louise and listening to the news bulletins on the radio. The whole country had its eyes on New Orleans. The protests against integration weren't only taking place outside the schools; violence was flaring up in the streets too. Shops in coloured neighbourhoods were being vandalised and Negroes were being beaten. Policemen on motorcycles and horseback were trying to keep the peace.

'We look like a bunch of racist hicks,' said Kitty, taking a sip of tea. 'It will be bad for tourism. Hopefully that will bring the moderates out of hiding to prove that we're not.'

Louise said she was thirsty so I went to the kitchen to get her some orange juice. Mae and Philomena were in there listening to the radio. I took a jug of juice from the refrigerator and Mae opened the cupboard and handed me a cup to pour it into.

'Is it true that you've been driving the white kids to school to help them integrate with the coloured kids?' she asked me.

I was sure that she was about to admonish me. Although I was a married woman and the mother of two children, I felt like a child again in her presence. Still, I couldn't deny what I was doing. 'Yes, it's true.'

She cleared her throat. 'Those white folks are making a whole lot of trouble for you. You thinking of giving up?'

I shook my head. 'No, we aren't going to give up, Mae. It's hard, but if we give up now, we'll always be giving in to those people. They'll tire before we do.'

She straightened and glanced at Philomena with a satisfied smile. 'I knew you wouldn't give up!' she said, turning back to me. 'You're a fighter. Always have been and always will be.' Then a gleam flashed in her eye. 'I'm mighty proud of you, Mrs Ruby.'

Since Mae had come to live in the Lalande household I'd noticed some changes in her. Clifford's policy was to pay his coloured help the same wages he would if they were white and to treat them like professional service providers rather than servants. It seemed to me that Mae was bolder these days and not afraid to look a white person in the eye.

'I'm proud of you too,' I told her.

Ned had cleaned out the glass from the car and covered the rear window in vinyl. 'No use getting it fixed,' said Kitty, when we were ready to leave to pick up Elsie and take her home. 'They'll only smash it again.'

I'd hoped that the crowds would have died down but they'd grown. Several television crews were there too, as well as vendors selling coffee and ice cream. I grimaced at the *White Mothers Only* signs on their trucks.

'It's like a circus,' I told Kitty, who was following the directions of the policemen to the rear of the school. 'One big grotesque circus.'

Because the other women volunteers from the Urban League were already in the school building when I arrived, we decided to walk out with the children as a group. The tactic worked better at keeping the crowd at bay, and although their language was so disgusting I had to cover Elsie's ears, we made it to our cars without incident.

As Kitty set off, I studied our little charge. Elsie's feet didn't touch the floor of the car and she used her hands to shift herself on the seat so she could lean against me. People glared at us through the windows and shook their fists at us. I was sure that the crowd's behaviour would have upset her so much that she wouldn't want to return to school the following day, but when I asked her about it she looked at me with wide eyes.

'Of course I'm coming tomorrow! School must be very important if all these people are trying to stop us getting here.'

Kitty glanced over her shoulder and we exchanged a smile. 'Out of the mouths of babes,' she said.

The police had cordoned off Elsie's street and had to move a barricade to let us through. When we reached the house, some neighbours were gathered on the pavement outside.

'I'd better stay with the car,' Kitty told me. 'Somebody might slash the tyres otherwise.'

When Elsie and I got out, I braced myself for more abuse. But the bystanders said nothing, they only stared. In many ways the silence was more unnerving.

I walked Elsie to her house, but before I had a chance to press the bell, the door swung open and I found myself face to face with a heavy-set man wearing blue overalls and a none-too-pleased expression.

'Pa!' Elsie cried. 'Let me tell you all about today!'

'Later, Elsie,' he said to her. 'This lady and I have something to discuss first.'

'Her name is Mrs Lalande,' said Elsie, skipping inside the house. 'And she's nice!'

Elsie joined her siblings, who were playing marbles on a rug in the front room. Her father indicated for me to follow him to an enclosed porch at the back of the house. As we passed the kitchen, I could see

Mrs Matthews busy cooking dinner but she didn't look in my direction. My heart sank. I was certain Mr Matthews was going to tell me he was taking Elsie out of William Frantz Elementary School, and I couldn't blame him. It was an enormous amount of pressure to subject a small child to, and unless he had an employer who could resist the White Citizens' Council, Mr Matthews could be fired from his job.

'I'm sorry about the people in the street,' I began. 'Have they been bothering you all day?'

He shook his head. 'Oh, we don't pay them any mind. They're amazed to see so much activity going on in our quiet street, that's all.' He indicated a patio chair. 'Take a seat, Mrs Lalande.'

I did as he requested, and he picked up a picture in a frame from a bookshelf and handed it to me. The photograph was of a young woman in a 1920s cloche hat and pearls.

'That's Elsie's grandmother,' he explained. 'Her dying wish was that Elsie get a good education. "That little girl has brains," she told us. "With a decent education she'll get a better shot at life."'

He sat down in a chair opposite me with his hands splayed on his knees. I waited for the crunch: how it would be difficult for Elsie to concentrate on her classes with all the commotion going on at the school.

'You see,' said Mr Matthews, 'my mother was part coloured. But she always hid the fact so she could get better wages. She denied her race on her marriage certificate and described herself as white, but when my father's family found out years later, they convinced him to abandon her. My mother brought up five kids on her own by working in factories and waitressing in cafeterias.'

I looked at Mr Matthews with interest. This was an unexpected twist to the story. I knew then that he trusted me, because if his mother was classified as coloured, he would be too. All it took was 'one drop'.

'Do you know about "passing", Mrs Lalande?' he asked, peering into my eyes. 'Although I look white, can you guess what I've had to endure to hide my past?'

He coughed, suddenly embarrassed at having revealed something intimate about himself. But I knew far better than he could imagine what it was like to have to cover up your past.

'I can,' I told him. 'It would be very difficult and lonely.'

He cracked his knuckles. 'Elsie doesn't know about having coloured blood, but if desegregation happens nobody will have to worry about that any more. We'll all be equal. That's why we're going through with this, otherwise we'd never subject our daughter to the harassment.' He leaned forward. 'Promise me that you won't give up, Mrs Lalande. Promise me that you'll take good care of Elsie and you'll get her to her classes and you'll encourage her. This could change her life for the better. It could change all our lives for the better.'

I shook Mr Matthews' hand before leaving. Mrs Matthews offered me some tea, but I told her Kitty was waiting in the car and we needed to be up early in order to get Elsie to school on time the next day.

The neighbours had already dispersed when I came out of the house. Before getting into Kitty's car, I turned to see Mr and Mrs Matthews standing on the porch and watching me.

'Until tomorrow,' I said, waving.

'Until tomorrow,' they called back.

I felt my chest swell. I was no longer the Ruby I had been in Avery's Ice Cream Parlor, too afraid of being called a 'nigger lover' to help Ti-Jean and his friends. Something had changed. I had found my courage by taking action, as Clifford had promised I would.

Kitty, Elsie and I, and the other women and children, faced those mobs every day for a month until the Federal Government saw the value in what we were doing and assigned US Federal marshals to look after the white children as well as the coloured ones. But our troubles were far from over. We had to find new jobs for the fathers who'd been fired for sending their children to an integrated school, which wasn't easy as the White Citizens' Council threatened to boycott any business that hired them. Then we learned that the home addresses of the members of Save our Schools had been read out at a White Citizens' Council meeting.

One night, Clifford and I were having tea in the parlour before going to bed, when three loud bangs sounded and the front window shattered. Clifford pushed me to the floor as shards of glass scattered about the room. We heard a car accelerate and then its brakes squeal as it turned a corner.

'Are you all right, Ruby?' Clifford asked, his face ashen.

I barely heard him over the pounding of my heart. I lifted myself on trembling legs. 'The children!' I cried.

We both rushed into the hall. Mae was coming through the kitchen to see what had happened. Dale was standing at the top of the stairs, wide-eyed and clinging onto the banister. Clifford ran up the stairs and swept him into his arms while I hurried to check on Louise. She was peacefully asleep in her cot as if nothing had happened.

I crouched down on the floor. My hands were shaking. If we'd been shot at a few hours earlier, when we were all in the parlour together, one of the children might have been killed.

The police came the following morning and inspected the damage, but they weren't too enthusiastic about following up who might have fired the shots.

'This kind of stuff is happening all over town,' the officer in charge told us. 'Not much chance of catching the culprits if none of your neighbours saw the licence plate.'

'They think it's our own fault for sticking our noses in where they aren't wanted,' I said after they'd left.

Clifford looked at me steadily. 'Ruby, you make the decision. Do we fight on? Or do we give up?'

I remembered Mae asking me not to give in, and the evening Mr Matthews had revealed his secret. People were depending on us. Nothing would change if we gave up now, and the world Dale and Louise inherited would be no better and no fairer than this one.

'We fight on,' I said.

Our determination to continue didn't mean a lessening of tensions. A week after the shooting, Philomena answered a ring at our doorbell but there was nobody in sight. Instead, a funeral wreath on a stand had been left on the porch. She called me and I looked up and down the street for a florist's van, assuming the wreath had been delivered in error. But then I saw the ribbon printed with the words: *The Lalande Family*.

A card was attached to it. I opened the envelope and read:

We're coming to get you.

Your caskets have been measured and made.

Your family will pay for its sins.

Fear gripped my stomach and my vision blurred. I could almost feel on my fingertips the malevolence of the person who had sent the wreath. But Philomena was watching me and I didn't want to alarm her.

'I'll take it,' I told her, avoiding her gaze as I carried the wreath and stand into the house. 'It's from a distant relative who has only just heard that Maman passed away.'

I tore off the ribbon and card before taking the wreath and stand out the back and asking Ned to burn them.

'The wreath has got oleander in it,' I told him. 'I don't want the children or Theodore to touch it and get poisoned.'

Ned took the wreath, but the way he held it away from himself told me he knew it was suspicious. It wasn't merely my lame excuse — after all, I could have had it sent straight to the cemetery — but Ned's uncanny ability to size up a situation in an instant and take the appropriate action. He put the wreath on a pile of dry garden scraps and set it alight. I'd always liked Ned and at that moment I found myself liking him even more.

But as I watched the flames, I thought of another time and the cross that had burned on the Thezan family's lawn. An ominous feeling came over me, as if something — or someone — had returned from the past. I shivered and went back into the house.

On my way upstairs I passed Clifford in his study, poring over some papers. He turned in my direction. 'Who was at the door, sugar?'

When we'd married we'd promised each other not to keep secrets, but I didn't like the pallor of his complexion these days and didn't want to burden him with any more worries than he already had.

'Just a broom salesman,' I told him, walking into his study and kissing him. But when he left in the afternoon for a meeting with Christophe, I drove straight to Kitty's house.

'Oh, those people are such chickens!' she said, reading the card that had come with the wreath. 'Everybody in Save Our Schools is getting death threats.' She opened the hall table drawer and showed me four notes that had been put together with cut-out letters from newspapers.

'Aren't you scared?' I asked her, cringing at the obscene words.

'When I get one of these, I ask myself how Mother would have reacted.' She tore up the notes, including mine, and tossed the scraps into the fireplace in her parlour. 'She would have said that these notes were sent by cowards, because only cowards write threatening letters and don't sign their names. So who's going to be afraid of a coward?'

Kitty's words got me thinking that the wreath might have been sent by Aunt Elva. After all, she'd been sick enough to show poor Ruby Nell Bridges a Negro doll in a baby casket. Well, I wasn't afraid of old Aunt Elva. She was full of hot air.

My mind was further set at ease by the bravado of the other women in Save Our Schools when I learned at the next meeting that several of them had been shot at.

'They just want to scare us,' Grace said. 'The most important thing is that you never let those crazy people inside your head. You mustn't let their distorted view of life get to you.'

I forgot about the death threat as things gradually settled down at the schools. The mobs thinned and white children began to return to their classes unmolested. Even little Ruby Nell Bridges didn't need the protection of the Federal marshals any more.

The following month, Philomena returned to Biloxi to help her elderly mother after she'd had a fall. The house and children were too much for Mae to handle on her own, so I helped out where I could. I didn't mind because it kept me busy. One morning, when I was trying to work out how to assemble the vacuum cleaner, I glanced out the window into the garden and saw Mae collecting the cut flowers for the day from Ned.

'Oh, my!' I gasped when I saw the way Ned smiled at Mae, and the way she blushed in return. 'How long has this been going on?'

I watched their giggling and eye-batting a little longer before I turned my attention back to the vacuum cleaner. Mae was in love! The thought of it tickled me pink.

Clifford and I had already planned to take good care of Mae when she retired, with a generous pension and a house of her own, and she would always remain part of the family. But I'd been worried that she would be lonely once she didn't have the children — or me — to look after any more. Now I was glad that she would have the company of a very good man.

My light mood was cut short when Clarita Galafate appeared at the door looking flustered. 'Ruby,' she said, 'Clifford collapsed at the office.'

My knees buckled. Terrible images of the day Helen died crowded my mind. 'What do you mean?' I asked, trying to catch my breath. 'Where is he?'

'He was stable when they put him in the ambulance,' said Clarita, taking my arm to steady me. 'I'll drive you to the hospital now to see him. It's exhaustion, I'm sure. You know how hard he and Christophe have been working.'

I told Mae we were going to the hospital and to look after the children. On the way in Clarita's car, I stared out the window and berated myself. I should have seen this coming. Clifford hadn't slept properly for months but had kept himself going on multiple cups of strong black coffee. I'd hoped that now progress was being made, he'd ease off. I wished I'd been more forceful with him that he needed to rest. What would the children and I do if something happened to him? He was their beloved daddy — and my best friend.

Clifford was dozing when we arrived at the hospital and were shown to his private room.

'I'll be out here,' Clarita said, taking a seat in the waiting area.

I sat in the visitor's chair beside the bed and took Clifford's hand. His face was so pale I could see the blue veins under his eyelids. 'Oh, Cliff,' I said. 'How did I let this happen to you?' His eyes flickered for a moment before they opened, and a smile stretched across his face.

'Hello, beautiful,' he said.

I tried to say something back but the words snagged in my throat.

He put his hand on his chest and looked rueful. 'The doctor said my ticker isn't in such good shape. Apparently I have the heart of a sixty-year-old man.'

I sighed and kissed his palm. 'You've got to slow down, honey. You've pushed so hard and things are changing. Let others take over for a while.'

He stroked my hair. 'You're right, Ruby. For your sake and the children's, I've got to pace myself better.'

We sat quietly for a while, then Clifford looked into my eyes and said: 'Do you even realise how exceptional you are, Ruby? You've been tested time and time again and yet you haven't broken.'

'We all break, Cliff. Maybe I've just never been pushed beyond my limits.'

Our conversation was interrupted by the arrival of Kitty and Eddie.

'What are you doing in the hospital, Cliff?' Kitty cried, smothering her brother in kisses. 'If you die, I'll never forgive you!'

She began bustling about the room, adjusting the window blind and ordering Eddie to find a vase for the flowers they'd brought. After she'd retucked the bedsheets so that Clifford looked like he was pinned under them and propped him up on two pillows instead of one, she sat down and sent him a stern look.

'Even the hardiest of us need a break, you know,' she said. 'I never would have survived the schools debacle if I hadn't kept up my tennis and gotten a weekly massage. Now as soon as you are out of here, I'm booking us all a cabin on Avery Island. We are going to have a family holiday together — and no arguments! You won't do anyone any good if you drop dead.' Then she turned and winked at me.

I was transported back to that tennis game where I had partnered with Clifford to play her and Eddie. Kitty had been so bossy then and it had annoyed me, but now I realised how lucky I was to have her for a sister-in-law. Sometimes somebody had to take charge.

When the visiting hour was up, a nurse arrived to tell us we had to go. As we were leaving the room, Clifford called me back.

'No matter what happens, Ruby,' he said solemnly, 'I want you to know that I love you and I love our children. If I had to live my life over, I'd do it all exactly the same way again. Promise me, if anything should happen to me, you will continue the fight. Our children deserve a better world. All the children deserve a better world.'

I was surprised by his seriousness. When I thought of all Clifford had achieved for civil rights, I felt immense pride. But when I looked at him lying in that hospital bed, pale and exhausted, I feared for our future. I didn't want to grow old without him.

'I won't give up,' I said. 'But you have to promise me you'll take better care of yourself.'

'You're looking exhausted too,' Kitty told me as she, Eddie, Clarita and I made our way to the parking lot. 'We can't have you collapsing as well. Let Eddie and me look after Dale and Louise for a few nights. That way you can care for Clifford without having to worry about everything else — and we'd be delighted to have them.'

I hated to be separated from the children, but I knew Kitty was right. I needed a rest so I could concentrate on helping Clifford recuperate. But when she and Eddie

484 • Belinda Alexandra

picked them up the following night, I despaired at how lonely the house felt without my husband and the children in it. I even missed Theodore, the dog. Dale, who was deeply attached to him, had taken him to Kitty and Eddie's home too, but I kept listening for his pattering paws on the floorboards and expecting the feel of his soft muzzle nudging me to get my attention.

I took a seat in an armchair in the sitting room and leaned my head back. From the garden came voices: Mae saying good night to Ned, who lived in the gardener's cottage.

'You put the potato poultice I made for you on that cut tonight like I showed you,' Mae said. 'It will be good by tomorrow. See you in the morning, sugar pie.'

I smiled and hoped she and Ned would announce their engagement soon. We could use the summerhouse for the wedding ceremony, like when Clifford and I got married, and Ned could choose the bouquet from his favourite flowers in the garden.

I heard Mae come inside and go to her room next to the kitchen. I picked up *Adventures of Huckleberry Finn* and read the first chapter, bringing back comforting memories of Maman and me reading it together. But the fire was dying and the room was turning cold. I decided to read more of the book in the warmth of my bed.

I turned off the lights and climbed the stairs to our bedroom. Once I'd changed into my nightdress and snuggled into bed, I picked up the book again. But I was exhausted and fell asleep with the bedside light still on. I dreamed I was Jewel again, on stage at the Vieux Carré Club, dancing to 'Chloe'. I turned and caught a glimpse of Leroy through the curtain with his band. A wave of tenderness washed over me. *You haven't gone*, I thought.

You've been with me the whole time, watching over me like you promised you would.

Then the music stopped and Leroy shouted, 'Wake up!' I jolted and opened my eyes. My thoughts were clumsy and slow and it took a moment for me to remember I wasn't Jewel on the stage at the Vieux Carré; I was in my bedroom in the house on Prytania Street and I was Mrs Clifford Lalande.

I rubbed my forehead and reached over to turn off the light. An eerie sensation sent a chill down my spine. I felt a presence in the room.

I turned to the door. A man was standing there, staring at me. Stark cold terror clawed at my heart. I knew him, although he didn't know me, as Ruby. He was older and rougher-looking, with a short beard and a scar under his eye. But his aura of malevolence was unmistakable. It was Jimmy, the former barman from the Vieux Carré Club.

'Hello, Mrs Lalande,' he said, in a voice that was chillingly calm. 'Isn't it a shame your husband's not home.'

A sickening sensation crept over my skin. I no longer had to guess who had shot at our window and sent the wreath. My gaze fell to the rope between his hands. I tried to scream, but I had no air in my lungs. A strangled 'Help!' that nobody would hear died in my throat. He moved towards the bed. I struggled to extricate myself from the sheets, but my foot got caught and I tumbled to the floor.

Jimmy grabbed me, but I managed to get myself on my feet and slip from his grasp. I ran for the door, but he caught the sleeve of my nightdress and dragged me back.

'Where are you going?' The stench of whiskey on his breath was nauseating.

He spun me round and slammed me into the wall. Then he pulled me forward before slamming me into it again. I tasted blood in my mouth.

'I've been watching you and your husband,' he hissed. 'You won't get away from me, you nigger-loving bitch!' His eyes looked up to the ceiling pendant. 'I'm going to string you up like one of those niggers you love so much.'

Panic ran through me. I struggled against him and clawed at the curtains in an attempt to get away. They tumbled down to the floor. Jimmy threw me onto the bed and put his knee in my back. I felt him slip the rough rope around my neck. I was going to lose this battle and there was something I wanted to know. Something that had disturbed me for years.

'Did you kill Leroy Thezan?' I gasped.

Jimmy turned me around to face him and squinted at me. 'I've heard your voice before,' he said.

It dawned on me then. That night he'd attacked me and Leroy, I'd forgotten my Jewel voice and screamed at him as Ruby.

'I know you,' he said, his eyes glinting. Then he realised where from and his eyes opened wide. 'You're that little hussy Jewel, ain't you?' He emitted a low whistle, like he'd just been given a million dollars, and laughed menacingly. 'Who'd have thought that grand Mrs Lalande is a slut!'

I sensed he was going to find killing me even more pleasurable now as he'd be settling old scores. There were only seconds of my life left and I repeated my question. 'Did you kill Leroy Thezan?'

He tightened the rope and frowned as if thinking over dozens of Negroes he'd killed, perhaps too many to recall. Then he sniggered. 'Yeah, I remember killing that nigger,' he boasted. 'I killed him like a dog I didn't need no more. He begged for his life but I killed him anyway.'

It took my last ounce of air to spit in his face. He slapped me so hard I almost blacked out. He stood up on my chest so I couldn't move and slung the other end of the rope through the light fixture. My arms flailed as he pulled and the world around me began to fade. For a moment I felt the terror of all the innocent souls who had perished this way.

There was a sound like a crack. I thought he must have broken my neck, but he let go of the rope. His eyes rolled back in his head and he fell to the floor.

I looked up to see Mae holding the cast-iron monkey I used as a doorstop. Blood dripped from it.

I rolled over and looked at Jimmy lying on the rug. His eyes were half-open but glazed over and his lips were curled back. For a moment Mae and I didn't say anything. 'Is he dead?' she asked, finally.

Blood was seeping from his mouth now. Mae must have given him one hell of a hit. I got off the bed and grabbed his arm, repulsed by the clammy feel of his skin, and searched for a pulse.

'He's dead,' I confirmed.

Mae sat on the end of the bed and rocked backwards and forwards. 'I killed a white man,' she wailed. 'They're going to hang me, Mrs Ruby. They're going to hang me or electrocute me like they did to that other woman.'

'Hush, hush,' I said and put my arm around her, still trying to convince myself that what had happened was real and not just a bad dream. The other woman Mae referred to had been a white woman, a cold-blooded killer who'd shot a salesman. She was the only woman ever to have been electrocuted in Louisiana. 'You killed this monster to save me, Mae.'

But even as I spoke the words, I knew she was right. With the current atmosphere of hate and fear that pervaded New Orleans, I couldn't be sure what would happen with an all-white jury in a segregated courthouse. Perhaps if Mae had defended any other white woman, that woman's testimony would be considered enough to exonerate her. But right now the Lalandes were one of the most vilified families in New Orleans for our stance on integration. Justice did not work in the South the way it should. Any of the white supremacist judges might view executing our loyal maid as revenge for our criticism of them.

I rubbed my head and tried to think. There was no way I could take the chance of calling the police.

'They're not going to hang you, Mae, because we aren't going to tell anybody about this,' I said finally.

Mae's eyes showed their whites, like she was a frightened horse. 'What are we going to do?'

I was too busy formulating a plan to answer her. 'Go wake up Ned and tell him to come quickly.'

TWENTY-SEVEN

Amanda

'That's why you won't let anybody repair the porch!' I cried.

I leaned forward and waited for Grandma Ruby to confess how she, Ned and Mae had carried Jimmy's body down the stairs, stripped it of all identification, removed the porch boards and, in the dead of night, dug a grave. Instead, she looked at me blankly and said, 'Amandine, have you lost your mind? Why would we have buried that monster here?'

She straightened her shoulders and lifted her chin. 'I called on Sam Coppola for the first time since I'd left the Vieux Carré Club. He sent some men to pick up the body. Jimmy ended up where he has always belonged — in the swamp!' Despite her proud posture, uncertainty flashed in her eyes. 'You can't expect me to be sorry. Not after what he did to Leroy! Not after what he intended to do to me!'

I wondered if I really had lost my mind from hearing too many revelations in one night. It was a moment before I could explain myself.

'It's difficult for me,' I told her. 'It's not as if everything is coming together neatly in a logical way. One moment I have a piece of the puzzle solved, and the next I'm swept off balance by a surprise revelation. I thought you were going to tell me why my father was drunk the night of the accident.'

Grandma Ruby lowered her eyes and twisted the rings on her fingers. I knew this was difficult for her too. She was telling me things that she'd never revealed to anyone else. I felt a kinship with her in that regard: the past wasn't always the pleasant, romantic thing we wanted it to be. My past felt like a shark that could emerge from the depths any time to take a chunk out of me.

'I understand about Jimmy,' I continued. 'He tried to kill you, and you had no choice but to protect Mae. I probably wouldn't have gone to the police either in those circumstances. But there is something under the porch that you don't want anyone to find, isn't there?'

She looked at me intently. 'When I hid what I did under the porch, I never expected it to be brought to light again, but time and nature have worked against me. The porch is rotting. It's like watching an old tomb crumble and not doing anything to fix it.' She clenched her hands together so tightly that her knuckles turned white. 'It's better we take it out together, and then you and Oliver can fix the porch. I wouldn't want anybody but you to see it. Perhaps I can be strong enough if you're with me.'

Goosebumps pricked my skin. What on earth was hidden under there? Something worse than a decomposed body? I wasn't sure if I was ready to know.

Grandma Ruby stood and walked to the door. 'Oliver keeps a crowbar and a spade in the potting shed. I'll get the key.'

'Now?' I said.

She turned back to me. 'If we don't do it now, I may never find the strength again to face it.'

The air had a tinge of coolness, but it was still humid. I stuck the crowbar into a gap in the porch floor and pried up one of the boards. Sweat rolled down my back and prickled my skin. A mosquito added to my discomfort by biting me several times on the back of the knee and causing itchy welts.

The floorboards were half rotted and I could lift them without having to saw them. Before long I found myself staring into the dark space under the porch. The earth smelled pungent. I wished we could've waited till the sun came up so I could see better, but it was Oliver's day for work and Grandma Ruby had insisted that it was now or never to uncover what was there.

'Do you have snakes here?' I asked. I'd come across enough deadly spiders and snakes in our garden at Roseville to be wary of digging around under old houses without taking precautions.

'We get garter snakes now and then,' said Grandma Ruby, shining the torch around the space. 'But they're harmless. Their fangs can't break your skin.'

The light caught a large rectangular metal object. I took the torch and saw that it was the lid of an army-green World War Two military trunk. I'd seen enough of them at vintage fairs to recognise one.

'There it is,' said Grandma Ruby, her voice trembling.

I grimaced. The trunk was large enough to hold a body if you twisted the corpse into a foetal position or ... cut off some of its limbs. I gulped and chastised myself for being so morbid.

'It's half out of the ground,' I said. 'The water must have pushed it up from the soil.'

Grandma Ruby shook her head. 'We never buried it. Clifford and I hid it under the floorboards. It must have sunk into the soil over time.'

'Clifford helped you?' I felt a surge of relief at the mention of my grandfather's name. From Grandma Ruby's description, he had been so noble, so upright, I couldn't imagine him burying anything sinister under his beloved home.

Then I remembered something Blaine had told me the day we drove out along the River Road: that during the Civil War many plantation families had buried their money and jewels in the ground. Perhaps Grandma Ruby and Clifford had been following a Southern tradition of burying their treasures.

'Do you want to tell me what's in the trunk before I take it out?' I asked.

Grandma Ruby opened her mouth, but emotion got the better of her and she shook her head. 'I'm not sure there will be anything left now.'

The relief I'd felt a moment before deserted me again. The situation seemed surreal, like I was overseeing a grim exhumation.

I used the shovel to clear the soil away from the sides of the trunk. Then I took the crowbar and held my breath as I prised the trunk out of the soil. The humid climate of New Orleans was brutal and I expected the metal to break apart at any moment with rust. But apart from some scuffs and scratches, the trunk was in good condition. It was also lighter than I'd expected.

'Is it all right if I turn it on its end to lift it out?' I asked.

Grandma Ruby didn't answer, and I looked up to see her standing at the end of the porch staring at the garden.

I managed to lift and then push the trunk up onto the porch, before climbing out of the hole myself. The front clamps were rusted, so I found a screwdriver and a hammer in the potting shed to break the locks open with. As I worked at them, I kept looking back at my grandmother but she was as still as a statue.

Dawn was breaking and the sun cast a soft orange light onto the porch. I remembered what Grandma Ruby had said to Leroy about them being vampires that disappeared with the morning. For a moment, I saw myself opening the lid of the trunk and an undead creature leaping out at me. I shook my head to get rid of the absurd image and turned my attention back to the task. Finally, the locks gave way and I pushed the lid open.

The first thing I saw was a layer of muslin that had yellowed with age. I put my hand on it and felt something soft underneath. I glanced at Grandma Ruby, but she remained with her back to me. My hand trembled as I lifted the fabric. It came away like a magician's scarf to reveal something red and sparkly underneath.

'Oh!' I cried, when I recognised what it was.

I remembered seeing a pair of cotton gloves under the kitchen sink. I rushed to the kitchen and put them on before returning to the porch.

'Grandma Ruby! Look!' I gently lifted the red sequined dress from the box. The matching bra and G-string were underneath. It was the outfit that Orry-Kelly had made for Jewel for one of her Mardi Gras performances.

Grandma Ruby turned slowly and the agony on her face transformed to wonder.

I'd learned enough about fabric preservation to know that we were witnessing a miracle. Although it had been packed in a watertight and airtight trunk, by rights the dress should have disintegrated from the changes in temperature or be covered in mould and mildew. But apart from some faded patches and a strong musty smell, it looked almost new.

I took it and the underwear inside and laid them out on the rug in the parlour. The sight of the costume brought not only Jewel to life before my eyes but Leroy too. The cut of the dress was exquisite. How could he not have been in awe of Jewel when she wore this?

Grandma Ruby stood in the doorway watching me, as if afraid to have any contact with the dress.

'Why did you hide it under the porch?' I asked her. 'Why didn't you store it in the attic?'

She was quiet for a moment before answering. 'I never got to say goodbye properly to Leroy. I got rid of everything from the room in Chartres Street, yet I couldn't bear to part with this costume. But I couldn't keep it in the house where someone might discover it. Clifford locked the costume away in his military trunk, but when we returned from our honeymoon and I discovered I was pregnant, I knew that I had to move forward. I told Clifford I wanted to bury the trunk. It would be the funeral for Jewel and Leroy that could never have taken place publicly.

'Clifford thought under the back porch was the best place — his mother so dominated that spot that nobody would disturb it. It was better than the garden where it might accidentally be dug up or float up after heavy rain. It was a good choice in the end, because Helen wouldn't have thought to interrupt her civil rights crusade by having anyone work on the porch. Back in those days, it was in good repair anyway.' A faint smile came to her face. 'You defeated me, Amandine. You and your strong will and your perfectionism. What a magnificent combination of your parents you've turned out to be.'

She sat down on the sofa but still didn't touch the dress. 'I was lucky to have been loved by two great men. Clifford was a good husband to me. He was never jealous of Leroy and did all he could to help me and to love me, including entombing the dress. If he thought it was absurd, he never made me feel it.' She paused, the beginning of a tear glinting in her eye. 'Every night of our marriage, when Clifford came to bed he would touch my shoulder and say, "I love you, Ruby. Sweet dreams!" In the morning when we awoke, he would put his arms around me and say, "Good morning, my lovely wife." Then one morning he didn't say anything at all. My beautiful loyal husband of nearly a quarter of a century was gone. He'd passed away quietly in the night. That was so like him, so gentle, not one to be made a fuss over. Even now, after all these years, I ache to hear his greeting in the morning.'

Grandma Ruby's description of Clifford's death made me think of Nan. I'd been furious with her only a few hours earlier for deceiving me about the circumstances of my parents' accident. Now the grief that she wasn't in my life any more came back as a heavy suffocating fog.

'Nan went too quickly, without any warning,' I said. 'There was no chance to say goodbye.'

Grandma Ruby looked at me compassionately. 'The longer you live, the more loss you will live with. I've had so many losses that at times I thought they would crush me. But something always came along to give me hope again. It was terrible to lose Clifford when he was only in his fifties, but nobody on his side of the family seemed to live to old age. Kitty had died the previous year, the same way as her mother, from a stroke. As hard as it was for me to bear the loss of my husband, it was harder still for Dale and Louise of their father. I had to be strong for them even as my own heart was breaking. But then your mother appeared like a burst of sunshine that saved us all ... and then you were born, Amandine. Your name means "deserving of love". Did you know that?'

I went to sit next to Grandma Ruby. Putting my arm around her and resting my head on her shoulder, I replied, 'No, I didn't know that.'

The sleepless night and the recovery of the Mardi Gras dress had drained Grandma Ruby. Her shoulders were slumped and her eyes drooped with exhaustion so I made her go to bed. Afterwards, I sat on the steps of the porch and drank a cup of tea to calm my racing thoughts. Despite not having slept either, I was too overwrought to go to bed. What I'd learned about the accident the previous night had unbalanced me, and digging under the porch for the dress had only intensified the feeling of coming unstuck.

Lorena arrived for work, but Oliver was late. I found a spool of yellow ribbon in a sewing box in the linen press and tied it around the porch posts as a safety warning. What Grandma Ruby had said about me being a perfectionist came back to me and I was seized by an idea. I went to my room and examined the restoration plan that I'd sketched out. A project was what I needed to restore my equilibrium.

Oliver would be pleased that we were finally going to repair the porch, but we needed a skilled carpenter to advise us on the tricky bits of the restoration. I knew the perfect person: Terence. The senior architect I'd worked with in Sydney had advised me to always use older carpenters. 'The younger ones will take short-cuts so they can get off in time to go to the beach,' he'd warned. I could see that Terence was detail-orientated and meticulous. I'd arranged to have another music lesson with him that day and I could ask him about it then.

I showered and changed before checking on Grandma Ruby again. She was asleep on her back with her head and body perfectly aligned and she looked peaceful. The red dress was on a hanger near her window. There was no need to hide it any more. If anyone asked about it, I could say it was something I'd picked up in a vintage store. I'd promised Grandma Ruby that I'd contact the textiles curator at the Powerhouse Museum in Sydney, who was a friend of Tamara's, to find out the best way to clean and store the costume.

I was on my way back downstairs when the house telephone rang and Lorena called me to the kitchen. 'It's your aunty,' she said.

'Hello, Amandine! I hope you can hear me?' Aunt Louise's voice sounded faint through the buzzing static. 'We've had trouble with our connections in the desert. From midday we're off on a trek. It's a retreat so we won't have any communication with the outside world until Monday. I wanted to check that you and Momma are all right?'

Apart from the dress upsetting Grandma Ruby, she seemed fine. 'We're good,' I told my aunt. 'Don't worry about us. You enjoy yourselves.'

More crackles and static interrupted the connection. 'I'm sorry about the phone — I think we're about to drop out. We love you, Amandine. I'll call you when we're back at the ranch.'

The connection cut out, but I stood holding the receiver to my ear as if Aunt Louise was still on the line. With a simple phrase that meant the world to me — 'We love you, Amandine' — she had calmed the mental tumult that had plagued me all morning. Despite all the ups and downs of the past week, I would have made the decision to come to New Orleans all over again, if only to hear those words from somebody who was related to me.

I put the receiver back and returned to the porch step, where I waited a while longer for Oliver. When he didn't come, I figured he must have gone to the garden nursery for supplies.

'I'll be back in a couple of hours,' I told Lorena, picking up my handbag. 'I'm going to visit a friend.'

'Amandine!' said Terence when he answered his doorbell. 'I've been looking forward to seeing you today.'

He invited me into the front room, then pointed to my knee-high gladiator sandals. 'I like your shoes.'

'Thank you,' I said, taking the seat he offered me. 'But the straps aren't so good for tan lines.' I opened my purse and took out my restoration plan. 'I wanted to talk to you about a project I'm going to start at my grandmother's home; she's got a porch in need of restoration. I've done all the measurements, but I want a carpenter experienced with New Orleans houses and the climate. I was wondering if you could come over and look at it?'

I was surprised when he hesitated. 'Oh, I'm retired now, Amandine. And my eyesight and my back aren't what they used to be. But I know a carpenter in Gentilly who would be perfect for the job. If he sees a joint you can fit a credit card into it drives him crazy. He's done a lot of restoration work too.'

I did my best to hide my disappointment. Not only would I have enjoyed working with Terence but I wanted to introduce him to my family. He'd told me what he thought of 'fancy folks', but I was sure Grandma Ruby, Aunt Louise and Uncle Jonathan would love him. I wouldn't push it for now. I might be able to convince him later.

'Maybe you could help me select the wood then?' I suggested.

He nodded. 'Yes, I can get you exactly what you want at the lumberyard at a good price. Those guys remember me. They won't dare cheat you.' Then rubbing his knees and turning to the piano, he said, 'Well, let's get started on our lesson. Since I saw you last, I've remembered a piece that your father told me he wrote for your mother.'

I flinched. The pain of the previous evening flooded back to me. I still didn't have an answer to what had upset my father so much on the night of the accident. 'Amandine, are you all right?' asked Terence, frowning.

I shook my head. 'I met a friend of my father's last night. He told me my mother was driving the car when the accident occurred. I'd always believed it was my father.'

Terence looked at me a long time, then took a breath before answering. 'I didn't know it was your mother driving. The details didn't make a difference to me. All I knew was an accident had taken place and two beautiful people had died.'

I tried to blink back the tears that were pricking my eyes. 'My nan blamed my father for my mother's death. I don't know if it was because she wanted to believe that, or she deliberately lied to make me hate him like she did. I wish I could talk to her, to ask her what she was thinking telling me that.'

Terence went to the kitchen and poured an iced water from the fridge. He handed it to me with an apologetic grin. 'I haven't had a chance to make more root beer yet.'

He sat down again and waited for me to continue, but I was too choked up.

Then leaning towards me, he asked, 'Do you mind if I tell you something as an old man who has seen much of life?'

I took a sip of the water. 'Go ahead.'

'When you're young, you have an ideal version of how you'll be when you're older. How you won't feel fear any more and you'll always know the right thing to do.' He sat back and smiled. 'Then you get to my age and you realise that, apart from some valuable life experience, you are still scared and you still do stupid things. In the end, we're all only human.'

I looked at him. His face turned serious again.

'It's a painful fact of life, but we can never know all the answers, Amandine. That your nan loved you, there can be little doubt. She brought you up, didn't she? But whether she was deliberately lying in telling you that your father was to blame for the accident is a question that can never be answered now. By asking it, all you're going to do is create so much pain that you can't ever go forward. And go forward you must ... because there's no going back.'

Terence was right, I knew it. Maybe I was more intimidated by the idea of creating a new life — my own life — than I cared to admit. If I took responsibility for myself, who could I blame if things didn't work out?

I took a few more sips of the water and steeled myself. 'Okay, let's work on the next piece.'

After our lesson, as I was about to leave, I asked Terence how he'd managed to become such a proficient musician while working as a carpenter.

He regarded me with a bemused expression on his face. 'In New Orleans it's quite rare to be a full-time musician. Most people have some other line of work besides their music. Nearly all the jazz greats, including Louis Armstrong, Bunk Johnson and Buddy Bolden, worked in trades, in factories or as labourers at some point in their lives. That's why the music here feels so real, because it's made by real people.'

I thought about how difficult it had been to keep up the piano when I was studying at university.

'You'd need superhuman energy!' I said. 'It's hard to hold down a job and follow your passion.'

He laughed. 'Who told you that? Passion gives you the energy. That's the difference between New Orleans and other big cities. In New York, you're a judge or you're a musician. You can't be both. Down here we're less pretentious. Our city coroner plays trumpet in gigs all over town. We've got judges and lawyers who think nothing of jamming with garbage collectors and city clerks. Jazz is a great equaliser. There's no reason you can't be an architect and a musician, Amandine. The only person stopping you is yourself.'

When I returned to the house in the Garden District I found Oliver moving the outdoor furniture into the potting shed. 'That tropical depression that's been hanging around the Bahamas is growing,' he explained.

I nodded, embarrassed that I didn't have a clue what he was talking about. I hadn't listened to the news since coming to New Orleans.

'Do you think it's going to threaten us?' I asked.

'At the moment, it could hit anywhere,' he answered, folding down a patio umbrella. 'But I'm following an old family superstition: When they give a storm a name, you better start preparing.' He pointed towards the dovecote. 'I'll take the birds to my mother's place in Natchez. I was planning to take my wife and kids to visit her anyway.' He peered at me like he'd just thought of something. 'You've got a plan, don't you, for you and Ruby to get somewhere safe?'

Aunt Louise had told me that she and Uncle Jonathan would be out of communication for a while. Did that mean they wouldn't have heard about a storm potentially heading for New Orleans?

Oliver took my hesitation for a negative answer. He went to his truck and opened the glove box, took out a pamphlet and handed it to me. 'That's the evacuation route out of the city. You better call some places in the non-coastal towns listed and make bookings. Even if you don't end up using them it's better to waste your money than have your grandmother sleeping in the car for three days. Especially in this heat.'

'Oh, no!' I said, horrified at the thought. 'Thanks. I'll make some calls.'

He indicated the garage with a nod of his head. 'Go fill the car now. This city is full of people who wait until the last minute before leaving. You don't want to be left short.'

He returned to his task of putting away anything that could become a projectile. It wasn't the right time to talk about fixing the porch. As I turned back to the house, I glanced at the neighbours' gardens. Basketball hoops, kiddie pools and garden ornaments were out in full view. If anybody else was worried about a potential hurricane, they weren't showing it.

I thought of something and called back to Oliver. 'What's its name?'

He put down the flower pot he was lifting and looked at me. 'Excuse me?'

'You said the storm has been given a name?'

'Oh,' he said, nodding to show he understood. 'Katrina. Tropical Storm Katrina.'

Lorena had already left for the day, but had posted a note on the refrigerator to say that Elliot had called. My stomach sank. I'd promised the previous night to call him first thing in the morning, but in all the excitement with the trunk I'd forgotten. He'd think I was a flake.

I dialled his number, but when he recognised my voice he sounded as cheerful as ever. 'Hey, Amandine! I tried your cell too but you didn't answer.'

'I was at Terence's,' I said. 'I'm sorry I didn't call —'

'You don't have to explain,' he said easily. 'I was wondering if you would like to come out tonight? I could take you to Snug Harbor.'

I would have liked nothing more than to go out with Elliot, but with all that had happened with the trunk I wanted to stay with Grandma Ruby.

'My grandmother's unwell,' I told him, then almost kicked myself. He'd think I was trying to blow him off for sure now. 'Would you like to come here?' I quickly added. 'I can make dinner.'

'Sure,' he replied. 'Your grandmother sounded nice on the phone the other day. I'd like to meet her.'

We agreed on six-thirty for Elliot to come over, then I went into a mild panic when I remembered his tiny but well-equipped kitchen. He was probably an excellent cook. What was I going to make to impress him given all Grandma Ruby's dietary restrictions? Did we even have any food in the fridge?

I opened it to see that it was well-stocked with condiments and fruit and vegetables. 'Thank you, Lorena!' That emergency over, I started thinking about my hair, which was sticking out in all directions from the humidity.

I put the pamphlet Oliver had given me on the hall table. Elliot hadn't mentioned anything about a dangerous storm. Perhaps Oliver was one of those people who became alarmed by anything.

Elliot arrived with a bottle of wine and a bouquet of red tulips for Grandma Ruby and one of blue delphiniums and hydrangeas for me.

'How did you know blue was my favourite colour?' I asked, leading him to the kitchen and filling two vases with water.

'Well, every time I've seen you so far you've been wearing something blue,' he said, his eyes travelling from my navy sandals to my retro strapless turquoise dress.

It made me smile to think Elliot was a man who noticed details. He was nicely decked out himself, in a spotted grey short-sleeved shirt and buff-coloured pants. But we were both outshone when Grandma Ruby sashayed into the kitchen in a billowy tropical tunic top teamed with white capri pants and a pair of strappy wedges. She was like a magnetic force field and Elliot couldn't take his eyes off her.

I held up the vase with the red tulips in it. 'Elliot brought you these.'

'Oh, how beautiful!' exclaimed Grandma Ruby, taking the vase and admiring the flowers. She patted Elliot on the shoulder. 'You are as cute in person as you are on the telephone. If only I was thirty years younger, you'd be my type.'

With her eyelashes fluttering, she caught Elliot in the beam of her Southern belle charm. Another girl might be annoyed at her grandmother flirting with her boyfriend, but I was grateful. The previous night and this morning had been emotional for both of us and I knew she was putting on a brave face for our guest.

Flambeau came strutting inside to check out Elliot too.

'You have a pet rooster?' Elliot said, crouching down to pat him. 'That's so cool.'

'Elliot has a squirrel named Duke,' I told Grandma Ruby.

'After Duke Ellington, of course. Is he as debonair as the man?' she asked.

'He tries,' replied Elliot, pushing his hair out of his eyes and looking up at Grandma Ruby. 'He likes grooming himself and likes to charm the ladies, but he's a noisy eater.'

Grandma Ruby laughed. It pleased me to see her and Elliot get along so well.

'Why don't you two sit down and have a chat,' I told them. 'Dinner is almost ready.'

While I warmed the soup, Grandma Ruby and Elliot went to the parlour. I tried to listen to what they were saying, but the sizzle of the onion I was frying for a risotto drowned them out. Flambeau stayed in the kitchen with me, watching my every move with curiosity. I gave him a strawberry and he pecked at it with relish, looking up every so often to make googly eyes at me.

'Well, it's only fair,' I said, nodding towards the parlour. 'Grandma Ruby steals my boyfriend, so I'll steal hers.'

'What are you two talking about in here?' asked Grandma Ruby, coming into the kitchen. She rubbed Flambeau's neck. 'I see Amandine is winning you over with treats.'

I'd intended for us to sit in the kitchen, but when Grandma Ruby saw that I'd laid out the placemats there, she shook her head. 'We are dressed up and it's a lovely evening; let's eat in the dining room. I'll light the candles.'

I thought of the dining room as her sacred place. If she was inviting Elliot in there, she must think he was pretty special.

When the soup was ready, I ladled it into Limoges bowls from the buffet cupboard in the dining room. When Elliot came in with Grandma Ruby, he noticed the extra place settings but didn't say anything. I felt like I was introducing him to my family. Then he impressed me again with his gentlemanly manners by pulling out the chairs for me and Grandma Ruby, and pouring the Chardonnay.

'Amandine, what delight have you made for us here?' asked Grandma Ruby, peering into the bowl I'd placed before her.

'That's sweet potato soup, and for the main we have sun-dried tomato risotto, and for dessert I've poached some pears,' I replied, feeling proud of myself for having produced a reasonable dinner from what was available in the kitchen.

Grandma Ruby and Elliot both murmured their enthusiastic appreciation. *This is how I want to live*, I thought. *With love, elegance and good company.*

Elliot's eyes sparkled in the candlelight as he looked at me. 'How are your lessons with Terence going?'

I stiffened. 'Oh, I haven't told Grandma Ruby about those yet. I was going to surprise her when I'd mastered the pieces a bit better.'

'Well, you've surprised me,' she said brightly. 'Who is Terence?'

I didn't want it to come out that he lived in the Lower Ninth Ward so I quickly answered, 'He's a jazz enthusiast who knew Dad.'

Dad! My mouth clamped shut as soon as I realised what I'd said. I'd never referred to my father as intimately as that before. He'd always been a stranger. I looked around the room where the whole Lalande family used to take their meals. For most of my life I hadn't even known some of them existed and now I felt that I belonged to them.

'Terence?' asked Grandma Ruby, as if trying to recall something. 'What's his last name?'

It occurred to me that I didn't know. I looked to Elliot.

'Bartholomew,' he said helpfully.

'Terence Bartholomew?' Grandma Ruby shook her head. 'I don't recall Dale mentioning anyone by that name. But my son knew so many people in this town — I couldn't keep up with them all.'

I was worried she was going to ask me more questions about Terence that would reveal where he lived. I wanted her to meet him first, so she would be assured that he would take care of me when I went to see him. I tried to change the subject by offering to play the pieces that I'd been learning after dinner, although I didn't feel I had them up to scratch.

'That would be delightful,' said Grandma Ruby.

When dinner was over, and I'd served port at Grandma Ruby's insistence, we moved to the music room. Elliot and Grandma Ruby sat down to hear me play and I realised as I opened the lid of the piano that I hadn't performed for anyone since my final examination in high school.

I played a chord progression to warm up, then stared at the keys: the same keys my virtuoso father had made sing with his music. I didn't feel ready to play those pieces for Grandma Ruby, and then I remembered that she'd called me a perfectionist. Was that what had always stood in my way? A desire to be perfect to make up for never quite feeling whole?

I wondered what my father would have done in the same situation. Then I recalled his words in the radio interview I had listened to with Elliot: *What I'm passionate about is music and being able to share it with others.* My father would have had a good time and been grateful that he could share his talent.

The tension drained out of my arms. I played the first piece that Terence had taught me, the one with a powerful swing pattern. I performed it much better than I'd expected and with feeling.

When I'd finished, Grandma Ruby stood up and applauded. 'What a granddaughter I have!' she cried. 'She's full of wonderful surprises. She's lovely, she can cook and she can play the piano!' Then she turned to Elliot, who was beaming with pride at my achievement. 'I really have to meet this Terence,' she told him. 'He's obviously a good teacher.'

Elliot glanced at me and saw my concern that more questions were about to be asked, so he jumped up and offered to play some pieces himself. He had a nice touch at the piano and a broad repertoire. He played 'You Go to My Head', 'Stormy Weather', 'Take the "A" Train', and other jazz favourites; and his version of 'Manteca' got Grandma Ruby up and dancing a sexy salsa. When he slowed down and started playing 'Summertime', I couldn't resist joining in and singing the lyrics. It was a sultry sensual tune, so perfect for a hot evening in New Orleans.

Elliot turned around and looked at me. 'I didn't know you could sing! What a voice, Amandine!'

'She's a natural,' said Grandma Ruby, clasping her hands together. 'She's so like her father, I can't believe it!'

I felt a wave of tenderness for them both. I was becoming a different person in New Orleans: more outgoing, more vibrant. Maybe all I'd needed was some encouragement.

After playing 'In a Sentimental Mood', Elliot glanced at his watch and apologised that he'd have to leave as he had a summer class to teach in the morning. Grandma Ruby yawned and excused herself to go to bed, but I knew she was only pretending she was tired so Elliot and I could be alone together.

We walked out to the entrance hall and Elliot's eyes fell to the escape route pamphlet I'd left on the table there.

'Oliver, the gardener, gave it to me,' I told him. 'My aunt and uncle are out of town so I'm not sure what to do. He told me I should book some hotels in case the tropical storm that's brewing in the Bahamas comes this way.'

Elliot touched my arm. 'I watched it on the news before I came. It's still out over the Atlantic. We've got some time before we'll know for certain where it will make landfall. Don't worry, if there is any danger, I'll come and drive you and your grandmother out of town. My sister has a big rambling house in Baton Rouge and loves guests. You'd both be welcome to stay a few days.'

Before stepping out the door, he kissed me so tenderly my toes curled with pleasure.

'I'll call you tomorrow,' he said. 'Meanwhile, stock up on bottled water, batteries and packaged food. Sometimes even when a storm bypasses us it puts the utilities out for a while.'

I waved as Elliot backed the car down the driveway to the street. *My knight in shining armour*, I thought. I'd never had one of those before.

I locked the door and walked up the stairs, revelling in the good feelings of the evening. Terence had told me that if I wanted to, I could be an architect and a musician. It seemed a world of rich possibilities was opening up before me.

TWENTY-EIGHT

Amanda

When I awoke the next morning, I lay in bed and stared out the window. It was a beautiful sunny day with a shimmering blue sky. Not the sort of day that signalled impending doom.

I sang 'Summertime' as I showered, recalling the fun of the previous evening, then dressed in a navy tulip skirt and a white top with a keyhole neckline. 'Looking good, Amandine,' I said, winking at my glowing reflection.

I dabbed moisturiser on my face but no make-up. I no longer felt I needed it. Optimism hummed through my veins. Blaine's Wiccan friend Zeline had said I was a young woman on the verge of a breakthrough. Was this it?

Lorena was vacuuming the hall carpet when I came out of my room. 'Your grandmother is downstairs,' she told me, turning off the vacuum cleaner. 'I don't think she's well. Perhaps you should take her to the doctor?'

My good mood drained away like water down a plughole. I rushed into the sitting room to find Grandma

Ruby lying on the sofa with her hand pressed to her forehead and her eyes closed.

'Grandma Ruby?' I asked. 'Aren't you feeling well?'

She let her hand slip to her side and opened her eyes. They were sunken with dark circles under them. She shook her head weakly.

I'd seen that look before when I was a volunteer for fun runs. The dry lips and pinched skin were signs of dehydration.

I went to the kitchen and poured a tall glass of water then added a slice of lemon to it.

While Grandma Ruby sipped the water, I dialled Aunt Louise's mobile number but it went straight to her message bank. I tried Uncle Jonathan's and the same thing happened. Surely when Aunt Louise had said they'd be out of communication until Monday, she hadn't really meant it? Who disappeared from civilisation these days? I'd try again later.

Even after a second glass of water, in which I'd dissolved a little salt and honey, Grandma Ruby wasn't looking any better.

'I'll take you to your doctor,' I told her. 'I'll call now and tell them we're coming.'

She shook her head. 'I'm not that bad, Amandine. As I get older the heat agrees with me less, that's all.'

The house was comfortably cool so I doubted the weather was the real culprit. I called directories and got them to connect me to Galafate Antiques.

When Blaine answered, my words came out in a rush. 'Grandma Ruby's sick. I think she needs to go to her doctor but she says she doesn't want to.'

'I'll be over right away,' he said.

When Blaine arrived, he took one look at Grandma

Ruby and said, 'Madame Ruby, we are not going to argue about this. I've already called Doctor Wilson and he is expecting us in an hour.'

'All right, I'll go,' she said, sitting up and smoothing her hair. 'But only because I'll have the two of you at me in stereo if I don't.'

'I suggest we go in Louise's Prius,' said Blaine, helping Grandma Ruby to her feet. 'We've got some time on our hands and Amandine should learn to drive American-style while she's here.'

It was a good idea. If there was an emergency and I couldn't reach him or Elliot, I needed to be able to take Grandma Ruby to the hospital myself.

The first thing I did after opening the garage door and helping Grandma Ruby into the back seat of the Prius was to get in the right side of the car when the steering wheel was on the left. I stepped out again and, with a sheepish grin, let Blaine sit there while I got into the driver's seat. *Thank God it's an automatic*, I thought, putting the key in the ignition. I didn't know how I would go shifting gears with my right hand.

I reversed down the driveway looking over my left shoulder when I should have been looking over my right.

'Now,' said Blaine, when I stopped at the gate, 'we are going to drive s-l-o-w-l-y around the block a few times before we head Uptown. Whenever I have to rent a car in England, I take a few moments to visualise how things are going to be different so I don't freak out when I get on the motorway from the airport. In your case, you need to be aware of three things: the oncoming traffic is going to be on the left; you have to go into the far lane when doing a left-hand turn; and at roundabouts you go counter-clockwise. Got it?'

I nodded, although I felt less confident than I had done when I was learning to drive a car. I'd been sixteen then and a know-it-all. I drove up Prytania Street so slowly that a kid on a skateboard overtook us and at the first intersection I stopped and looked in all directions twice over although I had the right of way. But as we continued on through the backstreets and I didn't run over anyone or cause a head-on collision, I gained confidence and started to drive like someone who'd actually had their licence for seven years.

'You know, Blaine, I would never have guessed it, but you're as cool as a cucumber in a crisis,' I told him.

He moved his hands over his mint shirt and cream trousers. 'A man who dresses right in the morning can handle anything life throws at him.'

Although I'd managed the road well, I was befuddled when we arrived at Doctor Wilson's office and I tried to do a reverse parallel park.

'I'll park the car,' said Blaine. 'You and Madame Ruby go up for the appointment. I've got some calls to make — I'll wait for you here.'

Doctor Wilson was a softly spoken man with a balding head and grey beard. Although his office had the ubiquitous cream-coloured walls and black leather furniture of a doctor's rooms, he seemed to have a fascination with horses. On his desk was a pair of prancing stallion bookends and a lamp with a bronze horse's head as the base. On the wall behind him, surrounded by his framed medical degrees, was an oil painting of a thoroughbred in a stable.

'So,' he said, studying us from under his bushy eyebrows, 'what symptoms have you been experiencing lately, Ruby?'

'I was dizzy this morning, but I'm better now,' she said. 'Amandine had a delightful young man over last night and I think that went straight to my head — and perhaps the glass of port.'

Doctor Wilson clucked his tongue, the traces of a smile twitching on his lips. 'Well, come sit on the bench and let's see what that ticker of yours is doing.' He listened to her chest through his stethoscope. 'You haven't had any pain? No shortness of breath?'

Grandma Ruby shook her head.

'We'll take a blood test to be on the safe side,' he said, strapping her arm and taking out a syringe. He turned to me. 'I had to increase her warfarin when she came last and that may be making her feel a bit off until her body readjusts. But all her vitals are good. The most important thing is that she keeps taking her medications exactly as instructed. Suddenly ceasing any of them is very dangerous, especially the warfarin. Stopping that can lead to a stroke.'

He helped Grandma Ruby off the bench and back into the patient's chair. Then he returned to his desk and wrote out a script. 'That storm in the Atlantic looks like it's gaining strength and might come this way. I'm writing a script for more medication in case you have to evacuate.' I shifted in my seat. That the storm might be turning into a hurricane didn't sound good.

Doctor Wilson must have noticed my alarm because he quickly added, 'It's a precaution. Better to be over-prepared than under-prepared.'

When we came out of the office, Blaine was in the car talking on his mobile phone. 'All good?' he asked, after he ended the call.

'The doctor gave us an extra script and took a blood test in case her warfarin level is too high,' I said, opening the car door and helping Grandma Ruby into the back seat. 'Otherwise everything seems good.'

'I was just speaking to a real estate agent friend of mine in Upstate New York,' he said. 'The furnishings of a deceased estate are going up for auction and he said they are magnificent. I've booked a flight for this afternoon. I'll write out all my contact details in case you need me.' He turned and smiled at Grandma Ruby. 'But Madame Ruby is looking much better already.'

After we'd returned home and Blaine had gone back to his shop, I tried to ring Aunt Louise and Uncle Jonathan again to let them know about the storm. I got their message banks again, so I called the ranch that had organised the trek.

'Echo Valley Ranch, how can I help you?' the receptionist answered.

'I need to contact Mrs Lalande-Barial. I'm her niece.'

The receptionist paused for a moment. I could hear her shuffling papers. 'I'm sorry, ma'am, Mrs Lalande-Barial and her husband are on our total silence retreat and won't be contactable until Monday.'

'It's an emergency,' I told her. 'I need to contact them immediately.'

'I'm sorry, ma'am, but the point of the trek is to get away completely.'

'But it's an emergency,' I repeated. 'I'm in New Orleans, I'm looking after my grandmother, Mrs Lalande-Barial's mother, and a hurricane might be coming our way.'

'Unfortunately I can't make contact. It is a condition of the trip that all participants leave their cell phones at the ranch.'

The receptionist remained polite but I could tell from her clipped tone that she was losing patience with me. I'd dealt with her type before. Whenever Julie at Tony's real estate office went on leave, we'd end up with temps who took their roles as gatekeepers far too seriously.

I sucked in a breath to calm myself, but before I could speak the receptionist added, 'You know, in the good old days, emergency or not, you would have had to write a letter and it wouldn't have gotten here for months.'

Was she serious?

'Surely their guide has a cell phone?' I said tersely. 'What would happen if one of the guests got sick or was bitten by a snake? Would he send the message for help on tom-toms?' The receptionist gasped and I knew I'd gone too far. 'Listen,' I added, in a more placating tone.

'I'm sorry,' she said. 'I've got another call coming in.'

The line went dead.

I took Elliot's advice and drove to Walgreens to stock up on bottled water, batteries and non-perishable foods. The store wasn't overly busy, but the customers all seemed to be surreptitiously checking out what everyone else was buying. I noticed handwipes were being snapped up so I got a couple of canisters myself.

Two cashiers were discussing what they would do if a hurricane started heading this way. 'You'd feel like a fool for evacuating if nothing happened, but an even bigger fool if you didn't and something actually did,' one of them said.

On my way back to the car, my mobile phone rang. It was Elliot.

'Hey, Amandine! I'm sorry, I won't get a chance to come over today. The university has called an emergency planning meeting and I think we're going to go late into the evening.'

'It sounds like things are getting serious,' I said. 'I've just come out of Walgreens and two of the cashiers were talking about evacuating. Grandma Ruby's doctor gave me an extra script for her medication in case we have to leave town.'

'Don't worry. We went through all this panic last year with Hurricane Ivan and nothing happened. Most likely this thing will bypass us again. But let's keep our eye on the news. I'll give you a call tomorrow.'

When I woke the following morning, Lorena was blending something in the kitchen and had the television news on so loud I could hear the voice of a weather woman.

'If you are in Florida you'll be pleased to know that Hurricane Katrina has been downgraded to a tropical storm again after making landfall last night as a category one hurricane. Let's show you what's happening with the storm on the radar. As you can see, the eye is now moving west over Florida and we are getting those bands of heavy rains and reports of trees down and about 1.3 million power outages.

'But while Katrina may be a tropical storm for now it's not likely to stay that way. According to the National Hurricane Center, the storm will work its way into the warm waters of the Gulf of Mexico, where it won't take long for it to regenerate its strength. Landfall is likely in the Panhandle of Florida, but there is a wide band of uncertainty. We could see landfall as far west as Mississippi and Alabama, maybe even New Orleans. But one thing is for certain: Hurricane Katrina is not finished with us yet ...'

When I went to the kitchen, I found Lorena staring at the television screen. 'That thing better stay in Florida,' she said. 'Have you ever been in a hurricane?'

'No.'

She clucked her tongue. 'They're not something you fool around with. My husband and I already have the car packed, and if the city says to go, we're going. We lived through Hurricane Hugo in Puerto Rico. We know what those winds can do.'

I watched the morning news programs while eating breakfast. They were giving advice about what to do to prepare for a hurricane, including stowing valuables and, if you lived in the lower-lying areas of New Orleans, moving furniture to the upper floors. When I thought of all the antiques and family heirlooms here that could be damaged, my stomach turned to knots.

I rang Blaine to see what he recommended. To my astonishment, he laughed off my concerns.

'Go see my assistant, Poppy, at the shop and get some bubble wrap and boxes to put away any fragile ornaments. If you want to, you can cover with plastic any furniture that might get wet if a window breaks, but that's really all you can do, honeybun. Stash Ruby's jewellery in the safe if you intend to evacuate, but looters will walk straight past the nineteenth-century Italian parcel-gilt chairs looking for televisions, computers and money.'

'What do you do about your shop?' I asked, thinking of all the treasures I'd seen there.

'We close the shutters, put the alarm on long-life battery and hope for the best,' he replied with a sigh. 'I love everything I've collected, but it wouldn't be practical to move it all each time we got a hurricane warning. That's why I have insurance.'

As I chatted to Blaine about the estate auction he was attending, my head throbbed. The only emergency I'd ever been in was the Sydney bushfires in the mid-nineties, but I'd been a teenager then and Nan and Tony had taken care of everything.

When I returned to the kitchen, Lorena was organising the refrigerator. 'I've moved all the perishables to the front,' she told me. 'If you end up evacuating, clear them out before you leave. The fastest way to ruin a refrigerator is to let food spoil in it.'

I went to check on Grandma Ruby, who was still lying in bed.

'How are you today?' I asked.

She placed her hand on her abdomen. 'My stomach hasn't been the best. I think it's the change in medication.'

'I'll ring Doctor Wilson and see if your results are in yet.'

She smiled weakly. 'It was sweet of Elliot to offer us to stay the weekend at his sister's place, but I don't feel like making a long trip in a car when I'm not well. This old house has withstood many storms, Amandine, and the Garden District is not prone to flooding. We'll be fine. Ask Elliot to come and stay here, and your piano teacher, Terence, too if you like.'

I was touched by her offer. 'One of Terence's neighbours is disabled and the others are elderly. He wants to look after them.'

'He can bring them all,' she replied. 'We'll make a party of it. It will be like the old days.'

It was time to come clean with Grandma Ruby. She might not be so enthusiastic when she learned where Terence and his neighbours lived.

'He lives in the Lower Ninth Ward.'

To my surprise she didn't bat an eyelid. 'What's wrong with that? Plenty of hard-working people do. You forget my little charge during school integration, Elsie Matthews, came from there. Through hard work that family paid off their mortgage long before many richer people manage to do, and they even sent Elsie to college. I heard that she became a fine doctor. I'm not worried about where people live.'

I put my arm around her and pressed my cheek to hers. Nan had been a generous woman too but I couldn't imagine that she would ever have opened her home to strangers. Grandma Ruby was exceptional and I was sure it was her scandalous and spectacular life that had made her that way. She truly did not judge other people by their race or economic status but solely on their character. It made me love her more. 'Thank you,' I told her. 'I'll let them know you've invited them.'

I went to pick up the bubble wrap and boxes from Blaine's assistant, a pretty Italian girl with pale skin and dark ringlets.

'Your grandma is right,' she told me. 'That old house of hers is well-built. As long as you stay away from the windows, you'll be quite safe. But where your aunt and uncle live could flood if the levees overflow.'

When I returned to the car, I called Doctor Wilson's office, but his answering machine said he was out of town for the weekend. I tried to ring Aunt Louise, but her message bank was full. I considered speaking to the uncooperative receptionist again, but decided I couldn't face it. I had the keys and alarm code for the house in Lake Terrace. I may as well go there myself and move the art objects to the upper floors and pack away any possible projectiles in the garden.

If New Orleans was in real danger, it didn't seem that way. I passed a high-school jamboree, a real estate agent sticking a sold sign on a front lawn, and a painter on a scaffold touching up the trims on a house.

When I reached Aunt Louise and Uncle Jonathan's place, I found one of their neighbours already putting the patio furniture in the garage.

'I'm Bob Kennard,' said the ruddy-cheeked man, offering me his hand. 'Johnny and I always keep an eye on each other's places when one of us is out of town. I had trouble reaching his cell, so I decided I'd best put everything away just to be sure.'

'Thank you. Are you planning to evacuate?' I asked, remembering the calm atmosphere on the drive over.

He shrugged. 'My wife said we should make a weekend of it. We're flying to San Francisco tonight. I'm kind of bummed to be missing the Saints game in the Superdome tonight though.'

'Is the airport still open? I thought they would have started cancelling flights.'

'Sure is. My daughter works there. The funny thing is, she told us that a bunch of Australian tourists arrived this morning looking forward to a weekend of partying. Nobody told them about the hurricane warning.'

Not so funny for them, I thought. *Who listens to the news when they're on holiday?* I thanked Bob for his help with the garden furniture.

'No problem,' he said. 'Don't worry about turning off the electricity and gas. I'll do that before we leave for the airport — that way the burglar alarm can continue to operate on battery for as long as possible.'

I spent the next few hours moving the Native American artefacts to the upper floors, packing as much as I could into the large walk-in wardrobe and adjoining ensuite, both of which didn't have exterior windows. As I worked, I noticed how solidly built the house was and that it had some hurricane protection in its design, including impact-resistant and well-sealed doors and windows. Wind getting into a house during a storm was what caused roofs to blow off and walls to collapse. Maybe contemporary houses had more merits than I gave them credit for — when they were well designed. But how it would survive a flood from a storm surge depended on the water level. The house was on the high side of the street, but it was built too close to the ground. If I'd designed it, I would have raised it.

My mobile rang, rousing me from my architectural fantasies. It was Elliot.

'Well, today was very ordinary until this afternoon when the National Weather Service started saying it looks like that storm in the Gulf might turn in our direction,' he said. 'Everyone in my building is now planning to leave town tomorrow, and I've heard the Hyatt has been fully booked by people who will feel safer there than in their own homes. It's weird. My colleagues who were deadset against leaving only a few hours ago are now saying this is the Big One!'

'Grandma Ruby doesn't want to leave,' I told him. 'She's not feeling well. She invited you to stay with us if you want to.'

'Let's see how things go,' he said calmly. 'If it looks like it's better to evacuate, I'll have to use my dashing charm to persuade her. Meanwhile, pack a couple of bags — one for her and one for yourself. I'm going to move everything to the upper floor of my apartment this evening. I'll come over in the morning. We should have a clearer idea by then of what this thing is going to do.'

Aunt Louise had already emptied her fridge of perishables before going on her trip. I unplugged it, along with the television in the sitting room, which was too large for me to take upstairs.

I got back into the car and thought about Terence. I took out the street directory and looked up how to get to the Lower Ninth Ward. But when I knocked on Terence's door, he wasn't home. I wrote him a note and slipped it into his letterbox.

Hi, Terence, I don't know what's going to happen with the storm, but I've got a car at the moment and I can pick you and your neighbours up if you want to stay with us in the Garden District. My grandmother says you are all welcome and wants to throw a party.

I included my mobile number and address. Then I returned to the Garden District, arriving just as Lorena was leaving.

'I've left my and my husband's cell numbers on the fridge,' she said. 'Make sure you pack your grandmother's medicine if you end up leaving. That's more important than anything else.'

Grandma Ruby didn't feel like dinner and went to bed early. I sat up with Flambeau, trying to make sense of the weather reports on the television. The Governor of Louisiana had declared a state of emergency, but exactly what did that mean? In the still, muggy air I could hear the bell of the St Charles Avenue streetcar, which was obviously still running, and the sounds of lively voices and glasses clinking emanating from the house next door. It sounded like a dinner party. People weren't rushing to their cars and speeding off. What sort of emergency was it?

Tired from all the work I'd done in the heat that day, I turned the volume down and drifted off to sleep with Flambeau resting in my lap. In the early morning I was woken by my mobile phone beeping. I reached for it and stared with bleary eyes at the screen. It was a text message from Tamara in Australia: *I've just seen the news. If you are still in New Orleans GET THE HELL OUT OF THERE! Call me as soon as you can! Tammy xx*

I looked at the television. Something was definitely happening. A panel of people were nodding their heads in a serious manner. I reached for the remote control and turned the sound up. The first words I heard were: *'It is now confirmed that New Orleans is in the cone. I'll repeat that again. New Orleans is now in the cone.'*

The cone of what? I wondered. *An ice cream cone? A traffic cone? Maxwell Smart's Cone of Silence?* It was obviously a term people who lived in the Gulf States understood immediately, but to my foggy brain it was gobbledygook.

I glanced at the clock. It was four in the morning. I wanted to call Elliot so he could explain what was happening, but he had sounded tired the previous day, and if we were going to spend hours in the car, I'd better let him sleep now.

I flicked to another channel. The blonde newsreader looked earnestly into the camera and informed viewers:

'It is confirmed that Katrina is now a major hurricane. While it's currently rated as a category three, there are fears tonight that as it gathers strength over the warm waters of the Gulf it will become a terrible category four, and perhaps even a catastrophic category five storm. Meteorologists predict landfall sometime on Monday. The National Weather Service has released a bulletin saying: "The bottom line is, Katrina is expected to be an intense and dangerous hurricane heading towards the North Central Gulf Coast." They warn that the threat should be taken very seriously, and anyone who is able to leave the coastal area while the roads are still clear should do so now.'

Trying to discern what was the truth and what was media hype was difficult. *Okay*, I thought, breathing more calmly. *It sounds like New Orleans is one of the possible places the hurricane could hit, but it's not confirmed.*

I turned the television off and went to bed, waking a few hours later to another beautiful sunny day and the humming of lawnmowers. Surely people wouldn't be doing their gardens now if they feared we were barrelling towards Armageddon? It was already hot and humid, and the air was completely still. If I hadn't watched the news report, I'd have no idea a dangerous storm was lurking out there in the Gulf.

I showered and dressed, and made breakfast using the last of the peaches, grapes, blueberries and coconut yoghurt in the refrigerator. Afterwards, I found two overnight bags in the closet under the stairs. I packed a couple of changes of clothes in the smaller of the two, along with my toothbrush, toothpaste, skin moisturiser and sunblock. As I shuffled through my suitcase for my passport, my hand touched something hard and smooth.

It was Nan's pendant with the pink rose. I'd forgotten that I'd put it away when I went to listen to my father's music at Elliot's place.

'Nan,' I said, putting the necklace on, 'please keep us safe.'

Then I picked up my digital camera and felt compelled to take pictures of my parents' room as if I was never going to see it again.

Grandma Ruby was sitting up in bed when I went to check on her, but looked weak and sweaty. 'Do you have a fever?' I asked, touching her forehead.

'I don't think so. I'm sure it's that warfarin. Do you think I should take the lower-dose tablets I had before?'

I shook my head. Grandma Ruby's doctor had been specific that it was dangerous to take the drug any way other than instructed. 'Stick with it until Doctor Wilson is back on Monday,' I said. 'He should have the blood results by then.'

I put the other overnight bag I'd found on top of the blanket box at the end of her bed. 'Pack a couple of changes of clothing,' I instructed. 'But leave some room on top so I can put your medications inside — in case we have to evacuate.'

'We don't *have* to do anything,' she replied irritably. 'They can't make you leave if you don't want to.'

A smile danced on my lips. I remembered Uncle Jonathan telling me that if something was forbidden it attracted Grandma Ruby all the more. She didn't like being told what to do. Was that really only eleven days ago? My life had so completely changed that I didn't feel like the same person. On the other hand, I felt as if I had just arrived in New Orleans and had come to love it. Now we might have to leave.

I left Grandma Ruby to pack her bag while I returned to the kitchen and put some supplies in a cooler box, including titbits for Flambeau who never seemed to eat anything as common as chicken feed.

'What do you think?' I asked him while he perched on a stool and watched me. 'Should we go or should we stay? Aren't birds supposed to be able to sense danger?'

Elliot arrived with some beignets.

'Firstly, how did you know that Grandma Ruby eats beignets in the morning?' I asked him. 'And secondly, how did you find a bakery that was open?'

'The Quarter looks surprisingly normal,' he answered. 'There are tourists walking up and down Bourbon Street and many of the shops are open.'

'Where's Duke?'

'My neighbour was leaving for Baton Rouge this morning. He took Duke and his portable cage with him to drop off at my sister's place. I thought that would give us more room in the car.'

Grandma Ruby came downstairs, and Elliot propped her legs up on an ottoman before serving her the beignets and a cup of hot water with lemon.

'I usually have coffee for breakfast,' she told him. 'And strong.'

'Not if your stomach is upset,' he said.

She rolled her eyes but drank the hot water and lemon obediently. I smiled. She would never have listened to me.

Elliot turned the television on and we watched the weather broadcasts in between stowing valuables away in the safe and wrapping up breakables and storing them in the cupboard under the stairs or in the bathrooms.

As I was sealing up one box I heard a male reporter say, '"Gassing up and getting out" is the catchphrase in

Louisiana, Mississippi and Alabama today as residents await confirmation of Katrina's dangerous track.'

I walked into the sitting room and stared at the image on the television screen. It showed a technicoloured swirl brewing in the Gulf of Mexico. The orange eye of the hurricane seemed to be growing bigger by the second.

The image switched to a diagram of New Orleans, which showed how the shape of the land and the levees did indeed form what looked like a soup bowl.

'*The worst-case scenario of this hurricane if it heads towards us or slightly west of us,'* continued the reporter's voiceover, '*is that the Downtown area of New Orleans could be covered in ten to fifteen feet of water. Of course, this is what many residents have been worrying about for several years now ...'*

'A lot of people talking and not a lot of action,' said Elliot, coming up behind me. 'That's why so many people are cynical about leaving. They can't believe there can be any real danger if the authorities haven't done anything to prevent the city being flooded.'

I thought of Terence and went to check my mobile to see if he'd rung. He hadn't. The low-charge signal was flashing. Because of the different power voltage between the United States and Australia, it took ages to charge my phone. I connected it to the charger on the kitchen bench, next to my bag so I wouldn't forget it.

By evening, the weather reports were becoming more dire. Max Mayfield of the National Hurricane Center was being quoted by a reporter as having said: 'This is the worst storm I've seen in my thirty-three-year history as a meteorologist. The conditions are the worst I've seen. The storm is the worst I've seen. This is the one that we have all been dreading.'

My stomach tightened. This wasn't some news anchor trying to improve ratings. It was the opinion of an experienced meteorologist.

Elliot noticed my concern. 'Landfall won't be until Monday,' he said. 'We've prepared everything we can prepare. We'll set off first thing in the morning. Hopefully Ruby will be feeling better by then. If not, we'll go to the hospital on our way out of town and get a doctor to check her before we go on to Baton Rouge.'

That night I sat with Grandma Ruby reading to her from a book I'd found on the shelf in the parlour, *The Bonfire of the Vanities*. Although I'd read it years before, it was only now that its racial themes hit home. Gradually Grandma Ruby's eyes began to droop and she fell asleep. I watched her chest rise and fall for a few minutes before turning out the light.

I made my way down the hallway to my room. Elliot had made himself a bed from cushions spread out on the floor and was fast asleep, sprawled on his stomach. I kneeled down and kissed his cheek. 'We could have shared the bed,' I whispered. He stirred and smiled but continued on sleeping.

The air in the room was motionless and a chorus of frogs was croaking in the garden. Sweat was dripping down my back from the humidity. I stood under the shower for a full ten minutes, letting the cold water stream over my burning skin. After going up and down the stairs so many times, I was dead on my feet and wasn't sure I even had the energy to reach the bed. When I climbed on top of it, I lay down on the bedspread —

still too hot to get under the covers. I closed my eyes then opened them again. Every nerve in my body seemed to have switched itself to high alert. 'Oh no!' I said.

'You all right?' Elliot asked.

I looked over the side of the bed to see that he was awake and watching me.

'I was exhausted a moment ago but now I can't sleep.'

He propped himself up on his elbow. 'That's called adrenal exhaustion. I get that sometimes when I'm marking final examination papers. I find a packet of Fig Newtons and a cup of herb tea usually does the trick.'

'Damn!' I said, tongue-in-cheek. 'We don't have any Fig Newtons.'

Elliot stood up and came to the bed, nudging me to move over and let him lie down next to me.

He smelled delicious, like coconut and lime. A warm thrill ran through me when he smoothed his hands over my hair and gazed into my face. 'You're getting the full menu of what New Orleans has to offer, aren't you?' he said, running his hand down my side then back again to my shoulder. 'This beautiful home in the Garden District, jazz, evacuating for a hurricane ... but I think you've missed out on a very important thing.'

'What's that?' I asked.

He kissed me softly on the lips then reached for the hem of my nightdress and drew it up over my stomach. Waves of desire stirred in my belly when he pressed his body against mine. 'The exquisite pleasure of making love in a four-poster bed that's going to creak like crazy,' he said. I laughed and lifted my arms as he pulled my nightdress over my head and dropped it to the floor. He brushed his fingers over the curves of my breasts and I quivered. 'Do you think you might like to experience that?'

I slipped my hand around his back and nuzzled into his neck, then whispered in his ear: 'Why don't you try me?'

TWENTY-NINE

Amanda

When I awoke the next morning, Elliot was already up. I lay back on the pillows and smiled when I recalled the pleasure of our love making. Then I heard him closing and lashing the shutters downstairs and remembered the impending hurricane. I went to the bedroom window and saw a stream of cars heading down Prytania Street. People were getting out.

The house was gloomy with the shutters closed. I searched for Elliot and found him outside nailing plywood boards to the parlour windows, which didn't have shutters.

He had his shirt off and for the first time I noticed the tattoo on his left shoulder, a treble clef and musical notes. I hummed the melody. It was the refrain from Louis Armstrong's 'It's a Wonderful World'. I sneaked up behind him and kissed it.

'I didn't notice that last night,' I said.

He turned around and smiled. 'I didn't think you noticed too much of anything,' he replied, kissing me on the lips. Then his face turned serious.

'I got up early and listened to the broadcasts,' he said. 'The Mayor has ordered a mandatory evacuation. It's the first time in the history of New Orleans that an evacuation has been mandatory. I'm not even sure if he can legally do it.' He finished securing the plywood then looked me straight in the eye. 'He wouldn't be doing that unless he was certain the storm was going to hit us and it was going to be a category five.'

While Elliot locked up the potting shed, I went to the kitchen and turned on the television. The station was replaying the Mayor's evacuation order: '*Hurricane Katrina will likely affect the Louisiana Coast with tropical force winds and heavy rainfall by this evening. Governor Blanco and I, Mayor C. Ray Nagin, have each declared a state of emergency. Every person is hereby ordered to immediately evacuate the City of New Orleans ...*'

I rushed upstairs and told Grandma Ruby that we had to leave and she'd better have a shower. I took her overnight bag downstairs. It was heavier than mine, but she was a snappy dresser so I assumed she'd included at least one pair of dress shoes. I unzipped the bag and placed her medicines on top of a couple of scarves she'd packed, checking and rechecking that I had included all four of them. I tucked the script Doctor Wilson had written in my own bag next to my passport.

Elliot took one of the cardboard boxes I'd got from Blaine's assistant and punched holes in it with a screwdriver. He went to the kitchen and returned with Flambeau, opening the box flaps to put him inside.

'He won't like that,' I told him. 'He's used to sitting on Grandma Ruby's lap.'

'I'm sorry,' said Elliot. 'But we can't risk him getting a fright and flapping off.' He put Flambeau in the box, took a permanent marker from his pocket and wrote my mobile number on the bird's wing.

'You think of everything,' I said.

Grandma Ruby came downstairs and rolled her eyes while Elliot and I did the final checks on the house. 'I'm only going along with this because of all your theatricality in making an evacuation,' she said. 'This house and its stories will outlast all of us. It's not going to blow away in any storm.'

Because Grandma Ruby's stomach was still upset, Elliot and I decided to go to the hospital before we left the city. We hadn't expected it to be so crowded. All the private clinics that were closing for the hurricane had sent their patients there and, as many of the doctors had left town, anyone who was sick had come too.

We found Grandma Ruby a seat in the waiting area, but Elliot and I had to sit on the floor. We hadn't wanted to leave Flambeau in the car because of the heat, but we knew there was no way he'd be let into the hospital, so I'd emptied the contents of my overnight bag into a shopping tote and put Flambeau inside with the zipper open at the edge for air. I'd expected him to protest about his captivity, but he seemed to sense something serious was at stake and kept quiet.

Storm updates were flashing on the television in the waiting room and were growing more ominous by the minute. *'A powerful hurricane is now predicted to directly hit New Orleans within twelve to twenty-four hours,'* said one newsreader. *'At least one half of*

well-constructed homes will have roof and wall failure.
All gabled roofs will fail, leaving those homes severely
damaged or destroyed. There is potential for great loss
of life.'

A convoy of ambulances arrived with elderly patients
from a care facility. Some of them were on ventilators. A
couple of nurses rushed past us towards the new arrivals.

'If it floods, we are in deep trouble,' one nurse said
to the other. 'Our back-up generators are below ground-
floor level. If they get water in them, they'll fail and we'll
lose our capacity for life support.'

I wondered what was going to happen to all the
people who couldn't evacuate the city: terminally ill
patients, women in labour, paraplegics, premature
babies, the homeless and the mentally ill. I slipped my
hand into my bag and patted Flambeau to calm myself,
but then started thinking about all the animal shelters
and the pounds. What about the zoo? Were they going
to get the animals out? And what about those Australian
tourists? The airport would be closed now. Could they
rent a bus and get away?

Panic seized me as the scale of the impending
catastrophe grew in my imagination. This wasn't some
tiny coastal town that was facing annihilation; it was a
major American city!

The woman next to me must have been thinking
similar things because she turned to her husband and
asked, 'What do you suppose they'll do at the prison if it
floods?' I assumed she was concerned about the welfare
of the prisoners who would be trapped there, until she
added, 'I guess the guards will leave them to drown, or
shoot them if they try to escape. And good riddance too.
It will save taxpayers' money.'

I turned to Elliot for comfort, but he was watching the elderly patients being wheeled into the hospital on gurneys and in wheelchairs.

'My grandparents used to shelter at the hospital during hurricanes in the 1940s and 1950s,' he told me. 'My grandfather was a doctor and my grandmother was a nurse. They'd bring sandwiches, flasks of coffee and their pet dogs and stay here the night helping with the patients until the storm passed over.' He nodded towards the nurses I'd overheard earlier, who were now directing the flow of patients towards the elevators. 'It sounds like they're worried how the hospital will hold up to this hurricane though.'

News bulletins continued to race across the television screen. I saw that the Mayor had informed residents that the Superdome would be a shelter of last resort for those who had no means to leave town. I thought of Terence, and took out my mobile to see if there were any messages, but the battery was flat.

'Are you all right?' Elliot asked.

'Terence is going to die in his home if he doesn't get out.'

Elliot frowned. 'He'll go to the Superdome surely.'

I shook my head. 'He told me that if his neighbours can't leave, he won't either. I left him a message to say he could stay with them in the house in the Garden District, but I haven't heard back from him.'

Elliot rubbed his arms and shuddered. 'After the doctor sees Ruby, we'll drive down there and persuade him to leave. We can give his neighbours a ride to the Superdome, or they can stay at my place. The French Quarter is on higher ground than the Lower Ninth Ward.'

I thought Grandma Ruby was dozing, but she must have heard our conversation. She suddenly stood up, looking perky. 'The other people here are far worse than me,' she said. 'I don't want to waste the doctor's time. Let's go, otherwise we'll be stuck in gridlocked traffic.'

Although I was still concerned about her, she was right. It would be hours before she could see a doctor, and if we stayed, we'd possibly end up weathering Katrina in the hospital. We could go see a doctor once we'd arrived at Baton Rouge.

As we drove to the Lower Ninth Ward, I had a sinking feeling that we'd left our escape too late. The traffic making its way to I-10 had slowed to a crawl. Elliot had to periodically turn the air conditioning off so his car wouldn't overheat.

We had brought only what was most essential, but some of the cars we passed were packed with not only adults, children and pets but also quilts, books, musical instruments and even paintings. I'd put Flambeau back in his box when we'd returned to the car but he had busted out and was now sitting on top of it, looking out the window. I thought it was cool that we were travelling with a rooster, but we were topped by a driver with his python draped over his shoulders.

It took us two hours to make the short trip to the Lower Ninth Ward. The wind was starting to pick up. It was the first sign so far that a storm was coming.

We parked the car in the shade of a crepe myrtle tree that was starting to bend in the breeze. Elliot left the tops of the windows cracked open, and I passed Grandma Ruby a bottle of water. 'We'll only be a minute,' I told her. I looked up at the sky, which was starting to grow darker. A minute was probably all we could spare before the heavy rains that preceded a hurricane starting pouring down, making the evacuation even more difficult.

The houses on either side of Terence's and across the road had plywood fixed to their windows and doors. I suspected he had installed that form of hurricane protection.

The sound of hammering came from the back garden and Elliot and I went around to find Terence securing plywood to his rear windows. He gave a jolt of surprise when he saw us.

'Amandine! Elliot! I expected you'd be well on your way out of town by now. I've heard I-10 is banked up already, even though they opened up the incoming lanes to outgoing traffic.'

'We've come to take you with us,' said Elliot. 'This storm sounds bad, Terence. Really bad.'

Terence shook his head. 'I can't leave. Augusta's son took her to the hospital, but I've still got elderly Mr and Mrs Williams across the road and the lady down the street with all her children. Then there's Jerry near the bus stop.'

'We can give them all a ride to the Superdome,' said Elliot. 'They'll be safer there.'

Terence grimaced. 'You know who's going to go to the Superdome? All the gangs, drug dealers and troublemakers. I went there during Hurricane Georges and got robbed at knifepoint. Those elderly people are too frail for that, and how's a young woman with five kids going to defend herself?'

'Hey, Ti-Jean!' called a man on a ladder from the house behind. 'You staying too?'

Terence nodded. 'And you?'

'Sure am!' the man replied. 'I got my arsenal of weapons. Any looter trying to get into my house is gonna get one hell of a surprise!'

'Why did he call you Ti-Jean?' I asked when Terence turned back to us. I remembered that had been the name of Leroy's brother.

'It's a diminutive, not a name,' he explained. 'My grandfather was named John Terence, and apparently I greatly resembled him so my family always referred to me as Ti-Jean — Little John — as a joke. I told my neighbour that story once at a crawfish boil and ever since he's called me Ti-Jean.'

'Well, that's the longest minute I've ever spent in a hot car,' said Grandma Ruby, coming around the corner with Flambeau under her arm.

She stopped in her tracks when she saw Terence and blinked. Then she brought her hand to her mouth, staring at him as if she'd seen a ghost.

'How can it be?' she said, her voice quivering. 'Is it you? Is it really you?'

Terence dropped his hammer. He was trembling from head to foot. For what seemed like an endless moment, neither of them moved.

Elliot and I exchanged a glance, confused. Terence and Grandma Ruby knew each other?

Terence tried to say something, but his voice died in his throat. He stepped forward, like he wanted to rush towards Grandma Ruby but couldn't move his feet.

Grandma Ruby edged back from him, looking bewildered. 'All these years,' she said. 'For all these years I thought you were dead. I saw you in the casket.'

My heart thumped in my chest. What was I not seeing? What was I overlooking? Then my mind jammed and

I stopped breathing for a moment as the realisation hit me.*When she came on stage the whole world stopped. She was mesmerising. She danced at the Vieux Carré nightclub, a classy place on Bourbon Street. It's gone now, of course.* I knew from Grandma Ruby's stories that black men weren't allowed to watch white strippers. Terence would never even have been allowed in the Vieux Carré Club unless he was in the band. What had been jumbled up started to make sense — but in a way that seemed crazy.

Now I understood Terence's deep love for my father: he'd loved him because he was Jewel's son. He was the one who had been leaving flowers at my parents' tomb. I also understood why he hadn't wanted to help with the porch or stay at the house in the Garden District. Terence didn't want to see Grandma Ruby because he was Leroy!

Tears ran down Grandma Ruby's cheeks. 'Why would you fake your own death? My heart was broken!'

'Every day, every second of every day, I always thought of you, Jewel,' Leroy said, his voice broken. 'I never left you. The Klan killed my brother Terence — Ti-Jean — because of his activities, but that wasn't enough for them — they went after my family too. And I could only imagine what they would do if they found out about you. When Terence was murdered, I begged my family to tell you that it was me who'd been killed. It was the only way I could set you free. No matter what I did or said, I knew you'd follow me anywhere, even to your own destruction. They only agreed because they loved you too, Jewel. They knew it was the right thing.'

It was clear now that Jimmy had lied when he'd told Grandma Ruby he'd murdered Leroy: he was the sort of person who would try to take credit for someone else's racist execution.

'It nearly killed me,' Grandma Ruby said, running her gaze over Leroy as if she still couldn't believe he was real.

'I watched you from afar. I wanted too much for you to be happy — that was the reason. The only reason. Not because I ever stopped loving you.' He sat down on the step, weeping now. 'I would never hurt you intentionally, never! You should know that.'

The grief in Grandma Ruby's voice intensified. 'Our son, our beautiful son! He never got to know you as his father.'

Leroy's head snapped up. 'What son?' Then, grasping the meaning of her words, he gave a short cry. 'Dale?'

Grandma Ruby nodded, and my whole world tipped over like a ship taking in water. My father was Leroy's son?

I leaned against Elliot for support and remembered the pictures I had seen of my father: the clean-cut, all-American boy. But if you knew what you were looking for, the clues were there: the sculpted cheekbones, the nose, the height, the tanned complexion.

I turned back to the man sitting on the step, the man I'd known as Terence. That meant he was my real grandfather, not Clifford Lalande.

Globs of rain began to fall from the sky but we had all forgotten about the hurricane. We were caught up in a storm of our own.

Elliot helped Leroy to his feet. 'We'd better all go inside,' he said, 'and sort this out there.'

Leroy had moved the electric piano upstairs, and with the plywood on the windows and doors, the front room was dark. Elliot turned on a lamp while I helped Grandma Ruby into a chair. I took Flambeau from her before sitting down myself. My legs were like jelly.

'Dale was our son?' Leroy said.

Grandma Ruby looked at her clasped hands on her lap. 'When I thought you were dead and I suspected I was pregnant, part of me was elated that I was carrying a legacy of the man I loved. But I was also terrified in case the child was born black. When Clifford proposed to me, I told him I couldn't marry him because I believed I was pregnant with your child.'

'He married you anyway,' said Leroy, rubbing his eyes with the heels of his hands.

'I didn't expect that of him, but he insisted. He made sure only a doctor he trusted was present for the birth. If the child turned out to be black, we'd say it was stillborn and find a good family to raise it.' She looked into Leroy's face. 'You can't imagine how torn I was that I might have to give up our child! I often thought that if it came to that, I would kill myself. How could I go on living? But Dale was born looking like a pure white child. God had been merciful to us. Clifford claimed him as his own.'

Grandma Ruby turned to me. 'I'm sorry for not telling you the whole truth, Amandine. I was scared of how you might react. I needed time to work up to it.'

'When I die,' Leroy said quietly, 'I'm going to embrace Clifford Lalande and tell him that he was the finest man this world has ever seen.' He drew a long breath before speaking again. 'Life is always taking turns we don't expect, isn't it?'

Grandma Ruby nodded. 'I still talk to you sometimes, like you're there and watching over me.'

He leaned over and grabbed her hand. 'I've always been watching over you. That's why I came back to New Orleans after my family settled in San Francisco. I took Terence's first name to honour his memory and settled in a part of town you were unlikely to visit. You were married to a good man and you'd had children. When I met Dale at Preservation Hall, I tried to avoid him in case he led you to me again. But he kept seeking me out to teach him piano. Then Amandine appeared one day with Elliot, asking about Dale. Life is strange. Of all the people in New Orleans, both Dale and Amandine had some magnetic pull towards me. It makes me believe in fate.'

'And you, Leroy?' Grandma Ruby asked quietly. 'Didn't you ever have a wife and children of your own?'

He shook his head. 'A man can live on his own with his memories. A woman can't. She needs a family.'

Grandma Ruby seemed to wrestle with something in her mind, then a change came over her. She sat up, her dignity and poise returned. 'You sacrificed a lot for me,' she said to Leroy. 'Clifford and his family were good people, that's true, and they were very wealthy. But in my heart I've always remained Jewel.' She turned to me. 'Amandine, get my overnight bag from the car.'

'I'll do it,' Elliot said. 'The wind sounds like it's picking up.'

When he returned, he brought all the bags in with him. He placed Grandma Ruby's in front of her. She unzipped it and took out the medicines and her scarves and dresses, then reached into the bottom and lifted out her red burlesque bra and G-string. Now I knew why the bag had been heavy. All those rhinestones!

'Do you remember these?' she asked Leroy. 'Of all the treasures in my house these are the only ones I brought with me.'

Elliot's eyebrows shot up and he looked at me. I wished we weren't all crammed together for such an intimate moment.

'When we have time, you're going to have to explain to me what's going on,' he whispered. 'Terence is really someone called Leroy, and he's your grandfather? But first I need to go and move the car to higher ground. Do you hear the rain? It's too late to evacuate. We'll have to take our chances and stay put. When I get back, we'll board up the back door and hunker down.'

I touched his arm. 'If you still have a chance to go, then you should. I can't now.'

He shook his head. 'I'm not leaving you, Amandine. And I know you won't go without your grandmother. I'll be back in about half an hour. Meanwhile make sure there's water, food and torches upstairs. Fill the bathtub and sinks with water too. Then when Terence ... I mean Leroy ... is ready, make sure he takes an axe up there and a can of spray paint.'

'An axe?'

He nodded grimly. 'If the water goes over our heads we'll need a way to break out.'

I kissed Elliot before he ran out into the gusty storm, and watched him until he turned the corner of the house. Then I looked back to Grandma Ruby and Leroy. Why had she thought I'd react badly? Then the truth hit me like a ton of bricks.

'Dad found out who his father was, didn't he?' I said to Grandma Ruby. 'Or at least he found out that it wasn't Clifford Lalande.'

Grandma Ruby slumped like someone had punched her hard in the stomach. 'I'd intended to tell Dale after Clifford's death that Leroy was his biological father, but then he mourned Clifford's loss so deeply that I was afraid for his sanity. When Paula came along, and you were born, he returned to his happy self again. I never seemed to find the right time. As it turned out, life did it for me. A friend of his at Tulane University was doing a study of DNA and asked Dale for a blood sample for his research. But after he tested the sample, he told Dale that one of his parents had been black. When Dale confronted me, I had to confess that Clifford wasn't his real father. It was a tremendous shock for him.'

'Was he angry at you when he found out?' I asked, sitting down next to her again.

'I tried to explain how much I'd loved Leroy,' she replied, dabbing at the tears on her cheeks. 'And that he'd been conceived in the greatest love he could imagine.' She turned away and bit her lip. 'Dale had no problem with being part black — that didn't bother him at all. It was the fact that Clifford wasn't his real father that upset him. But I believe he would have come to terms with that in his own time.'

She covered her face with her hands. 'Life is cruel. It snatched him away before he had a chance to embrace his own history. That's the bone I'll always have to pick with God: just as you start to get a handle on something, he takes it away.'

Now the events of that night were crystal clear. My moderate, responsible father had been in shock: that's why he had drunk too much and couldn't drive me and my mother. Grandma Ruby was right. From all I'd learned about my father, I knew he would have sorted things out in his mind with time. But he wasn't given any time, and all our lives were irrevocably changed because of it.

The wind was picking up velocity. It was whistling around the house like the scream of a ghost. I shuddered. 'I'd better move our supplies upstairs.'

Grandma Ruby repacked her overnight bag and I took it up with my bag and Elliot's. To my relief, Leroy had already put a toolbox up in the master bedroom along with bottles of water and food.

I called Elliot's mobile but there was no connection. I returned to the lower level and found Leroy getting ready to put the final piece of plywood on the back door.

'No, wait! Elliot's not back yet,' I said.

Leroy shook his head. 'He won't be able to get back now.' When he saw the alarm on my face, he put his hand on my shoulder. A shiver ran over my skin. His hand was ice cold. I'd noticed the coolness of his skin when he'd handed me the root beer that first time but I'd always thought it was because the bottle was chilled. Grandma Ruby's descriptions of Leroy having to warm his hands before playing came back to me. There had been many clues that Terence was Leroy, but they had not made sense to me until now.

'Elliot will be all right,' he said. 'The roads were probably blocked off by the time he went out. The police might have refused to let him back in.'

I calmed down. *Yes, Elliot is smart*, I told myself. *He'll be able to look after himself.*

It took both of us to shut the door and nail the plywood to it. It rattled like it was going to come loose and fly away until Leroy got the final nails into it. When we returned to Grandma Ruby, the quiet in the front room was eerie compared to the squalls outside.

Leroy turned the television on and set about making us dinner. 'Power's bound to go out,' he said, 'so let's enjoy the last hot meal we might have for a few days.'

Soon the delicious smells of onion, garlic, celery and jasmine rice permeated our hidey-hole. We ate together calmly. Not at all like three people whose lives had been turned upside down in the last two hours and who were now facing a deadly hurricane.

'We'll be all right,' Grandma Ruby assured me, patting my hand after she'd given Flambeau some of the vegetables from her plate. 'I've lived through worse than hurricanes.'

'Now,' said Leroy, pointing his fork at Flambeau, 'you have to explain the rooster to me.'

Grandma Ruby told him the story of how she'd acquired Flambeau. As she spoke, she and Leroy leaned closer and closer until they were holding hands and gazing into each other's eyes. 'You'll have to get used to calling me Ruby,' she said. 'You don't want to confuse our granddaughter now.'

Leroy grinned and brushed his hand down her cheek. 'I can call you "Ruby" if that's what you want. But when I look at you, I still see a bright, shining diamond.'

I wished I could give them some privacy — I could see they had many things they wanted to discuss — but soon the sound of the hurricane prevented all conversation. The wind had picked up speed and increased in pitch: it sounded like a freight train that never actually passed. The house shuddered and shook, and I could hear things banging and flapping in the wind outside. I tried to imagine what they were from the images being broadcast on the television. Street signs? Torn-off guttering? Roofs peeling open like sardine cans?

When the pictures changed to a radar image of an ever-widening circle of destruction heading directly for New Orleans, I looked away. 'Elliot, where are you?' I whispered. 'Please be safe.'

The power went out early in the morning. Leroy was prepared with hurricane lamps and a radio. But the static on the radio was too loud so we still couldn't tell what was happening. The wind was like a howling demon now, rattling at the doors and windows and shrieking constantly. I stared at the windows as if they were my enemies. The plywood was wet and parts of it were starting to buckle. If the wind got inside this house, it would collapse for sure.

Something crashed into an outside wall, something large, and I jumped out of my seat. Flambeau shot off his chair too and went running around the room in a panic.

I took a deep breath and tried to trust in Leroy's little shotgun house. Like 'Amandine', it must have weathered many a storm. I lifted Flambeau into the box that Elliot had made for him, seeing the wisdom of it now. I covered it with a throw rug to calm him. I wished I could put a throw rug over myself too; maybe it would help to quell my terror. I was starting to feel claustrophobic, but there was nowhere for me to run. I saw that my left arm was marked by strange half-moon-shaped cuts. In my trepidation I'd dug my fingernails into my skin and not even noticed.

As day broke, Leroy was able to get better reception on the radio. We could make out a few of the excited broadcaster's words: *'downgraded category three'* ... *'moved east'* ... *'New Orleans safe'*. We looked at each other in amazement. We were safe? The hurricane hadn't directly hit New Orleans? The three of us hugged each other with joy.

I felt like I had dodged death and took a moment to absorb that I'd ridden out a deadly storm with my grandmother and my newly discovered grandfather in the Lower Ninth Ward. What a story I would have for Tamara once my mobile was recharged!

Leroy checked the landline. It was dead. 'Never mind,' he said. 'I've got enough of everything to keep us going until the utilities come back on.'

It was still gusty outside when he unscrewed the plywood on the front door and ran across the street to check that Mr and Mrs Williams were all right.

'They're fine,' he said, looking relieved when he returned. 'I'll check on the other neighbours when the wind dies down.'

I took Flambeau out of his box. He looked dazed and didn't make a sound.

Grandma Ruby fetched a glass from the kitchen and gave him some water to sip. 'Don't worry, my love,' she told him, sitting down and scratching his head. 'We'll get you some treats in a moment.'

'I'll make some coffee on the gas cylinder,' said Leroy, rising from his seat.

A *boom!* sounded in the air, like a massive thunderclap, followed by a terrifying roar. Flambeau flapped to the top of the couch. Leroy knitted his brows. Grandma Ruby grabbed the sides of her chair as she started to move sideways. I wondered why her chair was moving, then I felt the wet around my feet. Water was coming in under the front door. There was a sound of shattering glass and it poured in through the lower windows too.

'Quick,' shouted Leroy. 'Upstairs!'

I lifted Flambeau and held him in the crook of my elbow. Leroy pushed me and Grandma Ruby towards the stairs to the upper floor. Grandma Ruby reached them and scrambled up, but my foot slipped and I fell. I grabbed for the banister but the water was too strong and it pulled me away.

Leroy had reached the stairs and he yanked me onto them too. I heard Flambeau squawk as he slipped from my grasp. 'No!' I cried, trying to reach for him. But the last I saw of him were his terrified eyes as he was swept away on a tide of water.

Leroy dragged me up the stairs with the superhuman strength that only adrenaline can give. I looked back. The water was less than half a metre from the downstairs ceiling. Curtains, pillows and dishes floated in the river that had filled the lower part of the house. If we'd hesitated even a minute longer we would have been washed away.

I turned to Leroy, whose teeth were chattering. 'What happened?' I asked.

He peered at the brackish water and shook his head. 'The levees must have been breached ... but there's so much water!'

Bile rose in my throat. I didn't think the levees could have been topped and produced a wave of water that fast. They must have collapsed under the pressure of the storm surge. This was the worst-case scenario we'd been warned about.

The wind started blowing again, whipping the water. The three of us lay huddled together on the bed in the upstairs bedroom. Grandma Ruby wept for Flambeau. I felt sick to my stomach as I relived the moment he'd slipped from my grasp.

'Lord have mercy on us, Lord have mercy on us, let the house hold,' Leroy prayed.

With my architectural knowledge, I couldn't see how the house could hold against the volume of water that was being thrown against it. I buried my head in a pillow, sure that we were going to drown in the flood. I'd come all the way to New Orleans and now I was going to die in the city where I'd been born. Was this why Nan had done everything she could to stop me coming here? Had she had some premonition of my doom?

THIRTY

Amanda

The three of us stayed huddled on the bed for what seemed like hours, with the humidity stifling and the water lapping downstairs. Finally, Leroy gathered the courage to go and check the lower floor.

'I think it's slowing,' he said, staring at the water. 'I think it's evening out.'

Was it really slowing or was he merely hoping it was? I was so stricken with terror I couldn't even make myself look. Poor Flambeau was gone, and where was Elliot?

'Amandine,' Leroy said, grabbing my shoulders and speaking firmly. 'Keep your head. We are going to get through this. But I need you to keep your head.' He pointed to the water and food supplies. 'Give your grandmother something to eat and drink.'

Leroy's instructions gave me a task to focus on. I remembered Grandma Ruby's medications. I opened her bag and found only three bottles on top of her clothes.

Where was the fourth? My stomach pitched when I realised the missing bottle was the warfarin.

I shook everything out of her bag and ran my fingers frantically through it, but I couldn't find the warfarin tablets. When she'd repacked her bag after showing Leroy her Jewel outfit, she must have missed that bottle. I wiped my sweaty palms down my legs and tried to calm myself. I had the script in my bag. As soon as we got out of here, I'd get it filled. Surely it wouldn't be dangerous if she took the medication only a few hours later than normal?

I put the other tablets into Grandma Ruby's cupped hand and she swallowed them in one go with some water without realising there was one missing. I sighed with relief — the last thing I needed was for her to panic as well.

I sliced some cheese and put it on the multigrain biscuits I'd brought with me. But when I offered them to Grandma Ruby, she shook her head. 'I don't have an appetite. How can I eat when Flambeau ...'

'Ruby, you'd better eat something,' Leroy told her, with tenderness etched on his face. 'We don't know what's happened to the rest of the city. It might take a while for anyone to come.'

While I was helping Grandma Ruby, Leroy went to the bedroom window and unhooked the plywood. I expected him to tell us what it was like out there, but he said nothing. He stared for a long time, as if he couldn't believe what he saw. Finally I couldn't stand it any more and went to see for myself.

My head spun at the scene before me. The Lower Ninth Ward had disappeared! It had been replaced by a rippled lake with smashed wood and an assortment of household items from beds to chairs bobbing on its surface. All the houses in Leroy's street were gone, washed away or crushed together. Further away, the houses that remained had water up to their eaves. Some people were sitting on their roofs looking dazed. But what about the empty roofs? Where were the occupants of those houses? I remembered Elliot instructing me to make sure Leroy had an axe upstairs and I realised those people had been trapped in their homes. They were probably dead.

My legs gave way beneath me and Leroy grabbed my arms. 'You've got to keep it together, Amandine. You've got to stay strong. It's the only way we're going to get out alive.' But even as he said it, his voice wavered and he fought back his own tears.

He turned back to the view outside the window and I followed his gaze. Mr and Mrs Williams' house was gone. It had vanished like it had never been there at all.

'That poor sweet couple didn't stand a chance,' he said, his chin trembling. 'I offered them to stay with us, but they said they wanted to sleep in their own bed like they have for the past sixty years.'

I sat down and rested my head on my knees. Surely this couldn't be happening? Surely it was a bad dream?

'Come to the window and keep hold of my legs while I write a message on our roof,' Leroy instructed me.

I did as he asked while he spray-painted: *SOS. Three people here.*

'What now?' I asked when he came back inside.

'We sit tight and wait to be rescued.' He collapsed onto the bed and Grandma Ruby rested her head on his chest. 'Never in my life did I expect to see this kind of flooding,' he added, rubbing his forehead. 'I can't take it all in.'

Later in the afternoon, the wind died down and we heard helicopters, but they were far away. Night fell yet the sounds of the helicopters continued, and I heard flares and shouting in the distance too. From somewhere closer came the haunting sound of weeping.

Dogs were howling around us, and I wondered if they'd been left behind in the evacuation ... or were they standing guard over their dead owners? The sound of their misery was unbearable. I covered my ears.

I didn't like how Grandma Ruby's pulse felt under my fingers. I'd been careful to keep her hydrated overnight with frequent sips of water but it seemed to me her pulse was racing. Was it her atrial fibrillation returning? Or was a racing pulse to be expected given that in the last twenty-four hours she had lived through a terrifying hurricane and lost her beloved pet, reconciled with the love of her life who she'd believed to be dead for the last fifty years, and was now trapped with him and her granddaughter in a house that was likely to collapse at any moment?

I grimaced and made up my mind not to feel her pulse any more. There was nothing I could do until we were rescued, and worrying about it wasn't going to change a thing. I had to concentrate on our survival, one step at a time.

It was boiling hot in the bedroom and it became difficult to breathe. Leroy opened the other upstairs windows in an attempt to get some cross-ventilation. The air smelled foul. It wasn't only the stink of garbage-strewn water now but something more sickening: the pungent stench of death.

Helicopters were moving through the sky again, but none approached us. I gave Grandma Ruby her medications and wondered how long it might be until we were rescued. Should I be rationing the drinking water? Then I thought of Aunt Louise and Uncle Jonathan. Their trek in the desert would be over now and they must have heard the news about the hurricane. They would be beside themselves with worry, but I had no way of reaching them.

Leroy lay down on the bed next to Grandma Ruby and cradled her in his arms. '"I don't need to go anywhere else in the world to be happy. All I need is to be near enough so I can hear your heart." I've always remembered those words of yours,' he told her.

She smiled. 'I have a question for you,' she said.

He gazed into her eyes as if he couldn't quite believe he was really holding her. 'Just one?'

'After Clifford died, why didn't you come and see me?'

He brushed his hand down her cheek before answering. 'I'd hurt you enough and I wasn't going to do it again. You had your own life, your own family. You didn't need me reappearing from the past and intruding on all that.'

She stared at the ceiling thoughtfully. 'We've been apart for half a century and yet it feels like no time has passed at all. You're exactly the same as you were fifty years ago. The sight of you still sends a tingle down my spine.'

It was awkward listening in on their reunion, but I had nowhere to go. The only rooms upstairs were this bedroom, an ensuite and a hall cupboard. Then I realised that considering we were in a house surrounded by floodwater, a lack of privacy probably wasn't their main concern.

Another day passed with no sign of rescue, and our supplies started to run low. I'd been thankful we'd survived the storm, but now the nauseating truth dawned on me. If we weren't rescued soon, we'd die of dehydration. The heat was so relentless that I was already suffering spells of delirium and Leroy kept stretching out his legs as if he was getting cramps.

I touched Nan's necklace and jolted when I heard her voice in my head. She was ranting against New Orleans: the drugs, the crime, the unhealthy food, the poverty, the racial tension, the lack of preparedness for a full-scale disaster. 'They can't even build proper levees like they have in Holland! I can't understand why anyone would want to live there!' But in those vicious words I sensed the undercurrent of fear. She'd been terrified I'd return to New Orleans and something bad would happen to me, like it did to my mother. Now, it looked like she might have been right.

I stood up and went to the landing and stared at the foul-smelling water. Even something as awful as Nan letting me believe my father had been responsible for the car accident paled in light of all that had happened in the last few days. It had taken this experience for me to see beyond Nan's anger and understand the hurt beneath it.

'I love you, Nan,' I whispered, and I meant it. Then I made a silent promise to her. *If we live through this, I will become the best person I can be. I'll help others and I'll make you proud of me.*

❧

I was watching the pre-dawn light slowly penetrate the windows when a sound — something familiar — broke the eerie silence outside. What was it? A squeaking door? A dog that had gone hoarse with barking? A horn?

I strained my ears and the sound came again — loud, demanding and close by. Cock-a-doodle-doo!

I jumped from the blankets I was lying on at the foot of Leroy and Grandma Ruby's bed and peered out the window. I couldn't see anything, but the crowing came again. I pushed myself further out and searched behind me. Perched on the roof of the camelback extension was a white rooster.

'Flambeau?' I called.

The rooster turned and looked at me. Was it Flambeau or not? Could he really have survived that violent rush of water? Then he turned again and I glimpsed the smudged ink on his wing where Elliot had written my mobile number.

'Flambeau!' I called out happily.

Leroy and Grandma Ruby joined me at the window.

'Don't go out,' Leroy said to me. 'You might slip.'

I gave my place to Grandma Ruby, who called to Flambeau. After some clucking and contemplation, he jumped onto the windowsill and she swept him into her arms. 'Flambeau!' she wept, burying her face into his feathers. 'My beautiful Flambeau!'

Leroy grinned at me. 'Let's hope it's a good omen.'

Flambeau's survival lifted Grandma Ruby's spirits. When I handed her the daily dose of tablets, she noticed the warfarin was missing but remained calm. 'Never mind,' she said. 'Now Flambeau is back I'm certain we will get through this.'

Indeed, Flambeau's return did seem to bring us luck. A short while later I heard a voice calling outside the window.

'Amandine!'

I put my head out and squinted through the bright sun reflecting on the water to see a man in a dented rowboat coming towards us. He was using a weatherboard plank for an oar. His denim shorts and his shirt were torn, his face was unshaved and his hair was wild. He shaded his eyes to better look at me. The skin on the back of his hand was red and blistered.

'Amandine? Is everybody all right?'

'Elliot?' My heartbeat sped up. Could it really be him? We'd finished the last of our water an hour ago and I wondered if I was hallucinating.

Leroy poked his head out of the window next to me. 'Elliot! I'm sure glad to see you! Where did you get the boat?'

Elliot secured the boat to a drainpipe and climbed in through the window.

Grandma Ruby embraced him fiercely. 'Thank God you are all right,' she said. 'I'm sorry we don't have any water to give you.'

Elliot sat on the bed. 'The coastguard gave me a bottle this morning. I didn't ration it though — I was too thirsty.'

'What happened to you after you left here?' I asked, sitting next to him.

'The wind had picked up too much for me to make it back here so I took shelter in a friend's house in the Upper Ninth.' He lowered his eyes. 'The house split in two when the flood came ... my friend didn't make it. I clung to the submerged roof of the neighbour's house thinking I was a goner until that old boat bobbed past like some kind of miracle. But when I climbed into it I discovered it was occupied by a rattlesnake. I tipped it out pretty fast and it swam away.'

'The water must be full of dangerous snakes,' observed Leroy.

'It's full of lots of things,' Elliot replied grimly. 'From what I've seen, most of the city is underwater. On my way here, I saw the coastguard picking people up. Some police and firemen are out in motor boats, but rescue is difficult because there are cars and other stuff under the water. Wildlife and Fisheries are using their flat-bottom boats to help.'

'The coastguard? Wildlife and Fisheries?' said Leroy, looking horrified. 'Is that all there is? They haven't got the capacity to deal with this kind of disaster! Where are the goddamn army and the air force? Doesn't the rest of America know what's happened here?'

Elliot shrugged. 'I don't know. It took me a while to make my way here.' He looked up at us and said with a thickening voice: 'Thank God you're all alive. From the way things appear here in the Lower Ninth, a lot of people haven't made it. The rescuers are dropping survivors off at the St Claude Avenue Bridge where they say they're going to be picked up. I'll take you there now.'

Elliot climbed back into the boat, then we each crawled out onto the roof — Leroy's first so he could help Grandma Ruby. She was more agile than I gave her credit for and manoeuvred herself gracefully into Leroy's and Elliot's arms without tipping the weatherbeaten boat. I realised I was going to have to trust in her resilience to get through this.

The roof was hotter than I'd expected and it burned my chest and stomach when I leaned across it to push the new box I'd made for Flambeau towards Elliot, who put it in the bottom of the boat. Then I passed him our bags. I'd put some of Grandma Ruby's medications in a bottle in my zippered pocket in case the boat capsized and we lost our supplies. I was learning to have a contingency plan for everything.

When I got in the boat, I kissed Elliot. His mouth was dry and his lips were burned.

'You're going to have to be strong for your grandparents,' he whispered. 'What's out there is pretty bad.'

Leroy plucked a wooden plank out of the water to use as an oar to help Elliot row. He looked over his neighbourhood with eyes clouded with pain. 'I can't believe it,' he said. 'It's all gone.'

'We've got to move slowly,' Elliot warned as he pushed the boat away from the house. 'I nearly got snagged on a live wire on my way here. One of the Wildlife and Fisheries rescuers said they've spotted alligators swimming around. Another guy claimed he saw a bull shark washed in from Lake Pontchartrain.'

I couldn't see how any living thing could survive in the oily toxic-smelling water. We'd have to be careful of cuts, which could quickly turn septic in the heat. I wanted to shut my eyes against the destruction around me, but I had to keep watch for anything that could pierce the boat. The water was so high that street signs and even traffic signals were submerged under the surface. Shoes, paper, toys, letterboxes and suitcases all floated in the water. Leroy's oar struck something and a shape drifted up from the murky depths. At first I thought it was a shark, but then I saw the eyes: human eyes, wide and staring. The man's shirt floated up around his bloated torso. Leroy pushed the body away as respectfully as he could.

'I've seen plenty of them,' Elliot said, his voice breaking. 'There was a whole family bobbing around near the overpass — mom, dad, kids and grandparents. I hope I don't come across anybody I know.'

We reached a bridge where people were sitting with plastic shopping bags filled with clothes on their laps. The towels on their heads were their only protection against the sun. They looked hot, dirty and exhausted. I glanced at our foursome and realised we looked the same.

'Have you heard if they're coming to pick you all up?' Elliot asked the people on the bridge.

A man nodded. 'A truck came about an hour ago. Dropped off some water and took some people. The driver said he'd be back.' He handed us a couple of bottles of water to share. 'Sorry there's not more,' he said. 'He didn't give us much.'

We thanked him and each took sips of the warm water, grateful to have something to drink.

Once we'd loaded our bags and Flambeau's box onto the bridge, Elliot got back in the rowboat.

'Where are you going?' I asked him.

'There are hundreds of people stuck on their roofs and trapped in their attics. They were calling out to me when I came to get you. I've seen dogs and cats too, clinging on to bits of wreckage. I'll never be able to live with myself if I don't help as many as I can.'

Our eyes met. I knew it was dangerous and that if he went out there again in that shaky little boat, he might not come back. It was a miracle that he'd survived the first time. My lips trembled and I leaned over and kissed him like it might be our last goodbye.

'Be strong for your grandparents,' he said. 'We'll find each other again.'

I watched him row off, back in the direction of the Lower Ninth Ward. It seemed like an insurmountable task for a few individuals to be rescuing all those people and animals. I clenched my fists and shut my mind to what could happen to him out there. Elliot was right — I had to stay strong for Grandma Ruby and Leroy.

There was no cover on the bridge and the sun beat down on us mercilessly. I found the escape route pamphlet Oliver had given me and used it to fan Grandma Ruby.

I looked at my arms and legs. They were darker than they'd ever been. Even as a teenager I'd been obsessed with premature ageing and had always smothered myself in sunscreen and never purposely tanned. It was like New Orleans was bringing out the blackness in me and this experience was happening for a reason I couldn't fathom yet.

Flambeau pecked at his box. He must be getting hot in there. I opened the lid and offered him some cracked corn, but he turned away from it. Even he didn't have an appetite.

We waited in the burning sun for another two hours. I stared out at what had been a busy neighbourhood but all I could see now were the tops of trees poking above the water, some submerged roofs and floating debris.

The absence of city sounds — traffic and sirens — was unnerving.

'Lord have mercy on the people trapped in their attics,' said the man who had given us the bottles of water. 'With this heat they are going to burn up like the bodies in the tombs in the old cemeteries do.'

I grimaced and looked back to the water. Boats were arriving with more people: rubber dinghies, aluminium fishing boats, canoes. I buried my head in my hands. If these were the only vessels available for rescue, those people still alive in their attics didn't stand a chance. At the sound of a motor rumbling I lifted my head. I expected to see an army truck but instead a rust-riddled courier van pulled up beside us and the long-haired driver beckoned. 'I can take four of you. It's all I've got room for in the back.'

The people who had been on the bridge before us declined. 'We're one family. We go together or not at all,' said one of the older women. She indicated to us. 'You can go. You're only three.'

I glanced back to the van's driver who was sliding open the rear door. His hair was greasy and streaked with grey and his overalls were covered in stains. This wasn't a time to be fussy about appearances, but who was he?

I glanced back to Leroy and Grandma Ruby for guidance, but they were both sitting on the hot concrete with their shoulders slumped. Grandma Ruby's face was beetroot red. She hadn't had her warfarin tablets and there was no more drinking water. I bit my lip. Who knew when any other means of transport would arrive? I nodded to the driver and helped Grandma Ruby and Leroy into the van, which was half filled with boxes. I put our bags and Flambeau's box in before climbing in myself. The driver slammed the door shut and we sat in the gloom as he turned on the engine and drove away. I stared at the back of the driver's head through the safety grille with no idea if we were being transported by a selfless citizen trying to help out or whether I'd just placed us all in the clutches of a serial killer.

After a short and bumpy ride, the driver brought the van to a halt and opened the rear door. 'This is as far as I can take you,' he said. 'If you keep walking up ahead you'll get to the Superdome. They've got food and water there. Good luck!'

I thanked him, ashamed I'd doubted his motives, and glanced at Leroy. I knew he had not wanted to go to the Superdome. But he only shrugged. There were no other options.

I linked my arm with Grandma Ruby's and guided her towards the Superdome, while Leroy carried our bags and Flambeau's box. We were walking up the steps when a young black man wearing only shorts and running shoes stopped me.

'You don't want to take elderly folk in there,' he warned. 'They're better off out here in the open. The electricity's off so there's no air conditioning and the toilets are backed up. It stinks worse than a sewage pit. Knife fights have been breaking out all morning and somebody committed suicide by leaping from a balcony.'

I recoiled. Suicide? Knife fights? This couldn't be real! We found a place on the dome's patio instead, with thousands of other tired, dirty and bedraggled people who had gathered there, most of them black. It looked like a scene from a refugee camp in a Third World country. Babies without clean nappies were sitting in their own filth, their parents looking lost and vacant-eyed. There was garbage everywhere. And that smell! I looked around and saw a corpse lying on the walkway, covered with a blanket. A curtain came down in my mind, closing out the horror around me. If I started to think of the implications of so many people gathered in such desperate circumstances with no rescue in sight, I would shut down. I couldn't afford to shut down. 'I'll go find us some water,' I told Leroy.

I'd only walked a short way when I saw a television crew arriving, with a young reporter. As she began speaking to camera, a woman with braided hair yelled at her, 'How'd you get here before the government? There's no water! No food! Old people and babies are dying!' She pointed to the covered corpse on the walkway. 'That woman over there had an oxygen tank but it ran out on her. She died where she sat. Ain't nobody come to collect her and she died yesterday!'

The cameraman moved to film the corpse, but then the woman who'd been shouting spotted me. She grabbed me by the arm and dragged me over to stand next to a white couple.

'Film the white people!' she screamed at the cameraman. 'Film the white people! You keep filming us black folks and nobody ain't ever going to come!'

The news reporter was about to ask me something, but a black man with a crying child in his arms rushed towards her and took her microphone. 'The National Guard brought enough food and water for the first couple of days, but now more and more people are coming and it isn't enough! Tell me, how can the government of the United States get to Iraq in a matter of hours and they can't even come to New Orleans to give their own citizens food and water? Is it because we're poor? Is it because we're black? Is it because we're the wrong voting demographic? We are goddamn citizens of this country! I've been paying taxes for years! Where is my government now?' The man broke down into sobs.

He'd articulated the desperate situation perfectly. Why *were* these people still here three days after the storm? And without enough food and water?

The reporter and cameraman moved on, and the white couple introduced themselves to me as Matty and Dave from Melbourne. I couldn't believe they were Australian.

'We haven't slept a wink,' Dave told me. 'Everyone keeps glaring at us like we're personally responsible for President Bush not doing anything. But we're suffering too.'

'How did you end up here?' I asked them.

Matty's shoulders stiffened. 'On Sunday morning the staff at our hotel said we had to get out. We went to the airport, but all the flights were cancelled. Then we tried the Greyhound terminal and the train station, but they'd closed too. We had no way out! We called the Australian embassy and they told us to come here. At first it was mainly homeless people, poor families and a whole bunch of backpackers who'd had no idea a storm was coming. It was all civil at first, but now that the conditions are deteriorating, fights are breaking out. One of the guards told me there are over twenty thousand people here.'

They asked how I'd ended up at the Superdome and I explained that I was there with my grandparents. 'I've got to get my grandmother some water. She has a heart condition.'

Matty reached into her bag. 'I've got half a bottle left — here, take it. Surely this can't keep going much longer? This is the United States, after all. I'm expecting Superman — or at least Arnold Schwarzenegger — to appear at any moment and save us all!'

I thanked them and wished them well before returning to Grandma Ruby and Leroy. Grandma Ruby was snuggled in Leroy's arms and they were deep in conversation. After giving them the water, I walked a little distance away so as not to intrude. What must it be like to have believed someone was dead for fifty years and then to find them again?

I stared out at the floodwater surrounding the Superdome. It wasn't as deep as in the Lower Ninth Ward. The speed limits and the lines painted on the roads were visible under the water. Army vehicles would have no difficulty getting through it — so where were the convoys? I looked at the tired and desperate faces around me and shuddered. Could it really be possible help wasn't coming because most of the people who needed it were black? Grandma Ruby's stories of the Civil Rights Movement flooded my mind and for the first time the implications of Leroy being my grandfather dawned on me. I knew that when I got to tell Tamara and Leanne that while in New Orleans I'd discovered I was one-quarter African-American, they'd think it was the coolest thing ever. Australians associated black Americans with entertainers and soul singers, but here in the United States things were different. Now, seeing all these people trapped here, suffering poverty and discrimination because of their skin colour, I saw nothing cool about it at all. It made me sick.

Grandma Ruby voiced a similar opinion when I returned to her and Leroy. 'I thought after all our sacrifices, New Orleans had changed. But look at these poor people. Nothing has changed! Does the government even think of these wretched souls as human beings? Why haven't they sent in planes with food and water for everyone?'

A National Guard sergeant approached me. 'Are you a foreigner?' he asked.

'I'm Australian,' I told him.

'We've got to get you out of here. You're not safe. We've got gangs, shootings and rapes. There are crack addicts wandering around crazed because they can't get a fix. Foreigners are easy targets. I'll take you to the basketball arena. We've already escorted a group of foreign tourists there.'

'I'm with my grandparents,' I told him, pointing to Grandma Ruby and Leroy. 'My grandmother has a heart condition and she hasn't had warfarin for three days.' I didn't tell him about Flambeau, who was hidden in his box again. I was worried somebody would steal him to eat.

'All right,' the guard said. 'There's a temporary clinic at the arena.' He eyed Leroy. 'And it will look better if your grandfather comes too. But walk with me real slow and don't look happy or relieved. There could be a riot if it appears like I'm giving you special privileges. But we take care of our guests here in New Orleans.'

To get to the basketball arena we had to pass through several armed barricades. The walk took us a long time because Grandma Ruby was unsteady on her feet. The sight of her weakness made me queasy in the stomach but I kept reassuring myself that she'd be fine again once she'd had a proper amount of food and water and was back on her correct medication.

The arena was dim inside, except for intermittent flashing blue lights from a smoke alarm nobody had switched off. At least it wasn't overcrowded like the Superdome.

The guard showed us to some seats in the stadium. 'You'll find the medics over there,' he said, pointing to a hallway.

Grandma Ruby was panting, so I gave her some time to rest before suggesting we head to the medical help area. Leroy took one of her arms and I took the other. Her flesh felt cold and clammy — too cold for the stifling heat inside the arena.

As we entered the hallway, the stench hit me like a punch in the throat. I gagged at the sickly smell of urine, vomit and faeces. Dozens of people, mostly elderly, were lying on army cots or sitting in wheelchairs while volunteers, equally as filthy and ragged as we were, fanned them with bits of cardboard. I could hear foreign accents, including a number of Australian ones, everywhere and no longer had to wonder what had happened to the unsuspecting tourists who'd come into New Orleans the previous Friday.

I spotted Matty and Dave and called them over. 'Could you help with my grandmother?' I asked. 'She can barely stand.'

Dave brushed a fly away from his face. 'There are no more cots — I'll see if I can get her a chair. It'll be a long wait until a doctor or nurse can examine her.' He returned a few moments later wheeling a push-cart trolley with a plastic chair placed on the platform. 'There aren't any more wheelchairs,' he said apologetically. 'I had to improvise with this wheeled cart.'

It was humiliating to put Grandma Ruby on something that was intended for moving boxes, but there wasn't any choice.

As Dave and Leroy took her arms to help her onto the chair, Grandma Ruby staggered. I steadied her and noticed her face was drooping on one side. 'She's having a stroke!' I cried.

A young nurse who had been taking a patient's blood pressure stood up and rushed over to us. She studied Grandma Ruby's face and asked her to lift both her arms, which she couldn't do. A frown wrinkled the nurse's face when I told her about the lost warfarin.

'It could simply be dehydration,' she said, pinching Grandma Ruby's skin. 'We haven't got any medications, not even aspirin. We ran out yesterday. All I've got left is IV drips. We'll put her on one and see if it helps.'

Leroy shot me a panicked look. 'Isn't there a doctor who can look at her?' he asked the nurse. 'She might be having a stroke!'

The nurse dragged her hand through her hair. 'I'll get one to see her, but they won't be able to do anything more than I can,' she said, her own frustration clear in her voice. 'I'll put that drip in now.'

I held one of Grandma Ruby's hands while Leroy fanned her with a piece of cardboard to keep her cool. My mouth was dry and it hurt to swallow. Grandma Ruby might be having a stroke and we couldn't do anything about it.

The nurse put the drip in Grandma Ruby's arm, but she continued to worsen. Her beautiful skin was drawn tight over her cheekbones and her body was curled up on one side. She tried to say something but all that came out was a raspy moan.

'Don't die on me now, Ruby,' Leroy pleaded, stroking her hair and weeping. 'Not now we've found each other again.'

I wanted to scream, but at who? Not at the other people who were suffering around us, or at the kind, overwhelmed and exhausted nurse who was doing the best she could to help. I pressed my face into my hands, as if by doing so I could make the whole nightmare disappear and transport us back to 'Amandine', where we would sit in the summerhouse drinking mint juleps and none of this would have happened.

A doctor arrived and checked Grandma Ruby's vitals. When he studied her face, his own expression turned grim. 'She'd better go to emergency,' he told the nurse, indicating a screened-off area at the end of the hallway.

'Can we go with her?' I asked.

'No,' he replied firmly. 'Help out here. I'll come and tell you about her condition when I can.'

A man whose entire head was bandaged except his nose and mouth tugged on my arm. 'They're not taking her to emergency,' he whispered. 'That's the morgue. They're taking her there to die.'

His words made the blood rush to my head. I tugged at the neckline of my top as if I were suffocating. 'No!' I said. 'That can't be true!'

'He's talking nonsense,' a female volunteer with a Danish accent said. She handed me a pair of latex gloves and a surgical mask. 'Ignore him and help us. We're desperate.'

THIRTY-ONE

Amanda

Leroy looked on the verge of collapse too, but he rallied himself, picked up a piece of towel and started cleaning the vomit off the front of an elderly man's hospital gown. Motivated by his example, I grabbed a garbage bag and collected the empty drink bottles and soggy adult diapers strewn over the floor. I worked like a maniac to push away my terror that Grandma Ruby might not make it through the day; or, if she did, she'd end up paralysed.

Someone poked me in the back and I turned to see a toothless woman staring up at me from her urine-soaked cot. 'You're an angel,' she said, pointing at the wing tattoos on my shoulders. 'I asked God for an angel and he's sent one.'

At first I thought I must be hearing things when violin music filled the air. I scanned the area to see where it was coming from and spotted a black man standing in the corner, playing Bach's 'Air on the G String' in the midst of all this despair. The beautiful music entranced me and for one brief moment I was transported from the hell around me.

'It's like the bloody *Titanic*, isn't it?'

The music's spell broke. I turned around and saw that it was Dave who had spoken to me. 'What?' I asked.

'You know,' he said with a sardonic grin, 'the part in the movie where the musicians keep playing while the ship sinks.'

Leroy and I spent the rest of the afternoon and night working in the medical area. Each time I saw the doctor, I'd ask him how Grandma Ruby was. He would only say that she was stable and refused to tell me anything else. He looked so ill and delirious himself in his sweat-stained scrubs that I wasn't sure he even knew who I was asking about.

When I told Leroy what the doctor had said, he bowed his head. 'I can't lose her, Amandine. Not now. If she dies I can't go on. When I returned to New Orleans, I made sure she'd never see me but I watched her from afar, always making sure she was all right. If she goes, I've got no reason to keep on living.'

There was a sign on the emergency-area screen that read: *Medical Staff Only Beyond This Point. No Volunteers.* I moved close to the screen and peered through the gap that served as a doorway. A nurse was squeezing air into a man's breathing tube using a self-inflating bag. A doctor approached them, felt the man's pulse and shone a torch into his eyes. 'He needs more oxygen than that,' she told the nurse wearily. 'And we're all out of oxygen.'

I stepped back and bumped into a National Guardsman. 'Get away from here!' he growled at me. 'The medics have enough to deal with without having to worry about busybodies!'

The following day, a guard announced to the medics and volunteers that the special needs patients were about to be evacuated. As the screens came down and the patients were carried or wheeled past, Leroy and I studied every face but Grandma Ruby wasn't among them. Panic rose in my chest. Had Grandma Ruby died? I ran my hand through my hair and my legs turned to jelly. I glanced at Leroy whose face looked pinched. A sickening feeling gripped my insides. Was this nightmare about to get worse?

I searched for the doctor who had treated her, but couldn't find him. I asked another nurse if Grandma Ruby's name had been on the list of patients to be evacuated.

She stared at me, then laughed like a mad woman. 'Girl, you think we've got a list? Where do you think you are? The Mayo Clinic?'

We were then told that the volunteers were to be moved to the Hyatt Hotel, along with the health-care workers and remaining patients. We were informed that the Hyatt was one of the few hotels that hadn't expelled guests during the hurricane, and Mayor Nagin was now using it as his command centre to inform the rest of the country how desperate things were in New Orleans.

'I'm not leaving till we find out where Ruby is,' said Leroy.

I didn't want to go until we found out what had happened to Grandma Ruby either, but I also suspected if we didn't take the opportunity to get out now, when it was offered, it might be days before we were rescued — and the food and water here had already run out. Leroy wasn't the strong looking septuagenarian he'd been a few days ago. He was unsteady on his feet and his eyes were dull. Whatever had happened to Grandma Ruby, I knew the she would want me to take good care of my grandfather.

'I don't think she's here,' I told him, doing my best to hide the tremble in my voice. 'They must have moved her and we'll have a better chance of finding out where if we go with the medical staff. One of them must know something.'

Leroy sighed and after a moment's hesitation agreed to my plan. We joined a group of volunteers being led to the lower level of the arena. There was a fruit and vegetable truck waiting for us there, and we climbed into the back. The water came to the rim of the truck's wheels and stank worse than ever. I was sure I could feel the toxic chemicals burning my skin when we had to wade through it.

Once Leroy was seated, I turned around and noticed an 18-wheel refrigerated truck parked some distance away. Had food and water finally arrived?

'That truck is for the bodies,' one of the health-care workers whispered to a colleague. 'I heard that two of them arrived a few hours after the storm passed. Isn't it strange that the Federal Emergency Management Agency got those mobile morgues here quickly but haven't done anything for the thousands of living people at the Dome and Convention Centre?'

I turned away. I couldn't even allow myself the possibility that Grandma Ruby might be lying in one of those trucks.

When we entered the Hyatt's lobby it seemed to be functioning as usual, apart from the plywood-lined walls. Some of the patients from the basketball arena were sitting in chairs around the lobby. A reservations clerk was handing them bottles of water. One of the patients got up to help her. My heart leapt ten feet into the air when I realised it was Grandma Ruby! She must have been transferred to the hotel along with some of the other less critical patients before the special needs patients were evacuated. Leroy recognised her at the same time and we ran towards her.

Tears brimmed in her eyes when she saw us. 'Thank God!' she cried, hugging us both. 'I was terrified we were going be separated.'

I clutched her in another fierce embrace. She still looked pale but much better than she had been when we'd arrived at the arena.

'I wasn't having a stroke,' she informed us. 'It was dehydration. The doctor told me to get a thorough check-up when I get out of here before going back on the warfarin.'

Flambeau wriggled in his box at the sound of Grandma Ruby's voice, but I couldn't risk taking him out in the lobby in case we got thrown out of the hotel. We went down a corridor and found an empty meeting room. 'Go to your henny,' I told him, taking him out of the box and placing him on the floor. 'Stretch your legs.'

Flambeau ran to Grandma Ruby who swept him up into her arms. 'You're a good boy,' she told him, nuzzling her face into his neck. 'But we aren't out of the woods yet.'

Someone coughed and I realised we weren't alone. I gasped as a man in a hotel uniform appeared from behind a chair. I opened my mouth, trying to think of some convincing reason why we had brought a rooster into the hotel but before I could say anything he lifted a ginger kitten that he'd been playing with on the floor. 'Don't worry,' he said with a conspiratorial smile. 'Your secret is safe with me. Reggie here has been hiding in my bag and I've been bringing him in here for exercise.'

The hotel staff were as helpful as they could be under the circumstances — finding water for us from their dwindling supply and even serving toast and cereal for breakfast the following day but the toilets were backed up and we had to use bottles and bags for our waste. I realised that I would never take civilised life for granted again.

Finally, the National Guard announced there was a convoy of buses waiting to transport us out of New Orleans.

'You will be protected by armed guards on your journey,' one of the soldiers informed us.

'Is that really necessary?' I asked him.

'There are snipers shooting at volunteers and police all around the city,' he replied. 'Law and order have broken down, and there's a possibility that the buses could be hijacked.'

Snipers were shooting at volunteers? I thought of Elliot and was sick to my stomach. What if some nutcase with a gun killed him for his boat? Or even just for the hell of it?

We were directed onto one of the buses. I sat in the seat behind Grandma Ruby and Leroy and took

Flambeau out of his box and put him on my lap, covered by one of Grandma Ruby's scarves. The bus was air-conditioned and I turned the vent to my face and let it blow soothing cool air over me.

As we drove through the city, I tried to fathom the destruction I saw all around. It looked like someone had dropped a bomb on New Orleans. Fires were burning unchecked. The windows of many high-rise buildings had been blown out and glass, sheets of paper and computer parts littered the streets. Street signals were strewn across the roads and cars lay upside down. I saw dozens of people wading through the foul water with their belongings on their heads, like they had no idea where to go.

The driver told us over the PA: 'Mid-City, New Orleans East, Gentilly, Lakeview and the Lower Ninth Ward were all badly hit. St Bernard Parish was totally wiped out. It's hard to get accurate reports on all the areas but it appears eighty per cent of the city has flooded.'

Some of the passengers burst into tears, while others sat like mute zombies, too dazed to take in the destruction of the city. One man hugged himself and wept over and over again, 'I don't know where my wife is, I don't know where my kids are, I don't know where my dog is ...'

I leaned forward and pressed my head against the back of Grandma Ruby's seat. We were the lucky ones but could life ever be normal again after going through what we had?

'Where are you taking us?' Leroy asked the driver.

'I've got instructions to take you to Dallas,' he replied.

'Dallas, Texas?' Leroy said. 'How long is that going to take?'

'Dallas, Texas,' repeated the driver. 'We'll be there in about fifteen hours.'

We arrived at the Dallas convention centre, which had been turned into a shelter, in the early hours of the morning. The first people I saw were a group waiting outside holding signs that read: *God has destroyed the City of Sodom and Gomorrah! New Orleans: Repent and Be Saved!* Grandma Ruby shook her head. 'People have lost their homes, their families and their lives and all those stupid people can do is judge and hate,' she said. 'They are like those women who screamed at the children outside William Frantz Elementary School during integration. Hate and judgement turn human beings into idiots, but they never seem to be able to learn that and behave differently.'

The volunteers inside the convention centre were much more welcoming. Despite our dishevelled and filthy state, they hugged each one of us and expressed their sympathy before directing us where to go next.

Grandma Ruby's condition was of immediate concern. Two volunteers helped her into a wheelchair. 'We'll take you straight to the medical command centre,' they told her.

'No!' she said firmly. 'You help the people who have no means. We'll go to a hotel and I'll get the staff there to call me a doctor.'

'The Westin has rooms,' one of the volunteers informed us. 'Let me go get you a cab.'

When the driver dropped us off, he refused to let us pay. 'God will pay me back, don't you worry. You look after yourselves now.'

It was humiliating to stand in the stylish foyer of the hotel in my filthy clothes and with my hair a rat's nest, while the immaculately dressed clerk checked us in.

She asked if we had any luggage and her gaze fell to Flambeau in my arms, wriggling and clucking under the scarf, but she said nothing.

'Let me send you up some room service,' she whispered. 'It will be on me.'

While Grandma Ruby took a shower and Leroy stretched out on the floor — he refused to lie on the bed until he'd cleaned up — I called Aunt Louise.

'Amandine!' she sobbed when she heard my voice. 'Oh my God! Where are you? Where's Momma? Is she all right?'

'We're fine,' I told her, nearly dropping the receiver as my hands began to shake. I burst into tears. The shock was wearing off and the trauma was setting in.

Aunt Louise was too overcome to talk, so Uncle Jonathan came on the line. 'A journalist acquaintance of mine got us through the National Guard on Wednesday. We found your note that you were evacuating to your friend's sister's place,' he said. 'But when we rang the number you'd left, Elliot's sister said none of you had arrived. She's beside herself with worry. I'll call her right away.'

'Elliot's not with us,' I told him, my voice trembling. 'I don't know where he is. When I last saw him he was rescuing people with a rowboat.'

Uncle Jonathan paused, then said, 'The house in the Garden District is undamaged, but the power is out and the city has turned off the water. Lake Terrace flooded in some areas, but according to one of our neighbours the water didn't reach our house. Our office building is a wreck though. We've rented a house in Baton Rouge until we figure out what to do. We'll book flights for you and Ruby to join us here tomorrow. Flambeau can come by pet transport. I can't see real estate being a booming business in New Orleans for a while.'

I glanced at Leroy; he'd fallen asleep on the floor. There was going to be a lot of explaining to do when we met Aunt Louise and Uncle Jonathan, but I'd think about that later.

'A good friend of Grandma Ruby's is with us,' I told Uncle Jonathan. 'He's lost everything in the storm. Can he stay too?'

'Of course,' he said without hesitation. 'Give me his name and I'll get a ticket for him as well. I'll call you back once we've booked the flights.'

Grandma Ruby came out of the bathroom after I'd hung up with Uncle Jonathan. She kissed Leroy on the cheek to wake him up. The natural closeness between them made them seem like an old married couple. It hard to believe that they hadn't been together all their lives.

Leroy offered me the bathroom next, but I told him I was waiting for Uncle Jonathan to call me back. I reclined in the armchair and thought about all the people in New Orleans, like Aunt Louise and Uncle Jonathan, whose livelihoods were gone: the tour guides; entertainers; hoteliers, restaurateurs and waiters; doctors and nurses; construction and council workers; teachers; hairdressers; cleaners and gardeners; accountants; lawyers; shop assistants; plant operators; and oil refinery and shipping workers. As the list grew in my mind, the full significance of what had happened and what the after effects would be hit me. Was New Orleans even going to be able to come back from this? Perhaps I had been witness to the last days of the city. Exhaustion overcame me and my eyes drooped. Despite my intention to wait for Uncle Jonathan's call, I surrendered into a deep sleep.

I woke a few hours later to see a good-looking elderly couple staring at me.

The man was wearing a golf shirt, khaki shorts and loafers. The woman was decked out in a Hawaiian-print pantsuit with a white beach hat.

'Well, you were lights out to the world, weren't you?' said the woman. 'We couldn't wake you for anything! Not even when Johnny called back, or room service arrived.'

'Oh my God,' I said, struggling to sit up. 'Where did you get those clothes? You look like a couple of escapees from a Florida retirement village!'

'The spare clothes we brought with us smell like the Superdome and resort wear was all we could find in the mall,' Grandma Ruby replied. 'We got some things for you too.'

'Oh, good,' I said, rubbing my face and discovering it was gritty with dirt. 'I'll take them into the bathroom with me. Did you see a doctor?'

She nodded. 'Yes, she checked me over and filled the script for the warfarin. I feel fine, Amandine. You've got to stop worrying. You're the one who looks like a wreck now.'

In the bathroom, I peeled off my skirt, top and underwear, dropped them in the bin and tied off the plastic bag. They stank like week-old garbage and there was no point trying to salvage them.

I caught sight of my reflection in the mirror. I was burned, peeling and filthy. Nan's pendant was still around my neck, and I took it off and rinsed it under the tap. Then I turned to get in the shower and saw the angel wings on my back.

'Thank you,' I said, brushing my hands over them. 'Thank you.'

I wasn't exactly sure who I was thanking. My mother for being my guardian angel? Or Nan? All I knew was that I was alive and that was something to be very grateful for.

When I stepped out of the shower, I smothered myself in the hotel's lavender-scented moisturiser, even though it stung my skin, then put on the clean underwear Grandma Ruby had bought me. She'd also acquired a floral shirt-dress, a pair of ankle boots and some aviator sunglasses.

'Not too bad,' she said with a giggle when I modelled them for her.

I put my mobile phone on charge and checked to see if there were any messages from Elliot. There weren't. But there was a frantic one from Tamara and I realised I'd never called her back.

'Oh, God!' she cried when she heard my voice. 'We've seen the pictures on TV! We were so worried when we didn't hear back from you. Come home, Amanda! You can't stay there.'

I rested my head against the back of the chair. 'I'll call you as soon as things settle down,' I promised her.

Hearing Tamara's voice was like being called back to another life, to safe Sydney with no guns, no hurricanes, and nice sane people. But those couple of weeks in New Orleans before the storm had shown me another life, another way of being. Crazy maybe, but also ... expanded, richer, full of possibilities. I'd seen the best of New Orleans and now it was gone, blown away before my eyes.

'Let's get something to eat,' said Grandma Ruby, touching my shoulder.

She'd rolled up a blanket so Flambeau could sit comfortably in an armchair with a bowl of oats she'd found in the mini-bar. Leroy put the *Do Not Disturb* sign on the door so the maids wouldn't discover our feathered companion.

When the three of us got in the elevator to go downstairs, we looked at our reflections in the mirror. 'I feel like I'm going to a Halloween party with my wife and granddaughter,' Leroy said. We all laughed so hard I thought my sides would split. I'd never imagined I could ever laugh like that again.

'I love you!' I said to Grandma Ruby and Leroy, my laughter melting into tears. 'I love you both so much.'

We hugged each other, then Leroy kissed Grandma Ruby and me. 'I love you both too,' he said. 'The storm took away everything I had, but it gave me a family.'

The waitress showed us to a table near the window. A gardener was trimming the hedges outside and the street was clean and free of debris. After being in a flooded city, the orderliness of our current surroundings was surreal. I tucked into my roasted beet risotto like I'd never seen food before. Grandma Ruby had ordered a green bean and wild mushroom casserole to build herself up again, while Leroy ordered shrimp and grits 'in honour of New Orleans'. We were silent as we ate, each lost in our own thoughts.

'Everything changes in fifty years and nothing changes too,' Grandma Ruby said finally. 'When I think of those people in the Superdome ... and the people who died in the Lower Ninth Ward ...' She choked back her tears. 'There were moments when I was sure we were going to die too, but the fact that we didn't tells me that we have something to do.' She clasped Leroy's hand. 'New Orleans is going to be hurting for a long time. The city needs our story. It needs people who will help it bridge the gap between its black and white citizens. And that is exactly what I intend to do with whatever time I have left.'

She ordered dessert and sherry for us, but I wanted to give her and Leroy some time alone to celebrate their reunion so I made the excuse of returning to the room to check on Flambeau and see if there were any messages from Elliot.

Before I left the restaurant, I turned back to spy on my grandparents from the doorway. They were holding hands and gazing into each other's eyes like young lovers. Despite all they had been through and the years they'd been separated, their expressions were serene. For a moment I saw them both as they had been when they were young: Grandma Ruby as Jewel in her red sequined dress, and Leroy in his sharp suit. Life had been cruel to them, but it had also been kind. Grandma Ruby was right: she and Leroy should share their story. It was a story of injustice but also one of love — a true New Orleans story.

I was heading towards the elevator when I heard someone call my name. I turned to see Elliot. A rush of warmth hit my heart. If I'd had the energy I would have leaped for joy. Instead I ran to him and threw my arms around him and pressed my face into his chest. 'Thank God, you're all right!' I cried. 'I was beginning to think I'd never see you again!'

'Easy,' he said, laughing. 'My ribs are bruised and I smell like a sewer.'

I didn't care how he smelled, I was so happy to see him. I took his hand and led him to the elevator. 'What happened to you after you dropped us off at the bridge?' I asked him.

'I ended up at the Superdome on Friday after my boat hit a submerged post and sank,' he explained. 'But I managed to get about one hundred and fifty people out and a truckload of cats and dogs into the hands of animal rescuers. I don't think that experience is something I'm ever going to forget.'

I gazed into Elliot's eyes, so thankful that I hadn't lost him. He'd rescued so many people and animals. He was a hero, but I knew he'd never call himself one. 'We've got a room upstairs,' I said, when the elevator doors opened. 'You can clean up and I'll order you some food. How did you find us?'

'I was moved to the Hyatt Hotel as everyone was being shipped out. I couldn't find you and was put in a group to be flown out to San Antonio. On the flight I got talking to a couple of Australians who had seen you and said you'd been sent on a bus to Dallas. I caught a flight to here then asked around at the convention centre until I traced you to the hotel.'

While Elliot took a shower, I turned on the television. It was the worst thing I could have done because all the news bulletins were showing ghastly images from New Orleans: the city underwater; bloated bodies floating in the muck or left on bridges and at other supposed rescue points; looters and armed guards roaming the streets because law and order had broken down and people were shooting each other simply because they could.

'We had a narrow escape in the storm,' I heard Elliot say behind me. 'A very narrow escape.'

He took a beer from the mini-bar and sat down next to me on the edge of the bed, a towel wrapped around his waist. There were scratches on his stomach and back, and blisters on his feet. I looked at my own blistered feet and understood then that we'd been through something that would bond us forever.

'You won't want to stay now, will you, Amandine? You'll go back to Australia,' Elliot said. There was a sad ache in his voice. 'It'll be months before New Orleans is habitable again, maybe even years, and many people probably won't ever come back. I'm not sure if the university is still there, or where all the students will go. I might not have a job to return to.'

He put his beer down and rubbed his face. 'Hurricane Katrina didn't kill people. Neglect did. Plain, criminal neglect. How do you ever recover from that? How do you make peace with yourself knowing that people were murdered by the corruption, arrogance and apathy of their own government?'

I turned the television off and took his hand in mine. 'Grandma Ruby thinks we survived because we have a duty to fulfil,' I said, and squeezed his hand harder. 'I'm not going back to Australia, Elliot. New Orleans is going to need people who love it to nurse it back to life. As well as its doctors, nurses, teachers and government employees it's going to need its storytellers — its writers and its musicians. And it's going to need architects to help people rebuild their homes. I'm not talking about big fancy plantation homes or mansions in the Garden District — there'll always be people to renovate them. I mean architects who'll work for free to help poor people rebuild their homes — and make them better than the ones they had before. Homes designed for the local conditions, that won't collapse so easily in hurricanes or floods.'

'Amandine ...' Elliot tried to say more, but he was too choked with emotion. Instead he curled his fingers around mine and pulled me towards him so I was nestled in his lap.

I kissed him like my life depended on it, then I pressed my face to his neck and thought back to that crazy night with Blaine in the Louisiana swamplands and the racoon and putting my wish in the cauldron. That wish had come true, despite all the horror and turmoil that had threatened to destroy it.

No matter what chaos we had to endure when we returned to New Orleans, I would stay. I had finally found the place where I belonged.

Southern Ruby
BOOKCLUB QUESTIONS

What did you think about Ruby's attempts to get herself, Maman and Mae out of financial difficulties? Do you believe her only alternative was to become a burlesque dancer, or did she have other options? Would you have made the same choice in her situation?

Burlesque striptease in the 1950s was an entertainment directed at men. But the revival of traditional burlesque led by stars such as Dita Von Teese attracts mostly female audiences.

- What is it about burlesque dancing that might be appealing to modern women?
- How do you feel about burlesque striptease personally – is it a celebration of female sexuality and empowerment, harmless fun or a form of repression?

Music plays a major role in both Ruby's and Amanda's stories. Have you been touched by music in a way that has changed or defined your life?

Amanda sees the world with an architect's eyes. The houses in *Southern Ruby* are richly described: Ruby's Apartment; *Amandine*; the Thezan's family home; Terence's house in the Lower Ninth Ward; Aunt Louise and Uncle Jonathan's house etc.

- Do you agree that the houses help demonstrate the inner lives of the characters and if so in what ways?
- The settings of Belinda Alexandra's books often focus on the symbolism of certain buildings. For example: Anya's home in Harbin (*White Gardenia*) contrasted with her new home in Sydney; the significance of the Paris Opera House to Paloma (*Golden Earrings*). Do you think the architecture and decor of your childhood home shaped your character in any way? Are there any buildings in your city that hold great emotional significance to you?

What does Estée's funeral scene represent to you? Some readers have been shocked by the graveyard scenes – how do the cultural ideas about death represented in *Southern Ruby* differ from your own?

Amanda is appalled by the racism of the USA's past – but what about the racism of the present? What do you think is the experience of black people in America today? Is it different from that of Ti-Jean and the young Leroy? Did the story make you reflect on racism in your own country or change your own views in any way?

Did anything you learned about New Orleans, the Civil Rights Movement, burlesque or Hurricane Katrina surprise you?

Do you think Ruby and Leroy could have been happy if they had eloped to San Francisco when they were young? What do your think the future holds for them now?

ACKNOWLEDGMENTS

I am enormously grateful to everyone who has been a part of the creation of *Southern Ruby*. Special thanks should go to my publisher at HarperCollins Australia, Mary Rennie, and editor extraordinaire, Nicola O'Shea, for their expertise and enthusiastic feedback on shaping the story and bringing the characters to life. Thank you also to the entire the team at HarperCollins Australia for their invaluable support, including publishing director Shona Martyn, CEO James Kellow, fiction publisher Anna Valdinger and the indefatigable marketing, sales, design and publicity teams. Historical novels include a lot of detail and I am grateful to the meticulous care of senior editor, Nicola Robinson, for all her hard work to make sure those details were correct and to Katie Lauve-Moon, Drew Keys, Annabel Adair and Pam Dunne for their careful readings of the proof-sheets, and to editor Scott Forbes for his help crafting the tennis scene.

I would also like to express my heartfelt thanks to my literary agent, Selwa Anthony, for all her guidance and encouragement. I am deeply appreciative of my beautiful family – including the much adored four-legged members – as well as my loyal friends, for their love and support through the long hours of discipline and solitude that are involved in writing a book. I am especially indebted to my husband, Mauro. He knows why.

Finally, I would like to thank the inspiring and resilient people of New Orleans for sharing their wonderful city and their personal stories with me.

My sincere thanks to you all.

Sapphire Skies

A love bigger than a war. A beautiful woman lost. A mystery unsolved ... until now.

2000: The wreckage of a downed WWII fighter plane is discovered in the forests near Russia's Ukrainian border. The aircraft belonged to Natalya Azarova, ace pilot and pin-up girl for Soviet propaganda, but the question of her fate remains unanswered. Was she a German spy who faked her own death, as the Kremlin claims? Her lover, Valentin Orlov, now a highly decorated general, refuses to believe it.

Lily, a young Australian woman, has moved to Moscow to escape from tragedy. She becomes fascinated by the story of Natalya, and when she meets an elderly woman who claims to know the truth behind the rumours, Lily is drawn deeper into the mystery.

From the pomp and purges of Stalin's Russia through the horrors of war and beyond – secrets and lies, enduring love and terrible betrayal, sacrifice and redemption all combine in this sweeping saga from Belinda Alexandra.

'Belinda Alexandra has unveiled another literary gem'
Courier-Mail